Upon the
FLIGHT
of the
QUEEN

HOWARD ANDREW JONES

St. Martin's Press
New York

First published in the United States by St. Martin's Press, an imprint of St. Martin's Publishing Group

UPON THE FLIGHT OF THE QUEEN. Copyright © 2019 by Howard Andrew Jones. All rights reserved. Printed in the United States of America. For information, address St. Martin's Publishing Group, 120 Broadway, New York, NY. 10271.

www.stmartins.com

Map by Darian Vincent Jones

Library of Congress Cataloging-in-Publication Data

Names: Jones, Howard A., author.
Title: Upon the flight of the queen / Howard Andrew Jones.
Description: First edition. | New York : St. Martin's Press, 2019. |
    Series: The ring-sworn trilogy ; 2 |
Identifiers: LCCN 2019028084 | ISBN 9781250148803 (hardcover) |
    ISBN 9781250148810 (ebook)
Subjects: GSAFD: Fantasy fiction.
Classification: LCC PS3610.O62535 U66 2019 | DDC 813/.6—dc23
LC record available at https://lccn.loc.gov/2019028084

Our books may be purchased in bulk for promotional, educational, or business use. Please contact your local bookseller or the Macmillan Corporate and Premium Sales Department at 1-800-221-7945, extension 5442, or by email at MacmillanSpecialMarkets@macmillan.com.

First Edition: November 2019

10 9 8 7 6 5 4 3 2 1

For my three favorite champions,
Shannon, Darian, and Rhiana

PLEDGE OF THE ALTENERAI

When comes my numbered day, I will meet it smiling. For I'll have kept this oath.

I shall use my arms to shield the weak.

I shall use my lips to speak the truth, and my eyes to seek it.

I shall use my hand to mete justice to high and to low, and I will weigh all things with heart and mind.

Where I walk the laws will follow, for I am the sword of my people and the shepherd of their lands.

When I fall, I will rise through my brothers and my sisters, for I am eternal.

Upon the
FLIGHT
of the
QUEEN

Prologue

As he shrugged into his khalat again, he couldn't keep from smiling, even though his fingers fumbled with the hooks. Earlier that night he'd been presented with the armored robe of the Altenerai, and now he donned it for the second time. He savored the moment and wondered if it would ever feel unremarkable to pull the garment on.

He glanced down at the sacred ring on his struggling fingers and willed the sapphire to light, chuckling a little that he could do so, that he had earned the right to wear it. He, whom so many had been certain would never rise past the second rank.

Still smiling, he thanked the sisters for a glorious evening. One was passed out upon the red coverlet, snoring lightly, her arms and legs akimbo, and he giggled. There was nothing very erotic about a drunken sleeping woman, he decided, even if she was mostly naked.

The other waved at him languidly and then lay back, accidentally bumping her sister in the thigh with her elbow. Neither noticed. He slipped out through the front door.

He hadn't remembered the route back to the Alantran citadel being quite so confusing, but eventually he found his way to the right hill, up to the entrance, and past the sentry, who saluted him crisply. He raised his bottle in acknowledgment and headed on for the barracks, where he performed a similar ritual with a similar sentry. Once inside, it seemed the hall tilted at an odd angle. What light there was burned too brightly in a lantern near the head of the stair.

There were more steps up toward Rialla's sickroom than he'd recalled, but he found his way at last, knocking loudly on the door. "It's me," he said, "Kyrkenall." His tongue felt thick.

He was leaning against the door so that when she opened it he almost fell in upon her, but caught himself on the verge, nearly dropping his bottle in the process.

Rialla retreated quietly.

He steadied himself against the frame, offered a grin of apology, and lifted the wine bottle.

Rialla wore a plain-cloth nightdress rather than the colorful silks of the dancers he'd left. Her short dark hair was in disarray, and she pushed it from her red-rimmed eyes, watching him.

A trio of candles burned upon the table beside the bed set in the narrow stone room. He stepped past her to peer through the arrow-slit window down across the length of Alantris. He saw sloping roofs, first, then a drop to the next level, and expanses of dark sward and the sparkle of moonlight upon the beautiful canals, and, distantly, the final, outer wall, rising blackly. The Naor would never break that, and the city supplies would sustain them until the enemies lost enough warriors and wealth to slink back where they came from. What a fine way to spend a war, he thought—running forays from a metropolitan base celebrating his recent heroism. He'd sure risen in the world.

"I brought this," he announced, "to celebrate. You should have been there."

"I knew you would come." Rialla's voice was solemn.

Kyrkenall couldn't help giggling at the unintentional double entendre. At her confused look, he attempted to mimic her solemnity. This resulted only in more giggles as he dropped into the single chair, beside the window.

She stood staring at him for a long while before he recovered and sat the bottle down upon the wooden floor with a clunk. He suddenly recalled that she was injured, and grew more serious. She'd been a very long time recovering from the spell to make N'lahr's sword. "How are you?"

"Better than you, just now. You brought no cups." Her flat pronouncement was characteristically perceptive with no hint of reprobation.

Kyrkenall fumbled at his khalat, and the pouch that he often hung upon his belt, searching for the goblets he'd meant to bring, but he found only the hilt of his knife. He had a panicked moment fearing that he'd lost both his wonderful sword and his amazing bow until he recalled that he'd left them in his room.

Rialla bent to retrieve the bottle and held it up to the starlight, looking at the label.

"Sorry about that," he said. "I had some, at some point this evening. Gods, I wanted you to be there." Then noticing how ably she moved, he said, "You look so much better."

She sat down on the edge of her bed. "I am still weary."

"You should have been with us tonight," he insisted. "Kalandra was the one who bore witness to my wisdom. Can you believe it? And you should have heard the toast Aradel gave us! She talked about how 'the future of the corps burned bright' because of us. She mentioned you, too. Everyone was asking about you."

He peered over at her, hoping he'd communicated the triumph of the moment. She didn't seem to be paying attention, and he frowned. It was unfair that Kalandra had declared her too weak to participate in the ceremony this evening.

"I have dreamt strange dreams," Rialla said. Her tone was intent.

But he hadn't shaken free his regret she wasn't sworn to the ring yet. "They'll give yours tomorrow, I expect. The ceremony won't be as big, but will still be amazing. And it will be all about you!" He willed his own sapphire to shine and chuckled in delight when it did so. "I hope they'll have the pipers again."

Rialla followed her own line of thought. "The Naor will fail this time, but they will return to break the wall in later years," she told him, or rather the bottle, at which she still seemed to be staring. "N'lahr rises. And Alten Aradel reigns as governor. Asrahn points the way. Kalandra loses herself, as does Belahn. You will seek, and fly, and stand with kobalin."

The information was already muddled for Kyrkenall. He raised one finger, then the other beside it, and tried to decide which of the statements was stranger. "Kobalin?" he decided. But he felt like he was missing something.

Suddenly she had put the bottle aside on the rumpled sheets and she was leaning forward. Her eyes were luminous and wide and strange. "But I am nowhere! Nowhere, Kyrkenall! There's nothing left of me but a statue in the dark."

"Hey. It's all right," he said, for he hadn't quite caught what she was saying, but could tell she was upset. "Statue in the dark" sounded lonely and bleak.

She wrapped her arms about her chest. "It's been a long time since I knew this fear." She was looking down at the wooden floor planks past her feet. "I thought we were strangers."

"You have nothing to fear." He tried a laugh but it sounded wrong. "You're the most powerful weaver to ever win the ring. Probably the most powerful weaver, anywhere at anytime."

"The ring? It won't save me. I don't even know why I want it anymore. I used to need it to prove I mattered."

He knew that she needed him to focus, and he was trying his best. "But you do matter. And you deserve the ring. More than I do, anyway." He'd said it impulsively, but recognized its sobering truth as he caught a piece of her mood.

Her gaze was like a physical force. "Kyrkenall, I think I'm going to die when the Naor come."

He shook his head. "That won't happen. You'll be using your hearthstone, well back from the front line."

"I'm not in control of it."

That was an absurd statement. No one could control them better. What was all this pessimistic gloom about? She seemed convinced she was doomed. "You're not going to die," he said, moving toward her before he remembered she didn't like to be touched. He lost his balance as he stood, and careened into the bed, then got tangled up with his foot against the post and tripped and landed half-stunned on the floor.

"I don't want to." Her voice from somewhere above him was hollow.

It didn't occur to him to be surprised, at first, that she helped him up and led him to bed. Head pounding, he was only vaguely aware that she unhooked his crisp khalat and made him lie back so she could remove his boots, and then she had thrown the blanket over him.

She climbed in on top of the covers and lay down near, but not directly beside him.

"Don't die," he said, not knowing he sounded as dependent as a tiny child. "We need you."

She smiled sadly, and it was that image that stayed with him as he drifted off to sleep.

The Dark Below

As the sun sank beyond mountain heights, the city's long avenues were stained in scarlet and shadow. Plumes of smoke twisted into the darkening sky from burning shingled roofs, and banners of no less than three Naor tribes fluttered above the invaders now striding red-handed through Alantris, hewing indiscriminately through knots of resistance and fleeing, frightened citizens.

There was nowhere for them to run. The Naor had breached each of the city's concentric ring of walls, flowing even to the foot of the citadel where Rylin watched from a high tower window. The sounds of the conflict washed up to him—the frantic trumpet blasts of defenders, the echoing horn call of the attackers, the clatter of hooves on cobblestone streets. The screams. Most of all, the screams.

Rylin's mouth shaped itself into an unconscious snarl. The capital's fortress loomed not only above Alantris, but the surrounding countryside, granting him an unrestricted view of the west wall and the gap blown inward by one of the great winged lizards flown by the Naor. Successive beasts had forced gaps in the rest. Generations of rulers had overseen the construction of those defenses, never guessing how simply their work would be undone.

Even as he stared, Rylin heard a nearby roar that set his citadel tower rocking. He cursed himself for permitting the horror to distract him. One of the Naor wyrms might at any moment focus its stone-shaking blast against the citadel and send its high towers splintering to the ground.

He turned and hurried down the narrow wooden stairs. He bore his friend and mentor over his left shoulder, garbed like him in the blue armored robe of the Altenerai Corps. He'd found no wound upon Varama, but her movements were feeble. The traitorous alten Cerai had attacked her magically and left her stunned, or possibly worse. Since he'd found her, Varama had only managed a few jumbled words uttered singly. It was another horror to contemplate that the most brilliant person he'd ever met might have been rendered a monosyllabic idiot.

He descended in gloom. Here and there, light shone blindingly through arrow slits looking down on crosswalks or courtyards, and he resisted the impulse to stop for longer looks. He would see only minor variation in the theme of destruction and futile defense. Alantris was already dead; it but flailed spasmodically as it expired. Somehow he had to get himself and Varama out of the citadel to somewhere safer in the dying city. Currently even that modest goal looked like an insurmountable challenge.

As he reached the next landing, he heard Varama mumbling something, and he paused, head turned to better hear her. Long habit had taught him that when Varama spoke it was worth listening.

"Can't hear you," he said. "We've got to get out of the tower before it falls."

Her hoarse voice struggled for greater volume even against a nearby trumpet blast. She spoke as if with great effort. "Entrance. Hid-den. Tunn'ls."

"Where? In this tower?"

Her grunt sounded as though it was in the affirmative.

"Where do we get in?"

"First. Floor. Near. Main. Stair."

"Right." Once he might have questioned her meaning. Now he trusted her implicitly. Her mind, at least, appeared to be working. She was aware of past and present, and planned for the future. It was the ability to communicate fluently which had failed her. Gods, he thought, let this be temporary.

He adjusted her weight on his already-aching shoulder and resumed descent, wondering even then why he prayed for one person when so many were dead, dying, or in danger even now. Probably because the magnitude of those horrors was difficult to contemplate, and this horror was immediate and evident.

A low, chest-shaking rumble set the tower rocking. He flung out his right arm to steady himself on the rail but increased his pace.

Close by, one of the Naor wyrms had unleashed the deadly energy that collapsed walls, and it pushed him to greater haste. He could all too easily envision their deaths among the crushing stones.

From below he heard a low horn call, and the shouts of men. There were sounds of booted feet on the stairs. "They're going out to fight," Rylin said to Varama, a little breathless. "And die."

He reached another landing. They'd finally descended the long vertical length of the west tower and emerged in the main portion of the citadel, though there were four stories yet between them and the ground. He dashed across an oaken floor covered over with a white flowered carpet, hurrying for the main stairs. "I should be with them," he said.

He was Altenerai, sworn to defend the realms and their people to his dying breath. "Must. Get. Others," Varama managed, her breath husky with effort. "In tunn'ls. Squires. Warriors."

"After I get you to safety." Rylin turned into the main stair. These were stone, and well worn by centuries of traffic. Indistinct shouting rose from below, followed by a horn call. Rylin understood its meaning: The Altenerai squires were being called to battle. A little late, he thought.

As he reached the second floor, a trio of men ran past bearing bows and quivers. The rear one slowed for a moment as he caught sight of their uniforms, then hurried after his comrades.

Starting down the last stairwell, he heard war cries and the clatter of blade on blade. An officer called out for her soldiers to pull back. A Naor bellowed that the Alantrans were on the run.

He eased Varama against the wall and was surprised to see her supporting herself, albeit dazedly. Finally, a stroke of good fortune. Rylin stepped to the inner stair rail and peered at the main floor.

Four Naor had advanced into the wide stone hall in a line, pressing three of the Alantran troops with spears set into the notches in the high corner of their shields.

No expert on the markings of the Naor tribes, Rylin nonetheless knew that the absence of crests on pot helms denoted them as low-ranking troops. They might lack experience, but they'd be eager to prove their ferocity and bravery.

He wondered why the Alantrans didn't press harder, then saw them shielding one of the city's councilors and the acting governor, obvious from the embroidered blue scarves wrapped about their heads.

His first instinct was to cripple the Naor with his sorcery, but he was already weakened from Cerai's attack. Varama had taught him to use the tools at hand, which was why he snatched a bronze flowerpot from a stairwell niche. It made a delightful clang when it smashed into the helmeted temple of the Naor on the left and crumpled him. He grinned to himself that Naor never seemed to take the time to properly pad their headgear.

Before the man had even hit the floor, Rylin vaulted the rail with sword in hand. His attack from on high cut through leather armor and shoulder alike and sent another warrior wailing to the ground. Rylin wrenched his arm pulling his sword from the body and just missed getting cut by an overenthusiastic Alantran charging into the sudden clear space.

Rylin cursed at him, but the wide-eyed soldier had already turned on the next Naor.

Attacked now from both front, flank, and rear, the last two Naor went down quickly. Rylin hurried to the citadel door, and was readying to slam it closed, when he saw a mass of Altenerai squires forming in a square and facing the ruined citadel wall.

He shouted to them; then, when they didn't turn, hurried forth, and screamed through cupped hands for them to fall back. Finally, the rear rank turned toward him, signaling those in front until dozens were hurrying into the citadel itself, along with some more of the city guards.

The acting governor lay her hand on his arm as he stood at the open door. He could just hear her over the approach of the squires. "Thank goodness you've come. You've got to lead these forces to battle, Alten."

He saw the fervent look in her eyes and wished he had something better to tell her. "I'd be throwing their lives away, Governor Feolia. The city's taken."

At those bleak words, she smiled gravely and looked to her own weapon. "Then we must die with sword in hand."

"Not today." He waved in the squires and pointed a familiar, square-jawed fifth ranker to the stairway he'd quitted. "Sansyra! Varama's on the steps. Get her down here!"

It took the young woman only a moment to register the instruction and then hurry up the stairs.

"You two—get to the windows on the stairwell and keep watch."

Still more squires filed into the hallway, along with some citadel soldiers, protesting that they should hold the wall.

He didn't have time to argue with them. "Close and seal the doors!" While this order was being carried out, Rylin turned again to the acting governor. "Varama knows of a hidden exit. Are you aware of it?"

Feolia cocked her head in surprise.

"Come along, then."

"What about the rest of our people?" the governor asked.

"I'm going to do what I can, but the odds aren't good for any of them, or us."

Sansyra returned, Varama leaning heavily against her. It might have been wishful thinking, but he thought he detected a little strength in the alten's step.

One of the squires he'd sent to watch from above called down. "Alten! The Naor are all over the courtyard now! Some more are coming closer!"

"How many?"

The second ranker fell silent. Presumably he was counting. From somewhere close by came the twang of bowstrings followed by a shout from outside, and Rylin guessed the small band of Alantran archers he'd seen earlier was finding targets.

The milling squires and soldiers, dismayed and shocked, parted for Varama as Sansyra guided her behind the stairwell. The pale blue alten stopped at the wall beneath it, her eyes roving over a gray stone partly covered over by the stiff tapestry of an archer on a hilltop under wintry skies. Her lidded gaze settled upon the stone where the fabric archer's arrow was pointed. She then pressed into it. Unfortunately, she didn't have much strength at her command.

"Sixty-six," the counting squire announced to a room whose interest had moved on. Someone outside the citadel let out a cry of agony that was abruptly silenced, and a celebratory whoop went off above. "Sixty-five."

There was nothing remarkable about the shoulder-high stone Varama labored against, not even when Rylin examined it with his inner sight. He dismissed the idea that Varama was confused or mistaken, then gently brushed her aside to place his own palms to the area. It was as cold and gritty as its neighbors.

There was barely space for two hands on the masonry, and Rylin found himself wishing his stronger friend Lasren were there. He'd been too busy to think about him for days. Somewhere in the wilds Lasren was probably still hunting the falsely declared enemies of the realms, Kyrkenall and Elenai.

Suddenly the stone gave way a little, sinking back into a recess, and Rylin halted in surprise before pushing further. He heard a low thunk, felt a vibration through his fingertips. The governor called to him, but he scarcely heard, for a jagged section of the wall in the shadow of the stairwell swung inward. The door was no higher than his shoulder and three feet at its widest. Its edge was uneven, so that when closed it would better blend into the surrounding wall. Rylin peered inside and saw the top of a wooden ladder secured against the far side of a stone shaft leading into darkness.

It wasn't the most inviting of openings even in these circumstances, but the squires shifted in expectation and the councilor beside the governor muttered a prayer.

"Where does it go?" she asked.

Rylin looked to Varama for the answer. "Deep," she whispered. "Far. Safe'ty."

"You heard her. You." He pointed to the nearest squire. "Get a lantern. And candles."

The councilor offered, "There's a supply room just down the corridor. I'll show you."

As she spoke, Rylin discovered an even larger band of people had arrived from deeper in the citadel and now waited behind them. Some were soldiers, and some were additional squires, but dozens were ordinary citizens, including children and elderly. Rylin searched their frightened faces, looking for Denalia, Aradel's niece, and didn't see her.

"Can all of these people fit?" he asked Varama.

She nodded. "Them first."

He frowned, but acquiesced. Varama for some reason wanted to remain behind until last; maybe she was gathering her strength to manage the ladder. He'd just have to work quickly. There were hundreds normally within the citadel and fortress and there surely had to be some still above. He couldn't fit the whole city into the tunnels, but he could certainly get as many as possible. Better to rely on those who knew the building.

"You six," he said, pointing to a group of Alantran soldiers, "come with me. We're going to search upstairs." He pointed to the squire Lemahl, and the governor and counselor. "Search the main floor. Get everyone that you can. Sansyra, stay here by Varama. You two, monitor the door. And everyone else—get down the damned shaft!"

He waved on his charges and they came with him up the stairs. "We have to move fast, and I don't want to leave anyone behind. But don't you dare shout that 'we've found a secret exit,' right? The Naor might hear."

That seemed to make sense to them, and they declared assent. They looked nervous but eager. Probably they were glad for the direction, the sense that they were involved in something that wasn't hopeless.

"You know this whole building better than me. You three, take the second floor. Spread out. Alert the archers to fall back to the window overlooking the main entrance. The rest of you come with me to the third."

From outside came another roar. Damn. He'd momentarily forgotten about the wyrms. How could he be so stupid? If he were to die pulverized by thousands of pounds of stone, then at least he'd be killed while he was helping people. But could he get Varama into the shaft before everything collapsed?

He left the soldiers to search the third floor and climbed to the fourth, racing from room to room, through open doors and calling every twenty paces.

He found a handful of frightened young servants hiding in a storeroom on the fourth floor and sent them down.

Searching beyond was another issue altogether, because above the fourth floor the fortress was composed of seven towers, some of which were linked by crosswalks but not all on the same floor. He climbed one, made his way to a balcony overlooking an inner courtyard and managed to catch the eye of another band of archers who'd taken up a post in the south tower. He waved them over and pointed to the ground floor and one of them raised a hand in acknowledgment.

He dared not be gone for any longer. He found the soldiers ushering a handful of additional refugees down the stairs, and joined them.

By the time he'd reached the landing leading to the second floor, the archer on duty at the window shook his head and pointed down. "There's a score of Naor in the courtyard and they're getting a ram to bash in the doors."

That hadn't taken very long. "Some archers are coming in from the south tower. I'm not sure where it meets up—get them here, and fast."

"Yes, sir." The bowman hurried away.

Below, Varama and Sansyra were still waiting. Alone. It was the first time he'd ever seen the squire's face brighten at the sight of him. He also noticed a large bruise rising on her cheek.

The soldiers he'd brought with him started onto the ladder. The rest of the hall was empty.

Sansyra sighed in relief. "Thank the Gods you're back, sir."

"I'd pray to them, but I'm not sure I'd thank them. Did the other three who climbed with me return?"

"Yes, with more soldiers and servants. They already descended."

He turned to Varama. "Where do the tunnels get you out of the city?"

"Just inside."

What was the point of that? "Just inside?" He couldn't contain his disappointment.

"Exit's in west wall. West wall fell."

Right. There'd be no way out from there. He'd have to get them out some other way, but on the bright side, Varama's sentence structure was improving. "Are there other entrances to the tunnels?"

She nodded.

"Where?"

She answered his question with one of her own. "Your plan?"

"Semblances," he said, unconsciously imitating her shortened manner of speech, and saw her gaze sharpen as she immediately understood. "I'll gather as much information as I can about our foes, find a way out for us. And sow a little chaos if I'm lucky. Do you still have your semblance?"

She fumbled with the pouch on her belt, and frowned as her own fingers obeyed only sluggishly. Sansyra hurried to help.

"You guard her with your life, Sansyra. Do you understand? We need her."

"Yes, sir. I know how important she is." Sansyra spoke with great sincerity, and an implied rebuke, as if to say she had always known and who was he to just now be noticing?

He deserved that.

Something huge rattled into the outer door, like a giant's fist. He glanced at the portal, saw it quaver. As impressive as the citadel walls were, the doors themselves looked more serviceable than fortresslike. Probably no one had ever expected that enemies would get so far.

Sansyra handed him Varama's small belt pack, her gaze seeking his, but he focused instead upon Varama, whose strange eyes fixed him with a particularly intense stare. "Three more entrances . . . simpler to find."

"Yes."

The oaken door bar rattled in its holdings as the Naor rammed it again. Up above he heard footsteps on the stairs. The archers. They'd damned well better hurry.

"Temple to Vedessa," Varama said, then paused to breathe. "North corner. Niche panel of praying man. Press."

"The second one?"

"Third tier. Below Merivan's Archway. Fountain of maiden. Third full stone left of her foot."

"Right."

There was the sound of splintering wood and Varama pointed toward the door.

"They're getting close," Rylin agreed. "You'd better get down. I'll ask about the third later. I'm going to use one of the faces from these dead Naor—"

"Throw down ladder."

"What?"

She rolled her eyes at him. "Stand up body. Look well. Then pitch down hole."

"The hole? You mean where the ladder is? Why?"

She stared at him. The archers he'd called to from the tower had finally reached the landing directly overhead, and the doors were splintering. It was hard to think. "Oh. Oh!"

Of course. The body of the Naor man whose face he meant to steal needed to be hidden so Rylin didn't look like a dead man's twin, one lying right in the path of the Naor, and easily visible.

"Sansyra, come with me." He raced to one of the dead men. "Hold that one up."

She looked puzzled, but bent to lift the corpse.

Outside the Naor counted, their meaning clear even though their borderland accent mangled the words: one, two, building to a three. There was a mighty grunt and the doors rattled. And cracked. He could see some light through the splinters, but for now they held.

Sansyra hoisted up a scruffy-looking Naor by the shoulders.

"Make him stand." Rylin had to make sure he got the height right.

The archers finally reached the spot just before the door, their eyes wide in alarm. More than fifteen of them.

Rylin thumbed them toward the ladder and they hurried on. One of them exclaimed in amazement before they started down.

Damned if that particular Naor body didn't have a nasty cut through his shoulder. That would look a little strange to take as a semblance, wouldn't it?

"Next one," Rylin said.

Sansyra released the dead man, and with a look over her shoulder at the door, lifted another.

This body was much better. There was a lot of blood on his cuirass and on his hands, but no noticeable injuries. His head lolled, of course, and his eyes were rolled back, and he smelled like he'd voided his bowels on death, but Rylin assumed the semblance he took on would move like a living person, and he'd work not to mimic the scent as well. He tried to imagine him with normal eyes.

After a long moment, he reasoned he had memorized the man's face about as well as he was going to manage. "All right, toss him down the shaft."

He stepped back to the opening to the shaft only to discover that four archers were left in front of the thing, watching as one of their fellows descended gingerly.

Rylin would have summoned his best "dressing down" voice if it hadn't been for the Naor within earshot. "Are you daft?" he demanded through clenched teeth. "Move your twice-damned asses! Go! Go! You want the Naor to find you?"

His urging brought a renewed sense of energy, but the door splintered with a resounding crash behind them. Rylin peered out from under the shadow of the stair and saw daylight shining through a head-sized panel in the door. The wood was bowed in around it. Two or three more good hits and the Naor would be through.

"Damnit!" Rylin gnashed his teeth as the final archer headed down.

He grabbed the shoulders of the dead man and, with Sansyra assisting, dragged him to the hole. A faint golden glow, as of a candle, pooled perhaps twenty feet below. Two archers hurrying down the ladder were dark blots. He might have reached down and touched the head of the nearest.

"On your left," he called into the shaft, then lowered the corpse out on the left side of the narrow ladder well, and released.

There was a frightened curse from below, cut off by the splintering smash of the door finally giving way.

As the Naor shouted, Sansyra kissed him on the cheek. "Luck. I was wrong about you," she said, and stepped to the ladder. Varama saluted him once, then got her hands on the rungs. She looked back as Rylin fussed with the recessed stone. He wondered why he hadn't bothered to ask how to close the thing. Fortunately, pressing hard popped it out and set the door sliding into place. As it closed, he watched his friend and mentor descending very slowly, carefully, closely warded by Sansyra. The door closed securely and then the seam vanished as if he had dreamed it all.

He heard footsteps behind, and grasped one of the two little semblance stones, willing it to life around him as he sank against the dark back of the stair. He wished he'd had a chance to examine himself in a mirror to make adjustments. The image of the Naor was laid over his own features, or at least all that he could see, for those boots and dark animal skin leggings weren't his own, nor was the blood-stained scale cuirass. The soldier he'd chosen didn't have the leather of the other frontline troops.

As he heard booted footsteps hurrying forward, along with the groan of soldiers on the move, he realized a proper scale mail shirt wouldn't be quite so flexible as it seemed to be in his slumped position, and so he shifted slightly.

"Something's moving!" a stranger's voice drawled. It was a man, naturally. There were no women to be found in the Naor military.

Two soldiers with bared swords hurried around the stair side to confront him.

So much for playing dead and then sneaking out behind them. Rylin would have to pretend injury and do some talking. A bad idea in front of agitated and highly suspicious soldiers, especially when he had no idea what his face looked like. Would he have a dead man's slack and staring eyes?

He groaned and shifted, put his hand to his face, his eyes half-closed. At least he hoped his eyes looked half-closed.

He peered through his fingers at the Naor who rounded the corner. They were in their twenties. Bearded, muscular, these must have been an especially valued regiment, for they were garbed in matching, well-fashioned mail shirts and metal caps with nasals. They looked competent and dangerous, probably experienced veterans meant for a quick thrust at the citadel.

He heard an officer barking orders to advance with caution, deploying men away to stairs and halls. The fellow's voice was heavy, with an accent that butchered soft vowels. "Scouts said at least a hundred withdrew inside here," he called. "Stay sharp!"

Rylin sat up, hand still to his head, as dozens of men hurried past in small groups, throwing open doors. Some marched swiftly up the steps.

One of the soldiers who'd found him first remained. His question held the barest hint of compassion. "Is that your blood?"

"Don't think so." Rylin hadn't heard the voice of the man whose image he'd stolen, so he was speaking with his own. He spoke haltingly, doing his best to imitate the roll of the Naor accent.

"What unit were you with?"

Damn. Of course they'd ask that. He groaned, mumbled a number, and rubbed the side of his head.

"Three?" the soldier asked. "Did you say three?"

He had, but he hadn't expected it to be heard.

The man's dry chuckle faded as he was joined by another soldier. Rylin pretended it took effort to rise, setting a hand against the wall behind him. He deliberately tapped his head against the wall and moaned. It had hurt more than he'd planned.

Before him now was a Naor officer, obvious from the blue plume in his helm and the better gear—the cuirass looked of sturdier make, the lines of the helm were better fitted and rounded, and a cloak draped his heavy shoulders. Impassive blue eyes stared at him.

"I think he took a head blow, sir," the soldier reported. "He said his unit number was three."

"He's one of that lot Tarjesen sent ahead," the officer replied crisply. "You have anything to report, soldier?"

"I'm not sure, sir," he said slowly. He approximated their drawl, but spoke thickly to disguise his voice. He needed to hear a little more of them actually talking.

The officer breathed out a swift sigh. "Do you know where the enemy went, and how many there are?"

Rylin had a sudden inspiration and held up three fingers.

"Three?"

The soldier's expression cleared. "That's what he was trying to tell me," he said by way of explanation.

"There were only three defenders?" the officer asked him. He looked doubtful.

"Three Altenerai."

The officer's eyes widened to show his whites. "Others. Archers?"

Rylin waved his hand down the hall.

"Upstairs?"

"Archers," he said.

Again the officer sighed.

"Which Altenerai were they?" the soldier asked him.

He blinked. How much did the Naor actually know about the Altenerai and what they looked like? Probably they knew the names of all the famous ones. Maybe even a common fellow like the man he impersonated would be familiar with N'lahr and Kyrkenall and Decrin and Enada—all the great war leaders from the last war, really.

"Describe them," the officer commanded.

He decided not to play thick this time. He wasn't sure what happened to useless Naor footsoldiers on the battlefield. "One was dark haired. Handsome."

"Handsome?" the officer voice held a mild revulsion, and Rylin realized he'd offered a descriptor Naor probably didn't use on other men.

"Wicked swordsman. Blinding fast." He supposed he was blinding fast as compared to the sorts of opponents the Naor usually faced. He saw the officer stiffen.

"Was he older, with dark hair, and tall?"

Who did they think he was talking about? N'lahr?

Of course. They wouldn't have heard of Rylin, so they assumed he was talking about the most famous Altenerai swordsman! He fought down a smile. Apparently that little joke he'd made to the Naor scout about being N'lahr returned from the dead had gotten through the ranks.

Rylin nodded slowly. "Yes. It was *him*."

The officer and his underling exchanged a horrified look.

Rylin straightened, risked a glance back toward the door. He still heard distant fighting, and the snorts of horses, but they seemed far away. The rest of the soldiers had moved down the corridor or up the stairs.

"You said there were two more," the soldier prompted.

Rylin nodded as he listened carefully for the sound of Naor above. Footsteps had receded there as well. He was alone with these two fellows.

The officer sounded impatient. "What did the others look like?"

"Your name, sir? Regiment?"

"I'm Commander Elchin of the Falcon Guard." The man sounded insulted, exasperated. Probably he wasn't used to being questioned by run-of-the-mill warriors from other tribes.

Rylin lurched forward as if losing balance, and when the other soldier reached forward to assist, he drove his knife straight under his chin and into his brain pan. The man spasmed as blood sprayed. Close at hand, Commander Elchin was surprised enough for Rylin to seize him with one hand, trip him, and drive him headfirst into the overhanging staircase.

The officer's helm clanked into the stone and he groaned. Rylin finished him before he could react further, and in only a few more moments opened the secret doorway, heaved both bodies into the ladder shaft, closed it, and left the fortress with a much more useful semblance. He was now Commander Elchin of the Falcon Guard. At his hip was Varama's pouch with its second semblance stone, hidden by the commander's actual cloak. He also wore Elchin's wineskin, and his own sword and knife, obscured by the same semblance that disguised his features.

The wine was good on his throat, a strong, clean flavor. The Naor commander had been possessed of decent taste. He held off drinking more, though, for the trickle of liquid reminded him of just how hungry he was, and alcohol on an empty stomach wouldn't do him any favors.

More troubling was his worry over the semblances. One night, during their long ride, Varama had used her hearthstone to take the things back to full power, which was wonderful, but still only gave him a few hours.

So, nothing challenging, really. He just had to wander into the dying city to gather intelligence, disguised as an enemy officer, hoping he wouldn't be detected as an impostor or accidentally killed by his allies. And then he had to find his way back into the tunnels. After that would be the small matter of getting his people safely outside Alantris. He didn't have a plan for that, yet, and hoped something would come to him as he explored.

If it all went poorly, he could always stick with his fallback plan—die in a blaze of glory and take a horde of the hastigs with him.

2

The New Commander

Tesra wished the designer of the exalt khalats had done more to distinguish them from those worn by Altenerai. She understood that the treated fibers naturally took on a blue shade, but surely the garments might have been tailored differently. All that distinguished the two kinds of armored robes was the red piping along the sleeves, cuff, collar, and edging, and that didn't seem enough. Not when she stood on a dais in front of a room full of Altenerai squires.

She wasn't completely sure why she felt a little like an impostor. It was the martial corps who had shown themselves corrupt. Kyrkenall had gone on a murderous rampage and killed two exalts and two Altenerai. And Rylin . . . She felt her face flush. He'd lied his way into the heart of the Mage Auxiliary, breaking one of the fundamental tenets of his oath as an alten. Then he and that weird alten, Varama, had broken into the Great Hall and stolen not only a supply of hearthstones, but the queen's special keystone, badly injuring Exalt Thelar in the process.

It had taken the concerted efforts of two healers to fix his arm, although as he stood quietly beside her, stern and grim in his own khalat, there was no knowing he'd been injured at all.

She was at fault for introducing Rylin into Thelar's training session, where he'd deeply embarrassed the dignified exalt by outthinking him during a duel. Afterward, Thelar had returned to treating her with icy, proper formality, which was his practice with all but a handful he considered close. That retreat was more painful than Synahla's blistering rebuke and even Rylin's betrayal, for she had no idea how long their working relationship would remain damaged, and whether repair was even possible. Synahla, at least, had accepted part of the blame once she'd cooled down. Thelar really wasn't talking to her anymore, and the silence as they waited for the arrival of the commander had grown strained.

She and her fellow exalt stood on the raised stage of the assembly hall in the third- and fourth-rank dormitory building, behind the stables. It was smaller and better appointed than the dorm for lower ranks. Most of the squires remaining in the city were actually first or second rank, yet there were so few of them, Commander Synahla had ordered the gathering here, lest the vast empty space in their own building further demoralize the troops.

The smaller hall hadn't made any appreciable difference in the manner of the thirty-odd squires facing them at parade rest. Though they were well-groomed, garbed in their immaculate gray dress surcoats—rank denoted on shoulder and left breast with red chevrons—the best that could be said for them was that they seemed subdued. Rylin and Varama had galloped off with the vast majority of the squire corps, and those left behind looked downright disheartened. Tesra felt for them. They could hardly be blamed for the actions some of their commanding officers had taken.

To left and right of the squires, the assembly hall benches had been stacked in an orderly fashion, under fading mosaics of fabled events from the Altenerai annals. On Tesra's right, robed Herahn bent one knee before Queen Altenera, who stood before him in old-fashioned armor and gazed proudly at the first sapphire rings, presented by the sorcerer on a silver platter.

A mosaic of Jessaymyr stretched along the wall to Tesra's left. The famous alten was central, bright hair streaming behind as she charged a rank of shadowy shapes with burning eyes while Kerwyn launched a blazing arrow from a nearby hillock.

Tesra heard the door open behind her, and she and Thelar turned as one, snapping to attention. Commander Synahla, leader of the exalts, had entered the room. Dark haired, violet eyed, she would have exuded authority even if she hadn't worn the exalt khalat. She didn't look as though she felt the least bit uncomfortable in her uniform.

She strode forward, her highly polished boots beating sharply upon the old stage boards. Her glance swept over her two exalts, and she paused briefly to return their salutes before halting to stare at the squires, now standing at full attention.

Thelar and Tesra turned to face the squires with her.

Synahla kept the young men and women at attention for a while longer. Finally she nodded. "At ease."

They shifted back to parade rest, hands behind them, feet a shoulder-width apart. The highest-ranking squire, a fifth-ranked man with short, curling brown hair, stood at their upper right, and he pivoted sharply to inspect the lower rankers before taking up parade rest himself.

Synahla stepped to the slim lectern in center stage and addressed the squires. "Thank you for coming."

Tesra, as Synahla's adjutant, had commanded their attendance, so the thanks was a formality. The squires seemed to accept orders from exalts under the circumstances, even though the question of rank priorities between the older and newer corps had yet to be formally settled by the queen.

Synahla continued. "We are at a difficult time in the history of the Altenerai, and of Darassus and the realms themselves. Many outsiders are saying that the loyalty of you squires has to be questioned, given that so many of your leaders have proven traitorous."

She let that statement hang fire for a moment before providing reassurance. "I think these fears are exaggerated. I know each of you has worked diligently for years to reach your current position. And I know few are as selfless as those who serve the throne as members of the Mage Auxiliary or the Altenerai Corps. So I want you to know that I will do my utmost to quash any rumors about your loyalty." Synahla paused to consider her listeners for a moment and brush a lock of hair from her brow.

"But you yourselves must not lend credence to these rumors by any of your own words or actions. It's come to my attention that some of you have openly expressed criticism of the Mage Auxiliary." She gripped the lectern edges. "I understand that some rivalry is inevitable, but it should remain good-natured, for we are all working for the glory of our queen and the safety of the realms. Some of this loose talk involves fallacious rumors that could be detrimental to all of us, and a few of them smack faintly of treason. I am certain that you are familiar with all or most of the accusations."

Tesra certainly was, and frowned that squires thought that the exalts plotted to usurp Altenerai power, much less that they had somehow framed the discredited Altenerai for crimes they had manifestly committed. Crimes Tesra herself had witnessed.

Probably Synahla did not expect a response of any kind, for she certainly hadn't invited one. But the fifth ranker took a single step forward, coming to full attention, and put his hand to his chest in salute.

Synahla paused with mouth partway open, staring at him. Tesra wondered what that measured look on her face meant, and whether she would ignore or chastise him.

She addressed him coolly. "There is something you wish to say, Squire Elik?"

"Yes, Commander. With your leave?"

Only the briefest quirk of the commander's eyebrow betrayed her irritation. She gave permission with the faintest of nods.

Elik resumed parade rest, left hand behind him, right hand sweeping toward his fellows. The alert blue eyes in the fifth ranker's broad face briefly caught her own. Like all squires, he was fit and muscular. His short brown hair curled naturally, and his chin had a pronounced cleft.

"I have spoken to the squires at some length, Commander," he said. "They have pledged focus upon their training and their duties, and will leave rumors lie. They recognize that unfounded accusations weaken the bonds that unite us. I wish to apologize, on behalf of the squire corps, for permitting gossip to gain footing among us. We will be vigilant henceforth."

Tesra saw only a sincere desire to please upon the squire's open, intelligent features. She had liked his pluck, and looked to Synahla for her reaction.

Synahla bowed her head in polite acknowledgment. "Those are nice words," she said, then added, "and I believe them heartfelt. I thank you for attempting to address the situation, but I think you are overmatched, owing not to your character, but to your inexperience."

Elik's brow wrinkled, but he said nothing further.

Synahla continued: "You cannot be blamed for that. But it is further evidence of the poor judgment of your commanding officers that they left a fifth-rank squire in command."

The exalt commander summarized for effect: in truth the departing Altenerai had abandoned their positions leaving no one in charge, and the fifth ranker had simply done his best in the absence of official orders.

"Which brings us to my next point," Synahla said. "Until Commander Denaven returns with the loyal Altenerai, effective this moment forward, I am placing Exalt Thelar in charge of the remaining Altenerai Corps. Some of you may be familiar with Exalt Thelar, for I am told he sometimes called upon the late Alten Asrahn. And you are likely aware that before joining the service of the exalted, he himself was a squire of the fourth rank. Thelar, would you like to say a few words?"

Synahla stepped aside and beckoned Thelar forward.

In profile, with his proud hooked nose and dark, brooding eyes, he appeared very much like some hero of legend. Thelar looked out on the squires and gathered his thoughts for only a moment.

"I thank you, Commander. Squires, I do not intend to supplant the legitimately appointed officers of the Altenerai Corps, but to aid them in this troubled time, and to ensure that its traditions, so exemplified by Asrahn Red Sword, are instilled in today's squires."

Tesra couldn't recall the last time someone had actually referred to Asrahn by his sobriquet, and struggled not to roll her eyes. Sometimes Thelar's formality bordered on the ridiculous. In her own squire days, they'd called the Master of Squires Asrahn Hard Ass. Behind his back, of course.

Thelar nodded to Elik. "I see that Squire Elik has reminded you of your duty. I will do my best to communicate your heritage. He and I shall work to ensure that emphasis is placed henceforth upon honorable conduct. We shall resume regularly scheduled training within the next hour. First, though, I believe the commander has a few more words."

He traded positions with Synahla.

"Thank you, Thelar." The exalt commander pushed back her hair once more as she resumed the lectern. "Until Commander Denaven returns from his mission, you are to refer to Thelar as 'Commander.' I fully expect that you will prosper under his leadership." Synahla paused, looked over her audience and then continued. "While I have full faith in the future of the Altenerai Corps, I believe we need to make absolutely certain that all lingering issues have been addressed. Which is why I wish to call forth two squires. Donahla, of the second rank. Hamar, of the third rank. Please step forward."

The third ranker, a tall, tanned man, took two steps from the front line. Donahla, a short-haired brunette woman, walked from the back. His manner was grim, almost challenging, and hers was furtive and uncertain. She drew next to him, glancing at him as if for solace. Not finding any, her gaze flitted to the two commanders, then to Tesra, who sadly met her eyes. Then the young squire fixed her gaze upon the middle distance, and she had marshaled her fear into determination.

Synahla looked sternly upon them both for several long breaths.

"My inquiries have led me to the two of you, who seem to be at the dead center of the most malicious web of lies. There is nothing honorable about those whom you have defended. Any of their past deeds have been overshadowed by their crimes. And you must realize this."

Tesra saw that Hamar's mouth tighten in anger.

"I can't imagine what either of you hoped to gain by your actions. I am giving you this one chance to speak the truth and apologize. Hamar, you may address me first."

The squire's eyes widened. His mouth worked back and forth, though he made no sound. And then, quite suddenly his expression cleared. "Commander, I always looked up to Alten Rylin, and I liked Squire Elenai. But it appears I was wrong about them. I . . . was trying to impress my fellow squires with defense of the rebels. But I realize now that I didn't understand the serious damage my comments could cause."

This was a remarkable admission, especially given what Tesra herself had learned from the stubborn young squire's records. His assessments recorded that he was habitually reluctant to change his opinion once it had been formed.

"Thank you," Synahla said, almost purring, and Tesra caught the barest twitch along the last two fingers of her left hand, gripping the lectern. Only another spell caster might have guessed she worked a spell, and even then, perhaps only one familiar with Synahla's habits.

She was weaving. Curious, a little apprehensive, Tesra opened her eyes to the inner world and beheld a breathtaking amount of energy linking the young squire to the commander. That Synahla could exert so much power without looking at all taxed was impressive. And a little alarming. But why was she casting a spell?

"I wish to say that I support you fully," Hamar continued. "And I'll not only refrain from further such speech, I'll report similar behavior by my fellow squires."

Tesra was aghast. Altering the perceptions of an enemy on the field of battle was one thing. But Synahla somehow worked the impossible and changed the very thoughts of someone as they spoke. And this was no enemy, but a young man whose only crime was that he didn't want to believe the terrible truth about the Altenerai Corps.

"Thank you, Squire," Synahla said, and her gaze shifted to the young woman.

If anything, Donahla appeared even more resolved than she had previously. Perhaps only Synahla and Tesra understood why the young woman's eyes were rounded. She had to have sensed something amiss with the young man beside her.

"Squire Donahla?" Synahla prompted.

The young woman was quiet. She blinked once, and then her eyes calmed. Watching through the inner world, Tesra saw that it took an even greater expenditure of power to control Donahla's thoughts.

"Commander, I'm dreadfully sorry," the woman said softly. She raised her hand to her face and wiped at her eyes. "I shouldn't have listened to what Hamar was saying. I didn't mean to question that proclamation you'd posted. I know that you and the queen are working to protect us all. I just . . . it's hard to believe that people we liked could take such terrible actions."

"Thank you, Donahla." The commander left off her spell and the squire fell silent.

Tesra studied them both as Synahla paused, wondering when they'd revert to their previous opinion. But their expressions remained clear, if troubled. Could it be that Synahla hadn't just temporarily altered them, but affected some kind of permanent change? Was that even possible?

"Squires," the commander said, "it is never easy to hear bad news. And it is doubly hard when you learn those you admired have failed you. It was right and proper to revere your leaders. But you couldn't know their weaknesses. Kyrkenall is a drunk, who was almost exiled from the corps many times. The Altenerai command ignored and excused his terrible habits for too long, and innocents have paid the price. As for Varama, well, she was always a strange one, far more interested in her studies than her duties. When the queen asked her to put aside her self-indulgent researches to aid the Mage Auxiliary, she fled the city. From notes Rylin left, I think it's fairly clear that he jealously craved attention and probably thought a grand apostasy could win him some measure of glory."

Tesra had heard nothing of Rylin's notes. What else might he have said in them?

Synahla continued: "The unfortunate squires deceived by these traitors may yet learn to see through their lies and rejoin our ranks. Remember. When you seek glory for yourself, rather than for your state, you are one step closer to failure. Follow the oaths you yourselves have sworn. And above all things, put your trust in the queen. There are strange and terrible challenges to be faced. But under her guidance, we will overcome them all. Thelar, you may assume command."

Synahla stepped to her side as Thelar walked to the stage edge and addressed the audience. "Squires! You will meet me on the practice field at the tenth bell. That leaves you less than a quarter hour to get into your training gear. Elik, move them out!"

"Yes, sir! You heard your commander! Fall out!"

Despite Elik's continued shouting, the squires knew their business already, for they moved quickly and orderly for the exits. Thelar trailed after, apparently content to watch Elik put them through their paces. Perhaps he was appraising the fifth ranker's abilities.

Synahla watched until most of them had departed, then turned a satisfied smile upon her adjutant. "You sensed what I was doing?"

How had the commander known? "There was almost no sign." Tesra didn't attempt to conceal her awe. "How did you manage it?"

Synahla shrugged one slim shoulder with false modesty. "I've been practicing. It's possible to draw upon the hearthstones and absorb a little bit of their strength for longer than I'd previously believed."

"It's not just that. It's . . . you changed their very minds. How did you do that?"

"Again, I have practiced."

But where, and with whom, and for how long? Tesra didn't press further, because she sensed she wouldn't get a real answer. One question, though, had to be pursued: "Why did you do it? Wouldn't it have been better to have won them over with the strength of your arguments?"

Synahla smiled drolly. "Their opinions were dogged and dangerous. And we're short on time."

"Will they . . . stay changed?"

"I believe so. Though I may need to meet with them a few more times to be sure. Why does this bother you? They were in the wrong, and they were the ones responsible for most of the grousing. This is better than kicking them out of the corps, isn't it?"

"I suppose so."

Synahla sighed. "What's wrong? Breath of the goddess. Don't you dare question my ethics."

Tesra had privately been doing that very thing, because mages weren't supposed to wield magic against unwilling targets unless they were foes.

"If we aren't careful, they will be our enemies," Synahla continued. "Their objections had to be stifled before things grew worse." Her commander looked at her sidelong. "Or is that not it? Does that look have something to do with Rylin again?"

"A little," Tesra confessed, although she hadn't currently been thinking about that particular part of Synahla's speech. The exalt had turned her from one troubling subject to another. "You said there were notes about his desire for glory. I didn't know that."

Synahla flapped a hand dismissively. "That was just a bit of improvisation."

So she'd lied? "He didn't leave any notes?"

"He might as well have. Clearly he was desperate to impress Varama and the other rebels. He was too easily influenced by the wrong people. Weak."

Tesra was struck by the irony that Synahla asked everyone to follow her and the queen without question, while criticizing others for obeying orders.

"You can take a lesson there. Be careful who you follow. If you hadn't trusted Rylin, we'd never have believed that nonsense about his wanting to join the Mage Auxiliary. He flashed his pretty eyes and you fell in bed with him. Dragging all of us with you."

Tesra felt her cheeks flushing. That wasn't exactly how it had happened.

Synahla continued, over-justifying. "You do understand that we'd have achieved the same results with those squires if I hadn't taken a shortcut? It just would have taken time we can't really afford."

"Yes."

"You don't look convinced."

"No, I'm fine."

"That's good. Because," she said, "I think you've seen I can be very convincing."

Was that a threat? Synahla laughed lightly, suggesting that she only teased.

Tesra forced a smile, feeling ghastly. "Yes. Yes, I've seen."

"Come. There's work to do." And so saying, she led the way to the door. Tesra glanced back once at the empty chamber, and brave Jessaymyr charging against her shadowy mosaic foes, then followed her commander.

3

Dragon Lord

Asrahn had drilled any number of lessons home to Rylin over those long years as a squire, and one choice statement came back to him as he paused before the battered and broken doors of the citadel. "The Naor don't think you're human."

The first time he'd heard Asrahn say that, the legendary Master of Squires had been lecturing first rankers on the practice field. It was a morning only a few months after Rylin had qualified for admission, and Asrahn had been uncharacteristically trenchant.

Though no one would ever have described the Master's instruction methods as gentle, his manner was usually a model of dignified restraint. Not so that day.

At that time the Naor war had been under way for two years, and N'lahr was riding toward Kanesh. Asrahn was training his unseasoned squires to follow as quickly as possible.

The older man was as immaculate as ever, from his polished boots to his well-worn but clean khalat, to his short brown hair, going to gray. He stopped in front of priggish Thelar, his weathered face heavy with a scowl. The hook-nosed squire nervously licked his lips and struggled for composure before his taller elder.

"You grew up in Alantris, didn't you, Thelar?" Asrahn's question might as well have been an accusation.

Thelar answered quickly. "Yes, Alten."

"A city boy?" The way Asrahn asked this, he might as well have been accusing Thelar of child abuse, temple desecration, and propositioning the queen.

Thelar gave Asrahn the confirmation he seemed to want. "Most of the time, sir."

"Taught that all men and women are equal, each presented with a divine spark, and sometimes a gift as well."

"Yes, sir."

Asrahn stepped away, back straight, hands clasped behind his khalat. His head turned and he met the eyes of the squires lined before him one by one. "The Naor don't see it that way. If you're not from their chiefdom, then you're an obstacle to be cut down. If you surrender, the best you can hope for is enslavement. Male squires, though, are a special prize." His voice sharpened. "They like to tear the hearts from you. They think their bloodthirsty gods consume the beating hearts of warriors. Let me be clear." He stepped up so that his face was thrust beside Thelar's. "They do their best to keep you alive while they're ripping your heart from your body."

To his credit, Thelar showed no obvious reaction, although Rylin noticed sweat beading his high forehead.

Asrahn stepped past Thelar and his eyes drifted over two lovelies: Gyldara, a blond woman strikingly beautiful, and Tesra, smaller, pretty, dark-haired and buxom. "They don't kill female squires. Don't count them as warriors. They use them for breeding stock. At least once. So you'd live for nine months the prisoner of some Naor king, which is better than being passed around the camps like any other non-prized woman. Your child, blessed with Naor blood, would be human, but you would never be. No. Sooner or later you'd end up on an altar, too."

"How can they . . . do that?" Tesra's voice was husky with disgust.

"Rape, you mean?" Asrahn asked.

It was a filthy word. In the realm of Erymyr and its allies, forced intercourse was such an astonishing social taboo that it was almost unheard of, and, like murder, certain to result in banishment or death.

"Are you uncomfortable with the word, Squire?" Asrahn asked. And then, surprisingly, he repeated it. "'Rape'?"

Tesra blinked long lashes, clearly affronted. Rylin wondered why Asrahn was conducting himself in such a mannerless way.

"You *should* be uncomfortable, Squire!" Asrahn stepped back and his voice rose. "If you ride out expecting quarter, you're in for a rude awakening. The Naor look on their own women as lesser beings, good only for labor and rutting. The Ushlekt clan routinely cuts the tongues from girls when they're born. Less trouble to remind them to be silent." He paced along the line, and Rylin made the mistake of meeting his eyes before looking straight ahead.

Pass me up, he silently prayed. Go on to Lasren on my right. Go on.

The Gods didn't hear, for Asrahn halted and faced him. "It wasn't so long ago the Naor spent most of their time squabbling over their own miserable little realms and splinters out there in the ass end of creation. All we had to worry about was an occasional raid. It kept our ancestors sharp. Do you know what changed, Squire Rylin?"

"Mazakan, sir." He'd quickly learned never to hesitate when Asrahn or any other alten asked him a question or gave a directive.

"You've just told me what any child over two knows. Is that how you plan to report should some shortsighted alten be so foolish as to send you on a scouting mission?"

"No, sir." Damn. This wasn't going well.

Asrahn's gray eyes narrowed. "Then provide specifics, succinctly! Strive for precision." He turned to Rylin's neighbor. "You."

"Yes, sir. Mazakan and his elder brother fought their way to the top of their own tribe and mastered it," Lasren answered.

"Too vague." Asrahn stepped passed Lasren to Sogahl, a lanky squire with astonishing endurance but no great aptitude. "How?"

"Um. His brother was a weaver, and Mazakan was a clever warrior, and they conquered a bunch of other tribes. One after the other."

"Passable. Speak with more authority. Unless you're guessing. You're not guessing, are you?"

"No, Alten."

Rylin would have said much the same as Lasren and Sogahl, and without hesitation, if Asrahn hadn't interrupted. But then, just as Asrahn had stated only a few minutes before, every child was acquainted with the information they had presented.

Asrahn walked on down the line. "Mazakan. The fearless leader of half a million. The god emperor. Now *he* could convince the other Naor, by fire and sword, that they were all human, under him. Any 'kings'—keep in mind they call any ruler of a Naor village, no matter how small, a 'king'—who didn't bow to his laws had his heart taken for the *olech*. The sacrifice of blood to benefit those in power." He paused for effect and turned to face the line. "But *we* will never be fully human in their eyes. They want our lands. They want our homes. They want our bodies to bring them pleasure and to work their unwanted tasks. And they want our hearts for their fires. But most of all they want to eradicate us as unholy offenses to the proper order of the universe."

Asrahn paced back toward him. "We are beneath contempt. Our men without beards are womanish, unmanly. Our women are exotic chattel. Our children vermin."

"Commander N'lahr said we should respect them, sir," Lasren said.

Asrahn's head turned very slowly. His voice, despite being suddenly softer, was somehow more ominous. "Did I say anything about respect, Squire?"

"No, sir. But—"

"Did I ask for your input?" Asrahn's voice rose.

"No, sir."

"Everyone: seventy push-ups!" he snapped. "And the last one done gets fifty more!"

Rylin dropped with the others, planted his hands in the dirt, and launched quickly into push-ups, privately cursing Lasren. Clearly the old man was in no mood for a conversation.

Asrahn's voice was a whip crack. Rylin saw his boots pass his line of vision as the Master of Squires strode once more to the right. "They don't value life as you do! They don't care about your morals, or your books, or your plays, or your poems. They don't care about your culture, or laws! They won't think like you. They'll not hesitate to take actions you would never contemplate! So don't you forget that when you face them!"

Rylin could no longer remember who'd ended up with fifty extra push-ups, only that it hadn't been him. But he did remember the lecture. It was only after being deployed along the border of Kanesh and facing the enemy had he understood what Asrahn really meant. The Naor had a completely different worldview inherited from birth. Not only did they treat others as less than human, they were reckless with their own forces, sending them forward in great masses despite crippling losses. Their commanders sacrificed their men and themselves in numbers the Allied Realms refused to contemplate.

It had taken the battlefield genius of N'lahr to counter those vast Naor numbers. He had lured the enemy into death traps that slaughtered enough troops that even the Naor had paled and withdrawn. Unable to face them on an equal battlefield, N'lahr had changed the way the war was waged, and he had won.

But now he was gone. The Naor remained in fear of him, but that fear seemed a pale rendering of the original. N'lahr's most talented pupil, Aradel, had perished in battle with the Naor only yesterday. Who was left to counter them? The other Altenerai were fantastic warriors, but the nearest thing left to a great troop leader was Enada. And her cavalry focus would be little help in the forested mountains around Alantris.

There was no one out there to counter the Naor this time, and inside there was only him. The Gods help them all.

The evening guttered to a close as Rylin exited the citadel tower. A pile of limp and broken Alantran soldiers was mounded where he'd spoken with Cerai on horseback earlier that day, their limbs draped across one another in the unfeeling embrace of the dead. Glittering in lurid lantern light, a ribbon of blood rolled out from the mangled bodies and armor and twisted along over the cobblestones.

Farther on, corpse parts projected through the rubble that remained of the innermost wall to the east. The roars from the wyrms he'd heard hadn't been directed against the citadel itself, only its protective barriers. The Naor probably meant to retain the fortress for themselves; walls could be far more easily rebuilt than the great towers.

He banked his burning outrage, clenching his fist beside his sword hilt rather than draw the weapon as he neared the Naor soldiers leading horses from the citadel stable. One man dragged a bloody stable girl by the foot toward the corpse pile, uncaring that the dead child's head clunked against the paving stones with each of the soldier's strides.

As Rylin drew closer, the Naor officer overseeing work noticed him. He was tall, his long chin coated with a sparse yellow beard. Like the rest of his group, he wore a long leather jerkin that hung to his waist, topped by blackened ring mail, and his muscular arms were shielded with metal guards. Despite the obvious rank of the appearance Rylin had adopted, the Naor soldier didn't come to attention like a squire or soldier in the realms would have.

"I've come for a horse," Rylin said.

The Naor was unimpressed. "These are for the general, sir."

It was no wonder the general wanted the mounts for himself; these were penarda, the finest in the Altenerai realms, bred for speed, endurance, and intelligence. The general would know that any horses in these stables would likewise have been highly trained as well.

"I'm taking that one." He pointed to Rurudan, his tall black.

"I'm sorry, sir." The soldier didn't look particularly apologetic.

"I'm glad you're sorry, but I have an important message for the general. The horse, now. I will give it to the general myself, in advance of the others."

The Naor didn't seem to like the sound of that very much. "Your name?"

"Commander Elchin." Rylin emphasized the first word.

"Take the horse." The soldier's bored tone suggested he was permitting a favor rather than following an order. "I'll make sure the general has your name."

Uncertain as to the appropriate response, Rylin frowned as he headed past. Would the real Elchin have dressed the man down, or did the blue feathers affixed to these men's helmets denote some prestigious unit, perhaps the personal guard of the aforementioned general or his clansmen?

He located his own saddle, grabbed a blanket, and found a suitable bridle with snaffle bit and reins. Soon he was mounted and leaving through the citadel's splintered gates.

The wails of men, women, and children hung in the night air. Dogs barked. Buildings burned, and the air was thick with smoke clouds reeking of timber and less savory scents.

Naor soldiers were everywhere, randomly defacing buildings and heaving contents into the streets. They reveled in destruction, carefully smashing heads and limbs from statues they passed. As Rylin rode over the canal circling at the foot of the second wall, he came to a square under an aqueduct where dozens of Alantran citizens were being sorted by Naor soldiery in the glare from nearby blazing market stalls. Rylin halted as one of the Naor smashed a woman in the face with a spear butt. The Naor's shield mate snatched a screaming toddler the mother had been shielding and raised his sword.

Rylin knew he should ride on. Too many lives depended upon getting through and scouting an escape. But he found himself kicking his horse ahead. He leaned from his saddle and swung his blade out to send the swordman's thrust off target.

The Naor swordsman whirled to find Rylin glowering down from his mount.

The soldier stared up at him. Everyone but the weeping, choking parent and mistreated child had been rendered mute.

He'd ruined his disguise now. What reason could any Naor have for stopping the murder of an Alantran child? And how much explanation would an officer give troops in any case?

On closer examination, he recognized the swirling green tattoos along their bared forearms. This was a contingent of the Naor clan Savesh, famed for their assault against The Fragments in N'lahr's day. They were especially bloodthirsty even for Naor. What to say to the dozen staring soldiers and horsemen?

He improvised, speaking through gritted teeth. "I want them all."

He'd assumed that there would be challenge, and that a bloodbath would then ensue. The simple statement, though, seemed to relax the warriors.

"Sorry, sir," the swordsman said. He didn't release his hold on the bawling child.

"Give that one back to its mother so they'll both quiet down. Then gather the prisoners and follow me."

"Yes, sir."

It was apparently enough for the soldiers that an officer had materialized out of the evening gloom and ordered them to bring prisoners somewhere. They must have assumed he intended the captured for an olech, a blood sacrifice.

Soon he was leading three dozen frightened Alantran men, women, and children, closely shepherded by a half-dozen Naor warriors.

He chafed all the while that he wasted time he could ill afford. He had but two semblances, and the power of the one he wore was slowly draining. Not only had he made no progress in how to get his charges safely out of the tunnels, he was trying to put more people inside. Yet he couldn't abandon them.

Nobody questioned him as he proceeded through the city, dark except for the areas being torched, for almost a quarter hour. Not the Naor soldiers he led, nor the large column of spearmen that passed them at a jog, nor the officers deploying soldiers through the square near the temple district on the second tier. From the shouted commands, Rylin understood them to be searching for snipers amongst the high roofs of government buildings, and he felt his back tense. As the Naor officer in charge of a prisoner contingent, he presented a tempting target, and it was easy to imagine an Alantran sharpshooter singling him out from on high to plant an arrow.

He turned down a quieter avenue, hopefully away from the attentions of local archers, and found himself riding under a carefully tended wisteria arch. The Sacred Quarter.

Cautious of both magic and the anger of deities, the Naor hadn't touched the unlit temple area. Presumably they'd have their priests correctly desecrate the houses of Gods with Naor blood rituals before indulging in any looting or wanton destruction. And that thought suddenly provided the inspiration he'd lacked.

Rylin guided his entourage past the fragrant gardens fronting the temple of Vedessa before arriving at the bottom of the seven curving granite steps that led to the sprawling temple, itself topped by three domes, black against a smoke-gray sky. He reined in and swung down from his mount. He bade the guards bring the prisoners up the wide stairs after him, and they did.

None questioned why he should open the massive open doors and walk under the archway, lettered with proverbs the Naor would never read. He skirted the alabaster-encircled pit where the eternal fire still burned among its coals and walked into the main temple chamber, a cavernous room lit only by the sacred fire near the opening and a pair of braziers hung in alcoves flanking the ceiling-high, robed statue of Vedessa. Human-sized wooden statues of Alantran ancestors looked down in silent disapproval from elevated alcoves as the clack of Rylin's bootheels echoed on old flagstones. He noted that tapestries, books, and sacred artifacts that should be here, weren't. Probably the temple tenders had quietly removed them as the first of the walls fell.

Rylin ordered the soldiers to close the door, then told the prisoners to kneel, their faces turned toward the distant statue of their god. They sank, frightened and resigned, and Rylin noted that the guards moved with some glee. They expected, possibly even looked forward to, the slaughter of these helpless people and cast their eyes covetously around at a few sparkling decorations left adorning the temple. The Savesh tribes didn't seem inclined to question the authority of an officer putting them first in line to access such treasures.

"Take a good, long look at the prisoners," Rylin ordered. He paced behind the six Naor soldiers like a drill instructor. "I want you to see how vulnerable they are."

A child began to moan, and an adult frantically tried to shush him. As a Naor moved forward with a growl, sword raised in readiness to still the noise forever, Rylin dropped the semblance. He drove his knife through the neck gap between helmet and armor of the advancing Naor and the man sagged, gasping. The closest warrior turned to see what had happened only to catch Rylin's second knife with his face. He dropped.

Two down, four to go. Rylin snarled and stepped to the right.

He came to grips with the third before the remainder could engage, beating his blade aside and driving his palm hard into the warrior's nose. He heard a satisfying crunch and knew he'd broken it. The man shouted, clutched his face, and tripped over prisoners, who fell desperately upon him. Three down.

The next two rushed at the same moment. Rylin veered left to put the first attacker between him and the second, parried, had his thrust turned by the soldier's ring mail.

The final soldier crept in from the left.

Rylin drove the closest Naor sideways with a flurry of slashes, then swatted his sword away and drove his blade deep through the man's scale mail. As the Naor staggered with a bubbling scream, he got in the way of his companion's attack.

If the third man had pressed on, Rylin would have been done for, but the Naor warrior's hesitation gave Rylin time to wrench his sword free with a spray of blood. Two left, and he not only saw the fear in their eyes, he all but smelled it on them.

The hesitant one tried to give orders to his thin-faced companion. "Attack left, Henzhar! Come—"

Rylin's next swipe separated Henzhar's hand from wrist, and the Naor's mouth opened in a silent scream as blood spurted after the plop of the hand onto the temple floor. The prisoners pulled him down and quickly silenced him.

The last Naor backed from him, eyes wide in horror. He thrust madly once, twice, and Rylin beat both attacks aside before driving his blade through his neck. The Naor toppled sideways.

Rylin turned to see what had transpired.

Most of the Alantrans were standing, staring, as Rylin panted. One of the children sniffed, and a few muttered among themselves in disbelief, but the sound was subdued enough that Rylin heard the drip of blood from his sword runnels to the floor.

The hoarseness of his voice surprised him. "I need to look outside." He wasn't sure why he said anything to them; perhaps it was the way they seemed to be waiting for him to speak. He paused to wipe his blade on Henzhar's pant leg, then jogged to the front door and peered out onto the temple grounds. His gelding, Rurudan, stood obediently where he'd left him. Firelight outlined the buildings to the west. He smelled smoke, and heard the awful screams of the injured and dying. Likely the screams of these Naor hadn't been noticed at all.

Once he returned to the temple, the former prisoners greeted him with thanks, and praise, although they were strangely subdued. A young woman gave him a cloth torn from her head scarf and blotted it at his face; it wasn't until she came away with blood that he realized the Naor had splattered him. He quieted the calls of what they were to do now, and what he planned, and posted a young man by the door to keep watch. Then he searched for the proper alcove.

Finding the trigger for the hidden door was harder than his combat against the Naor. His nerves were stretched tight and he was becoming increasingly frantic. It wasn't until he stepped back to swig from the dead commander's wine that he realized he'd miscounted stones, owing to a small triangular one lower along the rim.

Shortly thereafter he had pushed in and revealed a narrow doorway low enough that an adult would have to hunch. The light from the hanging lanterns outside showed him a ladder.

These people had no supplies apart from those carried by the Naor themselves, and so he raided the temple stores both for food and lanterns, then sent them down the dusty passage with vague instructions to keep quiet and to await his return. He wondered what it was like down there and hoped eventually to find out for himself.

It was still in the temple after he shut the door, leaving him with nothing but the memory of their muted, tearfully renewed thanks, and the dead men.

Before washing up in a back room, a macabre idea came to him. He hesitated only a moment before dipping two fingers into a pool of blood and writing N'lahr's name across the temple floor. The dead general was one of the few things the Naor seemed to fear. What might they think when they came upon these men here, with the name of the long dead Altenerai commander spelled out in their blood? He suppressed a grin.

Cleaned up once more, he shut the temple, like any good worshiper who hadn't just left six dead men behind him, and walked for Rurudan, who greeted him with a wicker of pleasure.

"Glad to see me, boy?" he asked. "You probably don't like this place any more than I do. I'm afraid there's worse to come."

He wished he had an apple for him, then shook his head. He wished he had apples for the refugees. He had to find a way to get them out of the city. They wouldn't store like produce in a root cellar.

Rylin resumed his semblance, glad to note it hid the gore splattering his clothing as he rode from the temple district. Soon he met long lines of Alantran prisoners shuffling past with hunched shoulders, under the eyes of not just a few guards, but whole marching troop columns. Maybe a band of Altenerai could have helped them, but not him, not by himself. He discovered that he clutched the reins in a death grip and forced himself to relax. He thought he'd longed for things in the past, but he'd never known such wanting as the fierce desire to save these people, too, and it was a deep cut to know that he was powerless to free them.

His hands tightened again as he turned a corner, for a contingent of the spiral tattooed Savesh Naor were systematically lining up dead Alantrans and hewing heads from their trunks. They were already well on their way toward a sizable pyramid of skulls.

How was he going to get anyone alive out of a city in the grips of such intense barbarism? Two of the soldiers were even mocking the contorted expression upon one of the heads as one grinning soldier lifted it by the hair.

Ride on, he told himself. Killing them would gain him nothing. Rurudan snorted as if in disgust.

He was still bereft of ideas for getting his people away as he saw a wyrm circling down for a landing just inside the city walls. It beat its huge wings ponderously against the dusky orange-streaked sky. Further information about them was certainly worth seeking out, and he paused to eye the men who rode on the creature's immense scaled back. The beast seemed crafted for nightmare, studded with boney spikes that jutted dangerously from random areas of its skull and spine and great leathery wings bearing sparse, vestigial plumage. Its four clawed feet spread as it dropped, readying for impact.

Its descent was nothing like Lelanc's graceful drops, for there was no sense that the creature thought about what it did. The eyes in its large horned head stared dully forward, and its jaw hung slackly, foolishly. Rylin remembered how one of the beasts had dropped from the sky when he had slain its pilot, a serious design flaw so long as you had ko'aye to carry the battle to them.

Once more Rylin fought a surge of anger at Cerai for stealing Lelanc and abandoning the city.

Flying against all of those wyrms would have been long odds, he knew, but he would have liked to have tried. If Cerai had backed him with her magic, it might even have worked. Instead she had ensorcelled brave Lelanc and fled. As she doomed them all she'd shouted that she hadn't the time for this nonsense, as though she were late for some vital appointment.

She would have to pay.

The wyrm landed like a meat slab thrown onto a table, shaking the ground as Rylin shook himself from his broodings. The creature had been guided into a field just within the outer wall.

The city of Alantris was once more populous than today, its numbers thinned by the last war with the Naor, so they'd turned a lot of the ground in the outer ring over to crops, the better to withstand more Naor incursions. Had Rylin held off those wyrms, the field before him would have helped bring vegetables to the tables of the city's defenders. Now it served as a landing field for abominations, scorched clean of any neat green rows. Five massive and variously colored lizards with thick bodies and necks and long tapering tails rested a few hundred feet apart from one another, and Naor workmen were pitchforking food in front of them from hay carts. Rylin saw animal carcasses and even what looked like some human arms and legs in their feed, although between the distance and the poor lighting on the ground it was hard to know for certain.

On the other side of the field lay a long intact portion of the outer wall. A dark banner, topped with a ko'aye skull, fluttered at the height of the gate tower. That was almost certainly where the Naor general had set up headquarters. At least until the citadel was cleared.

Rurudan disliked both the sight and smell of the wyrms, and Rylin had to urge him into obedience as he continued into the shadow of buildings at the north end of the landing field. The handful of Naor sentries saluted and let him pass. Rylin was soon riding west along the lane separating dark, silent houses from the fields where the wyrms had landed.

The monsters must not have been completely devoid of self-volition, for he saw no weavers, and the things were eating the food without having to be forced to do so. But he noticed that they looked neither to right nor to left, nor evidenced any curiosity about their surroundings. He wondered if they would simply consume whatever was placed in front of them. That, he thought, might be a very simple and effective way to damage or kill the things. Except that such large bodies would undoubtedly require a lot of material before they'd sicken. And right now he'd be hard pressed to find an apothecary or herbalist to obtain something poisonous.

"What are you doing here?"

The speaker had walked out from beside one of the wyrms with two other men. His companions retreated across the field toward the distant gatehouse, but this man planted himself in the midst of the roadway. His flowing fur cloak draped slim shoulders and his head was topped with a thick wool hat decorated with two upright feathers.

As if he weren't already ridiculous, the challenger's voice proved comically shrill. "Get down from that horse this instant. You know you're not allowed near the dragons! Who are you?"

Dragons? That was a new word. Rylin climbed calmly down. "I'm Commander Elchin," he said, noting with some relief that while there were numerous Naor beyond the road and field, none except those manning the food cart for the wyrms were closer than a hundred paces.

"You are to address me as warlord," the man screeched. "You approach the dragons, you do not give me deference—"

Rylin interrupted as he dismounted. It would do him no good if this warlord called down more attention upon him. "Your pardon, Warlord. I was sent to speak with the general. I have important news."

That brought the warlord up short. He peered at him. "There's a weird dweomer all around you, Elchin."

Damn. He'd run into a sorcerer. Could he have been the man who'd been controlling the wyrms? "I encountered an Altenerai sorcerer, up in the tower."

The warlord started. "The one who was flying on the wyvern?"

"I don't know, Warlord. But that's not all. I was sent to speak to the general about it." He feigned a sudden twinge and bent, putting hand to chest.

The warlord looked at him in alarm. "What's wrong with you, man?"

Rylin looked up at him, his lips moving soundlessly. "Important."

The warlord drew closer. Rylin lolled his head, carefully taking in the men and area around them. The food cart was rolling away; apparently the warlord's screeching was common enough to be of little interest. The back of the cart blocked the drivers from view. The outer walls were as yet empty of sentinels, and while Rylin still heard shouts, screams, and the occasional clash of arms, he and the warlord seemed very much alone in the growing darkness.

He pushed off his right leg and grabbed the warlord's throat.

The man's eyes bulged in anger and alarm. Rylin smashed him in the stomach to lower the fists that rose to counter him, and then he dragged his groaning victim into the shadow of the nearest abandoned house, through its doorway and over a dead Alantran woman lying with an arrow in her chest.

Rylin felt the warlord trying to reach his thoughts with a weaving. He dropped the semblance and, there, alone in the shuttered house, he allowed his ring to shine.

The warlord gurgled in horror.

Rylin grinned vindictively. "I'm the one who took down your wyrm, 'warlord.' I bet there's a lot you can tell me, isn't there?"

He turned his leg so that he took the warlord's knee to his thigh rather than his groin, than shook the lighter man. Normally Rylin didn't feel so powerful. But then the warlord was on the thin, reedy side, rare for a Naor. His weaker frame was probably only tolerated because of his magical skill.

The warlord didn't prove nearly as useful as he'd hoped. Rylin didn't have the mental strength to beat him down with magic, and the man proved heroically obstinate about answering any useful questions. It was only when Rylin presented a knife to the warlord's throat that the fellow's tongue loosened a little—he confirmed that the dragons were to be sent on to Vedessus, capital of Arappa, and then to Darassus. Unfortunately, it was in that same moment that someone outside shouted for Warlord Talkus.

His prisoner called out, presumably seeking help, but Rylin ran him through before more than a vague squawk was communicated.

He heard footsteps outside the cottage as the questioner called again for Talkus. Rylin kept his hand over the dying man's mouth as he lowered him to the scrubbed wooden floor, then jerked the cape off a slack neck. A moment later, Rylin was wearing Talkus' image, and called out that he would be along in a moment. It was a fair approximation of the warlord's high voice.

"The general's called a meeting, Warlord."

"One moment," Rylin replied, surprised by just how petulant he managed to sound.

He bent to strip the weird hat from Talkus' head, then used a booted foot to push the corpse deeper into the house, wiped his knife on the man's shirt, and sheathed it.

His first thought was to call the messenger in here to be killed so he could slip away unchallenged. He probably had only a few minutes worth of magical power left inside the semblance, and it was time to switch over to the second stone. He had just finished transferring the images to the other semblance when he heard a footfall and saw the outline of a man in the doorway of the home.

"Warlord, are you in there?"

"I am." Rylin stepped forward.

"The meeting's to begin promptly, and High Warlord Zhintin wants you there."

It would be very simple to kill this man and sneak away. But then if warlord Talkus didn't turn up, mightn't that get the Naor wondering where he'd gone?

Probably the chaotic nature of the attack upon the city would protect Rylin's movements for a while. In a flash of inspiration, though, other possibilities presented themselves. If he were in the same room with the general and top officers, might he be able to kill them all? Though he'd be unlikely to survive against the Naor's top amassed warriors, a sacrifice on his part might cripple their command structure. But would his death leave the refugees trapped?

He realized that he'd been more than a little lucky as well as a little smart so far. If he were to attempt something so bold as the action he now contemplated, he'd have to be very smart *and* very lucky. The potential amount of information he could learn, and the advantages it could give future warfare against the Naor, could not be underestimated. Yet wouldn't he be mad to try? He needed a little more information about what he was walking into.

"I'm coming," he said and started forward. "Why does Zhintin want me?"

The messenger still sounded respectful, but a little puzzled as well. "I'm sure he wants to hear your report on the downed dragon, my lord. The sub-commander said he saw you ride in. Were you able to look it over before your flight?"

"Of course," he replied. They exited the house and he judged they were on a course for the gate tower. He dare not ask who was assembled. Surely Warlord Talkus would be expected to know the commanders.

"What about the battle for the city?" he ventured.

"The dragons were a great asset, as High Warlord Zhintin predicted, and the city was ours almost as soon as the west and south walls fell."

"I know that," he snapped. He had surmised it, at least. "I've been busy. I want to know the state of our forces and what resistance is left."

"There's little organized resistance, Warlord. The attack force reached the citadel quickly after you breached the walls and rumor has it the governor is dead, along with the top leaders of the Alantran forces. We've had no important losses. Many captives have been rounded up. All the better for you, eh?"

The warlord he was impersonating must have some need for prisoners. Surely they weren't just chopped up for dragon food. By "no important losses" did this messenger mean all the commanders were unharmed? How many would he soon face?

As they neared the gatehouse, he saw no sign of the combat that must have taken place outside it, despite a generous amount of torchlight spilling from the ground floor windows. Many warriors, both Naor and Alantran, had doubtless been killed here, but no bodies lay beside the tower, nor were there broken arrows, swords, or other weapons of any kind, apart from the spears in the hands of the two tall sentries standing outside the main door. Slovenly about much else, the Naor were apparently organized with arms, command centers, and corpses.

The messenger who'd summoned Rylin hurried ahead to open the door for him, and the sentries ground their spear butts and came to attention. Rylin couldn't be sure what the salute from a Naor warlord looked like, or whether they even gave one to the rank and file, so he simply breezed past. He felt the cloak swinging from his shoulders as he moved, lending him a sense of dramatic importance. Apart from the absurd hat and fur-trimmed cape, the rest of his appearance was illusion.

Inside the gate's watchtower was a worn wooden staircase leading to the second level, and a door he knew would open to a mess hall. Once again, the messenger opened it for him. This time he stepped through less boldly.

Surely the table had never before hosted a meeting like the one now underway. He counted ten people seated in the bright rectangular chamber, well illuminated by pairs of sconces, two to each wall, and a lantern dangling from a ceiling beam that set their breastplates gleaming. A complex abstract mural suggesting a rolling, tree-topped landscape, rich with mountain browns and the green of grass and trees, wrapped each of the walls and intertwined the many mullioned windows, a sophisticated work completely at odds with the furred, murderous, and filthy occupants seated around the table in the room's center.

All but one of eleven chairs, inlaid with carved masterpieces of leaping game animals, was already occupied. The stench of sweat and body odor was almost overpowering. Rylin guessed that warlord Talkus had bathed a little more recently than many of the men here; he hadn't smelled this bad even after Rylin had killed him. Under the circumstances, sight of the table's mostly consumed feast—various animal bones, half-gnawed bread, and drink—was revolting, despite the length of time since his last meal.

The hulking warriors at the table paid him scarce attention as he walked in, for one of them was making a report.

Rylin stepped to the empty chair, idly wondering if the man he impersonated was always apportioned a position farthest from the table head, or if the chairs had been assigned on a first-come, first-serve basis.

A single look at the group before him persuaded Rylin that his mad idea about killing them all would result only in his own death. These were veterans, the quarters were too close, and there were countless warriors just a shout away. Had he just jeopardized all the lives under his charge by taking this risky step? Was he being bold and clever, or would Varama have chided him for not thinking the problem through?

As he took his seat, only one man, an older fellow with a long, thin beard, at the right corner of the table, paid him any heed at all. His eyes were searching, and Rylin wondered if the man might be a sorcerer. A furred cloak similar to Rylin's own hung from his shoulders, and in a moment Rylin guessed this was Zhintin, the lord of the dragons and his commanding officer. Probably wanting to know whether Rylin had good news or bad. Rylin gave a short nod, and the man relaxed, then gave his attention over to the scarred, red-bearded warrior addressing the meeting.

The speaker's voice was gravelly, as though he'd been gargling sand. The scars of an old neck wound showed above his scale mail when he turned his head. While he rattled on about the conditions of horses for various groups—all good to excellent, in his estimation—Rylin surveyed the rest of the table's occupants more closely. Half were men of early middle-age; the others were in their midtwenties, and all but one of them was bearded. It struck him as peculiar that the Naor would allow any men to be beardless, going on what he knew of Naor society.

And then he realized with a start that the one without a beard was a woman. She was a brunette with shoulder-length hair, sitting two chairs down from the general. She wore scale mail like all the others, but there was no missing the lack of a laryngeal bump along her throat. And despite a concerted effort to mask femininity through absolute absence of any refinements, she was pretty, even though her nose had been broken at some point. Rylin tried not to stare.

He let his eyes drift from her to the table head and contemplated the general, surprised to find such a young man seated there. His red beard was cut straight across only an inch below his chin and was waxed stiffly so that it looked almost like a comb. His eyes were green and rather small, though they were alertly centered on the reporting officer. Unlike many of his warriors, he wore no ornaments, and there were few flourishes upon his gear.

The gravelly, red-haired officer finally quieted and the young general turned to another warrior to ask for casualties.

Rylin listened patiently as reports were delivered. He learned that the information he'd obtained in the days previous was accurate—there were eighteen thousand Naor in and around the area, and some were already riding north to establish footholds in outlying regions. There was as yet no sign of reinforcements from other Dendressi realms—the Naor actually used the word "fae" to refer to the Allied Realms, which seemed to mean both "alien" and "wrong" at the same time.

As a black-haired cavalry officer was in the midst of his scouting report, the woman interrupted him. Her voice was low and rough, possibly in a deliberate attempt to sound more masculine. "Did you not find any sign of Altenerai near my encounter? It was a few hours outside the settlement they call Wyndyss."

The officer bowed his head to her, and addressed her with a male honorific. "We found nothing of interest there, Lord Vannek."

Her lips settled into an aggrieved frown. "Then you weren't looking closely enough. Kyrkenall was there. There were two others, in those armored Altenerai coats. And one of them looked a lot like N'lahr."

Rylin's ears all but rang. So Kyrkenall was still alive? And what was this talk of N'lahr?

"We found horse tracks," the scarred soldier beside Rylin spoke up.

The original speaker interrupted. "But they led up to a rock slide, and there was no way through it. It was a fae trick. Just like dressing someone up like N'lahr," the officer said with a smirk. "If N'lahr was really alive, don't you think he'd have turned up before this?" Rylin sensed he was no longer answering Vannek, but playing to the rest of the table in an attempt to score political points.

"Enough," the general said, and angrily slapped the table with his hand. For the first time he acted as young as he looked, but everyone around the table froze. "The account of my brother was verified by his officers. His honor, and his story, are beyond question, Tarsht."

Interesting that the general referred to the woman as both "brother" and "he."

"Of course, Lord General . . . ," the black-haired officer said quickly. Where he had seemed smug and certain mere moments ago, Rylin now saw his eyes wide in fear.

The general continued, his manner that of a hound fixed upon the kill. "Do you suggest a grandson of the great one provided a false report to me? Or that he is easily tricked?"

The "great one"—the woman was a descendant of the Naor ruler, Mazakan. Perhaps that explained why, even as a woman, she wielded power.

The Naor officer had grown ashen faced. "No, my lord."

"I think you do. Leave us."

"I meant no disrespect, my Lord General," Tarsht stammered. "Not to your family—"

The general looked at the man on the other side of the stammering officer and snapped a command. "Rolk, Tarsht does not obey. His spoils are yours."

"No!" The man named Tarsht backed away.

But the heavyset fellow beside him grabbed his long hair from behind and pulled him off balance, as Rolk was already plunging his food-stained knife once, then twice, into the officer's neck. Rolk stepped back and casually dropped the dying man on the ground behind the table. Rolk's graying beard writhed in a grim snarl of satisfaction.

The general glared around the table, then looked to Rolk. "Have someone get that thing out of here," he ordered.

"Yes, my lord." Rolk's voice was husky in answer. He moved swiftly behind their chairs and called out to soldiers in the hall. Everyone pretended not to notice as two soldiers dragged the corpse from the room. Rolk tossed the officer's empty chair in a corner.

Rylin hoped no one else could hear the thudding of his own heart, sounding as loud as a warning drum to him. Gods, it was madness to be here. So this was how Naor officers dealt with insubordination? Rylin didn't suspect it a method likely to promote independent thought. How would he cover if he were asked to report on . . . anything?

He tried to focus. But his mind turned to the talk of N'lahr. Wily as Kyrkenall was, he supposed the archer might have played a similar ruse Rylin used this very day, but what companion could he get to play N'lahr while he and Elenai were hunted outlaws?

As Rolk returned to his seat after obtrusively wiping his knife on his pant leg before sheathing it, the reports from other officers continued. Rylin learned that another leader, Chargan, was expected to arrive within the next week, intending to use Alantris as a staging point from which to attack golden Darassus itself. Apparently, an army led by Mazakan was already deployed about the city of Vedessus and awaiting arrival of the dragons. Those walls, the Naor expected, would fall even more easily than the walls around Alantris.

Rylin listened in dread. The Naor had planned all of this very well. The timing would limit any reinforcement from allied realms. Astonishing that the Naor could be so clever when they lacked insight about so many other issues.

As the reports dragged out, Rylin began to fear above all for the length of his semblance's duration. He activated his inner sight so that he might extend a sensory tendril toward the semblance and discovered it dangerously low. Lower than it should have been. He'd thought Varama had fully charged the item, but perhaps she hadn't managed it, or it might be that it required more power to maintain a more elaborate disguise. It wasn't as though he were simply wearing the illusion of a khalat with slightly different piping, as he had when he'd impersonated Exalt Thelar.

He couldn't be sure how much time he had left and didn't have the experience to guess. He tried not to fidget as he considered his options. If the thing dropped, he could leap for the door, or leap for the general. If he was going to die, he'd like to take out the Naor commander.

Rylin lost track of the conversation again, so he'd missed when the dragon lord, Zhintin, began to speak about the condition of the great beasts.

Zhintin's voice was thin, obsequious. Apologetic. "Using the dragons in battle proved far more taxing than my men had supposed, General. If they're to be used at peak efficiency against Vedessus my pilots need time to recover."

The general wasn't interested in excuses. His voice was cold and sharp. "They must be sent on to the Great Lord without delay. You know this, Zhintin."

"I don't make excuses, my lord." Zhintin bowed his head, quickly. "I merely inform. I tell you, it was harder for my men to control the great beasts than your brother Chargan had anticipated."

The general's little eyes were merciless. "Do you say he deliberately misled you?"

Zhintin held up a hand. "No, sir. Not at all. We don't each have the power and skill of your esteemed bloodline."

His commander's voice was heavy with disapproval. "Then you misjudged."

Zhintin spoke on courageously. "Yes, sir; it was very challenging to maneuver the beasts and attack at the same time, watching for enemy ballistae and spears. Our practice didn't take that into account. It left our handlers far more fatigued than we had expected."

The general stared at him, and Rylin wondered if Zhintin was about to get the same treatment as Tarsht. Maybe Zhintin wondered the same thing. The general turned to Rolk. "I'm not happy about this. What do you suggest?"

Zhintin visibly gulped as Rolk coldly eyed him then turned his head toward his ruler. "Wizards are weak, and magic is never dependable. There are no spares. They probably need the time."

That must not have been the answer the general looked for, because he frowned. He glared across the table and spoke as though he regretted being advised to mercy. "Give your men three hours. Requisition as many prisoners as you need for an olech."

There was no missing the relief in Zhintin's voice as he bowed his head. "Yes, my lord general. They will be far more successful moving forward with this rest that you've ordered."

Rylin wiped the rising snarl from his face at the thought of the citizens being rounded up for slaughter. When life was expended there was, indeed, a brief surge of magical power, but hundreds, perhaps thousands would have to be slain to generate enough energy to achieve anything noteworthy.

Rolk spoke up, his voice a hoarse growl. "My lord, we haven't had time to sort out the prisoners. We don't know the valuable from the useless."

The general nodded shortly. From this one, at least, he was willing to hear unpleasant information. He looked back to Zhintin. "Cull babes and the elderly, Zhintin. We need the able-bodied."

"Yes, my lord."

"Go. Now."

As Zhintin started to rise, Rolk spoke again. "Some of the weak ones will be bargaining chips, my lord. They may be relatives of some important—"

The general cut him off sharply. Apparently he'd taken enough advice. "No. Zhintin, you have your orders."

Dragon Lord Zhintin exited, fastening Rylin with a significant look he didn't understand before heading for the doors. Zhintin shut them behind him.

The general met Rolk's stern gaze, almost in defiance, for a long time, and then cleared his throat. He was doing his best not to look nervous, and failed. Rylin wondered if Rolk served as advisor or even monitor for Mazakan. "I appreciate your reminders of the god king's policies," the general said. "But I think Mazakan would be far more upset if we failed to send the dragons to Vedessus than if we anger a few cringing fae by killing their useless ones."

Rylin glanced at the graybeard beside him and watched him nodding his agreement. He looked neither cowed nor frightened.

The general's eyes then settled upon Rylin, who released his hold on the inner world, still doubtful about the amount of energy left him. A few more moments, probably. He wished he could be certain.

"What of the dragon felled by the Altenerai who fled?" the general asked him.

Rylin sought for meaning in his question. The Altenerai who fled? He stared, feeling immensely stupid as he tried to parse out a meaning.

At last it came to him. The Naor had seen him, Rylin, fighting the ko'aye on Lelanc, then witnessed Cerai departing upon Lelanc, and concluded that it had been the same person.

"Your report," the general snapped. "What's the dragon's condition?"

By the gods—he'd hoped the beast he fought was destroyed. Did that question mean that it hadn't been? He didn't have any way of knowing how it might be healed, or what it might take to do so. Yet the general didn't seem to appreciate bad news or challenge and he already looked irritated. The most important thing was to escape this meeting alive, and the odds of that would improve if he kept the general happy.

So he lied boldly. "Far better than expected, General. Little damage was sustained at the wings, which as you know, are especially delicate. The rib bones and supporting muscles are larger but much easier to heal because they're simpler structures." He hoped that sounded authoritative and vaguely technical, as he expected someone immersed in their field would sound.

It might have pleased the general. He wasn't sure, because he didn't smile. The man nodded once. "How long will it require?"

Damn. What would a realistic assessment be? Was the man expecting hours? Days? Weeks? He guessed. "At worst, three days."

"Three days?" Rolk asked. He nodded to himself and there was no missing his grunt of pleasure as he addressed the general. "I expected it would be far worse."

"A good weaver can surprise you," the woman, Vannek, said, then glanced down the table at Rylin.

"You said worst," the general prodded. "What's the best estimate?"

Damn. He'd hoped this scrutiny was nearly over. He'd have to keep the lies coming. Fortunately for his oath, he was speaking to the enemy during wartime. "If I have the support, sir, I might manage that in half the time." As he spoke, he realized how he might use the circumstance he found himself in to his advantage. "Though I will need a large number of prisoners for olech, to power the healing."

Rolk drummed fingers on the table, frowned, then nodded. "I'm impressed, Talkus."

The general continued. "Follow Zhintin and tell him to give you authority to acquire however much olech for your own needs. Go, now."

"Yes, General." Rylin rose, nearly tripping over his cape. As he turned his back, the semblance faded. It didn't run out with a pop or anything obvious, but he felt it slide away, and looked down to see the sapphire visible upon his hand as he reached for the door latch.

4

Beyond the Wall

Rylin bowed his head, fist pressed to his mouth to cough even as he dug into the pouch at his side. Would they see him? Would they notice that beneath the cape and hat of this Talkus fellow was a broader Altenerai?

The general was already questioning another officer, but what were the others doing? Would they see him fumbling at his belt rather than carrying out the order to exit?

His hands closed upon his semblance and he sent the image of Talkus into the thing and brought it upon himself as he opened the door.

The guards outside stared at him. What did they see? Had it worked? He closed the door as if everything were normal, and the sentries came to attention.

He frowned at them and stalked past, only then glancing down at his hand to see the sapphire ring absent. The first semblance, though, was likewise very low on power.

He found Dragon Lord Zhintin waiting outside only a few feet beyond the sentries. The man motioned him forward and began walking along the lane in front of the dragons. Rylin worried only a moment that he'd been found out.

"You survived your encounter with the general, then?" Zhintin asked in a low voice. "He must have been in a forgiving mood."

"He told me to round up prisoners for an olech."

Zhintin stopped in his tracks. "Did you actually tell him you could repair the wyrm with blood energy?"

"He suggested it; I accepted and departed."

Zhintin shook his head in sympathy. "That's going to go poorly for you. How long do you have?"

"Three days."

"Three days? Zhendek's balls. You'd need three weeks, at least, unless we could somehow take the beast straight into the Shifting Lands with a whole team of weavers!"

This was all wonderful news to Rylin. So the dragons weren't easy to heal, either in time or resources. No wonder the Naor had so few.

The dragon lord searched his face, looking honestly troubled for him. Rylin reminded himself that, while the Naor might think less of those who weren't from their culture, they must be capable of both love and loyalty. "What are you going to do?" Zhintin asked.

"I'm going to get as much blood energy as I can," Rylin said. "What else can I do? He told me to work with whatever I had, and to make it a priority."

Zhintin sighed. "Of course he did." He spoke on as if talking about one of his favorite subjects. "He doesn't really understand. He's fine with tried-and-true tactics, but none of them comprehend magic the way Chargan does."

Rylin said nothing, but recognized the name. This was the one expected to arrive next week with forces for Darassus, apparently another grandchild of Mazakan.

Zhintin continued. "If Chargan were in charge of this he wouldn't be letting all the tribes carve up different areas. Our takeover of this fae city would be a lot more organized. He'd also have brought a lot more spell casters to start with."

Chargan sounded uncomfortably capable.

Just as he'd begun to wonder how to gracefully leave Zhintin, Rylin noticed a cart moving along the lane in front of the homes beside the landing field where the dragons rested. As the cart came to a stop, two men hopped down and headed into the nearest home. A moment later they dragged out a pair of bodies. Of course. This was a cleanup crew, diligently collecting more skulls for their pile. And the home where Rylin had left the body of the man he imitated was just a little farther down the block for them.

Zhintin was returning to his original point. "But none of that matters. I just don't see how an olech can really help you. There aren't enough Dendressi to sacrifice to fix that dragon in the time you have." Zhintin's thin beard waggled as he shook his head. Rylin watched as the men with the corpse cart drew closer to the home where he'd left Talkus' body. Possibly they wouldn't recognize it. But wouldn't they still see it for Naor?

"You should drag out the process," Zhintin advised. "See if you can last until Chargan arrives. If you can show a little progress repairing the dragon, he's liable to be a moderating influence. I'll leave you our two cleverest weavers when we fly out. They don't have the stamina we're going to need anyway, and they might be able to help you along with the repairs."

The officer really did seem to have Talkus' best interests at heart. "That's kind of you."

Zhintin looked at him oddly.

Rylin groaned inwardly. He'd used words too genteel and wondered how the Naor gave thanks. "I meant only to thank you."

Zhintin grunted. "It may not be enough to save you." He glanced back at the guard tower. "I must be on with it. I'll have Tarften begin assembling some Dendressi for you. Fifty, do you think for a start?"

He meant to have far more than fifty. If this worked, everyone that he selected for olech would be walking free with him. "I want to start with a larger number, as the general ordered. I don't want to arouse suspicion. I'll only sacrifice them as need dictates."

"That might work. Very well." Zhintin frowned, following Rylin's gaze to the cart, continuing along the lane. The house where he'd killed Talkus lay only three ahead of them. "What is it you keep staring at?" Zhintin asked.

Rylin hesitated only a moment. Perhaps it should have troubled him that lies came so easily to his lips. "There's something I should probably show you. Come with me."

Zhintin looked doubtful. "Shouldn't we—"

"This is important."

The officer must have trusted Talkus, because after only a brief hesitation he followed Rylin toward the house where Talkus actually lay. Rylin moved into a jog as they neared the dragons, lying now with heads down between their forward claws. They showed no reaction to the presence of either Rylin or Zhintin as they hurried past, and he tried not to marvel over their vast dark bulk.

By the time they were beyond the dragons and approaching the row of dark houses, the corpse cart was drawing to a stop in front of the home where Talkus' body lay and a bulky Naor was already dragging the dead woman with the arrow out of the doorway.

"That's all you need to do here," Rylin commanded the young soldier.

The man swiveled quickly, and the light carried by his companion shone full on Rylin/Talkus and Zhintin. The fellow stiffened and came to attention, releasing his hold on the dead woman so that her hands slipped to the dirt roadway. He was a thick youth with a heavy jaw. His stare was almost comically stupid.

"Stay away from this house," Rylin said crisply. "This one's off limits."

The man with the lantern didn't seem much brighter. He spoke with a thick, guttural accent that Rylin had a hard time following. "Sir? We're removing all bodies."

"This home's off limits until further notice. Move along, and don't come back."

"Yes, sir." Both turned back to the cart, the larger of the two hefting the woman's body to his shoulder before hurling it amongst dozens of other corpses. Rylin tried not to focus overmuch on the arms and legs protruding from the cart.

"They don't breed them very smart in the marshes, do they?" Zhintin asked before turning back to Rylin. "What's this all about, Talkus?"

"Head on in. It's best that I show you."

"I don't have a light."

"I do. Give me a moment."

The dragon lord looked increasingly puzzled, but was still willing to follow Rylin's request, and so stepped into the dark space beyond the open doorway. Rylin closed the door only a moment after entering the building himself.

"Where's that light?"

Rylin willed his ring on. "Here." And he dropped his semblance as he reached for the dragon lord. His intent was to wrap his neck with his arm and put a knife to Zhintin's throat.

But the dragon lord wasn't so simple an opponent. He leapt away with stunning speed. Something sparkled in his hand as he tossed it toward Rylin.

There was no way for Rylin to avoid the shards. He shielded his face with one sleeve and was shocked to feel pain. Whatever the dragon lord cast cut straight through the heretofore impenetrable Altenerai cloth. Rylin's arm stung and, worse, something had jabbed his side.

He had neither the time nor the inclination to inspect his wounds; he advanced with knife ready, light playing across the room as the hand with ring shifted. He saw the dragon lord backstep into the central living room, with its table and chairs and the legs of dead Talkus.

Another stab of pain, this time from a spell that brushed past Rylin; protected as he was by the Altenerai ring, it didn't leave him completely unscathed. He winced, and his opening thrust at Zhintin was blocked by a swift arm. A second, more forceful blast of pain followed, this time centered on whatever had struck his side, as though Zhintin were twisting a dagger into him.

Rylin faltered, leaving the dragon lord time to draw his own blade. Zhintin stepped back to give himself more room, and that was his undoing, for he bumped into Talkus' legs and lost his balance.

Rylin leapt forward, swept his opponent's blade aside with such ferocity that it was knocked from the Naor's hand. He sent a numbing sleep command at the stumbling Naor.

The dragon lord caught himself against a low cabinet on the back wall, slumping a little. But he shook off the spell and reached once more for a side pocket.

Rylin swiped fast, striking deep into the reaching arm just above the elbow. The dragon lord's scream of agony was cut short by Rylin's second blow, which left the man a dying, gurgling, bloody mass on the floor beside the real Talkus.

Rylin stood panting, feeling with his inner sight toward the man's thoughts. These, though, were scattered and useless and frightened, and Rylin, out of respect for his enemy—even a little regret—withdrew so Zhintin could die without intrusion.

It didn't take long. Rylin set his knife on the counter and listened for a moment, fearful that the corpse cart men might return. But all he heard were distant shouts from some other part of the city where the Naor advanced and slaughtered. He then shone the ring's light upon his side and discovered a glittering object the size of an arrowhead piercing armor and skin. Other, smaller flecks stuck in the flexible khalat.

"That's surprising," he said aloud. So the Naor had been busy in the years after the war. They hadn't just developed the dragons, they'd come up with a counter to the vaunted Altenerai armor. The weapon must be rare or difficult to control, or he'd have found it used by other men he'd fought.

Rylin inspected his arm and saw he'd been struck by even more slivers. Though he couldn't be sure, it seemed none of the wounds was grievous. But each bled steadily through the armor.

"Fabulous." He'd been overconfident. The trick with the light had been arrogant. If he'd meant to take Zhintin prisoner, he should have managed it without dramatics. The end result had been that both the leader of dragons and his chief adjutant were dead, and that was good. But he'd botched things. Rylin hadn't managed to get any more information out of Zhintin, he didn't know how to arrange for the prisoner transfer, and he'd gotten himself wounded.

He discovered, upon touching one of the shards on his arm, that the cursed things were actually sharp all over. The tip of his finger bled freely until he pressed it and lifted it above his head. How the Naor had tossed them at him with such force without hurting himself surely had more to do with magic than skill. Unfortunately, Rylin didn't have time for long analysis. Right now, if he moved fast, he had an opening to walk out with hundreds of Alantran prisoners. What he'd do then remained to be seen, but he had a few ideas. The first task was cleaning his own wounds.

He wasn't an accomplished healer by any means. Rylin had no idea how to mend serious chest wounds. But like all Altenerai spell casters, he'd received rudimentary instruction about tending flesh injuries, and one of them was to simply lend energy to accelerate the natural process. Follow the thread, Kalandra had once told him. Just picture what the body was doing before it was interrupted by the injury, and make it whole. Sometimes that simply pushed out the bad, and while it wouldn't drive out a spear thrust through someone's shoulder, it might push out dirt or maybe even these metal shards, so long as they weren't embedded particularly deep.

It took more concentration than he would have liked to focus on his own body. He was too worried about losing himself in inner focus and being surprised by Naor intruders. But he felt the areas and sent little surges of energy through them. One by one the shards dropped away, and the skin scabbed, leaving a tingling afterimage of discomfort. Finally there was only the largest shard, in his side. He stared down at it, panting in exhaustion.

Removing that one proved almost too much. Already stretched a little thin, running low on magical energy, he was seeing black spots by the time he forced it free. It made a dull clatter as it dropped on the floor between the dead men. That, he thought, might be interesting to Varama, so he stuffed it into her satchel after wrapping it carefully in a piece of cloth torn from Zhintin's cape.

If he'd had more power—say, a third of Cerai's, or even a little of Kalandra's—or, better yet, one of the hearthstones Cerai had stolen, he'd have had much less trouble. And he might've worked out a way to re-charge the semblances.

But that was idle dreaming. He needed a better plan. In the darkness, if he were wearing the dead man's clothes, he stood a fair chance of getting by, so long as he didn't speak much. If, however, the semblance were to fade while he was still wearing the Altenerai khalat, he stood no chance at all.

Unlike Zhintin, Talkus was of his approximate height, though he was leaner. Maybe it could work. He quickly stripped the body, alarmed by the amount of thumping that took place as he maneuvered the corpse to leverage him out of pants and shirt. Every motion seemed to ram an elbow or boot or knee into the floor and cabinet.

There was the small matter of the blood all over the front of the dead man's shirt. He discovered a bucket of water someone had carried into the home. Probably that poor dead woman been planning to do some washing up in the evening, never dreaming the Naor would breach the walls and forever end her plans, even the mundane ones.

He poured the water into a smaller tub he'd spotted in a cupboard, and set to work cleaning the shirt, aided only by the glow from his ring. In the end he'd managed to wring out the worst of the stain.

The pants were fine, although on closer look they were a bit narrow, not to mention a bright green.

As he contemplated the pants that were too tight and the shirt that was wet and probably too tight as well, he wondered if perhaps this weren't as clever a plan as he'd originally thought. Unfortunately, it was the best he had.

As it turned out, the worst thing wasn't wriggling into the dead man's clothes. It was divesting himself of his Altenerai khalat. It wasn't just that it was superb armor that had been uniquely tailored for him. It was that, like his ring, it was a sacred object, entrusted to him to wear for the safety of the realms. Light and flexible it might be, but it was still armor, and it didn't roll into any sort of concealable bundle. How to explain carrying a large object with him?

In the end he decided he would wrap it in a blanket. He assumed he had enough rank to do what he wanted without challenge, and if he was questioned by a superior, he'd claim he'd found the armor and was planning to show it to the general.

The other option was to stuff it into the closet where he'd left the bodies, but he'd be damned before he let some Naor lord find his khalat.

With a little luck, of course, everything would be settled before the bodies would be discovered. But then he'd been pressing his luck for hours now. How much longer could it hold?

Please, he thought, whispering to Darassa, patron goddess and founder of the realm of Erymyr, let me get by for just a little while longer. I know I'm far from home, but these people need my help.

Rylin continued the prayer as he emerged into the moonlight and beheld the long line of dragons, still now and apparently sleeping. Naor pennants flapped noisily along the wall. Somewhere in the distance, Naor officers shouted commands.

He sighed and offered thanks at the sight of Rurudan. The big black was standing precisely where he'd left him. He knew his horse was well enough trained to stay where left, but he hadn't been sure the Naor were well enough trained to leave an officer's horse alone. He split the too-tight green pants climbing into the saddle and then decided to tear the shirt along the upper arm seams to give himself more range of movement before setting out, cloak and hat obscuring his features.

So far, bold action had proven the best option, so he continued in the same vein and briefly activated the semblance to impersonate Talkus while he asked a passing black-feathered soldier if he knew where the officer in charge of prisoners was to be found.

The man with the power over tens of thousands of innocents turned out to be fat and pig-eyed with a thin mustache and scraggly beard. Rylin found him in a finely appointed Alantran home. He got up from his candle-lit banquet table, struggling to smooth out a sash worn over his armor.

Rylin hadn't decided how to play the situation until he sensed the man looked a little flustered, so he kept his voice tight and clipped. "I want one thousand prisoners, including children, and mothers with infants—whole families if you can manage it—delivered to the west gate within one hour's time."

The man's face lit with a grin. "That's a whoppin' olech, eh?"

Rylin nodded curtly. "The lord general has commanded it. I'm to repair the fallen dragon."

"I will see that it's done, Dragon Lord. Do you want pretty ones?"

Rylin couldn't suppress a frown at the man's leer. "I want numbers; their appearance doesn't matter."

The Naor grinned. "Of course."

Rylin nodded sharply to keep from driving his sword through the officer, then turned away. "I shall await them at the west gate," he said over his shoulder.

Still sickened from the encounter, he disengaged the semblance, wondering the while how few moments of it were left him, and rode quickly back to the second level and the temple district, trusting that darkness and his Naor garb would be enough of a disguise.

He headed past the sentries around the temple district and then up around the maze of bushes surrounding the temple of Vedessus, riding his horse up to the porticoed entryway. As he dismounted he was dismayed to see two Naor guards slipping out of the darkness to draw close.

What if they'd seen the Naor bodies just beyond the temple door? "Who posted you here?" Rylin demanded. "How many are with you?"

He heard the scuff of a step behind him and pivoted sharply. The movement saved his life, for a spear jabbed through the space where he'd stood only a moment before. The figure from the darkness lunged with the weapon again. As Rylin stepped aside the man snapped at the others to hurry.

"Get him before he makes any noise," one on his right said softly.

The speaker didn't have a Naor accent, and none had beards. The ramifications of that information didn't occur to him until he blocked another spear thrust. It was only when he had the spear grasped in his off hand and his sword driving toward the man's throat that he recognized his attacker for one of the citadel archers. He managed to spare him only by a wild contortion that left him off balance. As one of the others leapt at him he threw himself sideways, willing his ring to glow as he rolled to his feet.

The two swordsmen disguised as Naor soldiers came at him anyway. Rylin maneuvered to the left, parried one savage strike with his blade, and said, sharply, "It's me, Alten Rylin."

Flush with battle lust, the men stared at him for a moment before realization finally dawned. He had the ring, but not his khalat, and apart from the sapphire light upon his hand the lighting conditions were feeble at best.

"It is him," the archer bearing the spear said breathlessly. He was a tall, powerful man with long dark hair.

"I'm wearing a Naor disguise."

"So are we. Praise the gods you alerted us," the archer said. "We might have killed you!"

More likely *he* might have killed them, but he let that pass. Rylin was disappointed that he hadn't thought of disguising some men as guards himself. "What are you doing here?"

"Waiting for you to report in, Alten. Alten Varama set us to watch for you."

That bode well. It likely meant that Varama's group had found the other refugees and she had taken charge of the situation here. "Is she doing better?"

"Better than she was, sir. She still seems weak."

"But she's speaking clearly?"

"Oh, yes. Did you find anything?"

"I think I've got a way out for a whole lot of us. Where's Varama?"

The archer brightened at the news, then pointed to the main door. "Just down the ladder, sir."

Leaving those three on guard, he grabbed his khalat and headed inside to the hidden entrance, and even with his ring shining had nearly as much trouble locating the proper stone as he had the first time. He divested himself of the strange hat and the cape, donned his damaged khalat, then pressed upon the stone to open the chamber. The revealed ladder led into darkness illuminated solely by a lamp at the bottom that pooled light against the final few wooden rungs. As an added precaution, he kept his ring lit as he climbed down.

Below he found squires, who greeted him like a long lost friend. Dust-covered lanterns hung in niches every fifty paces or so. Only a few were lit, shining feebly on refugees huddled all along the narrow hallway in both directions. There were far more than he recalled guiding to safety.

"Rylin!"

Before he knew it, a slim woman had thrust herself into his arms. She pulled back far enough to stare at him, as if searching his face to ensure it was really him. Denalia.

"I wasn't sure you'd come back," she said.

"Neither was I." He noted her glad smile and the bright eyes, and remembered again that she thought herself in love with him. He felt guilty that he hadn't thought about her for hours and that her own enthusiasm for their reunion was far greater than his. "How did you get here?"

"I led a band to the temple for shelter and the guards let me in."

There was probably more to it than that, but he was in a hurry. "I'm glad you're safe." Pleasantries would have to wait. "Where's Varama?"

"That way. What did you learn while you were out scouting?"

"I found us a way out, but we don't have much time. I need to see Varama."

Denalia nodded as if she understood, grabbed his hand, and forced her way past a group of staring youngsters.

Rylin was surprised by how far the tunnel stretched. "How extensive are these tunnels?" he asked. "Who built them?"

She glanced back with a smile. "There are all sorts of tunnels that run under the city: water tunnels and sewage tunnels and even some maintenance tunnels. When Alvor was governor, he abandoned some aqueducts and tore up a bunch of the city to add the canals. Varama says that while he did that he added hidden entry points and connecting tunnels to link it all together, and tie it in with an extensive cave system under the second tier. Apparently, the most hidden sections have been maintained by a select few ever since, under command of the Altenerai."

And apparently not just any Altenerai, for he'd certainly never heard of them. Rylin was swiftly lost in his own worries and oblivious to the touch of the young woman's fingers. The more he thought, the more tenuous his planning seemed. Right now the people in these tunnels were free and safe. If he was to lead them out he'd be exposing them to the Naor, and there was a very strong possibility that his plan would fail, in which case they'd be slain, or captured . . . and then slain. And what of the thousand prisoners he was promised? Could he convince the Naor to let him take the "olech" outside the city, as he'd thought when talking to the officer of prisoners? And even if he could get a group beyond the gates, what would stop the Naor watchers—for they'd surely send guards—from alerting the horde, who would chase after on horse and slaughter them all? Maybe he should just try to get them all into the tunnels, but would they all fit? And how long could they live with the surely limited supplies stored here? He couldn't see a way to get clear and could only hope Varama would be able to make something more of his efforts.

They passed several people who halted their activities to whisper or nod at him with questioning eyes, but none impeded their progress. Denalia stopped beside another lantern, where there was a door, and pushed it open. Varama sat behind a small, battered desk in a small, square room under an old-fashioned oil lamp, writing something on a piece of parchment paper. Sansyra lingered to one side. Varama saw him and set down the pen. As her long face turned up toward him, he felt a wide smile spread across his own. It was wonderful to see her again, and a delight to see her rising, even if it was slowly. The blue tinge to her skin seemed particularly prominent in the light, lending her an otherworldly cast. She stopped before him and slowly gave him a salute. "Hail, Alten."

"Hail. Feeling better?"

"I've felt worse and better." She nodded. "It's good to see you as well. You're wearing quite an interesting outfit."

He glanced down at his terrible Naor pants. "I only have one semblance stone left and it's nearly drained. You'll have to use it to conceal your appearance when we leave."

She blinked at him, said nothing. Sansyra looked expectantly between the two of them. Finally, Varama prompted: "Perhaps some of the questions I would ask in the wake of your pronouncement will be answered as you describe for me, precisely, what you've seen and done."

The door opened once more and Governor Feolia entered.

"Shut the door, if you please, Governor. Alten Rylin was about to present his report." She stared at him expectantly.

It had been such a pleasure to see her alert and normal again that he struggled momentarily to regain his focus. He noticed, too, that he was very, very tired. It took longer than he wanted to organize his thoughts.

He recounted chronologically, trying to include details he thought of most import to Varama. The adoption of Elchin's identity and the freeing of the prisoners. The killing of Talkus and the assumption of his identity. He conveyed all that he learned at the conference meeting, suddenly aware of the stunned regard of his listeners. He veered from strict recount to synthesize everything he now knew about the Naor leaders, from their names, to their plans, to their capabilities and behaviors. He moved on to the death of Zhintin, showed Varama a sample of the strange weapons the dragon lord had hurled at him, then returned to the subject of prisoners.

Tired or no, he found himself nervously shifting in the silence that followed his report. He concluded, somewhat self-consciously, "So the Naor are going to give me a thousand prisoners. But I'm not sure what to do next." He groaned inwardly that he should sound so hapless.

Sansyra and Denalia looked stunned.

Governor Feolia's worry-lined face was lit with determination. "You've succeeded beyond expectations, Alten Rylin. Not only did you gain valuable information, you've dealt major blows to their command structure and secured the lives of a great number of our people. This may be the providence we've needed to mount an effective resistance."

Rylin shook his head. "But the ones they release to me probably can't fight and they can't all live down here, right?" A hope flared as he turned to the still-silent Varama. "You haven't found a way out through the tunnels, have you?"

"The tunnel network is even more extensive and well stocked than I realized," Varama said. "But, no"—she looked at the governor before re-turning to Rylin—"it won't support a large number of people for long. And only one passage leads out of the city—it's currently impassable due to wall collapse." She crossed her arms thoughtfully.

"Then we'll have to get them out through the main gate." Rylin sighed. "I need a more plausible excuse to take the prisoners outside of the city."

A pregnant silence followed, broken by Varama's high timbre. "There's a spring with magical resonance a half mile from the city, where any ritual would increase in potency by nearly fifty percent. Tell them you intend to perform it there."

"I know of no such spring," Feolia protested.

"That's because I'm lying," Varama said. She spoke again to Rylin. "The Naor leaders don't know magic. They don't trust magic. They're likely to believe anything you say about magic if it's said with conviction."

He nodded slowly. There were a lot of steps missing—like how to take out the prisoners' guards—but he could assume Varama's keen mind had already worked out intermediate actions and he was more interested in the end point. "All right. Assuming we get that far, what then?"

"The village of Rilatrys. Some of the locals should know the way. It's in the mountains a half day west from here. Remote, accessible through a footpath that's easily defendable. There's a mountain lake with plentiful water, and they have storehouses for food because snow, and occasionally a strand of the shifts, precludes travel for months at a time."

"But the Naor will surely overrun that area soon," Denalia inter-rupted, and Rylin was surprised to note the same irritation he was sure Varama would register.

Varama's answer was clipped. "After Rylin escapes with his group, we'll be keeping the enemy busy enough that they won't have time to follow."

"Wait a moment." Rylin could scarce believe what he heard. "You're going to stay?" He didn't add that the whole reason he'd left the tunnels in the first place was to find Varama a way out. "You'll be discovered. There must be people out there who know about the tunnels, and the Naor might be questioning them even now. Whatever you intend to do here isn't worth the risk."

"On the contrary. Look at how much you have achieved in but a single night." Varama moved on as if the matter was settled. "I'll need most of the squires and many of the Alantran soldiers."

"I'm sure they'll be eager to fight for their city," the governor affirmed.

"The remainder will have to accompany Rylin, disguised as Naor, so that he has warriors at the ready. The Naor will assign guards to your prisoners—"

"—Unless we already have our own guards," Rylin finished. Of course.

"Exactly. We have a small number of Naor uniforms, including those acquired from the soldiers you slew in the temple. Additionally, we can hide weapons among the evacuees here. I wish you to take them with you. You can claim you rounded them up on your own."

"I will accompany them," the governor announced.

Varama turned to her. "You'll put yourself at more risk than if you remain."

"Yes. Should the gods smile and allow me to survive, I mean to rally help to relieve the city."

Rylin licked his lips and wondered how he could convince Varama to leave Alantris or if he should even try. He wanted to talk to her alone. "We're short on time," he prompted.

"We certainly are. Denalia, I want thirty warriors detailed with Rylin. Except archers. I'll need all the archers that can be spared."

"Right." Denalia nodded agreement and hurried to instruct her soldiers.

"Sansyra, go get the squires prepared for action. Feolia, you might spare a word for the evacuees."

"I will."

"Rylin, I want a word with you."

Feolia bowed shortly to Varama and left. Sansyra filed past him with a nod of approval. Denalia touched him again on the arm, smiling sadly, and then shut the door behind her.

Rylin sank down upon an old bench. It shouldn't have felt comfortable at all, but the relief was palpable.

Varama sat down across from him and passed over a flask. He took it gratefully, speaking as he uncapped it. "More fruit juice?"

"Only a little. We haven't much left."

He sipped, and the sweet pleasure of it was almost as much of a restorative as the cool tingle that spread through his body, for Varama tended to magically fortify juices with aid of a hearthstone. As Cerai had stolen all their hearthstones, it wasn't surprising the supply was limited.

He capped the now-emptied flask and passed it back.

"I want more specifics about the Naor dragons. It sounds as if they are crafted, living puppets, like Cerai's horse—powered almost entirely by the will of a pilot."

"Yes." Rylin hadn't thought about Cerai's disturbingly compliant equine in many hours. He wondered what had happened to the animal. What would the Naor think of it if they found the thing in the stables? He shook his head to clear it of idle thoughts. "If you really mean to stay here, killing the rest of the pilots ought to be a primary objective." Gods, he was starting to sound like her.

"Better to destroy the dragons, in any case. They could find new pilots. I want to hear about the security details around them."

He sketched in the information for her. As he concluded, Sansyra returned to report that everything was being readied.

Rylin nodded to himself, struck by an almost paralyzing wave of doubt. Suppose he were as blind to the inherent challenges before him as he had been to his own errors yesterday when he hadn't noticed the detail on the boots of the dead squire. How much could someone change in just a single day?

He wanted to close his eyes and sit against that wall and let everything stop. He wanted someone else to take the responsibility for these lives.

Varama put a hand to his forearm. That in itself was noteworthy. Then she squeezed it and met his eyes.

"Don't doubt yourself now, Rylin. You can do this."

"Before, it was just me. Now my scheme is putting more than a thousand at risk."

"I used to have faith in what you could be," she said solemnly. "Now I know that it was justified."

The day he'd been awarded his ring, he had been both exultant to receive it and torn by doubt that he truly deserved it. Now this remarkable woman told him that he had earned his place, and he felt a sense of satisfaction deeper than any he'd ever known.

She released his arm and he smiled, then shook his head. "You realize this whole thing's probably going to get us killed."

"Welcome to the ring," she said simply.

She went upstairs with him, moving a little stiffly still. Those about to depart assembled in the empty temple above. Compared to the overall population of the city, it was a paltry number. Yet the two hundred and sixty nervously watching his every move were a larger command than he'd yet taken. Among them were numerous children, some small enough to still be in the arms of their mothers. Another three were hunched with age and would be slow moving.

The majority, though, were fit enough, and nearly thirty were actual members of the Alantran guard force. And there were five squires, including two fourth rankers.

He stood before the Alantrans and warned them that they had to pretend they were cowed. That they had to fearfully keep eyes away from their captors. That while they could take their weapons with them they had to be careful to conceal them, and not even to reach for them until he gave a signal.

Time, he knew, was passing fast. The thousand Alantrans he'd requested were probably being marched from various holdings under the watchful eyes of Naor guards to the rendezvous he himself had scheduled before the gate. He'd requested intact families, but would such considerations be given high priority? He didn't know how much authority his assumed identity actually held. Would those orders be questioned? Was there enough energy left in his semblance to speak with any Naor at length while in full disguise?

Alas, with no hearthstones it was impossible to charge one. Some outcomes simply had to be trusted to luck, for instance that the bodies of Talkus and Zhintin would not be found and identified.

At a signal from Varama, he told them to ready themselves and to practice their expressions, and hurried to her side.

The alten looked wan and tired to Rylin, though she held herself erect. Denalia stood at her left with grim resolve. On sudden impulse, he passed over the used semblance. "In case," he said. He wasn't sure in case of what. Maybe she could use a little magic to charge it; even a half minute of assumed identity could be life saving. "I couldn't have survived without it," he added.

Varama accepted the tool without comment.

He put hand to heart and let flare his ring. "I can never repay you for your counsel. And your example. Someday, I hope to approach your wisdom."

A rare smile touched her lips. "Let's neither of us plan for the future, Rylin. Be not sad. If this be our numbered day, let us meet it smiling."

"Aye," he said, though his smile had passed, and he had to tear the words from his throat lest he choke upon them. "Hail, Alten."

"Hail."

He discovered that Sansyra and a group of squires had joined Denalia in staring at him and Varama. He motioned them over, for they were just as deserving of his regard as his friend. All but one were those he'd called in from outside the citadel tower late in the day. Saved, only for a later death. He soberly clasped arms with several. "Good luck to you," he said. "And good hunting."

"Good luck to you, Alten," the first whispered, and the others either nodded or repeated similar sentiments.

Sansyra and Denalia, he addressed last. Sansyra was more formal than she'd ever been with him, offering her hand in an arm clasp. Denalia, though, looked as if she expected something more, and when he offered his arms for an embrace, she all but threw herself at him, clasping him so tight it surprised him, something he was sure Sansyra caught as she met his eyes over Denalia's shoulder.

After a moment, he returned the embrace, and then Denalia took his face in both hands, leaned up, and kissed his forehead. "I shall live to see you," she told him softly.

"I'll hold you to that." He forced a grin.

It was long since time to be on the move, and he left Denalia and Sansyra and Varama and the other volunteers with a last salute. A few of the men grinned at him. Young love, he knew they were thinking.

He found it annoying that they thought he could be so distracted. He had much more important things to concern himself with.

As he rode at the head of his small column of refugees, prodded along by what looked to be grim-faced Naor guards, he thought they appeared convincing. It would never have worked in daylight, when it would be rendered very clear that most of the Naor beards were trimmed hair held in place by helmet chinstraps—Varama had already been making preparations for future events. But it wouldn't have to. It would either work now, or there was no point in trying.

He halted his procession at the entrance to the cleared market space before the west gate, astounded by the number of dejected Alantran citizens sitting under guard. Dozens of armed Naor paced back and forth around the seated crowd, and a stern-looking man sat his horse beside a lantern at the immense wooden gate that barred their exit from the city. Its three spearlengths of metal-sheathed planks had never looked so formidable before, or so far away. Rylin activated his semblance, silently praying that it would hold out for just a few moments longer.

Rylin had selected one of the fourth rankers as his second in command. He spoke in a hurried whisper to him as he started forward.

"Wait here, Donnis."

Rylin set Rurudan circling around the larger group of sad-eyed prisoners, most of whom didn't bother to look his way. Many were able-bodied women and men, with children sprinkled in among them, but a number looked elderly or infirm in some way. He hoped they'd be able to make the journey he planned this night.

There was no sign of the tubby officer of prisoners, whom Rylin had expected to deal with. Instead he faced a mounted and scowling Naor officer who offered only an abbreviated salute as Rylin drew to a halt. Having seen several other officers using the gesture—a hand lifted upright to the helm—he copied it himself.

"There they all are," the officer said with an encompassing wave of his hand. His face proved pinched and sour, his beard thick and curling. The officer's dark eyes burned with skepticism. "What do you want with so many good workers? And then you want children, too?"

Rylin spoke with dismissive arrogance. "I need them to gather sorcerous energy to heal a dragon."

The man's frown deepened. "Then why do you need any of them related? You just need life force, don't you? Given those you brought, shouldn't we keep the good ones back here for better use?"

Rather than justify, Rylin thought it best to go on the attack. He set his mouth in a prim line and was pleased by the whining, superior tone his imitated voice created. "Are you an expert?" He threw his head high and spoke imperiously. "There's a magical nexus located a mile east of here, and if you had the sorcerous talent of a toad you'd already have sensed it. Between it and the special olech I'm about to perform, I'll get enough of the right energy. But that's really none of your concern, is it?"

The officer actually growled. "You need to watch your tone."

Rylin had little idea whether he outranked the Naor, whose helm featured two yellow feathers, or if the fellow outranked him. "The lord general himself ordered me do this, as I saw fit, with as many as I needed for my olech. You've no right to question me."

The Naor officer's mouth worked silently for a long moment. Too long, Rylin thought, watching him.

"I will take this up with the High Warlord Zhintin," he said finally.

That would be hard, since Zhintin's blood-soaked body was lying in a home near the dragon landing field. Rylin felt an arrogant smirk rising and let it, thinking it played well with his role. "You go right ahead, but if you keep me waiting you'll have to answer to the general. He wants this done as soon as possible, to please the god king. And he's not particularly interested in excuses."

Rylin turned his back as he guided Rurudan past the man, pointed to the trio of soldiers beside the gate, and made a rising motion with his hand. To his surprise, they rushed to open the way to a dark track of road and grasses beyond.

The officer rode close to Rylin and leaned in, his voice cold. "I don't care who your father is, Talkus, when you're through with this olech I'm challenging you. We'll see how a scrawny rump rutter like yourself holds up against a real man." He turned the horse smartly and left.

Rylin felt his semblance fade. He shouted out to the guards about the prisoners and pitched his voice high, trying to talk through his nose as Talkus had done. "Up, up! We're driving the prisoners west. Quickly now!"

He had the snap right. He thought he sounded a little too much like a caricature, but the soldiers guarding the Alantran prisoners didn't seem to notice. Some of the Alantrans helped others to their feet. Rylin led the way through the open gate, his neck hairs erect, for he half expected someone to see through his disguise and call him out or simply hurl a spear into his back. He kept waiting for further Naor objections as he rode under the gate, but none came. Maybe in the dim light they couldn't see that his beard had vanished.

Rylin kept himself well ahead of the group and didn't look back until he was a hundred yards from the city itself. Plumes of smoke from burning buildings rose serpentlike to blot the stars. Behind him a mass of mostly slump-shouldered humanity was leaving the dirt road after them, shouted along by almost a hundred Naor guards, most of whom were on foot. A handful of them were his impostors and he carefully marked their positions in his mind. Some of the Alantran prisoners sobbed, thinking they were being marched to their execution. Well, with luck they wouldn't be tearful long. Some were looking around warily as if hoping for opportunity to attack or escape and he prayed they'd hold off until the time was right.

He wished there were a good excuse to send the real Naor guards away. Men and women were going to die when the time finally came to fight them, but if he ordered the soldiers off it would raise one question too many. Depending upon how successful that sour-faced officer with the yellow feathers was in expressing his displeasure, there could be trouble following them at any moment.

It was all he could do to keep from turning his head again to see whether units were being dispatched from the city. Surely that lone Naor wouldn't be the only one who thought it strange he was conducting the olech outside Alantris and far from the dragon he was supposed to heal.

Somehow, as they marched into the night, his luck held. It seemed an interminable time, with each pace a thousand year advance, but the walls were eventually more than a half mile off. Rylin rode on, back straight, hoping his arrogance and air of command would discourage any sort of challenge.

None came. From time to time, the Naor shouted for a prisoner not to delay, or to firm up their two column lengths, but there were no objections. He could scarce believe it.

A dense cluster of trees loomed between nearby hilltops just another quarter hour away, and he chose this for his objective. Once within, he'd be out of sight from the wall and the trees could be used as cover by the noncombatants.

As he glanced back to check on his charges, he heard the sound of hoofbeats. Another band of riders was charging at them from the darkness behind and to the left. He cursed. Luck had finally run out. But maybe these weren't Naor. There'd be no talking his way out of this now, so he raised his ring in slim hope and set it alight at the same moment an arrow slammed through his upper arm. It felt like he'd been jabbed with a hot poker. Altenerai armor had spoiled him, he thought regretfully as he struggled to pull his sword.

Rurudan suddenly collapsed under him, with a piercing scream. He rolled away, just managing to free his left foot before a horseman galloped up. The shouts and clangs and screeches of battle sounded in a darkness full of movement.

He blocked a blow from the slashing rider. It was only as another attack crashed into his chest that he recognized its wielder as someone in squire's gear.

And then he was down and he knew he was dying. The pain in his chest was overwhelmingly sharp and his breath had left him. His heart beat loudly in his ears, drumming out even the sound of the battle, which seemed now to be waged at slowed speed. Rylin fumbled to find the focus to cast a healing spell, even as he heard his name called out by Donnis.

The scent of the grass was very strong. Not a bad scent to die beside, he thought. He felt as though he might pass right through it and sink into whatever lay below.

5

With Clearest Sight

Tesra had always thought the queen's office a little stark. White shelves sat behind their glass doors, displaying long orderly lines of green and red leatherback books. At head height, the shelf near the queen's white birch desk displayed a line of glittering memory stones and a slim, elongated emerald, beside a single Altenerai ring. White wood paneling stretched above the shelves, though much of it was hidden beneath landscape paintings of forested scenes and one seascape looking from the Storm Coast out toward the palms upon the Isles of Koradel.

The room had once been orderly. Now stacks of paper were mounded across the table and upon all but one of the chairs in the overstuffed furniture group facing the queen, whose desk was likewise littered with parchment, much of which appeared to be covered with topographical maps showing mountains and rivers. Tesra knew better than to express surprise, but remained quietly perplexed.

Their monarch rose as she and Synahla stopped to bow to her, and this day at least she was a little more like her old self, for she beamed at them. Queen Leonara had thinned over the last year so that her clavicles protruded above her green blouse. Her neck was swanlike and her cheekbones prominent through her pallor.

Leonara hardly acted sick. Her movements were vigorous and her green eyes burned with secret fires. "Ah, Synahla! And Tesra. How good of you to come. Please, be seated. Should I call for refreshments?"

"It is our pleasure," Synahla said with a lesser bow. "And Tesra and I need nothing."

"Very good!" Leonara dropped into the chair behind her desk, her elaborately coifed and curled gold hair bouncing a little as she scooted forward.

Synahla immediately took the chair facing her monarch. The companion chair was buried under different-sized and shaded parchment paper scrawled with hand-drawn maps. Tesra glanced at it, then at the queen, then finally to Synahla, but no one seemed to note its condition.

Tesra sat the inkwell on the table behind the chairs and propped the blank papers in her arm over the little plank of wood she carried as a portable desk. She was used to having to record Synahla's ideas while following her on her rounds, so she was adaptable, if a little disappointed.

"I have decided to forego use of the keystone," the queen declared. "Let the traitors have it. I've spent the last days writing down all that I recall, so that my own impressions are in order."

"That's commendable, Majesty," Synahla said. And nothing more. Weren't either of them at all concerned that the keystone was needed to commune with the Goddess?

"I think we should begin final preparations," Leonara said, and smiled.

"That's lovely to hear, Majesty." Synahla smiled back. "We stand ready to help."

"Pardon me," Tesra said, a little surprised at the sound of her own voice.

Still smiling almost sweetly, the queen's face turned toward her.

She couldn't see Synahla's expression, but her disapproval was a palpable force. Didn't either of them recall the all-out desperation of their search for the keystone? That the queen had despaired for years that the way might never be clear for the Goddess without it? Did neither remember the queen's rages when the keystone had been stolen by Rylin and Varama shortly after its recovery?

How to remind them of that without implicating herself in its disappearance? "Earlier, Majesty, you expressed concern that you might not be able to . . . know the mind of the Goddess without the keystone."

"It is true that I did," Leonara acknowledged. "But my faith in my own powers has grown. I have used the hearthstones to aid my recall and reconstruct all that I saw when I studied the keystone myself. And I tell you now that it was like looking through the eyes of the Goddess! I have faith in my power, and in the visions I have witnessed, and I feel the hands of the Goddess upon my shoulders. We have no need to fear."

"Perhaps we might take a little longer to seek it," Tesra suggested. "There are still some hearthstones missing—"

"We have enough of them," the queen said curtly. "I've issued orders for attunement to begin today."

"Today?" Tesra repeated, feeling a chill.

Synahla spoke with icy disdain. "The time of her return draws nigh, Tesra. You yourself have felt her building heartbeat at the depths of the stones! Why do you object?"

Tesra gulped under the critical regard of the two most powerful sorceresses she knew. Somehow she found her voice. "I am as eager for her return as you," she said slowly. "But what happens if the ceremony doesn't work? We'll release all that energy, with nothing to constrain it. And," she added quickly, for she saw Synahla's mouth opening, "there are dozens of hearthstones missing from the matrix. Their absence makes the whole ceremony more likely to go awry."

"Oh, Tesra," the queen said. "I thought that you had faith in me." She smiled sadly.

"I do," she protested

"Then why do you question her?" Synahla demanded, waspish.

"It is but another trial," the queen said, as if to herself.

Someone rapped on the door. The queen hesitated, glancing first to her left, at a secondary entrance that led to her apartments, and then over Tesra's shoulder to the door by which she'd entered. From there came another knock.

"We are in conference," the queen announced.

"My queen, it's me," came the tense response, "Commander Thelar. I've urgent news."

The queen sighed and a frown pulled at her features. "Enter." She sat back resignedly in her chair as if troubles had fallen unfairly upon her shoulders.

Thelar let himself in, closed the door behind him, then advanced to stand stiffly before the queen, to whom he offered a formal bow. He nodded politely to Synahla, still his commanding officer no matter his own title, and caught Tesra's eye. She noted a vein throbbing at his temple.

"Yes?" the queen prompted.

"We've received a messenger from The Fragments. The Naor have invaded their realm and are laying waste to the villages as they advance upon Alantris."

Less than two days ago a messenger had reached them from Arappa, proclaiming that the Naor were marching through that realm, and heading for the capital, Vedessus of the plains. Tesra's mouth gaped in outright horror. "Two attacks at once?"

Thelar paused for a moment so that the queen might respond, but since she did not, he declared his intent. "I request permission to muster a force of squires, a force of exalts, and some Erymyran troops."

The queen quickly shook her head. "No. All our exalts are required for our final preparations. The Goddess is almost ready for her glorious restoration."

Thelar struggled and failed to mask his surprise.

Synahla explained, her voice kind. "That's too little to help them, in any case, Thelar. We sent all our available troops to Arappa. If we send any more there will be no one to defend Erymyr."

Thelar spoke bluntly to Synahla, though he glanced at the queen as he did so. "If the history of the Altenerai tells us anything, it is that a few men and women in the right place can accomplish the impossible. That's what the Altenerai and now the Exalted are trained to do."

"And which are you, Thelar?" The queen's tone had grown pointed. "Exalt, or alten?"

Thelar blinked in astonishment. But then he'd spent much less time with the queen and was unused to her sudden mood shifts. "Majesty, I have taken the oath of the Exalted."

"Then you know that the time of the Altenerai has passed. We can spare no exalts." She bestowed a beneficent smile upon him, as though it were a favor. "Besides. The sooner the Goddess returns, the sooner all this pain and suffering will be at an end."

Tesra understood why Thelar looked shocked. "But Majesty," she said, "there will be suffering in the meantime. Many may be hurt and killed."

Synahla's glare intimated that she should stop speaking immediately and that painful repercussions would surely follow this meeting.

"This is true," the queen admitted. "And perhaps you are right to question me." She then seemed to address not just them, but some audience watching beyond the room. Perhaps she thought the entirety of the future somehow looked upon her. "This is a weighty burden I shall bear. Many sacrifices have been made and I alone shoulder the blame. I wish it were not so, but it must be this way, and I gladly take up the responsibility. Those who know the Goddess shall be safe, and she shall make the world anew for us upon her waking." She smiled again and her voice was once more room-sized, her gaze upon the acting commander of Altenerai. "All will be well soon. No more than a matter of weeks."

Thelar, no dissembler, stood with mouth hanging partly open, like a dead fish. "Majesty, thousands are in jeopardy."

"We are all in jeopardy, Thelar," the queen snapped, "until the Goddess is once more in our lives."

Obviously dumbstruck, he glanced to Synahla, found no hope there, and mustered a response, voice rasping. "I would like to dispatch messengers to Ekhem and Kanesh, to ask them to send aid to The Fragments."

The queen sighed and sank back into her chair. "If it pleases you."

"I will also dispatch a return messenger to The Fragments. With your leave," he added.

"Yes, yes. You may go." Leonara watched as he offered another bow, retreated to the door, and departed, closing it behind him. She frowned fully upon Synahla. "Truly, Synahla, must all of your underlings question us so?"

Tesra saw the set of Synahla's jaw, and then the exalt commander turned to her. "You were quite rude, don't you think, Tesra?"

At the same moment, she felt a flush of horror as the commander's magic washed against her. Her own powers were far from negligible, but the block she attempted was blown away with the ease of dandelion fluff, and the spell enveloped her. As she struggled against its relentless pull she heard Synahla ask if she truly was as concerned about the queen's plans as she'd earlier proposed.

"Well?" the queen demanded, peevish. "Is she mute?"

It was then that Tesra apologized and accepted fault, fully believing each and every word she spoke.

6

———❧———

Crimson Dreams

Elenai woke, heart pounding, unsettled in the darkness of the unfamiliar room. It took a moment to remember she lay in the Altenerai garrison of Vedessus, upon a bed with mattress and pillows and blankets as clean and fragrant as she herself. She'd vowed earlier that night that she'd never take such luxuries for granted again, and yet now she had little thought for them.

She lifted her hands. There was only a vague suggestion of them in the darkness, and she knew that there would be no blood upon them. She had scrubbed so very carefully.

She shook her head, trying to clear the residual images from the nightmare that still preyed upon her. She took in a few deep breaths and waited for her pulse to slow.

She had dreamed of blood. Monstrous Naor warriors had charged again and again and somehow she kept them back. But her arm had grown weary and the soil around her foul. And everywhere was blood, coating weapon and boots and clothing and hair and eyelashes and skin until she was one hue with the corpses at her feet. Then, gruesomely, a slight figure rose, dripping, from the sticky red earth and looked about with piercing blank eyes—and through glistening crimson teeth the strange blood woman demanded to know if they had met before.

That moment had wakened her.

Lying in the safety of this room behind guarded walls, the stark dream terror fading, she wondered not at all at why her mind couldn't let go the dread from her recent experiences. But why had the dream changed who animated the gore? In life it had been a *male* sorcerer named Chargan manipulating blood.

Elenai shook her head wearily and found the mug of water some thoughtful squire had placed beside her bed. She drained the vessel, for her throat felt almost as dry as it had after the battle, and returned it to the nightstand, her pulse normal at last. She guessed it must be three hours before sunrise. She frowned and settled back between the covers because she had no business being awake after what she had endured for long weeks. Fatigue wracked her yet, and muscles ached as she stretched out to find a comfortable position.

Yet sleep would not return. And the distant sounds of revelry didn't help.

Eventually, with an irritated sigh, she cast aside the covers and turned up the flame on her bedside lantern. She noticed then that she had a clean, dry khalat folded over the nearby chair. The city squires must have quietly placed the garment after scrubbing for hours. There had been so much blood. . . .

She didn't have to imagine the process, as she had occasionally been involved in the care of the sacred garments herself. Hand washing over and over with astringent extracts left nails brittle and knuckles cracked; occasionally magical exertions were necessary to exorcize the most stubborn combat remnants, and most certainly had been used here as the cloth was already dry. They'd also taken pains to remove the red piping from this khalat and to replace the edges with gold embroidery, no mean feat given the toughness of the material. It no longer resembled an article worn by exalts, a castoff from a defeated enemy. It was now truly her own.

Most of the squires hadn't taken any active part in the battle, and she'd seen disappointment in their faces at the impromptu celebration that had swept up the city last night. Doubtless they had worked overtime on more than her khalat repair, hoping to distinguish themselves and be chosen for duty in the battles to come. They craved conflict and glory, just as she and her friends once had, not fully appreciating that they'd return soaked in blood if they returned at all.

From a pitcher nearby, she splashed water into a washbowl, then scrubbed her face, brushed back her hair, and peered at herself in the bronze mirror. She really didn't look like a killer, she thought. But maybe she didn't stare back fresh-faced, either. Those weren't just fatigue lines around her eyes. What she'd experienced was somehow etched there just in the way she held herself.

She turned with a contemptuous gesture and glanced over the bedroom. It was larger than her quarters back in Darassus, but she'd been so long in the wilderness that it felt constraining.

She pulled on a dark blue blouse and pants, then buckled on the khalat, noting dryly she didn't feel comfortable leaving without the armor even though it hadn't availed the woman who'd first owned it, someone she herself had slain. Ortala had been trying to kill you, she reminded herself, as she slid into her now well-worn parade boots.

The garrison corridors were still and empty until she reached the main entrance. The squire on duty there came to attention. Elenai was a little taken aback by the hero worship in the third ranker's eyes.

"As you were," she said, wondering at the crisply dismissive air in her voice.

She walked past him as though she actually knew where she was going.

No one was up, of course. What had she expected? The halls were quiet, the doors closed on people who had better sense to sleep or had taken their celebrations to the city streets.

And then, in an interior hall, she paused in mid-stride. She heard the scuff of bootheels on pavement, and saw the blaze of a light through a doorway to her left. She changed the course of her walk. Two lanterns burned brightly in the garrison courtyard, and a single man paced and pivoted between them. Shirtless in the warm night, N'lahr worked through a weaponless form.

She stood and quietly watched the perfection of his movements.

At rest, the commander's face was plain. But it was quietly expressive in motion, and his body was beautiful: long and well-muscled, flat bellied, glistening in a sheen of sweat. His movements were flawless, and as she looked upon him, she felt an unexpected stirring of desire.

Years before, she had idolized him. Now that she knew him as an individual, she'd thought her childish romantic inclinations a thing of the past. She supposed such a reaction was only natural. She knew the difference between love and lust. Who wouldn't be attracted to such a finely controlled physical specimen?

She stepped through the door as he knelt to deliver a blow to an imaginary opponent then rose to block others. She spotted his khalat and sword belt upon a nearby bench. Strange, that he wasn't practicing a fighting form with his famous blade. But then perhaps he meant to rehearse attacks he hadn't recently used. Irion had certainly been oft employed over the last two weeks. Or was it three? She realized wearily she had no coherent count of the days since N'lahr materialized into her life.

He paused, balanced on his left leg, his right hand ready to deliver a blow. For an impossibly long moment he perched there, and she was awed by his poise. Then he swept into a blur of motion as he delivered a sweeping combination of blows and kicks.

He came to a halt, breathing heavily, then looked up and met her eyes. "Hail, Alten."

He'd never greeted her thus. But then, she hadn't really been apart from him as an alten before.

"Hail, Commander."

"Why are you awake so early?"

"I couldn't sleep." At his quizzical look she added, "Bad dreams."

He nodded, once, as if he understood. "That will happen," he said, and from his manner, she knew that he accepted her as an equal, a recent development to which she hadn't fully adjusted. But then it struck her that he really *did* understand. His own eyes were at least as tired as her own. She remembered he always looked a little haunted. Is this what it was like then, to be Altenerai? He toweled off his face and asked an unexpected question. "Have you made time for your family yet?" He glanced at her before reaching for his shirt.

"I'm joining them for lunch."

"Good. Don't spend all your time with soldiers."

She hesitated, but impelled by the discomfort of strange regard she'd seen in her sister's eyes last night, blurted out: "Will it ever feel normal with them again?"

He slipped on his shirt, frowning. "No. But they can connect you to a shared past. And once you're with them for a while they won't follow you with upraised eyes. Kyrkenall could quote you the line."

She knew the poem he meant. "Fenahnis," from the Erymyran cycle. "'They lingered on my words, they followed in my wake.'"

"Yes."

"The squire on duty was looking at me like that just now."

"That's how you were looking at me until recently."

Embarrassment at the blunt truth in his words set her spluttering. "But, you've done so much. You're N'lahr the Grim, victor of countless impossible battles, returned from the grave, I'm just . . . me."

He held her eyes with a somber expression. "Elenai, you led an astonishing sorcerous attack to save your home city. You stood with five against a hundred. You were elevated from the fifth circle straight to the ring." He hooked the next-to-last button of his cool blue shirt and rolled down the sleeve, then spoke with an air of finality that carried neither pride nor condemnation. "You are Elenai Oddsbreaker now."

She felt the blush on her cheeks. And her eyes drifted over to his sword. To fill the awkward silence she asked the first thing that came to her. "Why were you practicing a form without Irion?"

"I can't rely on it alone."

A sudden cheerless insight dawned. "You were expecting the war to end when you killed Mazakan, weren't you?"

He smiled sadly as he hooked his khalat. "I'm not sure what to expect anymore," he said, and there was an uncertainty in his manner she hadn't seen before. "Rialla foretold I would slay Mazakan, with the sword. Nothing more. Yet the Naor power is hardly broken, is it?"

She thought of the image of the foul blood sorcerer last night bragging that Alantris had fallen and that Naor armies would soon take Darassus. "You killed Mazakan. You can kill Chargan if he really carries out an attack."

"Rialla didn't mention that."

"How many battles did you win that were never prophesied? More than you can count, probably." She didn't wait for an answer. "There was only this one that you knew about. That doesn't invalidate the ones that came before, and it doesn't mean no more will follow. And there's no telling if that enemy boaster will actually attack because we've destroyed the Naor army here."

His gaze was sharp then. "Early this morning a messenger reached us from Alantris. He'd been traveling at full speed for nearly three days. A sizable contingent of Naor were marching on the city when he left The Fragments."

She felt the hammer of her pulse. "You think the city's already fallen?"

"Chargan could have been exaggerating to frighten us. But either way, we have to field an army of our own because there are Naor soldiers in our lands." His voice grew taut with frustration. "And right now I have nothing to counter them but a few dozen garrison squires and a handful of Altenerai. So, in a few hours I'm meeting with the governor to request the aid of her troops."

"She'll help," Elenai said confidently.

"I hope so. I need also convince her to side with us in the matter of the queen. She was . . . reticent last night when I described Leonara's treacheries." N'lahr frowned. "If we didn't have Alantris to address we'd march straight to Darassus and charge the queen."

But they couldn't, not until any Naor invasion was stopped. She nodded as N'lahr spoke on, unusually loquacious.

"The last thing we want is for Leonara to have more time to scheme, but that's just what she's going to get. We must know what she's planning with those hearthstones!" His teeth bared in a silent snarl, and then he buckled on his sword belt. He sucked in a deep breath, let it out slowly, then raised his eyes to her own. "I shouldn't burden you with this."

"It's a burden we must share," she answered. "I'm Altenerai now."

He nodded to her and suddenly, through a subtle change in the set of his shoulders and face, she was no longer his confidant, though his manner was not unkind. "We must ready for the fight. And that means rest. You've a few hours before dawn. You should be able to sleep now. Sometimes it works that way."

"What way?"

"After you've been up and thought or done something else for a while."

She was very tired still, and wondered if he might be right.

He spoke on, as though he'd decided something with minimal reflection. She'd never known him to do that before. "Join me at the governor's. For breakfast. I'll send someone around to wake you a half hour before."

She felt honored. "Yes, sir. Thank you."

He nodded and headed for the door. She realized that was a dismissal, and followed him out.

With so much to think about, she really only returned to her bunk to humor him, and was surprised to find herself deep asleep when the squire touched her shoulder hours later. Disappointed as she was to be awake, it was exciting to be included in N'lahr's plans, and reassuring to learn herself still capable of sleep untroubled by dreams.

When she left the barracks with N'lahr, the sun had risen as though a normal day was come. But so would it have risen, she knew, if the Naor had laid waste to the city.

Dogs barked and carts creaked in the streets as Vedessus struggled sluggishly to rise. It was an uneven awakening after the revelries of the previous night. Many houses still were shuttered, but scattered bands of people lay in the parks; a distant few staggered homeward in a happy haze.

Vedessi buildings were built mostly of tile, brick, clay plaster, and stone, wood being a rarer commodity on the plains, and few rose more than two stories. It was a city of low hills and beautifully tended gardens, arranged for the most part in straight lanes. The windmills that drove the pumps and other machinery soared above all, facing into the west wind. The city had a spare, geometric beauty, especially in comparison to the ornate artistry everywhere evident in Darassus. After having been away for so long, she saw the place with new eyes.

A few unaccompanied children played in the streets, chasing each other with sticks and arguing about who should play Altenerai and whom Naor. At the sight of the solitary Altenerai pair striding purposely along, the youngsters stopped cold to regard them with naked awe. One girl who couldn't have been more than five came stiffly to attention and offered a perfect salute with a grimy hand.

Elenai heard the group jabbering excitedly after N'lahr returned it.

An occasional adult shopkeeper, busying to open their concern, stared at her companion. They didn't try to interact. Elenai could see in their faces and prayerful motions the undiminished reverence she'd noted the night before—his presence was proof of divine intervention in their lives. No matter the mundane details of treachery, hardship, skill, and sheer luck that underpinned the miracle, the Gods had, for them, simply sent N'lahr back from the dead in the city's hour of need.

She realized with a start that once again she'd neglected her morning prayer, and swore to herself that she'd stop forgetting. With their rushed schedule in the last week, there'd been so little time for so many things, but that didn't fully excuse her inattentive behavior. She wondered if Kalandra's casual blasphemy about the Gods' early activities had unconsciously influenced her own actions.

The Vedessi palace lay just off the city's center, an ugly, flat-faced building of four stories with six separate towers. One tower climbed from each of its four corners, one rose from its front entrance, and a thick one, with a bell, half again the height of the others, stuck up from its center. The building's brick had been painted a startling light blue offset with elaborately painted tiles around the openings. It had always struck Elenai as garish, although it did set the building apart.

"This has bothered me for years," N'lahr said, indicating the palace.

"The color?"

"No. The design. Someone with an idea of defense but lack of actual practice. Look: arrow slit windows but too many gates and doors. Any decent force that breached the city walls wouldn't have difficulty taking the palace. There's not even a protective wall."

She'd grown up with the building, but immediately understood and agreed with N'lahr's assessment, wondering why she hadn't noticed before. A seat of government should serve as a fallback position for as many critical assets as possible. N'lahr was a tactical genius, true, but she was certainly capable of noticing such deficiencies herself.

Once beyond the gate guards, a servant conducted them past expensive wooden doorframes and paneling to a sunny oval dining room with a small table. The servant told them the governor would be along shortly, and Elenai scanned the room while two attendants in dark livery kept their eyes forward resolutely. Five leaded windows looked into what was likely an interior courtyard, admitting light but little detail. Beautifully scrolled panel doors were interspersed with built-in drawers on the cabinet opposite them. Most likely the pale green tablecloth, plates, and utensils now adorning the oval table were normally stored within. Six chairs were in place, although there were settings only for four. She guessed N'lahr had sent a messenger ahead informing the governor he'd be bringing a guest. A door stood closed on either end of the room, one by which they'd entered and one behind the head of the table, where the most ornately scrolled chair back was positioned.

While the two Altenerai waited, a small army of servants arrived in waves. The first group set small plinths before the windows to support vases holding blooming blackthorn and rockrose. Next came the food, borne on lidded bronze platters, and drink, carried in slim white pitchers set along the cabinet's surface.

Silently the servants had come, silently they left, and it was Elenai's stomach that intruded into the quiet, for the aroma of fresh baked bread, cooked eggs, and some kind of sweet sauce awakened her hunger. She longed to reach for the lids.

N'lahr smiled conspiratorially at her, an unguarded human moment broken by the opening of the door behind the table head. Elenai looked up expectantly. A fox-faced older gentleman entered, dressed in a dark red robe threaded in silver. He nodded politely and stood to one side of the door.

Only then did Governor Verena join them, smiling warmly.

Elenai had seen her several times over the years, most recently last night. Verena had risen to rule the decade before, proving her competence through many challenges. In the light of day, Elenai saw that age had thickened her middle even as it had softened her squarish face. This morning, her gray-streaked auburn hair was piled loosely behind her, cascading to rounded shoulders. Her eyes were well and darkly lined, her cheeks lightly rouged, and a low neckline revealed generous cleavage. She wore a light blue dress reminiscent of the color of khalats, probably meant to honor the Altenerai, although it emphasized her eyes as well.

She advanced to extend hands to the commander, her dress hem swirling about pretty ankles. "Alten N'lahr! It's a pleasure to see you again so soon." Her voice was strong and clear.

"Likewise." He briefly touched fingertips with her, his beneath hers, then bowed his head respectfully. She didn't offer her hands to Elenai, but nodded, and Elenai lowered her head.

"A pleasure to see you again, Elenai Dartaan. And let me again offer my congratulations upon your well-earned promotion."

"Thank you."

"This is my chief counselor, Alusus Garl."

The gray-haired man nodded solemnly. "It is a pleasure," he said. Elenai suspected she had been introduced to him last night, but much after the battle was blurred to her recollection. There had been so many people who wished to greet them all.

Verena bade them to be seated, and they took their chairs, Alusus on her right hand, N'lahr on her left. Elenai had been placed nearer N'lahr than Garl. Quickly, the liveried servants stepped forward to serve the food—steamed greens, pan fried eggs, fried tubers seasoned with cinnamon, and fresh fried trout coated in bread crumbs.

It was all Elenai could do to keep from shoveling it in like a teenaged boy. Though the impromptu feasting last night had been excellent, she hadn't dined this well in months, not since she had helped Elik celebrate his twenty-third birthday. Idly, she wondered if he was still in Darassus, and what her friend had heard of her. Would he believe her a traitor, allied to the purported murderer of Asrahn, Master of Squires?

Verena was eying N'lahr over her cup. "How long has it been since you've had a day off, Alten?"

"A long while," he admitted, and Elenai noted that the governor didn't address him as commander. A slip, or a slight? He continued, "Today won't be a respite, either. There's much to be done."

"I hope you have the time at least for a leisurely breakfast. And that my company doesn't require too much work." She eyed him through her lashes as she sipped again.

Elenai stared. Was the woman flirting with him?

"On the contrary." N'lahr paused to butter a slice of steaming hot bread. "But I can't tarry long. I'm sure you've received the same news as I and appreciate the need for haste."

A smile pulled at the corner of Verena's mouth. "Are you always so serious? Do you hurry so quickly from your lovers in the field?"

N'lahr's eyebrows rose. He actually sounded caught off guard. "In the field?"

"Do you rush from Kyrkenall?" she explained, as if it were obvious. "Or do you favor the lovely Elenai?" Verena glanced over at her before appraising him once more.

Elenai blinked a little in surprise and resumed chewing her greens. It had never occurred to her anyone would assume her involved with Commander N'lahr.

N'lahr returned her gaze with a level expression of his own. "Elenai is but newly promoted and it would be inappropriate to have a relationship with a subordinate," he said, which should have been blindingly obvious, but it intrigued Elenai that he dismissed the idea with that argument and no other. "And Kyrkenall isn't my lover." He added the last as if he'd addressed the matter before.

"I thought you went everywhere together. And he's more beautiful than I am. Surely." Verena bent to cut one of the eggs into smaller pieces.

"You undervalue your charms," N'lahr said.

If she'd been astonished at Verena's flirtations, she was even more surprised by the frank appraisal in the commander's response.

Verena smiled knowingly. When she spoke once more, she adopted a heavier tone. "You're here to convince me to send soldiers and supplies with you to The Fragments. But you know I must always keep the needs of my people foremost in my thoughts. What if the Naor return while our strongest sons and daughters are gone? If they go with you, how would my soldiers fare against a force said to be many times their number?" She paused, her eyes shining. There was nothing remotely playful in her manner now. "Why should Vedessus weaken rather than fortify itself? Especially since, by your own report, we face invasion from without and corruption from within our own alliance."

Every one of those was a legitimate question, as much as it annoyed Elenai to hear them.

N'lahr appeared lost in thought.

Garl, silent apart from the clatter of his cutlery until that moment, spoke with a flat authority. "Vedessus is recovering from a siege and can ill afford expenditures on behalf of its neighbors."

As N'lahr seemed disinclined to speak, Elenai offered, "If Alantris falls, the Naor will use The Fragments to regroup and resupply and then resume their attack on Vedessus. We're all safer if we drive them from our lands now."

Verena addressed her directly. "Why can't you just fight the Naor in Alantris with another herd of eshlack?"

Elenai should have guessed that would come up. But before she could manage an explanation, N'lahr answered. "Because that tactic would fail. The circumstances here were unique and cannot be duplicated in The Fragments. We struck at night with no warning over plains and at great speed. The few Naor who escaped the battle will tell others how they were defeated, so precautions will be taken against a similar attack. And cattle cannot be moved quickly over forested hills and through river valleys undetected all the way to the walls of Alantris.

"As to your other concerns," he continued. "You know my reputation; the soldiers of Vedessus will not be wasted in battle." He held Verena's eyes a moment before adding. "Vedessus remembers its own straits, only yesterday, and will soon know that Alantris finds itself in the same situation today. Your people will want to fight. And they'll want their leaders to make the way clear."

Verena sat against the back of her chair and brushed absently at her necklace, her expression thoughtful. "Share your plan. What dangers would my people face?"

"I require eight hundred of your foot troops and all three hundred of your cavalry. That will leave a minimal but adequate defense should a Naor force return, though I intend to keep them busy around Alantris. A third of the cavalry will be sent forward with Altenerai scouts, and the main force will approach through the Cenahra Pass to minimize chances of detection. My chief concern is supplies. I will need approximately one hundred wagons of rations and fodder. As for my plans against the enemy, those will be determined once I understand their disposition."

Elenai forgot to eat. She was astounded that N'lahr had worked all that out in the handful of hours she'd managed only sleep and worry. The governor nodded gravely. "There's another matter I wish to discuss. One hardly insignificant."

"You refer to the queen's betrayal."

"That's not at all how I refer to it," Verena said bluntly. "I understand you believe your freedom was traded for Naor hearthstones, but it sounds as though Commander Denaven was the offender, not Queen Leonara. He tried to kill you and lied for years to maintain his hold on power. And he's already paid for his crimes. You need further evidence if you wish to prosecute your claims against the queen."

N'lahr put down his fork. "Even if Leonara were ignorant of the conspiracy to imprison me, its existence without her knowledge hardly speaks well of her management. She sat in Darassus for seven years staring into hearthstones while Mazakan built up his armies and our own defenses were left to rot. She pulled our brightest mages out of public service to aid her obsession. She remained unengaged while our Master of Squires . . ." He seemed choked for a moment as if struggling to speak the words ". . . Asrahn, was murdered and our best defenders divided in a misplaced manhunt against one of their own. Denaven's hunt for Kyrkenall resulted in the death not only of several promising squires, but Belahn the Bear and Decrin of the Shining Shield."

Verena sipped from her cup, watching steadily.

"Leonara's attention has been focused inward, not outward to the care of her charges. She has all but abandoned any day-to-day governance of Erymyr, much less the realms, because she is consumed with the study of magic. Specifically, the study of the hearthstones, aided by her Mage Auxiliary. And need I remind you, Denavan was her choice to replace me."

"It seems to come again and again to hearthstones." The governor set the cup on its dish. "While much of what you say is opinion or speculation, the queen's infatuation with the stones has been noted by the governors and members of the Erymyran Council. And the secrecy she enforces around that subject is a source of growing irritation." Verena toyed with her fork, but only Garl showed any remaining interest in the meal as he precisely moved carefully chosen bites to his mouth. "What would you have me do?" she asked, watching through her lashes.

"Gather the governors with the council," N'lahr said simply. "And replace the queen. For the safety of the realms. Her flawed judgment has endangered the lives of every man, woman, and child in every one of the five realms. If not for her disastrous choices, the Naor would never have come close to your walls, or those of Alantris."

"If I champion your charges," Verena said slowly, "I place my own position at risk."

"There are few rewards without risk," N'lahr said. "But someone must step into the void the queen's absence will create."

"Indeed," Verena said with a shrewd smile. Elenai understood that she'd arrived at that conclusion long since. "And which of the many hopefuls will receive the blessing of the Altenerai commander?"

Gods. Was that what she had been angling for this entire time? Elenai looked first to one, then the other, watching the way their eyes locked. And she realized that the governor had finally referred to N'lahr by his appropriate title.

"I am no queen maker," N'lahr said. "But I will support someone with a proven record of sound judgment. Someone who sees beyond the border of her own realm to weigh the people of all our lands equally. Someone who is not afraid to make the right choices, even when they come with challenges."

The two, governor and general, looked at each other for a long time. Elenai barely breathed while Garl continued calmly eating. Finally Verena signaled for an attendant and indicated her cup. As the young man hurried forward, the governor addressed Garl. "Give him what he asks. Ensure that he receives the best wagons. Market price only please."

Garl bowed his head. "As you command."

"All needs be done swiftly. Commander N'lahr will seek to leave on the morrow." She looked across the table at N'lahr. "While it is true that we store surplus for times of need, Vedessi stock is not inexhaustible. If the winter is hard this year this expenditure will be felt keenly by my people. I understand that some supplies were recovered from the Naor. I expect you'll use what you can of those?"

"I'm accustomed to making the best use of what's at hand," N'lahr said.

"Yes," Verena said with a faint smile. "You've ably demonstrated that. I'll contact my fellow governors on the subject of the queen and the charges against her. It would be helpful to have a written account from you, signed by your own hand. I'll include it in the dispatches."

"I'll dictate one and have copies sent to you."

"Most excellent."

The rest of the meal passed pleasantly enough, and consisted mostly of small talk. Verena inquired about Elenai's family and what her future plans might be. For all that, she devoted most of her attention to N'lahr, who proved more gifted a conversationalist than Elenai had expected. As she listened to him she realized that apart from his tactical brilliance, one of the secrets of his battlefield success might be the acute way he could read people and adjust his conversation.

It wasn't that he was facile; he seemed uninclined to present himself as other than he was. But somehow he was capable of presenting a different footing and to meet those he spoke with on ground he used to his advantage. This he had done with Verena, and Elenai began to wonder if he had done likewise with herself at some point previous. Probably he had, and she simply hadn't noticed.

As they left the palace, they discovered a city better wakened, although the streets still looked emptier than usual this time of morning.

"How do you think that went?" Elenai asked.

"Almost as expected," N'lahr said.

So apparently he'd anticipated both Verena's initial objections as well as her reactions, and passed it off as nothing remarkable. Typical of him, she thought. "Do you really want her to . . . take over for the queen?" Somehow phrasing it in a different way sounded less traitorous.

"She's intelligent and decisive." N'lahr seemed to read her feelings. "You don't like her."

"I've always respected her, but I didn't realize what a game player she was." And the governor had been flirting with N'lahr, which Elenai had only recently discovered she found bothersome, even as she recognized her reaction as petty and a little ridiculous.

N'lahr shrugged minutely. "She cares about her people and is involved with their welfare. She makes wise choices on their behalf. And her motives are less opaque than the queen's."

"That wouldn't take much."

"True," N'lahr agreed, then promptly changed the subject. "There's something I've been meaning to speak to you about. I'd like you to look at the shards of the hearthstone I was trapped in."

His customary calm was in place, but somehow strained. "Is there something wrong?"

"Do you think," he said, then hesitated a moment. He cleared his throat and continued. ". . . that there's such a thing as hearthstone sickness?"

"The power's addictive."

He shook his head slowly. "That's not what I mean. I think my years trapped inside of one might have altered me."

"Altered you?" she repeated in alarm. "How?"

He eyed her soberly as they turned onto the street that led to the barracks. "It's hard to describe. But it's getting worse."

7

Allies on the Wing

Elenai would have asked for details then and there, but as she and N'lahr rounded the corner they discovered a crowd gathered in front of the barracks building, one apparently more agitated than festive. A couple dozen people were talking with the squires on duty outside. Judging from their hand wringing and wide gestures the questioners weren't liking what they heard.

A man on the edge caught sight of Elenai and N'lahr, and at his prompting all eyes swung to watch them as they neared. The crowd quieted, although one gruff voice called that there were kobalin in the city, and a matronly woman demanded to know if it was true.

"I've not heard this news," N'lahr answered calmly.

"But we saw kobalin being brought in through the gates," a young woman said.

"Only one," an older man clarified. "But it was huge, and black."

A gangly man with a cobbler's apron stepped forward. "Was he a prisoner?"

Another chimed in. "It was with Altenerai. Why would they bring one into the city?"

Elenai relaxed. There could only be one kobalin entering the city with Altenerai. Ortok had arrived.

"That's no prisoner," N'lahr said. "He's come to help us fight the Naor." The crowd regarded him in stunned silence as he explained. "There's no danger. You're safe. This kobalin has aided us before, and will do so again. And he'll be leaving the city tomorrow." He strode among the gathering, returned the salutes of the sentries, and stepped through the door they opened for him. Elenai came after. She had a sense that her commander was amused, though he wasn't smiling.

Elenai had last seen Ortok a number of days before, when they'd had to leave him in the shifts with some squires and the formidable elder alten, Tretton. All had been wounded, and unable to keep up with Kyrkenall, N'lahr, and Elenai as they raced to save Vedessus.

From the squire at the duty desk, they learned healers were seeing to the squires but Tretton had already been tended and would be in the mess hall. They found him putting down his knife and rising smoothly the instant he caught sight of N'lahr. His eyes were tired, but there was no other sign of fatigue in the man's manner. There wouldn't be. He effected a dignified salute with his off hand, for a white sling supported his right arm. "Hail, Altenerai."

Elenai had to remind herself to answer with N'lahr. "Hail."

Alten Gyldara, seated nearby, had likewise risen, smiling warmly as she acknowledged them. She sought Elenai's eye particularly, and Elenai was pleased to have earned the regard of the long-admired instructor after fighting at her side through wave after wave of Naor warriors.

Ortok, a hulking shadow over the largest pile of food Elenai had ever seen, turned on the bench with a wide grin on his furry face and his dark eyes glinting in the reflected light from a nearby window. "Greetings!" he boomed. "Fine food has been brought. And lady magickers have helped the arm of Tretton. He can move it now."

To demonstrate, Tretton raised his arm in its sling and flexed his hand in a fist.

"How does it feel?" N'lahr asked him.

"Almost normal."

A single nod from N'lahr acknowledged he was glad to learn this news. More likely relieved, for it was his blade that had injured the man. "The squires?"

"Still being tended," Tretton answered. "Yeva has an infected wound, but the healers thought she had a fair chance. They're not sure Renn's shoulder will recover fully, but Dalahn's just about ready for service now."

Once more N'lahr nodded. "You made excellent time."

"Yes," Tretton agreed.

Ortok looked confused as he bit off a slab of roasted meat. Kobalin had a terrible sense of time, Elenai recalled, because the length of seasons and even days in the shifts, where they made their homes, had few set patterns.

Yet it seemed the kobalin had more important matters in mind as he spoke up, his resonant bass carrying clearly. "Gyldara tells that you have now finished your great battle against Naor." He half turned and scooped scrambled eggs into his mouth with his fingers. Tretton's gray mustache tightened a bit, though Elenai wasn't sure why until the kobalin swallowed and climbed from the bench. "With the battle over, we should duel. Unless you wish to eat first."

Ortok was a head higher than N'lahr and half again as wide. His power-ful, furry arms stretched nearly to his knees. And Elenai had learned he was swift, too.

Gods. Surely he wasn't still serious about fighting the commander? Here and now?

Ortok grinned, showing huge pointed incisors. Tretton stepped to one side, ostensibly to retrieve his goblet, although to Elenai's eye he was ready to assault Ortok's left flank.

Gyldara watched tensely from the right

Tall though he was, N'lahr raised his head to meet the kobalin eye to eye. "If I fight you now, Ortok, one of us dies."

"Yes."

"I can't die right now. My people need me to defeat the Naor who are attacking one of our cities to the southeast. I must lead an army to fight them."

"Then you will have to kill me to help them."

N'lahr shook his head. "If I kill you, you won't be able to kill any Naor, either. I'd rather we were both alive to do that."

"It is good to kill Naor," Ortok agreed. The kobalin waited, as if mus-ing, silent.

"I release you from your debt, Ortok. You've more than repaid it. But I won't fight you. I wish for neither of us to be killed or injured."

"You will not fight me?" The kobalin's voice rose indignantly.

"No. I hope you will accept a different pledge. The debt of friendship."

Ortok puzzled over that, his jaw outthrust. "You wish me to take your debt?"

"I wish us to exchange debts."

Ortok's brow furrowed. "If we exchange debts," he rumbled slowly, "then we cancel them, unless one is heavier than the other."

"That's not how friendship works. Kyrkenall and I are indebted to one another because we're friends."

"You are his superior."

The explanation was too simple. "I was his friend before I became his commander."

Ortok mulled this over while saying nothing.

"Don't you have any friends among the kobalin?"

"Of course!" Ortok shook his head as if N'lahr was an amusing idiot. "But we always know who leads. And you and I cannot decide that with-out a duel."

"I suggest we consider ourselves equals," N'lahr said.

"How can I be equal when you have an army and I do not?"

That was a reasonable objection. "If you can get an army," N'lahr said, "you can command it at my side."

Elenai wasn't sure what to make of that suggestion, but the kobalin scratched his head, apparently giving the idea serious thought. He must have decided to accept it, for after a moment he returned to his central concern. "And after we kill more Naor, then we duel?"

"A debt of friendship doesn't lead to dueling."

"I like the words you speak about armies, and equals." Ortok smacked his chest. "Better than fighting at your side is leading an army at your side, although this will take some planning. But best still is fighting in the end, after we kill Naor."

"That's not how it's done between friends."

"This"—Ortok paused to point at himself and then N'lahr—"is not how it is done between kobalin and Altenerai."

"Not usually."

"Well then. If this is different, then so is our end. We will duel, after we kill the Naor, but until then I accept your debt of friendship. How is friendship done?"

Elenai wished for a different result than this. At least N'lahr had bought some time. She'd grown fond of Ortok and hated to think of him dying. She supposed it was just possible he might kill N'lahr in the battle. Neither prospect was remotely appealing.

The commander raised his hand. "We clasp hands."

"Are there words of power to say?" Ortok asked.

"Give me a moment." N'lahr was silent for a good while, then lifted his hand, palm out. "When we take hands, we pledge to aid and counsel one another in peace and war, and to safeguard and protect the allies, friends, and possessions of the other so long as those friends and allies do not bring harm to our other friends, possessions, and allies."

"Will we share food?"

"Of course," N'lahr said. "We will share supplies."

"It will be as though we are elders," Ortok said, "but with bloodshed."

Elenai wasn't sure what the relationships between kobalin elders were like.

"Your pardon," Tretton interrupted. "What do you mean about elders and bloodshed, if you don't mind me asking?" His phrasing was impeccably polite, though his eyes were ice cold.

Ortok looked over at him as if explaining to a child. "Elders no longer prove might with combat, but N'lahr and I do."

"I see." Tretton hadn't remotely relaxed his ready stance, and Gyldara, who had backed to cover Ortok's right flank, also looked grave.

Ortok raised his hand and then lowered it to N'lahr. "It is a strange thing, this debt. What if we don't like it?"

"Then we must talk about it."

"Talk, but not fight?"

"Some friends fight. Usually not to the death."

"Huh. Maybe only good friends do that."

"I don't think so."

"You fae are strange. Here is my hand." The kobalin thrust it forward, fingers extended widely.

There was that word again. The Naor had begun using it to distinguish the people of the realms from the "true" humans, they themselves. It was odd to hear that it had worked its way into kobalin speech as well.

N'lahr extended his own hand. Elenai heard Gyldara suck in a breath as the commander clasped about half of Ortok's great lower arm. The kobalin's fingers closed completely about the commander's forearm.

"You are so small, N'lahr. If I didn't know better, I would think you were weak."

"He's not at all," Tretton interjected.

"Oh, I know," Ortok agreed. "That is why you are so confusing. Do we say other words to close the ceremony?"

"Friend," N'lahr improvised.

"Friend," Ortok said with a growl, then grinned at him, displaying an impressive number of teeth. N'lahr released his grip and the kobalin did likewise.

"Now I have fed, and we have talked. I should like a time of rest."

"We can arrange that. Do you have quarters yet?"

"We have not discussed a sleeping place."

"Stay here for a moment and enjoy some more wine. The four of us will go find a place for you."

"I do like the wine," Ortok said, and ambled back to the table. The wood creaked as he resumed the bench.

"Ortok," N'lahr said, "you are clear that there's to be no dueling between you and my friends and allies?"

Ortok paused in mid-reach for the wine jug. His eyes gave a very human roll, as if N'lahr were exasperating. "If I duel them and die, I won't be able to kill you, and then I would break my word. Surely you know me better than that."

"Of course," N'lahr said.

Ortok shook his head. "I will never understand why you make simple things so complicated."

N'lahr motioned the others after him and then headed into the hall-way. Gyldara came last, closing the door behind them as Tretton reached N'lahr's side and stared at him.

"That agreement won't protect us," Tretton said. "You can't truly predict what he's going to do."

N'lahr spoke. "You traveled with him. You know he'll never break his word."

Tretton frowned. "He'll hold to the letter of his understanding, but we don't fully understand the rules he lives by and he really doesn't understand ours, and someone's going to be hurt. Probably not you. An alten or some squire or some poor soldier who's been taught that kobalin are the enemy."

He had a point, and Elenai looked to N'lahr to see how he'd react.

"He's a tremendous asset, Tretton. He's like having another alten serving with us."

Tretton stiffened and his breath came in a great sniff. "You compare the refined discipline of an alten to a chaotic kobalin?!"

"He has the power of an alten," N'lahr said. "Stop looking for problems. You know what I meant. The Naor are marching on Alantris and we need all the help we can get. Kobalin help included."

Tretton clearly did not like the sound of that. "I'm aware of the Naor threat. But keeping company with a kobalin is a dangerous policy."

"We've little spare time, and almost none for pointless debate. Are we going to have a problem, Tretton?"

Tretton eyed him steadily. The oldest alten still in service, he was the product of a different time. Like Asrahn had been, his manner was formal, but unlike Asrahn he wasn't obviously convivial even with his colleagues. Cordial was as close as he ever seemed, although there was clearly depth of feeling in him, judging by the way he'd reacted to Decrin's death. And during Elenai's second year as a squire, she'd heard a rumor he'd gotten publicly, scandalously drunk with Alten Enada on one of her rare visits to Darassus, singing bawdy songs with her while propped up against an old fountain on the main esplanade.

But he customarily held himself apart, as though he were wary of forming close connections. Elenai supposed that was reasonable, given that everyone Tretton had begun service with was dead or retired. And most of those retired ones were likely dead as well.

It could be, though, that Tretton was aloof because that was his nature. The preeminent scout and tracker among the Altenerai, he was as famed for his iron will as his implacable spirit. His talent in the wilderness was so great it bordered upon magical. Having heard that he could hold a post without moving for days, Elenai wondered if he might be planning that now.

After the slightest nod of acknowledgment to his commander, Tretton responded. "I asked too few questions of Denaven. I deferred to his rank even when I disagreed with his judgment."

"Does that mean you don't intend to defer to my rank?" N'lahr, too, sounded calm. Stern, but calm.

"I intend to question. Once, you had Asrahn and Kalandra and Aradel to counsel you. And Kyrkenall, I suppose." There was a dismissive note that Elenai didn't feel was entirely fair.

Tretton continued. "Those three aren't with us, and all the rest of these lack wisdom, no matter their skill and worth." The older man didn't look at either Gyldara or herself, nor did he seem troubled about speaking of them as though they weren't present. "Having learned from previous errors, I intend to question you."

"Noted," N'lahr said. "I'm still the same man I was."

"So it would appear. But it's not the same world."

"Also noted." And with that, the moment between them seemed resolved. At least for now. Tretton didn't object to the subject change when N'lahr asked Gyldara if she knew where Ortok should sleep and which squire might be best suited for assisting him there. They stopped at the duty desk to assign the younger alten's recommendation, then the commander sent another to fetch Kyrkenall before leading the way to the small square room he'd adopted for his office.

At N'lahr's gesture they took to the benches, Gyldara and Elenai choosing the one on the wall facing N'lahr's desk, and Tretton selecting the one opposite the door to the courtyard. Elenai could see where N'lahr had exercised this morning, just visible through the door's hazy glass window.

"What about Alten Lasren, sir?" Gyldara asked.

"Let him rest," N'lahr said. "I'll have work for him soon enough."

Lasren had been wounded by Kyrkenall even before the great battle, only after which it had been apparent he'd been in far more pain than he'd let on. The healers had seen to him, but he'd likely need time to recover.

N'lahr took his chair behind the desk and looked over to Gyldara. "What did you learn from the Naor prisoners?"

Each of them turned to look at her, a far from objectionable thing. All of the Altenerai were healthy and well-formed, but Gyldara in particular was a lovely woman, with flawless skin, bright eyes, and fine features. Her golden hair shone with sunlight pouring through the window in the courtyard door.

"I spoke with seven ranked prisoners at length and separately," she said. "I kept a weaver squire on hand to monitor surface thoughts. In summary, the Naor have developed a new weapon." She then spoke quickly, describing terrible creatures that were something like their old allies, the ko'aye, feathered reptiles. Except that these beasts were far larger and had the power to tear down city walls. "That's why the Naor last night didn't have siege engines," she said. "These 'dragons,' as they call them, were supposed to fly to Vedessus just as soon as they smashed the walls of Alantris. Praise the gods they did not."

Elenai tried to imitate the solemn manner of her older companions, who might have been alarmed by the news but revealed only mild concern.

"Aradel must have found a way to stop them," Tretton suggested.

"Chargan claimed he'd already taken Alantris," Elenai remembered suddenly. The mage's image in blood had said as much last night.

N'lahr, it seemed, hadn't forgotten at all, for his nod was slow. "How many dragons do the Naor have?"

"The officers weren't sure, but I got the sense they were limited in number. Apparently they're hard to get and hard to control. They're dangerous to groupings of defenders, but would have trouble picking out individuals to attack. And, like ko'aye, they put themselves at risk if they fly low enough to assault us."

Gyldara continued, her voice growing strained. Probably she'd put hours into her questioning before rolling into bed, only to rise in time to report. "I confirmed that Chargan, the weaver who spoke to us last night, is one of Mazakan's grandchildren. He's reputed to be a very capable magic worker. But I suppose that was obvious."

It had been fairly so, since the man had apparently sent his image to talk to them from hundreds of miles away.

"I've also confirmed he's part of a final force meant to rendezvous with the one already in Alantris," Gyldara continued. "Mazakan's plan was to hold both Alantris and Vedessus and then advance with the bulk of all three armies for Darassus."

"Just like Chargan boasted last night," Elenai said. "But if he's such a powerful sorcerer, why is he in the rear? Shouldn't they have had him with either of the first two armies? To make their success more likely?"

"Maybe they meant to protect him," Gyldara suggested. "Although I suppose they could have placed him to the rear of either of the besieging armies, and kept him safe that way."

"Certainly," Tretton agreed. "Elenai's question stands."

"I can think of two possible reasons," N'lahr said. "First, magic workers are accorded honor, but still have lesser status than Naor warriors. He probably wouldn't have been allowed to lead an army against one of our cities—that would have been left to someone of higher status—but as a scion of Mazakan he might be given some authority over others for specific lesser tasks. Second, someone has to be responsible for recruiting or subduing these dragons. That may be Chargan, in which case he'd remain behind to collect more for the assault on Darassus. How far out is his army?"

"He's due to reach Alantris about a week from now. His younger brother's troops were to reach it at about the same time these Naor arrived at Vedessus. In all likelihood they're already at the walls. Or through them," Gyldara finished grimly.

N'lahr paused for only a moment. "I want to move out tomorrow. If the Naor are in the city, we'll find a way to root them out. And if they're not yet there, we'll have to defeat them before Chargan turns up with his group." He was starting to brief them about the troops the governor was turning over to them when someone rapped on the hallway door. "Enter," N'lahr ordered.

Elenai fully expected Kyrkenall to come through, and then, upon seeing a third ranker poke in her head, realized the alten probably wouldn't have bothered knocking.

The squire stepped inside and saluted. The younger woman looked more uncomfortable than she should be, even accounting for the fact she stood before four Altenerai.

"At ease, Squire," N'lahr said. "Report."

"Kyrkenall is in the stables, sir. He said that . . ." She paused minutely. "That he doesn't have time for a meeting right now."

N'lahr stood.

"Did he say anything else?" Elenai asked.

"Not . . . Yes, but . . ."

"But not that bears repeating," N'lahr finished. "All right." He turned to Tretton and Gyldara. "Get started organizing and cataloguing the supplies we need. It's a tall order to get it all ready in the time we have but I know you can do it. The Naor had a lot of smoked meat we can use. And

Gyldara, good work." He caught Elenai's eye while striding to the door. "Come with me."

She followed him out of the room, wondering at his speed until he explained.

"Kyrkenall's heading out to look for Kalandra."

"He wouldn't do that—not without permission," Elenai said.

He shot her a look. "That's why he didn't ask for any."

"But that's a terrible idea," Elenai objected. "There's too much going on. And what about the storms in the shifts? And how remote the last little fragment was—he needs to travel with a weaver. Isn't he thinking about any of that?"

"Of course not. Because he doesn't want to."

They pushed their way into the outer courtyard. There were target markers stored to the left of the doorway they exited, and stables built into the wall to right and left. Kyrkenall was leading a horse quickly toward the thick double gate. Lyria, his sturdy dun, was saddled.

He didn't look especially happy about their arrival, but paused and faced them. He was fully dressed for an expedition, complete with travel kit and extra bundles of arrows. His great black bow was stored in Lyria's saddle holster.

"You can't look for her right now," N'lahr said as he strode forward.

"I didn't ask."

"Your horse is even more exhausted than you are," the commander pointed out, which was a line of attack Elenai hadn't considered. "And you're bad enough. The bags under your eyes have bags. You're going to get yourself killed."

Kyrkenall frowned at that and absently scratched the side of Lyria's nose. She snorted. "I won't press hard until we reach the border."

"I know you want to find her. *I* want to find her. But we made that mistake before and we barely got here in time to save Vedessus. Naor have already marched on Alantris. They've probably got it surrounded."

"Then coax up another miracle. You don't need me. You've got more Altenerai now. I hear Tretton's back, too. And the Kaneshi cavalry's probably on its way as well."

Elenai had only learned at breakfast that the governor had sent word to the nearby realms as soon as the Naor had been spotted in Arappa.

"I'm glad you're keeping well informed. Did you hear about the dragons?"

"'Dragons'?"

"Naor secret weapons. Great winged beasts, larger than ko'aye, that can knock down walls with ease. They've likely already been used against Alantris. And they're overdue here."

Kyrkenall's brow furrowed. That was apparently a bit of news he hadn't learned.

"We need to counter these dragons with aerial forces of our own. I need you to make peace with the ko'aye."

Elenai inwardly shook her head, amazed both that N'lahr had already devised a strategy to counter the Naor "weapons" and that he'd struck on an argument to intrigue Kyrkenall, maybe into changing his mind. The commander could just order him to stay, but that didn't seem to be how it worked between them. Unfortunately, the alliance with the winged lizards had been broken years before, and from what Elenai had learned, repairing it would be no simple matter. Did he really expect Kyrkenall to serve as diplomat?

Kyrkenall let out a dry barking laugh. "The queen royally pissed them off. I told you that. When the Naor attacked their holdings, she didn't help them like they'd helped us. They were driven from their own hunting grounds and we didn't lift a finger. I would have—if I'd known."

Probably when all that had happened he'd been out in the wilds on his long, fruitless search for Kalandra.

"We'll have to make amends," N'lahr said

"How would I even start?"

"Do we know where the ko'aye went?" Elenai asked.

"Deep into kobalin lands, in the shifts, where I'm sure the hazards are innumerable and the hunting is thin," Kyrkenall answered. "Toward the northeastern tribes there are some fair-sized fragments."

"Which is why Ortok will show the way, and act as negotiator with any kobalin." N'lahr looked hard at his friend. "And you'll negotiate with the ko'aye."

The archer shook his head. "You're out of your mind this time, N'lahr. No, I'm going after Kalandra."

N'lahr didn't say anything for a very, very long time, and the dark-eyed archer looked back and forth between him and Elenai. "Aren't you going to tell me I can't go?"

Still the moment stretched on. N'lahr stood motionless.

"N'lahr?" Kyrkenall asked.

Finally the commander responded. "I'm going to ask you who's better to send," he said simply.

"Well, there's Aradel."

"I mean right here. I'm sure she's quite busy in Alantris. And you know that."

Kyrkenall growled. "Damnit to the darkest pits, N'lahr . . . you think we're going to be able to talk to the ko'aye?! They'll tear apart any one of us that gets close."

"Gyldara, Lasren, and Elenai have never met them. Tretton will never be in the air. And I can't go. You've flown with more than one of them. They like you."

"Liked."

"You're all I have, Kyrkenall. If Kalandra's survived this long by herself, she'll manage a little longer."

Kyrkenall cursed colorfully, then sighed in profound disgust. "Why do you always have to be right?"

N'lahr smiled sadly at his friend and turned to Elenai. "I want you to go with him and Ortok. They need a weaver if the storms get bad."

She should have expected that, because it's an argument she had made a moment earlier. She swallowed. "Yes, Commander. How soon do we leave?"

"Tomorrow morning. Right now I want you to go spend time with your family, as you promised. I'm sorry," he added with quiet sincerity, "that it can't be longer."

"They'll understand."

Kyrkenall's voice was low, resigned. "What do you want me to offer them in exchange for joining us?"

"Find out what they want, but let them know that I have returned, and that I will honor my promise. I will help them recover their homeland. We should have bound all the Altenerai to that oath."

Now that Elenai better understood the history, she frowned at the thought of the queen's slippery reasoning. She had justified the annulment of the agreement with the ko'aye in part by saying that it was only N'lahr who'd pledged to aid them, something a dead man couldn't do.

N'lahr was thinking along similar lines. "This time I hope you and Elenai and the others will join me."

"Happily," Kyrkenall said fiercely. "But what if they won't trust us again?"

"The queen kept me from keeping that word, but she won't be able to stop all of us. Tell them that. Even if they're not interested, they should know the Naor are out in force and away from their own holdings. It might be the ideal time for the ko'aye to retake their ancestral lands. If they don't join us, they can still weaken the Naor in that fight. But they are our friends, and they were our allies. Find a way to remind them."

Kyrkenall looked doubtful.

"How are you going to convince Ortok to guide us?" Elenai asked.

"He said he wanted an army. Maybe he can find one out there to lead."

"And bring back? You want an army of kobalin on our lands, too?" Kyrkenall asked.

"As I told Tretton, we need all the help we can get. Now give Lyria and yourself a little longer to rest. Tomorrow morning is soon enough."

Frowning, Kyrkenall turned and clicked his tongue, and Lyria plodded after him toward the stables.

"I expected it would be harder than that," Elenai said softly.

N'lahr smiled a little. "You need to get on your way, and I need to speak with Ortok."

She was briefly confused, thinking N'lahr was changing his mind and ordering her into service now. "And you should probably change out of your uniform," he continued. "I'm sure they'll want to see you in it, but it will feel a little more like home if you're not in your khalat."

Her khalat. It still felt strange to think of it in a possessive way. "What about . . . that matter you wanted to ask me about? The hearthstones?"

"It will keep. We'll talk when you get back."

She started to object that she wasn't actually that hungry, not after the breakfast, then nodded her agreement. "I'll check in this evening."

"You don't need to hurry. Our lives will be nothing but hurry after today."

Clearly he was wasn't slowing down, and she wondered briefly if she should stay to help him more, but she merely nodded again, wondering where she'd find a change of clothes. She'd fled Darassus with nothing but the garments she was wearing.

Fortunately, Gyldara had a spare blouse, and some squires offered a selection of leggings that fit fairly well. She felt almost naked without the khalat and sword, but once she was a few blocks away from the barracks she realized that she was free—no longer was she instantly recognizable, and people went about their day without halting their work to stare, congratulate, or thank her.

This anonymity proved so pleasant that she was almost saddened as she turned down the side street of the main square and drew in sight of home.

It wasn't an impressive a structure from the front, typical of all those on this street. Within though, she knew it was spacious, with a wide courtyard that her father found ideal for entertaining—after-parties for cast members, business meetings, and sometimes rehearsals were held there. All this activity to grow his theater and provide for his daughters, she'd realized later, might also have helped drown the silence in his wife's absence.

When last Elenai had visited three years ago, she'd hesitated, because it no longer felt quite like her home, but then opened the door without knocking. Today she raised her hand to the fading red wood, and rapped it.

From within came the sound of laughter and talking. It seemed that no one had heard, and she was lifting her fist to knock again when she heard the distinctive tread of footsteps. The door opened before her.

Elenai didn't recognize the young woman who brightened at the sight of her. She was of average height, dark-skinned, with curling black hair bejeweled.

"Oh! Elenai. I'm Ahzelia. Caslia's girlfriend," she said quickly, seeing no sign of recognition in Elenai's eyes. "It's such a pleasure to meet you." Belatedly, the woman stepped to one side and gestured for her to enter. "Please, come in, it's your house."

"Thank you." Elenai stepped over the threshold and onto a new green rug stretching down the entry hall. She waited politely while Ahzelia closed the door, feeling out of place.

"Your sister's told me so much about you," Ahzelia went on. "She's always looked up to you."

"Has she?" Elenai found that declaration implausible. She'd always wanted a close relationship with Caslia and seldom had one, and certainly she'd never seen much evidence that Caslia wanted to emulate her.

Ahzelia laughed in a self-conscious way. "She told me how determined you always were. She said you took a target and a spear into the courtyard and practiced every morning for hours."

"She hated that," Elenai said, remembering Caslia shouting down from the balcony to stop the clatter.

They moved out of the entry hall and into the central living space fronting the courtyard. Two of her three aunts and their husbands were placing napkins and utensils on a long table while some of her younger cousins chased a pair of brown spotted puppies. It was her grandmother who saw her first, turning with pitcher in hand and then flinging water from it as she threw open her arms. "Elenai!"

All those fears about feeling apart from things evaporated in the explosion of cheerful greetings. Her grandmother's embrace was exactly as she'd remembered: strong, no matter her protests that she was growing "feeble in her old age." Her grandfather had aged more obviously. There was little left of his hair but fringes along the side. His smile was warm as ever, though, and he still smelled of wood and resin from his carpentry shop. Her aunts complained, as they had before, that she was too thin, but added this time that she needed sleep.

"She'll have to stay a while with us," bosomy Zianna cried, "and we'll fatten her back up! Remember what a chubby toddler she was?"

Everyone parted for her "uncle" Crenahr, waiting politely with a huge grin. Her mother's cousin had been a steadfast if somewhat remote presence all of her life. At first she'd thought him stern, only realizing as she matured that he'd always been painfully shy.

She opened her arms and they embraced.

"It's so good to see you," he said, then, beaming, stepped back to take the hand of a small woman with a gap-toothed smile cradling an infant somehow sleeping through all the ruckus. "This is my wife, Mahra."

Of course—she'd received his letter announcing the date, astonished the old bachelor would settle so late in life. She'd always thought of him married to his job, overseeing the windmill-powered pumps that brought water from the deep aquifers below the city.

"And our son," the graying man said proudly, "Reynahn."

She teared up at that, and hugged him once more, for Crenahr had honored Elenai's mother by choosing the male form of her name.

There then came a blizzard of greetings from younger cousins, all far taller than she recalled. Her father was the oldest of five children, making her the eldest of her generation in that family. She scarcely recognized some of her cousins, or they her, and the youngest goggled at her.

And then her pretty aunt Irehna, only four years her senior and something like an older sister, took her by the hand out into the courtyard where her father and uncle were putting finishing touches on a slew of baked goods. A second table was arranged out here, in the sunlight, and various of her father's friends were either helping set up or standing in little groups talking. These shouted her name and raised hands in greeting.

Her father looked up from his work over the stove, beamed at her, turned his utensils over to a handsome, graying brunette Elenai didn't recognize, and came toward her with open arms.

Jenahl Dartaan still had a thick shock of black hair, still threaded naturally—though it looked theatric—with strands of silver. He had a square, open face lined with laugh and care. His embrace was even tighter than it had been last night.

"By the gods it's good to see you." He held her close and then thrust her apart, looking hard at her while he gripped her shoulders. "Last night you looked a little like a frightened wild animal."

She'd felt like one. She and the other warriors had hastily cleaned up, but the cheering throngs had been too reminiscent of the crowding Naor, eager for her blood, and she'd been tense even with those she loved. Her father must have noted a similar look now, for he turned and used his penetrating director's voice: "Give her some room! Don't smother, for goodness sake!"

They laughed a little and faded back, and then her father steered her past a rack of trout suspended over coals, and brought her to the handsome brunette woman overseeing some blue and green peppers split open on searing hot rocks.

The stranger was waiting with an expectant smile, and Elenai's father put his hand to the woman's arm while still touching Elenai, as if being in contact with both somehow brought them closer.

"Elenai, I want to introduce you to my . . . to someone I've been seeing. This is Kelindra."

"It's such a delight to finally meet you," the woman said.

Surprised both by the woman's name and by what was apparently an important relationship she'd heard nothing about, Elenai hesitated too long. After the awkward silence she strove to explain her reaction. "I'm sorry—one of my friends is in love with a woman named Kalandra, and it caught me off guard." Realizing that sounded foolish because most people had heard of Alten Kalandra, she added: "I mean, Alten Kalandra. My friend, Kyrkenall, the alten, is desperate to find her . . . it's a similar name. Of course, different people can have the same name, or similar ones . . ." She stuck her hand out as if to ward away the inane babbling that probably sounded like name dropping. "I'm so happy to meet you."

Kelindra clasped arms with her cautiously, still seemingly uncertain what to make of her. Elenai didn't blame her. She'd sounded ridiculous.

Her father laughed and squeezed her shoulders from behind. "I've managed to render my daughter speechless. I'm sorry, my dear. I didn't mean to surprise you."

"No, it's fine." Elenai looked back to smile at him, and then turned her head to share it with Kelindra. "I'm happy for you. Did you meet in the theater?"

"I'm an old friend of Crenahr's," the woman said. "He introduced us. I'm afraid I've dreamed of your father from afar for ages."

"What do you think of that?" her father said with a laugh, and a shoulder pat.

Elenai managed to sound almost normal as she turned to greet her father's brother, and then worked her way through her father's friends, wondering the while where her sister was.

This was all made clear when Caslia turned up with two more cousins, each carrying baskets of fresh baked bread from a nearby bakery.

What a difference three years had made. No longer was her sister hunched defensively. Now she held her head high, even if that meant she was a handspan taller than nearly everyone. Once gawky and stork-like, Caslia had filled out a little, but more importantly, moved with assurance. If not classically pretty, she radiated charm and confidence that was attractive in itself, something Elenai hadn't noted during their brief conversation the night before. But then she'd been a little overwhelmed by the reception and distracted by the crowd.

Once the food was ready, her father clapped his hands and called for attention, then hopped up on a bench with the dexterity of a younger man. His voice, often deployed on the stage, had no trouble reaching everyone in the courtyard and living areas beyond. He commanded everyone to fill their cups, and once this was done, lifted his goblet.

"Now I know all of you are almost as eager as I am to throw yourselves at this food."

Elenai felt a little pang of regret, for she was still mostly full from the governor's breakfast.

"So I want to say a few words before they're drowned out by the babbles and mastication!"

This elicited a few chuckles.

"The last time I saw my eldest daughter, she was a quiet squire newly risen to the third rank. She never said it to me, but I knew she worried whether or not she had the mettle to keep on rising. I knew. I think most of us always knew. Now she's returned to us, not just an alten with a field commission, but as one of the saviors of our very own city. My dear, I am so proud of you, and only wish your mother could be here to see you now!"

"Hear, hear!" a male voice at the rear echoed.

Elenai felt tears welling and managed not to cry. Nor did her father, though she saw him struggling. "Welcome home, Elenai. We are all grateful for your service and your presence in our lives. Here's to your health, and to the Altenerai! Long may you both prosper!"

He raised his goblet, and the answering chorus of relatives and guests cried, "To your health, and to the Altenerai!"

She drank, feeling her face flush a little at all the attention.

"Now," her father said, "let's get to the eating!"

With that, the uncomfortable moments were mostly over. The food was as excellent as ever, and family stories and old jokes and the mundane trials of daily life were exchanged around, about, and with her. The courtyard felt almost like home, and at least familiar. The affection was real, and not the mindless adulation she'd been seeing in the eyes of the squires.

Over the course of the afternoon, she fielded occasional questions about the battle, and the Naor, and what she thought would happen next. Her answers downplayed the violence and played up the hope. Younger children wanted to see her ring light, and ask about the bizarre magical storms she'd witnessed in the deep shifts, and hear the tale of Kyrkenall vanquishing the kobalin Vorn. She followed that up with tidbits about steadfast Ortok and his friendship with N'lahr.

More than a half-dozen children of relatives and friends were gathered at this point, in a half circle before the old wooden chair she'd taken in the corner. Her aunt Irehna had wandered up to listen. "So what's N'lahr really like?" she asked.

Elenai saw an amused glint in her aunt's dark eyes, and remembered in a flash how she'd once confided her interest in the great swordsman to Irehna. That was mortifying.

"Did he really come back from the dead?" a little redheaded boy asked. She'd lost track of who he was, apart from being the son of one of the theater hands.

"He wasn't really dead," she said. "He was trapped in a huge crystal and sealed in a tower. Kyrkenall and I rode nearly to the world's end to free him."

That pronouncement was absorbed with wide-eyed wonder.

"Children," Irehna said as she stepped carefully through them, "I'm going to borrow Alten Elenai for a little while myself."

There were a few disappointed sighs as Irehna dragged Elenai up by the hand and headed for the stairs. She'd slid off her sandals earlier, as was Irehna's habit, and padded barefoot up the steps to the balcony ringing the courtyard.

She managed to be showy even in bright loose leggings and off-shoulder blouse, for she was wide hipped and small waisted, a woman secure with her own appearance so that she was beautiful however dressed. She sat down in the shadow of the awning near Elenai's old room, her legs hanging out through the gaps in the slats supporting the balcony rail, and passed over a wine bottle as Elenai sat. Her smile was mischievous. "So I finally have you to myself for a little while," she said.

Elenai drank deep. All that talking had been thirsty work.

"How are you, really?" Irehna asked.

"I'm not sure, really," Elenai confessed. "I was afraid I wouldn't belong anymore. But it's still home, even if it feels different."

Irehna brushed back her mane of curling dark hair, her eyes fixed upon Elenai. "Is that because you've grown up, or because of what you've seen and done?"

"A little of both. I mean, I think I've grown up because of some of the things I've seen and done."

Irehna took another pull and, at Elenai's demur refusal, sat the bottle between them. "Remember when we used to sit here in the evenings?" she asked. "I had such a crush on that actor Oramahn. What was that play?"

Elenai laughed, remembering how her aunt had worked so hard to get the young man's attention. But Oramahn had always remained politely distant. *"The Rise of Myralon."*

"That's the one! Do you know, he came by the furniture store last year to look me up. He'd decided the stage wasn't for him, and does tile work or something."

"What did he want? Was he still handsome?"

"Oh yes. He apologized for avoiding me those years ago. Here I'd been thinking he was only interested in men. But he said he hadn't wanted to date the director's sister!"

"That wouldn't have stopped most."

She smiled. "Some use it as an introduction."

"So did you get together with him?"

"No. He's married. And he's a little dull, so it's all for the best. Now tell me truly—you used to *dream* about N'lahr. How has that worked out?"

She should have known her aunt would come back around to that, but she was still surprised. "Oh. There's nothing going on. He's my commander."

Irehna might actually have decided upon restraint, for her next question wasn't teasing. "Is he really as humorless as everyone says?"

"No. I mean, he's direct, but he's . . . he's really a very nice man, and a sad one. And I'm not sure I've ever met anyone as intelligent. He's always focused clearly on what he needs for the objective, but he's also paying keen attention to what's happening moment to moment. He's planning ahead but not missing anything at the same time. I don't know how he does it."

"And what about Kyrkenall?" Irehna asked. "What's *he* like?"

Despite herself, Elenai flushed a little, and Irehna laughed.

Elenai quickly held up a palm. "There's nothing like that between us, either," she said.

"But you wish there was?" She didn't wait for an answer. "By the gods but he's a beautiful one."

"I could introduce you," Elenai said. She rather thought Kyrkenall would enjoy meeting Irehna. Probably most men would, and many women. "But he's in love with Kalandra, and she's missing."

"I'd love to help him try to forget her," Irehna jested.

"He's a handful," Elenai cautioned.

"I like a handful," Irehna said with a laugh, then reached out and patted Elenai's wrist. "But I think my niece has first claim."

Elenai shook her head, for she had no claim upon Kyrkenall. And she didn't think she'd want to claim him. How might she convey her conflicted feelings about the brave, reckless, cunning man, haunted and deeply loyal and a little mad? Maybe he couldn't really belong to anyone, which was why it might be best that he'd given his heart to someone who wasn't really there.

Her aunt recognized her change in mood and wisely shifted from talk of relationships. "What's next for you? There are rumors the Altenerai have to move out soon. People say Alantris may be under attack."

It certainly hadn't taken long for the news to spread. "They are. And a lot of the Vedessi Guard is leaving with them."

Irehna was no fool, and read between the lines. "But you're not?"

"I've another mission."

"A secret mission?"

"It's secret so long as I don't tell anyone."

Irehna chuckled. "Is Kyrkenall going with you? Ho ho! I see from that blush he is!"

"It's not like that," Elenai said, wondering why her body was reacting like this to her aunt's prodding. Perhaps knowing Irehna had always been a creature of strong sexual appetites, spending time beside her put her in mind of her own.

"If your relationship ends up being less like you think and more like you wonder about, make sure you've the proper protections."

"Always," Elenai said, a little aghast she should be talking about such things, much less considering the possibility of them happening on an urgent mission into the deeps. With a kobalin nearby, no less. She worked to change the subject before it grew more embarrassing. "Tell me about father. Is it a good match?"

Irehna frowned a little. "He seems very happy."

"You don't like her?"

Irehna sighed. "She's nice enough. She wants to change things around the house, though, for no real reason. She's changing the way he dresses, too. Making him over a little. But maybe it was time for a new wardrobe," Irehna admitted. "Every woman wants to put a little bit of a stamp upon her man, I suppose. But she seems just a little fussy. He's fine with it, though."

"And what do you think of my sister's match?"

"Oh, they're young still, but they're good for each other. Ahzelia has a pretty singing voice. And she just dotes on Caslia. But then Caslia's really blossoming now. Her last play was something to see. She based it on an unfinished play your mother had written."

"I didn't know," Elenai said. Her mother, a talented actor and gifted singer, had been dabbling with playwriting in the years before her death. Her sister had been determined to follow in her absent mother's footsteps from a very young age, but Elenai hadn't known she'd worked on anything their mother had written. Much less that any of Caslia's plays were more than trial pieces.

"It debuted two weeks ago," Irehna said. "It's this dreamy swashbuckling fantasy with moments of high humor and mixed identities and love. It was all anyone was talking about until, well, the Naor turned up."

Elenai looked down across the crowd and saw her sister in the midst of a group of laughing people, the center of attention as she shared a story.

"No wonder she looks so confident."

"She has a lot of talent for someone so young. But she grew up surrounded by wonderful stories, so any kind of natural knack was going to get fertile ground."

That made sense. She was happy for her sister, and a little sad, too, for the gulf that had long been between them. "Her girlfriend says Caslia's told her all about me."

"You sound skeptical."

"We never really got along."

"You were sort of an impossible older sister, though, weren't you? Good at everything and pretty and successful?"

"That's not how I remember it." She recalled years of frustration and struggle.

"That's because you were constantly striving to better yourself. Caslia was painfully jealous."

"It hadn't felt like jealousy. I think 'hateful' is the word you're looking for. You can only hear 'I wish you were dead instead of Mom' so many times before you start to think she might really mean it. I know she loved me, sometimes, but I never got the sense she *liked* me."

Irehna nudged her. "Think how she felt. Always younger and worse at everything than her pretty, accomplished sister, who had five years more experience. *And* she was competing with you for the attention of a distracted, grieving father. I know Jenahl's a good man, and he tried, but he can be absent even when he's there. And he missed your mother so terribly. He built her up so much your sister practically worshiped her memory. It's no wonder she set herself up to follow in her footsteps, is it?"

"It sounds like she's done it. I guess she gets the love of theater naturally."

"Probably so." She nudged Elenai again. "I don't know how to explain you; though your father's strong for his size, he's no athlete. I guess you're determined."

"I'm just stubborn. And maybe too stupid to give up."

"I don't think there's anything stupid about you, Elenai. I never have. I'm very, very proud of you."

"Thank you."

Irehna then asked a question outside her usual interests, and it sounded odd to Elenai's ears, perhaps because she was being consulted as an expert, not a relative. "Do you think you can save Alantris?"

"I think it's going to be difficult. The Naor have brought another large army."

Irehna grew grave. "Do you think the Naor are coming back here?"

She shook her head. "Vedessus is safe for now, and probably for a good long while. But we might be in for another long war. And there's more to it than that . . ." She fell silent, wondering how much she should say about the queen and the conspiracy, even here, within her own home and to one of her very favorite relatives. In the end, she decided to provide more detail. Word was going to go out to the populace one way or another, and it would be better if some of it was the truth. "The queen's the one who betrayed N'lahr," she said finally. "She knew he was alive, locked him away, and spread the lie that he was dead."

Irehna's elegant eyebrows rose in astonishment. "Why?"

"She's completely caught up in magical studies," Elenai said. "And she traded him for more magical secrets. Dark ones, we think." That was a fair enough summary of what they guessed was happening, even if it left out the specificity of the hearthstones. "She needs to be brought up on charges. But that's going to be kind of hard to do right now with an invasion under way. Queen Leonara sent people to try and kill Kyrkenall and me, once we found out about N'lahr. And we're worried about what she's going to do now that N'lahr's back and exposing her misdeeds."

Irehna could only stare. "By the grace of Elahn," she said. "Why didn't you say something sooner?"

She shrugged. "It's not something you mention in casual conversation, is it?"

"What are you going to do about it?" Irehna asked in growing alarm.

"N'lahr presented testimony to the governor this morning. We'll try to let the governors handle it. Meanwhile, we have to find a way to win the war."

"Hail, Alten Elenai," Irehna said quietly, and reached for the bottle. She raised it in salute. "And here all I was asking about was whether you were sleeping with any Altenerai. You're really in the thick of it, aren't you? Like a hero from legend."

Elenai snorted.

Irehna drank. "I won't be surprised if your sister ends up writing a play about you."

"Gods," Elenai said. "I don't even want to think about that."

And then her aunt spoke with surprising insight. "You just want to be you, for a little while, don't you? Before you have to run off and play soldier some more."

Elenai answered her softly. "I'm kind of afraid that I've become a soldier, and I had to run off and play Elenai."

Her aunt put her arm around her shoulders and kissed the top of her head. "You still seem like Elenai to me. Just sadder, and wiser. And a lot more dangerous, apparently."

"And you certainly seem like Irehna. Beautiful and flirty and a little dangerous yourself. Are you still breaking hearts? Is there anyone important in your life?"

Irehna laughed. "I opened my own little shop across the street that specializes in more high-end work. Lots of ornamental railings and decorative wall hangings and that sort of thing. Between that and arranging the timber shipments, I've been very busy."

"But not too busy?"

Irehna smiled, pleased with herself. "There's a certain broad-shouldered potter who's been taking up some of my time," she admitted. "He's a little intense. And very brooding."

"That sounds like nearly every man I serve with," Elenai said. "I'd be mad to get involved with any of them."

"There's involved, and there's *involved*. But you be careful," she admonished, as though she might instill caution when she herself practiced so little.

Late that afternoon, as Elenai made farewells to all, she reflected on Irehna's admonition and how it dovetailed with that of her father's and her sister's. Nearly everyone had told her to be careful. She hadn't dared tell them a whole host of things she'd been involved in over the last month. It wasn't that she hadn't attempted to act with care, but that dangerous things were occurring to her with astonishing frequency, and no amount of care would shield her from experiencing them. Skill and planning could compensate, but a careful person wouldn't be readying to ride off into the shifts with Kyrkenall the Eyeless and a kobalin lord sworn to slay the commander of the Altenerai.

There had been no point in trying to explain or discuss any of that. They wouldn't have truly understood.

Her visit hadn't been easy, but she knew a sense of loss as she passed through the streets on the way to the barracks. People hurried back and forth from the markets with last minute purchases for supper, and there was something about their bustle different from that she'd seen after the city woke. She realized that word had spread that the Vedessi Guard was leaving. The city's unease was palpable, though whether it was because they feared for their departing warriors or for their own welfare with them gone, she couldn't say.

Once within the barracks, she bypassed a line of squires queuing up to eat, asked N'lahr's whereabouts, and found him in his office.

He opened the door and gestured for her to enter. "How was your visit?"

She took the bench across from him and waited while he retook the chair. A square of light thrown from the window illuminated his desk and the paper, inkwell, pen, and blotter awaiting his return.

"It was good," she said.

"Did you see both sides of your family, or only the one?"

"Both," Elenai said. "One side is rather small. The Naor wiped out my maternal grandparents' village," she explained. "While my mother was visiting."

"I'm sorry."

She was surprised she could speak of it so plainly. "One of my mother's cousins survived because he happened to be visiting a library in Vedessus. And she died because she happened to be visiting her parents."

He nodded solemnly. It was enough. She knew his own background was even more dire—in a similar raid he'd lost most of both sides of his own family.

"He's just gotten married, and has a small child, so I guess that side of the family's a little larger now." She wasn't sure why she told him that, but his expression cleared a little. "How are things here?"

"Much to do and little time, as you'd expect. You could have stayed away longer."

"It was time to leave," she said. And that seemed explanation enough for him. "Now tell me about this hearthstone problem you're having."

N'lahr opened a lower desk drawer. From it he withdrew a pair of fragments and set them on the dark old wood. "My hearthstone."

He didn't have to say as much—Elenai recognized the two small halves. Seven years ago he'd sliced it in two with Irion and ended up encased in a crystalline prison.

Knowing that N'lahr never wasted words, she looked to him for an explanation.

Yet it was a while in coming. The commander was silent in thought for a long moment. "I can feel the thing when I'm away from it," he said, with the air of someone admitting a minor infraction. As though he'd been caught filching desserts.

He'd asked for the pieces back as the celebration had wound down last night, and she'd obliged without question. "I assumed you'd wanted it for security reasons."

"I wanted to test my ability to know its precise location in relation to me. Even over in the governor's palace I could feel right where it was, down to a finger's width. Is that what it's like to be attuned with one?"

"Not entirely." Her first instinct was to reassure him, for there was no missing his concern, muted though it was. But she didn't want to mislead him, either. "Mine's in my quarters. Give me a moment." She paused to slip into the inner world and reached out with her senses, encountering his life force, the glow of Irion, the duller energy of the shattered hearthstone, the life forces of all those in the building, and after a time she latched on to the faint energies of the inactive hearthstone in her quarters. The moment she did so she felt that longing to open it that had so begun to worry her, so she resisted its pull.

With a breath of effort she let go of her magical sight and spoke to the commander. "Do you sense other things when you're reaching for it?"

"I don't reach for it. I just know. And I don't sense anything else. Only the stones."

She stepped up to the desk and held one of the pieces up to the square of light framed by the door's window. Even in her grasp she barely felt its power. She knew from before that the shattered remnants held only a fraction of the energy of a fully formed hearthstone, but she considered it with her inner sight and confirmed her earlier impression.

"Do you sense a connection between it and me?" N'lahr asked.

"No. But your life force was enmeshed with this stone for years. I guess it's not too surprising you have a connection to it."

"It goes beyond detecting the thing," he said with mild annoyance. "My sense of time is off. And I think it's getting more obvious to others."

At her hesitation, he continued. "Kyrkenall thought I was simply pausing too long during our chat this morning, didn't he? It didn't even seem a pause to me, until he started prodding. From his tone I gathered it wasn't the first question. How long was I quiet?"

"A good long time," Elenai admitted. She was growing more troubled about the symptoms and their possible dangers. "What about when you delayed during the breakfast, or held the one-legged stance so long this morning? Were those the same things?"

His blank expression changed to one of true unease. "I didn't realize I'd done anything of the kind."

Elenai wasn't sure what to say. "Suppose that happens while you're in the midst of a battle?"

"Yes." Being N'lahr, he didn't bother stating obvious worries.

"Does your sense of time ever seem to speed ahead?"

"No. But then that's not what being imprisoned was about."

"Maybe we should keep it farther away from you," she suggested.

"Do you think that's the answer?"

"I'm not sure." She thought. "I might be able to tell more if I opened one. Unless you think that's dangerous."

"You tell me."

She considered the possible dangers and decided they were slight. "I'd like to try it. I'm going to step out into the courtyard so I'm a little farther away from you, but so we can signal one another."

He acquiesced with a nod and opened the door for her.

She walked over the old pavers and moved for the point farthest from the door, in the shadows of the second-story eaves. Once there, she labored to focus on what she had to do and not upon N'lahr's well-being, but it was a challenge. What if N'lahr were to get worse and worse? What if he were on his way to becoming a permanent statue?

For that matter, though, who was to tell what would happen if she tinkered with a broken hearthstone? Slicing it open the first time had introduced a completely unforeseen and catastrophic result. Suppose just poking at it when the stone was damaged did the same? To her? Or would it act against the person it was apparently linked with and encase N'lahr again?

The more she thought about it, the more she realized she'd too quickly dismissed the dangers.

She had an errant thought that she ought to consult with someone who knew something more about hearthstones, instead of relying upon the limited knowledge of an amateur like herself. But while there were certainly more experienced mages in Vedessus, when it came to hearthstones she was the best resource N'lahr had. And that was a little surprising.

Opening a hearthstone had grown simpler and simpler, but this proved a challenge. She searched and searched for the flaw and got to thinking it might be on the other half. Rather than return and search that piece, though, she considered the dead center of the stone, usually unreachable, and touched it with a clockwise spiral of energy as she would when facing an actual opening.

The stone flickered to life in her hands and she felt the soothing brush of its power, dull though it was. When contrasted with the blazing heat of the activated hearthstones she was familiar with, this thing was but a coal lately removed from a dead fire. It retained only a hint of energy. It seemed uninclined to encase her in crystal, or to subdue N'lahr once more. She glanced over at the commander, peering with interest through the window and suddenly she was in his thoughts.

She had practiced a few linking exercises over the years, where two mages shared memories, but this was nothing like that. She was suddenly aware of everything he thought and felt.

He ruminated upon an old memory. A dust cloud billowed. His oft smiling, now wide-eyed father shouted to mind his sister and whirled from the horses and new plow to snatch a hoe. He, N'lahr, was pulling the little girl away from the seedsack and dragging her into the drain ditch, feeling her shake with each fresh scream from their mother or older sister. He pleaded with her to stay quiet, even when the screaming stopped and the hairy strangers grunted and cheered. He was filled not with fear, but impotent rage.

She didn't know he'd sheltered a sister. N'lahr was famously the only survivor from his village.

She died of high cough in the refugee camp later that spring.

"You can hear my thoughts, too?" she asked, thinking it at the same time.

I can. The rage, she felt, had never fully left him.

"I'm so sorry," she said. "About your family." She worked to set aside the deep grief and anger he'd shared, and looked down at the stone, seeking in vain for some sign of obvious connection between it and the commander. There was nothing visible in the outer world, much less glowing threads of energy in the inner.

Intrigued, Elenai shut the stone down, relieved when it cooperated with little effort. She walked back to N'lahr. He opened the door and eyed her, apparently waiting for her judgment, but she still wasn't sure what she'd say. Finally, she began with the obvious. "This could be very dangerous in the wrong hands."

He seemed unfazed. "How far do you think you can go with it?"

That question didn't truly make any sense to her. "What?"

"How far do you think you can take it and still communicate with me?"

She answered honestly. "I have no idea. I don't even know how it works."

"Do you think the other stone needs to be near me for the trick to work properly?"

"I don't know. But I'm not sure you should keep either near you."

"All right. You can take one with you. I'll have someone else hold the other half, but keep it away from me. At the rear of the baggage train, say."

She didn't care for that at all. "You should leave both pieces here, where the Naor are in no danger of getting hold of it. You'd be in extreme danger if this stone were to fall into enemy hands. I'd just as soon see both pieces destroyed, if I knew how."

He shook his head. "There's an advantage here you may not appreciate. It's just possible the stones can give us a way to communicate from a distance."

The full force of his idea caught her off guard. "You think that I can reach you while we're traveling?"

"We know a talented weaver can use a hearthstone to send messages, even between realms. Why not send a message to me? I'm no mage, but I'm somehow attuned to this stone."

"Not in a good way. Or in a controlled way, at least."

He turned over his hand, as if casting off a worry. "We should experiment. I'll have you ride to the far side of the city, on the wall, and try there."

"Of course, but—"

"Good. And then if that works, it may work when you're farther out. In either case, it will be farther away, which may limit the stone's effect upon me."

"I suspect. I don't know for sure."

He nodded. "Good. I want to be kept abreast of your progress."

Didn't he understand the risks? "You're overlooking the dangers of your connection with this broken hearthstone. I have no way of knowing what prolonged involvement with it, or proximity to it, is going to do to you."

When he met her eyes, she realized that he understood completely. "It's a risk I'm willing to take." He jabbed a finger at the broken pieces. "That thing stole seven years. It's about time that it helped me for a change."

8

A Brother's Word

Alone among the dozen or so weavers Vannek had met, Syrik had a warrior's physique. He was broad shouldered and deep chested, with massive legs and thick arms. If he didn't spend so much time studying spell work, he'd probably be even bigger. Almost all Naor mages were mocked, even if they were feared. The most powerful were only disparaged behind their backs. No one, though, ridiculed Syrik, in part because he was born from one of Mazakan's lesser sons, and thus had some blood of greatness in him, but also because he could land a solid punch if you crossed him. He'd been pulled unwillingly into the company of mages during his twelfth year, soon after he had personally slain an adult wyvern—what their enemies called ko'aye—in the most elite rite of passage available to aspiring men.

By ancient traditions, children who had visions or other weird behaviors were turned over to the mages, no matter their birthright. Syrik had kept his oddities secret for longer than most, but Vannek's eldest brother,

Chargan, had eventually noted Syrik's magical taint in his aura and secured a confession. Thus the young man had been forced into training and, outside of occasional forays, his hunting days were now over.

Vannek had grown up surrounded by cousins and sons and daughters of other lordlings and chieftains and kings. Syrik had been a favorite. He was blessed with strength and speed but didn't make a show of it. And he possessed a rare ability to laugh at himself when he made mistakes. Vannek had no idea how he'd developed that particular quirk, for his father had been a brash and sullen braggart and his mother inconsequential.

When Vannek was eight, he had sometimes wondered if Syrik, only two years older, might make a good husband. One who would listen, and maybe be kind, and not take too many other wives. But then Vannek had been declared a man, and he could no longer look on men in a womanly way.

Sometimes Syrik still looked on him as though he were a woman, and he did so today as he finished drawing the sigils over the horse trough. There was an appraising look in his dark eyes, a warmth that there should not have been when looking upon another man.

Such looks from Syrik made Vannek uncomfortable, and yet he never quite managed to dismiss the mage from his service, in part because he valued Syrik's meticulous work ethic. Any other senior magician would have his apprentices draw the sigils, but Syrik wanted them created just so, even if he had to bend and strain and even crawl into position to carve them perfectly before standing back to nod in satisfaction.

At Vannek's waved assent, Syrik motioned apprentices and slaves into place. None were Alantran slaves, who couldn't be trusted. These were men from other tribes. They hobbled the horses and then slew them, one by one, while their stablemates whinnied in fear and rolled their eyes and stamped in their stalls until their own turn came.

Vannek disliked killing the beasts; the plow horses would have been useful for years yet. He hated the blood, too, and the sight of the butchered animals being dragged away, and the reek of their terror, but there was no help for it. The ritual required blood.

Just as the chanting from the five kneeling apprentices was really beginning to irk, Syrik raised a hand. "Enough." The barn went quiet. The apprentices stepped back, their foreheads running with sweat.

"Place the stool," Syric said. "And be gone."

"Yes, master," the lead apprentice replied, breathing heavily. He stepped over to where one of the burly slaves waited with a battered, three-legged stool, accepted it from the man, then set it into the trough, filled to the brim with steaming blood.

The slaves and apprentices left them alone, closing the barn door. It didn't keep out all the noise from beyond, for someone was shouting orders for a unit practicing drills, and it didn't restrain sunlight pouring in through windows and slats, but there was the suggestion of privacy.

"Are you ready?" Vannek asked.

"Cousin, I am yours."

He didn't like how Syrik said that, but Vannek nodded. "Begin."

The mage raised thick fingers and then swept them through the air, almost as if he wove invisible cloth. Sweat beaded his brow, too, as his lips parted to show strong white teeth. Vannek noticed again that he took pains with his beard and hair, trimming and combing them carefully.

At Syrik's command, long tendrils of glistening crimson liquid snaked up from the trough. Vannek felt his skin chill at the ugly sight. No matter how much time he'd had to spend near sorcery, he'd never grown used to its unnatural manifestations.

The rising strands of blood twisted into ropes that quickly shaped a complex framework. In a few minutes a scaffolding took shape, over which recognizable forms grew distinct: a torso, a head, a mass below that which was flowing and vaguely fishtail-like until it was revealed as the bottom of a robe.

The head shape then became overlaid with more specific features, and long strands of the blood hung down to either side of the head. In only a few moments more, Vannek looked upon a sculpture of her oldest brother, Chargan, fashioned in liquid scarlet and reeking of fresh death. His image seemed to float upon an invisible chair, a few inches over the stool. The one time they had dispensed with the stool, Chargan had looked almost comical when he materialized, so Syrik had ever after insisted on its use.

The mage stepped back and leaned against a post in the barn, breathing heavily. His hands dropped shaking to his sides.

Chargan blinked bloody eyes and spoke, his voice heavy and somewhat distorted, as if with mucous. "Something's gone wrong, hasn't it?" he asked. "I expected an update sooner."

"The city's secure now," Vannek said quickly. "But there were complications. An alten killed one of our dragons."

Chargan stiffened in his seat, somewhere far away. "How did he manage that?"

Interesting that her brother assumed the alten was male, even when there were many formidable women warriors amongst their enemies. Still, in this instance Chargan was correct, at least according to the Alantran prisoners. "It's a new alten, named Rylin. He rode a wyvern against our forces during the assault on the city, and he managed to take out the driver."

Chargan's bloodied face frowned. "What are you doing to catch him?"

"He's escaped. And another alten tricked his way out of the city with a thousand Alantrans. We don't know which one that was, although some think it was the same one."

Chargan's mouth widened, displaying a crimson gap. "How did they get so many prisoners out?"

"They were clever. But our brother was negligent," Vannek summarized.

"How surprising," Chargan said with distaste.

Vannek glanced back at Syrik. By the Sacred Three, the mage had best hold his tongue, for he had heard enough of their scheming over the last months to doom her and Chargan both. Syrik's eyes were slitted, for the spell required much concentration.

"It's worse than any of that," Vannek told Chargan at last. "That same alten was responsible for killing both the dragon lord Zhintin and his assistant Talkus. So that's our three best dragon masters gone. The other dragon masters were far more exhausted than expected. We were unable to send them on to Grandfather. Perhaps tomorrow—"

"There's no need," Chargan said, darkly.

"What do you mean?"

"Grandfather's dead." Chargan delivered the news with deadpan calm. No grief could be expected, for Grandfather had been fierce and terrible. Their devotion to him had arisen from fear and awe and not from any especially close bond. Still, one might as well say that the ground had dropped away, so certain was his presence in their lives.

Vannek gasped in wonder. "How did it happen?"

"It's not just him. Most of his army died with him. The Altenerai ensorcelled a huge oxen herd into charging late at night, while the soldiers slept. They were expecting the arrival of some oxen for supplies and were less cautious than they should have been when they heard hoofbeats."

"The oxen killed Grandfather?"

"N'lahr killed Grandfather. The oxen destroyed our army."

Vannek sucked in a breath. "I told you he lived! I spotted him in The Fragments only a week and a half ago! With Kyrkenall!"

"Yes." That's all Chargan said. There was no apology for laughing at Vannek, or mocking him. "Well, you were right. Are you happy now?"

"No." Vannek would have been more pleased with an apology, but he knew better than to suggest one. "What does this mean?"

"It means I'll have my hands full keeping things together until we can take Darassus."

"You still mean to do that?"

The bloody image's teeth gleamed. "By the Three! Yes!"

"But you're coming here first, aren't you?"

Chargan laughed. "No. If I actually turn up near Alantris, Koregan will take command." He continued venomously: "This is my army. And I am going to lead it to victory."

Horrified by this change in plan, Vannek struggled to frame an objection that didn't sound oppositional, but Chargan went on as if convincing himself. "I will not aid Koregan in securing his rule. And think. Even if I was comfortable with our idiot brother in charge, so long as Darassus stands the fae will send warriors from their other realms to fight us in The Fragments. If we destroy Darassus, they'll retreat to secure their own lands. Even with N'lahr returned from his grave."

Vannek could withhold protest no longer. "That's not certain, but if we push on to Darassus we'll be too far extended. We can hold The Fragments. We don't need Erymyr. The Fragments have more than enough land for us all. And the kings and warriors know how instrumental you've been—"

Chargan cut him off, sharply. "That won't make me god king! I must slay their queen and break their walls to show I am the strongest. I have to do better than plan the victories for Koregan to take credit. If I'm to unite the clans under my rule I have to be a warlord. And when I rule," Chargan's chin rose in pride, "we will finally be secure. It won't matter if I'm a 'weak' spell caster," he said with a sneer, "or that you are a woman."

"I am a man," Vannek countered. He'd more than once had to follow those words with a duel to the death, but that kind of anger served no purpose here, so he deliberately relaxed his clenched fists.

"You haven't the parts of one, and none of the kings truly believe those lies. But think; you can do as you please, once we're in power. No one would dare question you under my rule, even if you did admit you were a woman."

Chargan was arrogant and infuriating. But of his two brothers, Vannek vastly preferred him over the spoiled, boastful favorite son of the favored son, Koregan. Chargan was a stronger man, no matter that he was a mage, and a smarter one, and he would be a better king. And unlike Koregan, who saw Vannek as an embarrassment to be defended only to preserve his own dignity, Chargan actually valued Vannek's abilities. They shared a measure of trust, a rare and valuable thing.

Chargan, noting the hesitation, spoke on, derisively. "Don't tell me you think you can count on Koregan's love to see you through?"

"You have my support. But what will I tell him? Koregan has to be informed of Grandfather's death. And the other kings will challenge more when they learn you're not coming."

"Tell him that I've been delayed because of trouble with the dragons, my sister brother."

Vannek frowned, for he hated being addressed that way. No one but his brothers would dare call him that, and it was in bad taste for them to do so. "He's not going to like that. And the kings will think that means your sorcery is weak."

Chargan laughed. His smile was satisfied and confident and ghastly, with his lips of blood. "All will be fine with the kings when they learn I was destroying Darassus. I've managed a new surprise that may even be better than dragons. And neither our brother or the fae are going to be able to stop me."

"Cousins," Syrik's voice was a hoarse whisper. "The energy fades. . . ."

"No matter," Chargan said. "We've touched on all that's important."

"But what should I say to Koregan?"

"Tell him to hold position. He has more than enough troops to do that. I'll bring good news. Take care of Syrik for me." He said the last with a smile, and then he was nothing but raining blood.

Vannek's cheeks flushed with both anger and shame, and he stood glaring at the liquid-filled trough, roiling still from the influx of blood fallen from Chargan's failed image.

When Vannek had mastered himself at last and turned to face the mage, he found Syrik calm but pale. He was breathing hard, but quietly, and his dark eyes seemed to bore into Vannek's own.

Vannek stepped closer to Syrik. "You heard treasonous things today."

"You need not fear me."

"I don't. I fear *for* you if word gets out."

Syrik held Vannek's eyes, and he wondered if his cousin worked a spell, for he felt flush and uncertain, rather than menacing as he'd intended.

The mage continued as though he hadn't noticed. "My apprentices are loyal. They can be counted upon to serve with discretion and they hear nothing of your discussions."

Vannek wasn't sure what else to say. Finally, something other than threats, or words more dangerous, came to him. "I'll relay that you're to begin working with the dragons. I think it's vital you learn to fly them. And soon." Vannek turned on his heel.

Syrik's voice was smooth, liquid. "I will be ready, when you are."

He hadn't said what he'd be ready for, and Vannek didn't ask.

9

The Tracks in the Outpost

Two balconies wrapped the stage floor in a horseshoe pattern, one recessed above the other. Elenai recognized the place immediately for the theater where she'd spent much of her youth, except that there were no curtains or backdrops visible, or even the old brick wall to the stage's rear. Instead, the boards where the actors would have walked were vastly deep, and suffused with a bright yellow glow, as if the sun shone with the cheery hue of a dandelion rather than damning brightness.

She saw no actors, though she heard their voices and even the creak of their tread, a notion she realized should have disquieted her, and she wondered a little at her detachment. In the seats all about her, she discovered the audience was composed only of shadow.

On reflection, that didn't bother her, either, and it was then she knew she must be dreaming. She was idly disappointed that her mother hadn't appeared even as she was glad that she wasn't experiencing another vision of blood.

The audience of shapeless shade tittered at lines mumbled by invisible actors, and Elenai rose to leave the theater, supposing she might wake if she did.

As she started up the aisle toward the exit, someone addressed her with a solid voice rather than the suggestion of one. "Has he jumped yet?"

Elenai searched through shadows, which faded as her eyes passed over them. Vanished, too, was the indistinct noise of actors mouthing lines, and most of the theater. Nothing was left but a row of chairs where a woman sat in the yellow brightness from a distant doorway.

The stranger looked familiar to Elenai, but she couldn't place her, no matter the woman's Altenerai robe. She looked to be about Elenai's age, with a high forehead and pale blue eyes that assaulted Elenai with the force of her personality.

"Did who jump?" Elenai asked.

"You have to tell him about the jump," the stranger insisted, and climbed to her feet, revealing herself to stand almost a head shorter than Elenai. She had a curiously direct way of speaking, as if every word were impossibly vital and could only be understood if it was stated earnestly. "It's the only way to protect him."

Somehow she knew that "him" was Kyrkenall. "Protect him from what?" she asked.

But the strange woman answered her question only with one of her own. "Have we talked yet?"

"We're talking now."

The high forehead furrowed and the wide mouth curled in annoyance. "That's not what I mean. Have we talked before?"

"No. Never."

"Then maybe I have the right Elenai."

It was then recognition struck. She knew who this alten was, whom she had seen only as a statue. And then once a few nights before, emerging as a bloody image in the place of Chargan. "Rialla?" she asked.

"No, I'm Rialla," the woman replied, exasperated, then pointed at her. "You have to tell him to jump left! He has to be there when the world ends."

"Left?" she asked. And then she wakened to find a cool wind blowing through a twilight land.

She and her companions, she recalled, had laid their sleeping rolls on a plateau amid a rocky wasteland where the sun was forever halted just above the horizon. She opened her eyes to the same hazy, tired orb cloaked by gray clouds. Jagged peaks reared in the distance, outlined starkly against the sky. There were few sounds in this region of the shifts, but above the wind and the crackle of a fire, she could hear two voices in low tones. There was no mistaking the grumbling bass that answered the archer's fluid words. Ortok was talking with Kyrkenall.

Elenai blinked, wondering at the disquieting dream. While she gathered her thoughts, she turned over to find the veteran alten several paces off shaking his head and grinning at Ortok seated across from him. His teeth glinted in the light from the little fire.

"No, see, that's exactly what I mean," Kyrkenall said. "Tell me again how you described him."

Ortok spread huge furred arms, opening fists the size of mattocks. "He was mighty. He was bold!"

Kyrkenall's lovely features twisted into a wry smile. "You have to paint the image in the mind of your listener. What do you imagine if I tell you he was mighty?"

Ortok scratched his furry chest. "A big fellow, with great muscles."

Kyrkenall pointed at him. "See! That's what you should say. It draws a better picture."

She was a little embarrassed that her companions had let her sleep longer, even knowing that Kyrkenall often subsisted on very little rest.

Elenai rolled out of her blankets and slipped barefoot into the dark sand that surrounded their hillock. After relieving herself and washing and putting on her boots, she settled back on her bedroll, focused herself, and prayed to all four of the gods. She pushed aside her worries over Kalandra's claims that the deities who'd shaped the realms were merely people. She would honor them as they deserved.

Still hooking the front of her khalat closed, she walked to the ring of boulders where Kyrkenall and the kobalin had taken their seats. "Good morning. What are you two doing?"

Ortok grinned at her. He had a larger mouth than a human, one that seemed crammed with teeth. "Good morning! Kyrkenall speaks for improving my storytelling."

Kyrkenall explained. "If we meet kobalin there's going to be a ritual exchange, and a story contest. I've been giving Ortok a few tips to help him win."

"My stories are always loved."

"That doesn't mean they can't be loved more, does it?" Kyrkenall countered. "Let's try it out. Describe me while Elenai's grabbing breakfast, then we need to get going."

Ortok sat and thought, his breath rumbling deep in his chest. Elenai helped herself to the last griddle cakes, and some dried fruit and yellow cheese from Vedessus. The road fare, even honey drenched, was no comparison to the feast her father had served: crisp river trout drizzled with herbed butter and breaded with crushed nuts, fresh baked bread, and greens and citrus on the side, and berry pie for dessert. But she was hungry and her mouth watered in anticipation.

Ortok spoke at last. "You seem small and puny, but you are swift, and mighty!"

Elenai snorted but managed to hold back a chuckle when Ortok looked over at her.

Kyrkenall cleared his throat. "That's better. But it doesn't describe what I look like, does it?"

"You are small," Ortok said. "And you look puny."

"I suppose," Kyrkenall admitted grudgingly. "But what's distinctive about me?"

His strange eyes, Elenai thought. Obviously. And his elongated eye teeth.

"Your height," Ortok said.

Kyrkenall's reaction was carefully blank and Elenai could almost hear the dry rejoinders he didn't speak. "Let's try this. When you're describing someone, to make them distinctive, your listeners can usually only hold on to about three characteristics. Make them stick. For instance, in Elenai's case I'd describe her as striking, with hair like autumn leaves and eyes like a misty morning."

"Striking?" Ortok rumbled.

"Pretty in an unconventional way," Kyrkenall explained.

Elenai liked the compliment, though she strove not to show a reaction.

"It is not very precise," Ortok objected.

"All right," Kyrkenall said waspishly, then breathed out, paused a moment, and was calm once more. "Be precise about me."

"Hmm." Ortok pushed out his jaw so that his lower fangs protruded over his upper lip. It gave him a doglike appearance. "Your eyes are black like night and like the deadly bow you hold."

Kyrkenall brightened. "Good!"

"And you are puny, but deadly."

Kyrkenall closed his eyes, his mouth tightly clamped. Elenai waited for the expected sarcasm when he opened his eyes again, but heard, instead, a polite statement: "You're getting there."

"Thank you!"

"Certainly." Kyrkenall's tone suggested that he might not be entirely happy. "Maybe think about how you'd describe the lands while we travel." He climbed to his feet.

As the archer bent to grab his sword belt, Elenai wondered whether she should say anything about her dream. She watched him for a moment as he tightened his buckle, and then he vented his suppressed ire with a snapped question. "What are you staring at? Do I have food on my collar?"

Owing to the way his pupils blended with his sclera, it could be a challenge to know where he was really looking. "No." No time like the present, she thought. "What did Rialla look like?"

His eyebrows arched and he swore. "What in the deepest dung pit does that matter now?"

She had expected avoidance but not anger. She bit her lip and persisted. "Humor me. What did she look like?"

Kyrkenall glared for a long moment, then said, grudgingly. "She was about my height."

So she was short, Elenai thought, though in Kyrkenall's mood she didn't say it. "What else?"

"Broad hipped. Thin waist. Sort of a high forehead. Lovely eyes, though."

"What color were they?"

"You gave more than three things," Ortok pointed out.

Elenai glanced at the kobalin and nodded shortly. She returned her attention to Kyrkenall. "What color?"

"Blue," he said, simply, then spoke with a poetic undertone, as if he'd decided to resist his natural impulse no longer. "A pale blue, going to gray, like you'd see on a clear winter day. Except that there was a bright intensity behind them."

"Oh, that was nice." Ortok sounded as though he might want to take notes.

Elenai wondered briefly if kobalin knew how to read or write down their stories, then returned her full attention to Kyrkenall. "I never knew what color her eyes were. I've seen her statue, I think. I suppose I only looked hard at the most famous ones."

Though Kyrkenall frowned still, his tone was more curious than challenging. "Why are you suddenly interested?"

"I dreamt about her."

He grunted in surprise.

"Who is Rialla?" Ortok asked, climbing to his feet.

When Kyrkenall didn't answer, Elenai offered, "One of Kyrkenall's old friends. An alten and mage."

"Ah. Dreams can tell you things you saw but never noticed."

At this sage observation, Elenai looked more closely at Ortok but saw that he looked as open and guileless as ever.

The kobalin continued. "Is she living, or dead?"

"She's dead," Kyrkenall said with finality, and there was a challenging set to his stance, clear indication he wanted the conversation over.

He always acted strangely about Rialla.

Ortok didn't pick up the human cues, and spoke blithely on. "Sometimes when the dead speak in dreams you must listen. But sometimes demons from the waste take the shape of trusted dead ones to spread fear and hurt."

Elenai pressed on. She hadn't gotten to the most important factor yet. "The thing is, in my dream I saw her eye color. But I shouldn't have known that. I never saw a single tapestry or painting of her."

"There aren't any," Kyrkenall said bitterly. "Maybe you heard me talk about her."

"No. Any time I ask for more information about Rialla, your mouth seizes up like a rusted clamp. I think it was a true dream. I think she might have been real."

"Oh," Ortok interjected. "When a mage has a true dream, you should pay attention, Kyrkenall."

Kyrkenall was famously quick to anger, yet she saw him breathe in shortly, then sigh audibly. He was far more patient with the kobalin than she'd ever seen him prior. In some ways, Kyrkenall treated him like a child unused to social niceties. "Thanks, Ortok," he said quietly.

"You're welcome."

Ortok was apparently indifferent to or unaware of the tension. "What makes you think it was a true dream, Elenai?"

She answered him, but looked at Kyrkenall. "I knew I was dreaming even before Rialla appeared. But the moment she did, nearly everything else faded away. And I felt that she was real."

"Why would she appear to you?" Kyrkenall demanded, sounding a bit injured now.

She shook her head. "I tried to ask her that, but she kept asking nonsensical questions. She wanted to make sure you jumped left."

"What does that mean?" Ortok asked.

"I didn't know, so I asked her to clarify, but it didn't seem like she was making sense at the end."

"What more did she tell you?"

"She was wanting to make sure I was the 'right' Elenai. And," Elenai said, hesitating briefly before deciding to plunge straight on, "she warned me that you had to be there when the world ends. Before I could ask more, I woke up."

"So I have to jump left, and I need to be there for the end of the world." Kyrkenall shook his head.

On repetition, her whole dream conversation seemed nonsensical.

She'd expected Kyrkenall to tease her, but that would have required him being in a good mood. "If it was really her," he groused, "she wouldn't waste time with cryptic jokes."

"Was this Rialla a powerful mage?" Ortok asked.

"One of the greatest weavers the Altenerai ever fielded," Kyrkenall answered. Suddenly he sounded tired. "Better than Commander Renik."

"Mighty Renik!" Ortok declared with pleasure. Only a few weeks ago the kobalin had expressed great interest in the long-missing alten, a man so revered by those who served under him, Elenai had yet to hear any of them, even Kyrkenall, refer to him without mentioning his rank. "N'lahr said he was the best at both sword and spell."

"He was," Kyrkenall said sadly. "But Rialla would have grown to be better. Maybe she already was, that day she died."

And she had died the same day she had won the ring, Elenai knew. She had the shortest service record of all the Altenerai whose plaques she'd polished as a squire.

"If she was a great mage, the matter is clear," Ortok announced. "Her spirit went to Elenai's because she, too, is a magic worker."

Kyrkenall seemed almost to be talking to himself. "I'm more sensitive to the inner world than most non-mages. She can speak to me any time she wishes."

"I've been using her hearthstone," Elenai reminded him. She still carried it, though she'd yet to activate it on their current trip. So far she'd resisted the temptation. "Maybe she could find me more easily through it than she could find you."

He threw up his hands. "She doesn't even know you! You think I should move left whenever I have to jump? Or that I should continually jump left?"

"That would look very foolish," said Ortok, and then laughed. "I can picture it!"

"I think," Elenai said slowly, growing annoyed Kyrkenall would pretend to be so dense, "that you shouldn't dismiss what I say out of hand."

"Sure," he said, and turned away. He forced lightness into his voice. "We'll worry about the world's end some other time. We've enough on our plate right now. You two keep your eyes peeled for any sudden drops. In case I have to jump."

They didn't take long to load up the camp and did so in silence. She and Kyrkenall had brought one horse apiece and a pair of pack horses. Ortok rode a huge white gelded plow horse recovered from the Naor invasion. If a little slow, the animal had proved remarkably sturdy and unfazed by the often peculiar aspects of the Shifting Lands. He had also shown no fear of Ortok, or inclination to unseat his inexperienced rider. The kobalin had no inkling of how fortunate he was. His only prior experience with horses had been hunting them. While he claimed to enjoy riding, she noticed he still clutched the reins in a death grip as they headed downslope.

A storm had recently swept through the shifts. All was stable now, but they saw its remnants. It looked as though some mad deity had dropped geometric monoliths upon a distant line of irregular hills. Immense, perfectly square onyx and celadon blocks had embedded in three of the nearer ones, and the slopes were littered with smaller cubes of gray and green.

The faded red orb of the sun was their constant companion, ever balanced upon the line of the left horizon. Behind them, all was darkness, and ahead was nearly so, a condition that never changed no matter how long they traveled. The rare grasses were dark as well, though they seemed ordinary in other ways, for the horses ate them without hesitation or ill effect. Kyrkenall seemed to trust Lyria's instincts on the matter, so Elenai followed suit. Occasionally they passed little copses of twisted trees with sickly red boughs that all of them kept clear of.

After what seemed hours, she sensed that they approached a long section of unwavering reality, very different from these fragile shifting lands through which they'd traveled. This place, she knew, was solid. A storm might cause it damage, but would never destroy or completely remake it. Far smaller than a realm, it was still large enough that an edge was a few miles on, so it was a fragment rather than a splinter. Unlike the famed realm known as The Fragments, though, there seemed no other nearby formation of similar size.

"Be on your guard," Ortok told them. "We are in kobalin land."

"How do you know?" Elenai asked.

"The winds sing to me," Ortok answered simply.

"What's this place called?" Kyrkenall asked.

"This is Gray Sky holding. We will ask those here where the ko'aye have gone, if the winged ones truly left this way like your people say. First we present ourselves. If we have the approval of a clan mother, the hunting groups might be less challenging—although with your Altenerai markings you shall tempt the brave and foolish."

"Shouldn't we have seen hunting groups before now?" Kyrkenall asked.

Ortok raised hulking shoulders in a shrug. "They will be chasing something."

As they advanced, though, no kobalin appeared, and Elenai wondered if they might be watching from the brush, or the little rock piles, preparing an ambush. Ortok led them onto a trail winding through the scrub, and they followed that up through some green hills, passing for a time beside a cheerful burbling creek that seemed straight out of a Darassi folktale.

It was then that they saw the first body. It was larger and thicker than a human, and three odd horns projected from the front of its skull. Ortok called a halt, and the three of them readied weapons, though whatever had picked these bones clean was probably long since gone. Beyond that body was another, and another with elbow spikes, stretching on toward a flowering place between the hills, under a chalky cliff.

Silently, carefully, they worked their way up to what appeared to be a large campsite, complete with a burned-out fire pit. Kyrkenall signaled her to watch, and then slipped off his horse as Ortok, looking a little confused, considered the devastation on every hand.

Skeletal remains were scattered over a wide area circling the fire pit; rib cages, pelvises, arm and leg bones, and heavy skulls. As Elenai studied one long thigh, she realized with a chill it had been gnawed upon and broken in two, probably to suck out the marrow.

In mute dread, Elenai tore her eyes from the killing field and scanned the distance for enemies, then the nearby ground. She realized that the piles of rocks at key points were likely deliberate defensive points. Here the knots of dead were thicker.

In search of something less grisly, she let her eyes drift to a pile of large stones, where she'd glimpsed something colorful. She discovered an immense display of swirling, childlike figures inscribed upon the stone with bright reds and blacks. Some appeared to be dancing in circles, others bearing gifts. Perhaps the extra limbs upon some were artistic license or denoted the lack of skill of their makers, but they might also have represented kobalin as they actually appeared.

Kyrkenall fixed upon something he spotted in the dirt. He followed a trail he alone could see, tracking it through the massacre site.

"What could have killed so many kobalin, Ortok?" Elenai asked at last.

The kobalin's answer was muted. "I haven't seen a thing like this before."

"Are there any kind of . . . hunting beasts in these lands?" Elenai asked.

"None powerful enough to do this."

Elenai fought a rising sense that the place was a death trap and that they should flee on the instant.

Ortok lowered awkwardly from his saddle. He chose his footing with care so that he didn't step on part of a broken rib cage. Almost she asked if kobalin would have done this, but held back. She wasn't entirely clear that they wouldn't kill and eat each other, but if she were wrong that assumption would be terribly insulting. And Ortok *had* said that he'd never seen anything like this.

Their hulking, hairy companion moved gingerly toward the fire pit, sidestepping a misshapen bulbous skull, then advanced upon the tallest pile of boulders, before kneeling, head bent either in sorrow or curiosity.

After a moment, Kyrkenall crept silently around one of the piles of rock. He worked his way past his dun mount. Lyria's slowly turning head appeared to demonstrate her grave consideration of the situation.

The archer stopped at Elenai's stirrup and looked up at her. His voice was strained with false nonchalance. "Remember that thing we fought at N'lahr's tower? The lizard creature with too many legs and the long tail?"

"I do." She didn't expect she'd ever forget. The creature had been beautiful, for its scales displayed shifting patterns of colorful light. And it had been deadly, owing to its inexplicable power to share any pain it felt with any who inflicted it, something Kyrkenall had learned to his regret. "Do you think that's what did this?"

"Judging by the tracks I think that at least five of those did this."

Elenai regretted paying so little attention to any markings near the tower where they'd found N'lahr. It reminded her once more that, for all of his idiosyncrasies, Kyrkenall was a veteran Altenerai, and she still had habits to acquire and skills to refine. "Fighting one was bad enough."

The archer pointed behind him. "I think the things caught a foraging party on its way back to camp." He swung his extended finger to the defensive points. "The kobalin here tried to hold them off, but it didn't matter."

Elenai knew that was because kobalin males usually traveled in packs, separate from the matriarchal groups that were true kobalin society. Only young and aged males were usually welcomed among the females. And this would have been a fine grouping, with lots of fierce defenders and wise leaders.

"The older ones tried to make a stand on the other side of the firepit, but it didn't do them any good," Kyrkenall finished.

She never thought that she'd be touched by the death of kobalin. But this sad little battlefield moved her. "How recent was this?"

"A month or more, I think. Judging by the bones." He shrugged. "But it's hard to know. Environmental conditions aren't always what we're used to in these outland fragments."

Ortok rose, his fists tight at his sides as he strode toward them.

"Was this place important to you?" Kyrkenall asked.

Ortok grumbled deep in his chest. "It was an oasis, a peace place. One that I had sometimes visited." He pointed to a hilly slope strewn with purple-leafed bushes. "The klektik grows here, and we gather it for long journeys. It sweetens things. And there are the roots that are good to eat, in abundance. Always enough."

"Did you ever see any long lizard beasts, about half as tall as a horse?" Kyrkenall indicated the size of the creature they'd seen by lifting his hand and patting the empty air. "Very fast, with scales the color of shifting water struck by a rainbow?"

Ortok pointed at the space beneath his hand. "I see what you described. You gave me a picture with words."

"Yes. Have you seen anything like that?"

Ortok shook his shaggy head. "No. Why?"

"Elenai and I fought one when we found N'lahr. I think they're what attacked this place."

"Are they always this hungry?"

"It seemed pretty motivated to eat us," Kyrkenall mused.

"What do they taste like?"

Kyrkenall could only look back blankly.

"We didn't sample it," Elenai replied, and changed the subject. "If we encounter them, you have to be careful, because any hurt you cause them, they magically share with you."

Ortok's brows furrowed at that, but he asked no questions.

Kyrkenall turned and considered the horizon. "Guess we'd better keep an even sharper eye out for surprises." He walked over to Lyria's right, slid his bow into the saddle holster, and dropped his arrow into his quiver.

As he was doing that, Elenai couldn't help noticing Ortok hadn't moved. He continued to stare at the bones.

"Are you going to be all right, Ortok?"

"I am fine for now." He turned abruptly and stalked back to the other side of the fire pit, kneeling once more in nearly the same place.

Kyrkenall, now in the saddle, watched him. "That's where the elders fell," he said softly. "He must have lost someone he cared about here. I guess we should give him a little time . . . but . . ." He offered empty palms. "N'lahr is going to be hip deep in Naor battles soon and we need to find him his ko'aye."

"If N'lahr were here, he'd give Ortok more time."

Kyrkenall nodded distractedly.

"Do you think we should give him an update yet?" She had reluctantly, and successfully, experimented with N'lahr's shard on the far side of Vedessus. And she'd briefly tested the fragmented stone's range yesterday, discovering the link was as strong as ever.

Kyrkenall shook his head. "We still have almost nothing to report," he said, and returned to scanning the distance.

Partly to fill the silence, Elenai made a confession. "I know so little about kobalin and their habits. Is this a village? I don't see any huts or anything."

"They don't really have settlements. They get all they need from the land. They have favorite places to camp, and routes their tribes take, but they're so resilient they don't really feel the need for shelter." He smiled thinly. "They make us look pretty soft."

"So do you think this is where his . . . mate was?"

"I don't think they breed for life. Maybe this was where his mother was, or some siblings."

"You think we should ask him?"

He looked at her sidelong. "You want to talk to him about his love life or reminisce with him about his family?"

"He seems pretty upset."

Kyrkenall sidled closer, his voice just above a whisper. "He's kobalin. Don't forget it. He might hunt with you, but keep your fingers clear if you hand him food. I still have no idea what will really set him off. Do you?"

Elenai disliked the analogy. "He has a pretty strict code of honor."

"Seems so. But do you entirely know what it is? I don't think I understand it."

She started to tell him she could hazard a guess about a lot of Ortok's code. But she couldn't really define its borders. And she realized that maybe she *had* become a little too trusting of him.

It didn't change the fact that she felt for Ortok when he walked back and climbed into his saddle. He fought to turn his horse around. "We should leave this place."

"Are there any other tribes in this fragment?"

"Sometimes. But I think they would have cleaned this camp, if they had come. We will have to try elsewhere." Ortok shook his reins and his incredibly placid horse started forward.

"Great." To Elenai, Kyrkenall said quietly, "I never thought I'd be so eager to talk to kobalin."

He'd already been caught off guard by Ortok's excellent hearing before, so she was a little surprised that he started a bit when Ortok responded over his shoulder: "There are many surprises today. Mine are less pleasant than yours. But I do not wish to speak. It is a silent time."

Ortok's pronouncement felt final and apt, and Elenai rather wished she'd been able to declare such a sentiment at certain times and have it honored so quickly.

The kobalin led until they left the fragment, whereupon Kyrkenall rode up beside him. "With no one here, where should we go? I've got to find the ko'aye, and your people are our only lead."

Ortok gestured vaguely to the horizon. "There are little places before us. There may be hunting parties in any of them, if they have not been eaten by monsters."

"Any larger settlements?"

"Eventually. But not so close to this one. We will find hunting parties first."

Kyrkenall struggled for a patient tone without entirely succeeding. "Which direction should we go to find a tribe? In case we don't find a hunting party?"

Scratching his elbow, Ortok looked off to their left. "A place of elders lies in that way. But they are hard to impress and dislike new things. They might send challenge to you and me. We might kill them, but that will delay speaking of ko'aye." He considered the right. "We should go that way."

"So there's another fragment out there?"

"Sometimes. One tribe that often comes this way brags too much of things they have never done, but they gather stories. They may be useful."

"All right then. That way it is. And we can hope we're still in the general direction of the ko'aye."

Ortok grunted assent and led them on.

The shifts kept their peculiar twilight status even as the terrain grew rocky. Elenai scanned the sky, wondering if they might find ko'aye without assistance from kobalin.

"How did you meet the ko'aye in the first place?" she asked Kyrkenall. "Did you have to be this far out?"

"No." Kyrkenall shook his head. "They were fleeing fragments closer to Naor lands." Kyrkenall shifted Lyria around a conical boulder, then continued. "Naor kings hunt ko'aye. It's a mark of honor to bring one down, even if you have to use a huge hunting party. Hunting like that doesn't seem especially honorable to me, but it's the symbol that counts, not the getting of it. Anyway, I was on patrol with Kalandra and we noticed a large winged birdlike lizard following us. It was a ko'aye named Drusa. She'd seen that we kept fighting the Naor, and winning, but was very wary of us. Kalandra, though, could be persuasive. She eventually coaxed it down to communicate."

"Is Kalandra the one who brokered the alliance?"

"By and by. First the ko'aye started acting as long range scouts to help us hunt Naor. Then Aradel—who'd become friendlier with one of them than the rest of us—wanted to head up into the air with her. After a little while several of us were invited aloft."

"Who?"

"Aradel, of course. Me. Kalandra. Temahr and N'lahr went up a few times. Oh, and Sergahn."

Sergahn, Elenai recalled, was a veteran alten from Asrahn's generation who'd died near the end of the war. And the swordsman Temahr had been about the same age as Decrin of the Shining Shield. He had been slain by Mazakan.

"The ko'aye can't actually carry us very well," Kyrkenall went on. "We're a heavy burden. Varama engineered some saddles."

This was the first Elenai had heard of ko'aye saddles. "What do they do?"

"She enchanted them so that they displace our weight—that way we only weigh about half as much to the ko'aye. You can ask Varama about the how of it sometime. Anyway, I was pretty friendly with Drusa, by the end. We got good at killing Naor together."

"How do you think we'll be received?"

He flashed a droll grin. "I don't expect very well, do you?"

"Do they hold grudges?"

"You mean do they hold them longer than we would? Probably. They're not very trusting by nature and they're not stupid. They've no reason to trust us after what happened."

"What are you going to tell them?"

"I'm still working on that."

As the endless day wore on, swirling violet clouds spun lazily to their east. They steered clear of the scarlet downpour drenching the lowlands and rode on through blue sands that gave way to orange and then amethyst grounds. Overhead the skies gradually transformed to a lighter gray. Still, the lands themselves showed no signs of dissolving away, as had so often occurred during Elenai's first outings into the shifts. It was as though the chaotic energies that lay behind the mad changes of the

Shifting Lands were feeling more charitable this week, or less determined to kill.

They took a brief rest on a tiny splinter of solidity and traded off napping, then plunged back into a landscape suddenly somber with browns and blacks. Even the occasional plant thrust up from the cracked soil was dull, with fuzzy gray leaves. Kyrkenall advised riding well clear of them.

"There's usually something wrong with the truly odd-looking plants out here," he said. Lyria made no attempt to near them.

"Poisonous?"

"Usually. Sometimes you only have to touch them to get hurt, or even ride very close, if the wind blows the spores at you."

Ortok, who'd remained gravely silent, spoke quietly. "Some are good to eat. Not that one, though. You can tell by looking," he added.

Elenai had yet to see any plant she'd want to sample out here. "Why did Sartain make so many useless things?"

Kyrkenall snorted and flashed her a knowing grin.

His amusement irritated her. "I'm serious. Even if you believe what Kalandra said, and none of the Gods were gods, Sartain was still the one in charge of making things for the shifts. And most of it's useless."

"There are many useful things out here," Ortok objected.

"He's right," Kyrkenall agreed. "And our legends got so many things wrong, what makes you think that part is right? Maybe Sartain was the best plant maker of them all, and the others killed him because they were jealous."

"How can you say that?" She blurted out. Sartain had universally been labeled a schemer, envious of the other gods. "He murdered Syrah, and nearly destroyed her creations in the process—we're left with The Fragments! No one disputes that!"

Kyrkenall shrugged off her outrage. "Are you sure that's true? Maybe everything you've heard about the gods is wrong."

"You spend too much time with God talk," Ortok offered. "The ways of Gods are unknowable. Their moods are strange. They play with the sky and the ground and the air. They play with our fates and give us different strengths and weaknesses. They are cruel, but they provide mighty challenges and great beauty. There is no more to it than that."

"There's a lot more to it than that," Kyrkenall began. He looked as though he was about to speak on, but raised a hand to warn silence, all pretense of humor vanishing from his face. He stared left.

Distracted by her anger, at first Elenai thought the distance Kyrkenall contemplated was unremarkable. And then she realized a vibrant blue, multi-legged object was darting over a distant slope. She felt herself tense as it disappeared into the shadow of a hill. It wasn't until she saw another scurrying after it that she realized they were all in mortal danger.

A half dozen of the creatures scampered behind the first two, each running on multiple legs, heading toward where she and her comrades guided their mounts. The beasts at the rear were lit by internal energies so that they seemed alive with shifting stars and lightning bolts. The closest, only a half mile away, was mostly matched to the shadows it crossed.

It was a pack of hunting lizards.

Kyrkenall cursed and nudged Lyria. The animal bolted into a ground-eating canter. Elenai and Ortok followed quickly.

"Can't you shoot them?" Ortok demanded.

"Harder than it sounds," Kyrkenall shouted back.

"No," Elenai called to him. "They'll hurt you back." Didn't he remember her warning?

Picking up on the mood of their riders, the horses snorted nervously to one another and strove to keep tight together.

She glanced over her shoulder as they moved into stubby brown-orange grasses. The lead creature hadn't gained, but it hadn't lost yet, either, and two others were just behind it.

"Kill them from much distance," Ortok urged.

But Kyrkenall shook his head and kept them moving. He set Lyria and the pack horses he led into a gallop and pushed on toward a bluff, heading diagonally up the gentlest part of the slope. He slowed as he led them through a field of boulders and loose shale.

Looking over her shoulder once more, Elenai discovered the creatures had halved the gap and raced only a few hundred yards behind. And unlike the horses, they appeared untroubled by the change in terrain. She remembered the monster that they'd fought at the tower hadn't been able to climb very well, so perhaps the steeper ground would slow them up. She hoped so. She struggled to think of a magical attack that could destroy them without injuring herself.

Kyrkenall reached the bluff and passed over.

"This is ground to fight on," Ortok said as his own horse labored after, and Elenai briefly wondered if Kyrkenall meant to do just that.

But as soon as she reached the height and saw him heading into the hills beyond, she knew he'd kept his sanity. Ortok, though, was slowing, and shouted at them both. "Stop running! This is time for fighting!"

The kobalin reined in even as Elenai called to keep moving. "No, Ortok!"

He ignored her and slipped from his horse with a fistful of spears, the highly polished, lovingly fashioned weapons that were the pride of the elite order of Arappan warriors. N'lahr had personally presented them to Ortok from the Altenerai armory in Vedessus.

She wheeled her mount with a warning cry to Kyrkenall, some small part of her wondering what those spear makers would think to see their weapons in the hand of an avowed enemy of the realm.

Ortok stood on the edge of the bluff, and even as Elenai reined in, still shouting at him not to throw, he launched one, then another.

She saw the first weapon sink into the lead creature. The second spear was still airborne when Ortok dropped with a groan in the instant after his spear plunged into the thick neck at the base of the lead monster's skull. The beast squirmed a little and was still. Ortok, too, was inert. Below, the second creature was struck in its flank. It turned in a half circle to tear at the spear with its weird, side-hinged jaws.

The other six monsters ran forward.

Elenai considered and discarded the idea of wrestling Ortok onto his horse. She didn't have the strength. She'd have to do something with magic.

Wishing she felt more reluctant, she reached out to the hearthstone she'd kept quiescent in her pack and willed it to life. In a moment she smiled, even as the beasts climbed closer, for power coursed through her frame. A quick glance showed her that Ortok still lived, though his energies had ebbed to a low yellow.

The creatures' bodies leapt with energies, cauldrons of living force that threatened to boil over.

She'd already rejected her first learned spell, to lash out with fear. She couldn't be sure an emotional attack would even affect the monsters, and the assault would probably reflect back against her. And then, again with a smile, she realized that she'd overlooked the obvious solution. Seeing that the lizards had followed up the slope, she reached through the framework nature of the reality of the shifts and swept the final ten feet away into so much dust. In a single breath, the final distance to the bluff where she stood and Ortok lay had grown nearly vertical.

The creatures milled back and forth along the bottom of the cliff, confused. The one Ortok had pinned was still unmoving, and she saw that its life energies had almost completely drained into the soil of the shifts. The other he'd wounded succeeded finally in pulling the spear out, then joined the others pacing back and forth along the bluff. Their behavior was reminiscent of ants she'd seen in search of a trail forward.

She didn't think that they'd hesitate long.

Kyrkenall had returned and dropped to the ground to check Ortok.

The lizards came to a decision at the same moment and began scrabbling energetically up the side of the bluff to the right side of the steeper grade.

Elenai scoffed inwardly, then swept the terrain into its component pieces right beneath the creature at the head of the line. As the soil beneath it disintegrated, the animal slipped, struck its back against the creature just behind it, and plummeted to the soil twenty feet below. The others continued to climb.

Growing both bold and a little desperate, she tore up the edges of the framework over which the soil was positioned and shook it like a rug. A couple of the creatures held on and the closest managed to get two legs over the top of the bluff, only three feet to her right. She had a very good look at the scaled jaw that opened sideways, for a cone-like tongue slipped out between rows of sharp teeth.

No way was that thing getting anywhere close to her or her friends. She had already tested the fragility of the Shifting Lands here. Now she grasped at the tenuous soil with the full force of her powers and bent the form until it broke, almost as though she were grabbing plywood scenery in the theater and smashing it over her leg.

She didn't hear a resounding crack, but she saw reality beneath the creature give way entirely. As the thing was leveraging up over the edge it suddenly found itself falling through a gap opened in the ground and into the starless void over which the whole of the Shifting Lands truly lay. Elenai extended that tear and pulled with all of her might until all the beasts were falling away into darkness. They continued to move their clawed feet as they drifted, desperate to grasp hold of something.

The cliff itself began to fall into the gap she'd torn and Elenai spent the next few minutes mending the destruction she'd wrought. After a time, the surface looked normal once more, even if the underlying structure felt flimsy.

"I think that will hold." She breathed with satisfaction. "I'm not sure I'd walk over it, though."

"I did not know you had powers so great," Ortok said, reverence apparent in his voice.

She hadn't realized he was up, and she turned to see him sitting, his huge eyes blinking slowly.

Kyrkenall acknowledged her accomplishment with a casual salute, then nodded to the kobalin. "She learns fast. Where did those things go, Elenai?"

"Into the void beyond the shifts." She sounded more certain of the destination than she believed.

"I never have witnessed so much magic," Ortok said. "All the colors flowing and churning. You were very mighty."

Elenai realized something about the kobalin she hadn't before. Ortok hadn't just seen the outward manifestation of the energy she used. He'd seen the inner world. "Can all kobalin sense magic like you, Ortok?"

"Yes. Can you not?"

"They have to," Kyrkenall explained. "Otherwise they can't make it through the shifts. Kobalin are far more sensitive to disturbances and storms out here, and far more resilient to changes."

"One is coming," Ortok said.

"One what?" Elenai asked.

"A storm." He scrambled to his feet, wobbling a little. "I think you called it when you brought so much magic in one place."

She wanted to ask him a host of questions, starting with how he could be sure and how a storm could be "called" but Kyrkenall cut in as she opened her mouth.

"How close? How strong?"

"It is beside us," Ortok said, then stumbled forward. Elenai hurried to his side and offered an arm. But the kobalin lord seemed confused by her gesture and righted himself.

"Why did it hurt so to throw those spears?" he asked her

"When you injure the lizards, they share their pain," Kyrkenall replied. "That's what Elenai's been trying to tell you. Didn't you hear her?"

"I thought you were not mighty as I am."

Kyrkenall grinned and scooped up the trio of spears Ortok had dropped when he'd been stunned.

"But they had bad magic that was more mighty," Ortok concluded. Even in close proximity to him, Elenai noted again he had very little scent.

She accompanied him toward his mount. For once, the big steady plow horse was nervously flicking his ears.

"I will remember," Ortok said, then grasped the saddle and pulled himself heavily into it.

Elenai hurried to her own horse, surprising herself a little when she used the magical power of her hearthstone to push herself easily into the saddle. She'd done it without thinking. Putting aside guilt and worry, she told herself to focus on the task at hand. To her eyes, nothing around her was amiss. The sky was calm. But beneath the fragile shell of pseudoreality, she sensed energies gathering around the weak point where she'd broken into the void. She had no need to urge her horse to flee with the others.

They were only a few hundred yards out when the ground shook. Elenai gentled the minds of the animals, then sent tendrils of will toward the ground beneath and ahead of them. The surface vibrated when a terrible explosion occurred behind, sounding like some monstrous entity had just torn open a mountain.

Looking back, she discovered the earth splitting wide in an uneven crack, one that gained on them. "Keep going!" She curvetted her horse as the others galloped on, then stared down the storm. If she had called it, maybe she could disperse it. She must at least try, for if the tear opened to the void the lizards might return.

She touched the storm with tendrils reinforced by the hearthstone. Violent pulses flowed out from the stone, past her, and into the maelstrom. The strange artifact was actually tapping into the storm's energy! She understood now that it must have been low on power, for the hearthstone took on a brighter sheen.

She shouted in a mad mix of joy and abandon, and worked her magics. This time she strove not for a bandage, but to relink the pieces of this land's matrix, soothing and mending lines of force. It was like taking a shattered timber from a bridge frame, righting it, and smoothing it into place, except the entire time she did so wind roared and lashed at her.

She felt the void below her, and tried not to think of the hungry entities she had sensed there the time she and Kyrkenall and N'lahr had fled a storm so dangerous it had completely stripped all pretense of reality from the shifts. What would she do if some of those waited below?

She smiled, awash with power, knowing she could master anything, be it monstrous being or glowlizard or a mighty storm. She laughed to think of the fears she'd once had when manipulating the stuff of the shifts, discovering that the task grew simpler the longer she worked. In the hearthstone's glow, all things were easy.

When she at last had everything restored, she put hands to hips and regarded her work. No sign remained of the damage, and nothing was left of the storm but a few rough winds.

Normally when she finished working with a hearthstone she disengaged, but now she tried to remember why she'd want to relinquish the godlike power. Because it isn't safe, she thought, and laughed.

This isn't right, she told herself, and again strove to recall exactly how hard it had been to untangle from the stone after she'd fought Denaven.

But that was as nothing, so she thought of the withered husk that Belahn had become after long immersion in his own hearthstone. While she knew that would never be her fate, she found impetus enough to withdraw her own energies from the stone and spiral it closed.

She sat silent and whole, trying to recognize herself again for who she truly was, like an actor who had immersed herself in the role of majesty.

Kyrkenall grinned at her as he trotted up on Lyria. "That was fantastic! Do my eyes deceive me, or did you just completely quell a storm in the shifts?"

"Yes." She couldn't stop smiling, thinking all the while that was because of the lingering tingle of pleasure from controlling so much energy.

"You've really gotten good," Kyrkenall said.

Was it her getting better, or was the stone getting good at working with her? Her eyes drifted to the saddlebag where she kept it.

Not for the first time, she thought back to what Kyrkenall had once suggested about hearthstones being alive. Had the thing made a deliberate choice to feed from the storm, or had she directed it?

"Are you all right?" Kyrkenall asked.

"I feel fine," she said, and wondered if she lied.

10

———≈———

Challenge in the Shifts

They halted when Ortok nearly fell off his horse. The kobalin seemed woozy, though he refused to admit that he was impaired in any way, even after it happened a second time.

Elenai could have kept on for hours longer, even days. She was comfortable, confident, and ready for action. In the first few weeks of hearthstone use she'd had to make a conscious effort to recharge after wielding her hearthstone. This time it had happened with little to no effort on her part.

She felt so strong that it was hard to muster much inclination for concern. She'd managed to deactivate the thing, after all. Maybe her stone was less addictive than Belahn's, or perhaps she was less prone to getting trapped in it. She supposed it would be nice to consult with someone who knew more about the hearthstones, someone with more experience. Unfortunately most of the true experts left alive were numbered among their enemies.

And so as Elenai bedded down beside her comrades in a tiny splinter of reality deep in the shifts, she thought of Rialla. If Elenai really had spoken with the dead alten's spirit in a dream, she could return again. If she did, Elenai wouldn't just ask for more details about the warning meant for Kyrkenall, she'd ask for help with the hearthstones.

While she lay fighting for sleep, she rehearsed the questions she'd ask, afraid she'd have little time to talk during a dream visit. Thinking and rethinking kept her awake deep into Ortok's watch, until she drifted off at last, her dreams alive with confused images of rafting upon a river of stars with her mother.

Kyrkenall woke her with a hand on her shoulder. His voice was low. "We've been found. Get dressed."

"The glowlizards?" she asked groggily.

"Kobalin. Ortok says it's a hunting party. They've crept close for a look."

Waking was unpleasant, owing to the onset of cramps no longer abetted by the hearthstone's power. She was sorely tempted to tap its energies once more and restrained the impulse. The night's sleep had brushed out foolish optimism like a broom taken to corner cobwebs. The hearthstone should always be a last resort; Belahn had surely thought himself in control as well. The stones were deceptive that way, and when you were flush with their power you felt invincible. Remember this, she told herself. Remember how Gyldara had to physically shake you back into yourself after that battle in the shifts. *You could lose who you are.*

Elenai had long since learned the mind-over-body exercises drilled during squire training, so she rose without voicing complaint, surreptitiously scanning their surroundings.

She saw no obvious sign of kobalin watchers. Orange clouds spiraled over craggy hills thick with dark blue grass and tough clumps of reedy bushes topped by broad, cinnamon-scented flowers. Despite the chill and unwelcome wind, it was one of their more attractive stops in the last few days.

Kyrkenall had his bow ready and studied the lands opposite her, arrow nocked but not pulled back.

Ortok stepped past them both, smote his dark hairy chest with both hands, then spread his arms and lifted his voice. "Cease your stalking! I am Ortok, Hunter of Beasts! Slayer of Nemrose! I have journeyed long.

I have traveled deep! I have seen rare beauties and horrors, and trod the lands of Dendressi! I have earned the friendship of N'lahr the Grim, and dined with Altenerai!"

Apparently they weren't going to play this coyly. Elenai wondered why he mentioned only N'lahr by name, but supposed it was the commander who'd officially named him friend.

It looked as though Ortok was addressing the wind until a distant bush rustled and a tall, brown-scaled manlike thing crept from behind it. The creature held a spear in a fist dangling at the end of arms so long they reached to its calves.

Then, at fifty yards out, more kobalin stepped from the cover of rocks or lifted themselves up from the ground. There were almost twenty of them. Two looked nearly human; the rest were strange amalgamations, covered with fur of varying lengths. Many boasted horns or scales, and one strange entity even had a third eye in the center of its head.

Kyrkenall raised his bow, arrow nocked to string. The long-armed kobalin drove its spear point into the ground with sudden violence, then struck its chest as Ortok had done.

"I am Qirok!" It cried in a querulous alto. "I am slayer of Red Tongue, slayer of Four Patch, and master of the Five Corners. You're foolish to dare our lands! You're foolish to enter with none but Dendressi!"

Ortok chuckled. He indicated his companions with a sweep of his arm. "These are Altenerai! The mighty Kyrkenall the Eyeless, great archer and sharp swordsman! Elenai Oddsbreaker, enchantress of stunning potency! We have no fear, and we are no fools! We have no need of your meager lands. We pass through them to better places!"

The watching kobalin muttered among themselves. Elenai studied them calmly. She knew how swiftly Kyrkenall could kill, and had learned herself capable of the same, but even so, twenty to three on even ground wasn't especially good odds.

"What do we do?" she whispered to Kyrkenall.

He answered without looking away from the kobalin. "Leave it to Ortok."

Qirok stamped a foot beside his spear and sent dirt billowing. "I say that you lie, Ortok! You have built a fire! You claim this place for your own!"

Ortok laughed again. "We do not want your flowers or your clouds. We travel far to test our might! Already we have overcome many dangers!"

The challenger took two steps forward and puffed out his chest. "Why would kobalin travel with Altenerai? I say that you lie! Dendressi do not belong here. If you won't kill them, I will!"

Elenai looked to Kyrkenall, who subtly shook his head.

Ortok raised his hands. "They are mine to kill if I wish it, not yours!"

That was a startling pronouncement, Elenai thought as she recalled Kyrkenall's warning.

Snatching up his spear, Qirok stomped forward.

"This is about to get interesting," Kyrkenall said, and for some reason he eased the hold on his bow. The watching kobalin seemed to relax as well. Elenai didn't understand what was happening until Qirok stopped six paces from Ortok, re-drove his spear into the ground, spread his arms, and addressed him boldly.

"I say that you are a liar who spent his last years hiding under a rock in the Dendressi lands!"

A ritual challenge had begun. Elenai had only seen one before, but she was familiar enough with stage portrayals of them. Elenai looked to Ortok for his answer.

The black kobalin spoke with great ease. "You are only a sand eater who wanders from sight and returns with lies of great victories!"

Qirok smirked. "You are only a pet of these Dendressi, who groom you and feed you treats!"

Ortok crossed his arms. "You are a boaster, who lacks cunning and grace."

"Hah! You are no great champion, or you would have better phrases! Mine are masterful, for I have practiced long and won many battles!" Qirok then jeered, as though he had delivered a death blow, but Ortok merely shook his head.

"You need more than words to be great. You need strength, and skill, and wit. These are strangers to you. You pretend before your band of weak ones, but must bow to true greatness."

Qirok let out a high-pitched shriek of rage and sprang at Ortok, who flexed his knees and raised knotted fists. The challenger came in swinging his two absurdly long arms. Ortok ducked one and batted the other aside before slamming his opponent in the kidney. Qirok yipped, his momentum carrying him past.

Elenai leaned toward Kyrkenall. "Why aren't they using weapons?"

The archer seemed as curious as she did. "They've always attacked *me* with weapons. Maybe it's different when they're fighting each other."

Maybe, Elenai thought as Qirok swung at Ortok's head, their hand combats were deadly enough without weapons. The shot clipped Ortok's cheek and he grunted. He threw up two clenched fists to block another blow.

Qirok danced forward on his long legs and threw two accurate, powerful punches before leaping back. Elenai was a little dismayed to see Ortok merely blocking, turning to face the shifting, ongoing assault. On the whole his defense was effective, for only an occasional blow slipped through as his opponent circled and hammered, but Ortok's forearms absorbed a tremendous amount of punishment.

Qirok leapt back and stepped high, shouting gleefully. "You're slow and weak! Ortok the warrior! I call you Ortok the dullard!"

The spectators seemed to share Qirok's assessment, for they crowded close and grinned wickedly.

"Here is another, and another!" Qirok pivoted and shifted all about Ortok, raining blows upon him. "And here—"

Ortok caught Qirok's right arm in his furred left hand, pulled him off balance, then hammered him in the face with his right. Again and again he punched, and as Qirok sagged, Ortok drove a fist into his stomach and then kneed him in the face. Elenai winced at the crunch she heard.

Qirok slipped to the ground, groaning, and curled into a protective ball.

Ortok slowly turned to regard the others with baleful gaze. Before long, their heads sank in shame, as though they were hounds who'd failed their master.

Thrusting one hand at the defeated kobalin, Ortok barked a question to the watchers. "You chose this one to lead you? Look how easily I defeated him! You are a lot so sorry I don't even wish you as followers. I will permit only that you walk with us until we reach the border, so you can be eaten by any beasts we meet. Now. Provide us with food, and do not sicken us."

The kobalin hurried forward with bent heads, crying that they had guessed his prowess from the first, promising their allegiance and asking whether they should finish Qirok for him. Ortok roared at them to fetch food and drink and they scattered.

They brought forth sacks of small, headless furred creatures and weird, orange roots. Though they peeked continually at Ortok and the two Altenerai, none made direct eye contact. Nor did they pay any heed to Qirok, who slunk away with his bloodied face in his hands.

Elenai had about as much interest in sampling kobalin cooking as she had in gnawing her boot heel, but she sat down on a boulder near Ortok and watched the kobalin drive sticks through the juicy tubers and put them over the fire. Kyrkenall leaned between her and Ortok and softly addressed the combat's victor. "Why didn't you kill him?"

"Did you want me to?" Ortok asked.

"No. I was just wondering."

"If I killed him I'd have care of his band. I don't want them. Do you?"

Kyrkenall laughed. "No."

"What's going to happen to Qirok?" Elenai asked.

"When I am gone there will be other battles to see who leads."

Three of the kobalin finished erecting a wooden frame over the fire, then hung slabs of now skinned meat.

"And you'll ask about the ko'aye soon?" she suggested.

Ortok leaned forward and attempted to keep his voice low. "I told them I want nothing from them. I have to think about how to ask."

She wished they could be more direct and get on their way, but she supposed there were some kobalin social graces after all, and that they'd have to be followed.

"I'll do it," Kyrkenall said. "Once we sit down to eat."

"That will be fine," Ortok murmured.

Before long, Qirok, nose dramatically swollen, returned and declared that the middle hunk of meat was clearly the best and must be saved for Ortok. He then plopped himself down in the center of the first of the serried ranks formed opposite Ortok.

Elenai was surprised that the meal smelled enticingly sweet, particularly the tubers. But Kyrkenall quietly advised her to eat from their stores, and none of the kobalin seemed to mind when neither alten tried their fare.

The attention of the kobalin centered upon Ortok, and once the meal commenced they begged him to tell a story of his deeds.

"We all want to hear that," Kyrkenall agreed, then spoke boldly to Qirok. "But first we want to hear what you know of the ko'aye here."

"Oh, yes." Qirok raised his head from one of the fire-blackened vegetables. His voice was more nasal than it used to be, perhaps because of his broken nose. The left side of his face was swollen as well. "If it pleases Ortok I shall happily speak of it."

Ortok nodded his head seriously. "You have my permission."

Qirok puffed out his chest. "Ko'aye nest in the direction of where the war god sleeps, but not quite so far—"

Ortok's brows knit as he interrupted. "There is no such place here. You mean to send us to nowhere and laugh at our confusion."

A gasp of astonishment swept through the ranks of the kobalin, as if those with such wicked and sharp-toothed faces had heard something indecent.

"No, oh no, mighty Ortok!" Qirok spoke quickly. "Forgive me. It may be you know the place by another name, that of the Round Stone Home. That is what it is sometimes called. By those who are my betters," he added, anxiously licking thin lips. "If you go to that place you have gone too far. There are several named lands between here and there and these the ko'aye have seized for hunting, for they are swift and have many claws."

Their black-furred friend looked as though he were still mulling over whether he believed this information.

"How many ko'aye are there?" Kyrkenall asked.

Qirok shook his head. "Who can count so high? I have never tried. There are many more than we have here."

"As many as a great mother group?" Ortok asked.

"I never saw that many at once," Qirok answered with a bob of his head, "but I am no fool to go to a land with so many claws. But then," he added quickly, lest his information be deemed an insult, "I am not so mighty as great Ortok. Do you go to battle with them?"

Ortok grunted. "We go to ask them to battle with us against an even bigger foe, one your feeble mind could not hope to understand. It will be a brave fight, and one for which we shall be long remembered."

At that the other kobalin grew eager and begged for details with the fervor of children hoping to stay up past bedtime.

"I will tell you of brave battles." Ortok paused to tear off a big hunk of meat. Fat and juices dripped from his teeth as he chewed and swallowed, then he wiped his mouth with the back of his hand. "First, I want you to tell about the lizards with many legs. When last I passed here there were none of those things."

The kobalin all tried to answer at once, a confusing blur of information from which Elenai only understood a few phrases: "Much trouble . . . hungry and cunning . . . pain when you hurt them . . . hard to slay . . ."

Ortok cut them off with a shout. "Qirok, you answer! How many are there?"

The wounded leader smiled at those to his right and left, preening a little to be singled out. "There is a pack as many as my fingers. And they are close. Perhaps," he added slyly, "you are mighty enough to kill them."

Ortok dismissed this with a slash of his hand through the air. "Elenai has already destroyed those with sorcery."

The kobalin turned as one to stare at her. She had never been regarded with such naked awe, not even in Vedessus, and she felt her cheeks flush.

This awe was then turned upon Ortok. "Your pets are mighty, too," Qirok breathed.

Ortok grunted. "The strong do not keep company with the weak."

"Are there more here?" Elenai asked. And then the kobalin fixed her with their strange gazes. Being studied by them was different than being watched by humans, where there was a standard uniformity of distance between eyes and certain givens in shape. Some kobalin eyes were very far apart, or set high upon their head, and some looked in two or more directions at once.

"There are many of the glowlizards these days," Qirok said bitterly. "But usually they hunt alone."

"Bad enough when they are alone," lamented a kobalin with four horns atop his scaly head.

"I don't have time to hunt the ones that walk alone," Elenai said, effecting Ortok's nonchalance. "But if I cross the path of many, I'll kill them." Beside her, Kyrkenall chuckled before sipping from his wineskin. "Do they hunt along our route to the land of the ko'aye?"

The kobalin seemed uncertain about this and debated amongst themselves for a lengthy time.

"Cease your squabbling," Ortok growled. He lowered the thigh bone he'd been gnawing so it resembled a club in his fist. "Is there a pack of glowlizards between us and the ko'aye?"

"We do not think so, oh mighty one," Qirok answered. "Scattered ones may haunt the path, but packs are more interested in the mother groups, and there are few toward the Round Stone Home."

"Where did they come from?" Elenai asked.

"From the pits," said one of the kobalin.

"From the void come all things, good and bad," answered another.

Kyrkenall leaned close to her ear. "They won't know," he said softly.

Elenai replied to him just as quietly. "I'd like to know how long they've been facing them."

"These are kobalin. Their sense of time is pretty vague." He gestured to the motionless sun. "No way to follow it. No dependable seasons. What would knowing more about it do for you, anyway?"

She shrugged. "I wondered if they'd been sent deliberately."

Kyrkenall eyed her blankly, and she suddenly felt very foolish. "Unlikely," he said. "Nothing's in control in the shifts. And there are plenty of surprises even the greatest travelers have never seen. You know the old tales of lost and forgotten realms, lands with lush grasses and rich game and smooth rivers?"

"You believe them?"

"Not really. But I'm sure there's some weird fragments and splinters out there still and these things probably found their way in from some of them."

While Elenai and Kyrkenall talked quietly, the kobalin returned their attention to Ortok, pleading with him to tell them about his battles.

"I shall tell you one story," he said, and the kobalin fell silent attentively.

"It was a rainy day. With clouds. And wind. That was when I saw the Naor. There were many of them. On horses. With swords. And helmets." He looked over toward where Kyrkenall and Elenai sat and winked broadly. "They rode at me. The one in their front was larger than the others. He had on shiny armor, and his beard was yellow."

Kyrkenall chuckled softly.

"What is it?" Elenai asked.

"He's giving exactly three descriptions of everything. I should have known he'd take my advice to the letter."

As Ortok continued his narrative it grew even more obvious that he'd taken Kyrkenall's counsel absolutely to heart. If his descriptions had been bland before, they were now tedious. Yet the kobalin stared in rapt fascination, and the story of Ortok's encounter with Nemrose the Naor King and his bodyguard set them murmuring appreciatively. She leaned close to Kyrkenall. "I guess that if they're used to hearing tales the way Ortok used to do this must be very impressive."

"They do seem to like it," Kyrkenall agreed. "Turns out I'm a pretty good tutor."

She couldn't keep back from a skeptical snort, at which he chuckled.

"And how are you feeling?" he asked.

"Tired. But ready to keep moving. I can't help worrying that all this effort may come to nothing."

"I know," Kyrkenall admitted glumly. "We don't have much time to spare, and N'lahr will be reaching The Fragments soon enough to scout out the situation. Assuming I can work a miracle, the ko'aye can fly to him a lot faster than we can ride. But I'm still not sure how I'm going to convince them to trust us."

Ortok must have borne their mission in mind too, for when he wrapped up his story—which mostly consisted of drawn out details of his axe cleaving and the wounds inflicted upon his enemies—he told his audience he must be going. Qirok volunteered to guide the way toward the ko'aye lands, suggesting two others. Ortok chose different ones, and

Qirok quickly agreed Ortok's was the superior selection. Elenai couldn't tell whether their ally was simply being contrary or if he'd actually observed that the other two would be more useful.

Soon they were packed and on their way. Qirok loudly proclaimed it would be their joy to witness other great deeds Ortok and his allies might accomplish.

Those left behind begged Ortok to return and lead them so they would be remembered in his stories. He ignored them, and they stood in a long line watching as the Altenerai and their companions headed into the wilderness.

Long-armed Qirok ambled alongside Ortok's stolid horse. With him came a narrow, hunched thing with horned head. It had somewhere acquired a dirty kilt, in imitation, she supposed, of the one worn by Ortok. The other wore old leather armor over its scaly orange skin, a round shield hanging from its right arm.

"Do you think he's in danger?" Elenai asked Kyrkenall.

"Who? Ortok?"

"They could surround and attack him."

"No. They'd lose too much respect. They have to meet him in the open, in a challenge. You see how they work now, don't you?"

Elenai did, and even understood now why N'lahr and Kyrkenall had stopped to speak over the body of the mad kobalin who'd fought the archer in The Fragments. "They're really not so bad, are they?"

He met her eyes in disbelief. "If they think they're stronger than you, they'll take whatever they want. It's only if they think you're equal or superior that they act with honor. Don't forget some of the things they've done on the border—killing and looting and setting things on fire for the fun of it is just the start."

"They seem less evil than the Naor."

"There's little calculation in their actions," Kyrkenall agreed, "unless some kobalin lord or elder stirs a bunch of them into action."

"They remind me of children."

"Murderous children."

"Do you think Ortok's going to build an army with them?"

"He said he wanted one," Kyrkenall said. "But I don't see him trying very hard with them." He shrugged. "Who knows. Maybe N'lahr convinced him of just how important it was to find the ko'aye and he's focused on that."

They journeyed on through the starkly beautiful land for countless hours. They were nowhere close to a splinter or fragment when the storm built in the sky to their left. A few weeks ago, Kyrkenall's innate sense about the Shifting Lands had confounded her. Now Elenai didn't even have to be looking toward the storm's darkening clouds to feel the change in atmosphere.

The kobalin pulled themselves away from Ortok to point at the storm. Their champion awkwardly guided his horse in a circle back to Elenai and Kyrkenall.

"A bad storm is near," he said.

"You'd better have all of them gather close." Elenai turned to Kyrkenall. "Unless you think we ought to keep moving."

The archer mulled that over. "Let's not risk it unless this storm takes a while to move past."

"There is a ceremony we must do," Ortok said.

"What kind of ceremony?" Elenai asked.

"A warrior ceremony." Ortok shook his reins with far more force than was required and guided his mount back to the others.

"He's going to hurt that horse," Kyrkenall muttered.

"What kind of ceremony is he going to do?" Elenai asked.

The archer smiled faintly. "Didn't you ever learn about the kobalin?"

"I wasn't sure how much of it was true."

"It depends on what you heard." He nodded toward the little group. "They're going to pray to the storm goddess to thank her for the coming challenge. They'll plead with her to make death swift for the fools too slow to change." He grinned. "They're crazy, but I can't help but like them a little."

"I thought you didn't."

"I don't *trust* them. That's different from liking them. I respect their outlook, you know? They don't ask for their god to spare them, they don't think she's angry and ready to punish the unjust. They just look on the storm as an opportunity to prove themselves."

She looked from the anvil-like front and decided she didn't feel like trying to break up another storm. Especially one that size.

Ortok had dismounted to lead the other kobalin in prayer. The four of them genuflected toward the storm and were repeating some phrases after Ortok. The wind, already whistling, carried most of them away from her.

"If we'd been raised out here," Kyrkenall said, speaking loud enough that his voice would reach her, "I can't help wondering how our culture would change. How we'd handle ourselves. And I wonder if I'd be as crazy as they are."

"Maybe you already are," she said, and smiled as he laughed.

He grinned at her, and went to gather Ortok's horse.

She activated the hearthstone, rationalizing the excitement of its proximity by telling herself she was simply keyed up by the storm. I will not lose myself in power this time, she told herself.

She sent threads of will through the hearthstone and into the inner world. She saw immediately that the storm wasn't as large as it looked. The changes rippling along behind weren't severe enough to unmask the void beneath the Shifting Lands. It was almost simple to firm up the little circle of land where they stood, and she calmed the animals with negligent ease, a little astonished that she'd once found both actions challenging. She resisted the impulse to reach deeper into the stone, or to attempt greater manipulation. She would keep to the surface, and not dive deep. Not this time.

She called to the kobalin to retreat into the protective circle, but they only leapt and shouted and waved their arms as the wind hit them.

Kyrkenall touched her arm and shook his head. "I thought I explained. They'll stay where they are."

"They could be killed out there."

"That's their choice. Let them be."

As she watched them, the light harshened and the dark, rocky soil under their feet transformed into white sand blazing under a tropic haze. The kobalin crooned, then they themselves began to shift. Startlingly, Ortok shed his thick, black fur and his skin rippled into a shorter, light gray hair covering. Elenai had heard kobalin were shape changers but until that moment had thought it exaggeration.

When the flat terrain was replaced everywhere but their safe circle with mountainous slopes, Qirok's hands lengthened to claws and the hunched one grew hooves, the better to balance on an impossibly steep slope. The orange one thrust new elbow spikes into the soil. Ortok didn't change, relying upon his strength to clasp to a rock upon the slope, nor did he alter when the ground leveled into a little river valley, soon flooding into a marsh where he and the others stood hip deep in watery bog.

Elenai and Kyrkenall and the horses remained dry and secure upon the rocky ground she'd rendered solid.

Before long, the marsh dried away into a parched desert, blasted now by a furnace-like red sun hanging directly overhead, and Ortok changed once more, for most of his fur sloughed off. He transformed into a creature of gray scales, touched only here and there by light patches of hair. It was disconcerting to see him thus, for he little resembled the person she'd come to know.

When the storm blew itself out a few moments later, the kobalin turned and spoke to one another, pointing to their bodily changes with pride.

After, they resumed their journey, under blistering heat, and Kyrkenall warned Elenai to shed her khalat and to cover her head and neck. She copied his example, draping part of a spare shirt over her forehead. They rode with these protections for hours, streaming with sweat. The kobalin drank greedily from their stores.

And then, finally, in a land where three clawed peaks soared into the sky, they saw the ko'aye.

ᑙᑙ

≈

Among the Dragons

When Varama lifted the dead officer's signet ring close to the lantern light, Sansyra saw her smile. Seeing the alten so pleased was a rare thing, and the squire barely contained the urge to pull out her battered sketchbook. Knowing her superior would find the activity a distraction at best, Sansyra instead strove to memorize the expression on her features. She noted again the sagging and darkening of the skin beneath the clever eyes, as though Varama had aged years in the last few days.

All of them were under pressure, though, even those who never left the tunnels beneath Alantris. They lived under the constant threat that their hiding place would be discovered by the Naor and that their hundred-odd force would be rooted out and destroyed by enemies renowned for their cruelty. The stories reaching them about rapes, dismemberments, beatings, and random slayings alternately disgusted, infuriated, and depressed. Every man and woman in the Resistance longed to aid their people, but immediately dislodging the Naor yoke when they were outnumbered more than eight hundred to one was an impossibility, no matter Varama's brilliance.

And if those factors weren't the source of enough tension, they'd learned a few hours before that the second Naor army was due to arrive in only a matter of days. Accompanying that force was an infamous blood mage—

grandson of Mazakan no less—who was sure to order massive organized "sacrifices" of Alantrans to fuel his dark arts.

Circumstances Varama commented upon with a dry frown as "less than ideal."

Yet now she smiled. Seated, Varama's height wasn't so readily apparent, but her leanness was, for she was built on rangy lines, rather like the racing hounds of the Storm Coast, save that their fur was usually black, and Varama's skin held a faint blue cast, even by lantern light.

The folk of the realms boasted many different skin tones, but a smaller number were truly unique, like the healer in Sansyra's home village who had rounded horns upon either side of his head, or Kyrkenall the archer, whose eyes had no whites. These few blessed by the Gods with distinctive appearance often carried extraordinary abilities as well and were more often found among magical practitioners and elite warriors. Varama could be mistaken for no other person in all the five realms.

Her mentor lowered the ring. "This should provide us with some entertainment." She looked up sharply, and Sansyra wondered if she had guessed her mind was wandering. "Did any of his men get away?"

"No," Sansyra answered proudly. She'd led the ambush against the little Naor patrol herself.

"And how long ago was this?"

"No more than a half hour." She'd followed Varama's instructions absolutely. Over the last few days, she'd repeatedly quelled her subordinates' confusion and complaints about missions with less obvious purpose. Most of the squires and all of the Alantrans were unfamiliar with Varama's foresight, and a few of the locals even grumbled anxiously at the series of tasks she'd set Sansyra to accomplish almost from the moment Rylin left.

That first night in the tunnels, Varama had still been a little slower in her speech, though her mind had been razor keen as always. First Varama had set a team of volunteers to sewing expensive silky fabrics liberated from the temple above, promising that the strange patterns would prove useful in the coming week. Then she had dictated detailed instructions to Sansyra: "I require several dozen intact glass bottles and a great quantity of spirits."

Sansyra had thought that a little challenging, although not impossible.

Varama had continued: "Send parties to city gardens and recover all the bee canopy plants, leaves and blossoms, and a good quantity of lark stem. Sketch them to show the squires what the plants look like."

Sansyra had bobbed her head. The bee canopy plant was known for producing a toxin useful as a numbing agent in small doses. In the days since the plants had been acquired, Varama had rigged a clever distillation system to concentrate alcohol from the spirits, then extracted the poison from enormous quantities of fan-dried plant parts. Sansyra guessed what her mentor planned to do next, although she had no idea how Varama would transport the bottled poison past sentries and down dragon gullets.

Varama had relayed even more orders, though. "I need two buxom female volunteers proficient at both sword and shield for an especially dangerous and unusual duty. Lastly, I'll need the signet ring of a high-ranking Naor officer whose death won't immediately be discovered."

That last had been the most challenging assignment of all, and Sansyra had handled it personally. Now she watched with profound satisfaction as the alten set the ring down on the old desk with a muted clunk, the rough oval symbol pressed with the ring's twin spears facing outward. "This is ideal."

Sansyra loved those rare moments of praise from Varama, or the suggestion of it.

They had precious few supplies with them in the long tunnels beneath the city, but they'd discovered ink and paper in the desk in the cool gray room Varama used as her headquarters. By the light of the single lantern suspended from the ceiling hook, Sansyra watched Varama retrieve them from lower drawers.

"Let me see his orders again."

Sansyra unfolded the papers she'd taken from the dead man's belt and handed them over. "What are you planning, Alten?" She'd been curious for days.

Varama answered without looking up. "The Naor are going to give us the remaining supplies we need to kill their dragons. I'm going to write some orders. Then we must move with speed. See that I'm undisturbed."

Of course her explanation wouldn't be detailed. It would have to serve, for Varama hated repeating herself. "Yes, Alten."

Sansyra stepped to the door, ready to intercept any attempt at interruption. Varama herself stared unblinkingly into space for prolonged moments, tapping her long blue chin. Then she bent to examine the sloppily worded orders, penned in their looping script. She pressed the paper flat to the right side of the desktop, stared at it a final time, then dipped the pen into ink and set to work, scratching quickly across the paper. With her choices made, she acted without hesitation or even pause, as if she'd completely worked out what she'd write before she set to work. Probably she had.

Some squires disliked Alten Varama because of her odd habits and awkward mannerisms, and accused her, to each other, of being arrogant and brusque. Sansyra preferred her direct manner of speech. She had never actually witnessed arrogance, only certainty, borne up by Varama's thorough understanding of her own strengths and limitations. Sansyra delighted in anticipating Varama's needs, carrying out her brilliant schemes, and occasionally offering a suggestion that her mentor found useful.

Though she'd have never wished it, the situation in Alantris was somewhat of a reprieve for Sansyra. Before much longer she'd have to decide if she wanted to apply for her sixth brevet, or leave the corps. Not only were sixth rankers supposed to venture widely, acting much like junior Altenerai, she'd almost certainly be shifted to another post, nominally under supervision of a different alten. And she didn't want to leave Varama's service. Once the alten saw them through their current difficulties, Sansyra would have to decide whether to accept the promotion that was almost certain to be offered, or to ask Varama if she'd consider using a civilian adjutant—after all, Varama worked with talented craftspeople and engineers who weren't in the corps, and who couldn't be promoted away from her, so perhaps she'd consider an assistant outside of the military structure.

Sansyra shook herself out of reverie as the alten finished with a flourish and motioned her over. The squire hurried to take the paper, blotting it dry with a rag she'd brought as Varama began composition of an entirely new letter. Over the next few minutes she drafted four sets of orders, sealing each with wax stamped by the ring. By the time she'd finished, Sansyra was ready to succinctly confirm her understanding of what must be done. She then departed to send messengers in captured Naor uniforms hurrying to deliver the forged documents and organized all the other tasks required to further their plans, afterward grabbing a few hours of sleep. Though excited by what lay ahead, she was experienced enough with Varama's irregular habits to take sleep when it came, even if she delayed a few minutes to sketch Varama smiling.

Sansyra was roused deep in the night to don a leather cuirass with reinforced metal studs, favored by one of the Naor tribes, then led her similarly outfitted force through the deserted streets, stopping just shy of the cross street where Alvor's Oak thrust its great thick branches toward the bright stars. It stood near the canal ringing the rise to the second tier, in one of the city's innumerable garden spots that the Naor hadn't gotten around to destroying yet.

Varama was waiting for them in the shadows with a small force of archers that included the young warrior Denalia, niece of the late governor, Aradel. Their taciturn commander made no mention of the first part of their mission, which had obviously been a success, for they now possessed a cart, horses, and more Naor uniforms. Of the Naor who'd followed Varama's forged orders to deliver these supplies there was no sign, though Sansyra could easily guess their fate. Their bodies had been dragged into a deserted house where the words "N'lahr will come for you," or something similar, had been written in blood upon a nearby wall. With the Naor, primitive threats seemed to work better than any other and Varama had encouraged this tactic whenever opportunities arose.

Sansyra motioned her people carrying the bottles full of distilled bee canopy toxin forward, and Varama took each and carefully applied them to the foodstuff packaged in five large baskets on the cart.

The alten wore a Naor officer's get-up from the Ferasht tribe, complete with fur ruffle and feathered helmet. At close range she'd never be confused with a Naor man, even with darkness cloaking her distinctive features, but by the time a Naor was as near her as Sansyra he'd either be dead or Varama would have activated her semblance. The alten couldn't afford to leave the magical disguise active all the time; there simply wasn't enough power within the tool. The energy currently filling this one had been painstakingly donated by the mages among them, a little bit from each, a little at a time. Their hours of effort had resulted in only a few useful minutes of energy. But even a little moment of illusion might make all the difference.

Varama handed Sansyra a helmet. "Squire, here's yours."

Sansyra slipped on the captured Naor helmet earlier prepared for her use, oversized and fuzzy with its ridiculous horsehair beard and mustache, anchored in place by the cheek guards.

Varama checked over the soldiers, quietly reiterating instructions. Though she disliked repeating herself, she tended to do so whenever she was uncertain that important information was thoroughly absorbed by her listeners. Sansyra had noticed more repeating in the past two days than at any other time in their acquaintance.

The squires Iressa and Nereal were the only two among them not garbed in armor. Instead, they wore Alantran dresses and head scarves. They packed shields into the bottom of the cart, along with their weapons. While Iressa adjusted a dark rumpled blanket over them, Nereal fussed with her dress front, pulling down on the cloth to reveal generous cleavage.

"No Alantran woman goes out without an undershirt," Denalia scolded as she stepped in close. "And your scarf is done up wrong."

The blond squire squirmed a little, jiggling. "Goodness, am I too scandalous? I'd hate for the Naor to become distracted."

Curvy, fine-featured Iressa joined her. "Quit shaking those around before someone gets hurt."

Denalia pointed at their skirts. "Alantran women don't slit their dresses like that."

"I don't think the Naor soldiers will care," one of the Alantrans muttered from the side. Sansyra recognized him as Tevrik, an archery officer.

"Shouldn't you be on guard?" Sansyra asked.

"I'm testing the distractibility of the lures, here. Good job, Squires."

Iressa smiled slyly at him.

Sansyra was getting ready to mouth a rebuke, but Denalia stepped forward. "At least let me help with the scarves," the young officer said. "You've both gotten the front folds wrong. And Nereal, you have too much hair showing."

"A little more alacrity if you please," Varama said.

Denalia fussed for only a moment before stepping back, still looking dissatisfied, but Varama ordered them under way. The alten marched at the column head, immediately followed by Sansyra, who led the cart. Iressa and Nereal came after, shadowed by Tevrik, pretending to guard them. The archers ranged at the rear in two semi-orderly columns, as they'd noticed Red Feather bowmen tended to march.

They passed shuttered houses. No lights shone from within, and no cookfires sent smoke from chimneys. Some few refugees probably hid within portions of the city, but most Alantrans had been forcibly moved from their homes and were kept under guard in larger spaces, when not directed to prepare food, care for animals, labor on Naor engineering projects . . . or other tasks that no one wanted to visualize.

Apparently the Naor didn't see the defensive utility of a staggered gate system, thus walls and homes were coming down for the construction of straight throughways from the outer gates to the city's heart. They passed near one gaping rent, astonished by the wanton destruction of the ancient wall and nearby houses, now nothing more than wrecked timber piles or empty foundations.

The city was mostly quiet. The wind rustled herbage and creaked abandoned doors. Every now and then a dog barked, which was unremarkable. The outbreak of terrified screaming from somewhere west of them, abruptly cut off, was not. Were these ordinary times, they'd have immediately diverted to investigate. This night, though, they had a vital mission more important than seeking evidence of another of the innumerable tragedies visited on the people of Alantris by their occupiers.

As they advanced they passed within a block of a dully glowing square, but no one turned to look. This was the source of a continual greasy smoke that clung to surrounding structures, a special fire fed not only with wood, but the flesh of the blood-drained vanquished. Sansyra shuddered to think about the ash that fell upon her and feared what she might smell, but the scent of burned timber overwhelmed all else.

They marched over bridges and streets and presented themselves at a checkpoint, receiving only rudimentary examination. The "prisoners" Nereal and Iressa drew the male gaze just as readily as Varama had intended. It wasn't just their distraction at work, though. The Naor hadn't imagination enough to suppose the Resistance would walk freely into the most heavily guarded sector of their captured city with a wagon and two "helpless" women.

They passed through two barricades before they arrived finally at the outskirts of the flat field in the outermost ring of the city where the dragons lay.

The buildings that had once housed the farmers who'd worked these fields had been cleared away over the past three days, apart from one home to the far northwest and another to the southeast. A crude sentry platform had been erected upon the roof of each. More than a half square mile of slapdash wooden fence now sealed off the field and presented only one entrance, which they approached. The outer wall beyond was a black slash defining the horizon, ominous and threatening now that it lay under enemy control.

Their escort of archers fell back in the shadow of the last line of houses. Their moment would come.

Only Tevrik stayed with them, behind the costumed squires walking with downcast eyes, miming the part of downtrodden citizenry. Varama donned her semblance as they drew close to the sentries at the dark dragon field's entry point. The alten had transformed into a slim young man with a wispy beard. She arrogantly pushed back her shoulders as she stopped before the Naor guard.

Four of the six Naor had been playing dice, but rose with their commander to receive the wagon party. Lanterns hung from nearby poles ruddied their beards and hair and the one in charge carried himself as though he hated his job and personally blamed them for being stuck with it. He bade them halt in a gravelly voice and saluted with a hand to head.

Varama returned the salute. Sansyra noticed the soldiers glance briefly at her and Tevrik, but the men's eyes slid over to the comely squires and settled there.

"I am Dragon Lord Torzhek," Varama said in a reedy voice, and passed over more of her forged papers. "I have supplies for the dragons."

The sentry officer took the papers and stepped closer to a lantern to read them.

Sansyra knew what was written there—a terse set of lies about Torzhek's imaginary arrival from General Chargan's army to assist with the dragons, authorization to access the beasts, and the command that his orders regarding them were to be obeyed without question.

The sentry folded the paper and handed it back to Varama. "Everything looks in order, Dragon Lord. Is that more food? They were just given a bunch of uncooperative Alantrans a few hours ago."

Sansyra's lips curled beneath her scratchy faux beard.

Varama answered coolly. "A spell has been worked into this food to make their scales tougher. Let us through, while the magics remain potent."

The sentry officer turned to two of his men. "You heard the dragon lord. Get the gate open."

"And," Varama said, as if it were an afterthought, "I'm supposed to convey this pair to the general when I'm through. Would you like to keep them here or shall I take them with me?"

One of the guards whistled appreciatively.

"You'll keep hands off," Varama snapped. "They're for the general alone."

"It's not my hands I want to touch them with," the guard joked in a low voice, and he and his comrades laughed.

"Silence that," the officer snapped, then nodded to Varama. "They'll be safe with us," he promised.

"See that they are." Varama raised her head. "Come," she told Sansyra, then advanced past her without looking. Sansyra led the cart after her. She feared little for Tevrik and the lower rankers. All the squires had to do was distract the sentries for a few moments as the archers came up.

Soon they were in the fields where artichoke and fennel had been stamped flat. Sansyra could imagine no reasonable explanation for ruining crops that could just as easily have fed invaders.

A lane that had once separated fields from vanished houses still ran past the space in front of the clear spot where the dragons rested. While the darkness hid the dragons themselves, it could not hide the huge awnings thrown over them yesterday. She felt exposed and vulnerable in the flat empty space as they made their way toward the monsters.

She wasn't aware that Varama had shut off her semblance until she heard her speak quietly, in a rare attempt at rapport. "Things are going well enough so far."

"Yes," Sansyra agreed.

"If we are challenged on our way out, remember that many of these are young men out on their first foray. The last war did not leave the Naor many veterans."

She'd said something similar in a brief speech several days earlier, and Sansyra appreciated the reminder, although their edge in skill would only count if they could keep clear of the overwhelming enemy numbers.

As the cart rumbled forward, their proximity revealed the outline of their monster targets at last. The five great beasts lay beneath individual awnings, arranged some forty paces apart, with their snouts a few paces back from the edge of the lane. The outer wall was only a few hundred feet beyond the last. There was no missing the silhouettes of watchers on the wall and towers. Sansyra spied four of them making their rounds. "What will the men on the walls think of us?"

"That we obviously belong here because we passed through the gate." She must have been keyed up because she elaborated. "Those are sentries charged with watching for the terrible fae cavalry. They are apt to be both nervous and bored, but all of their suspicions will be focused outward, especially after yesterday's incident."

From what little they'd been able to glean about life beyond the walls, some uncaptured Alantran cavalry were bedeviling the Naor. Yesterday they'd reined in at extreme range and unleashed a volley that cut down two Naor sentries and wounded three more. A liberated work gang of Alantrans had been elated to pass on the news they'd overheard from their slain minders.

Sansyra risked a glance over her shoulder and calculated that they were a quarter mile from the gate and the sentries. She hadn't heard a sound from them, and that was probably a good sign. Maybe the archers had already finished off the Naor behind them and assumed command of the sentry post.

Varama drew to a stop beside a stinking wooden trough near the first dragon's head.

The dragon itself was still. The resistance scouts reported that the beasts moved little, except when food was deposited in their feed troughs, at which point they lurched to life, so eager to eat that they'd once snared one of the slaves forced to feed them.

Two evenings previous, Sansyra had considered them from a hiding place high on the second ring. The dragons were broadly similar in that their central bodies stretched on for at least twenty horse lengths, their tails longer yet. But each was different. One with a greenish hue had a variety of added spikes upon nearly every leg and shoulder joint. Another had a beautiful, almost iridescent sheen, like an insect's wing held up to the light, and Sansyra had found that such a stark contrast to its brutal outline she'd later sketched it from memory. The ugliest, though, was a deep blue with a heavy jaw and especially large spikes, and this was the one they neared first.

The horses shied as they stopped in front of it, and Varama stilled them with a word and what Sansyra sensed was a brief magical force. Surprisingly, the winged lizards smelled like very little at all, or perhaps their scent was completely disguised by the reek of blood-soaked soil.

Varama hung a lantern on a pole standing up from the corner of the cart, then unshuttered it to narrowly direct its beam toward the rectangular trough. If not for the dull light gleaming on the cobalt scales of the dragon's snout, the creature would have seemed black. It lay with eyes closed, spiky head between its massive front feet, dark wings folded along its sides.

While Varama watched, Sansyra hurried to the back of the cart, hefted the first basket, and carted it to the trough. Her eyes locked upon the dragon's features as she upended the raw meat, heavily soaked in poison, and sent it sliding into the container. The dragon did nothing. Sansyra stepped back, glanced to her commanding officer.

"Stand watch," Varama said. "I'm going to wake it."

Varama seemed no different than usual; distant onlookers would only have seen her staring at the great lizard. Her mentor was one of the least demonstrative spell casters Sansyra had ever encountered. Likely at this very moment the alten was deeply enmeshed in a weaving, connecting her mind to whatever mind the dragon possessed.

Sansyra noticed nothing along the wall. Back at the gate the guards were no longer silhouetted by their lanterns.

Torchlight reflected upon the whites of the dragon's huge open orbs. Sansyra swore softly in surprise.

Varama stood absolutely still even as the beast craned its neck within a few feet of her and lowered its maw toward the poisoned food. It tipped in its head, bared its knife-sharp teeth, and dropped in a black tongue to slurp up the meal.

Sansyra smiled triumphantly. One down, assuming that such a creature could be killed by the poison Varama had harvested from flowers.

After it had lapped up the food and, for better measure, licked the wood where it had rested, the dragon stared past them, closed its eyes, and slowly lowered its head. A function of Varama's spell work, Sansyra knew, for she recognized the alten's concentrated look.

Sansyra only realized she'd been holding her breath when she let it out at the same time as Varama, who relaxed and turned away. "Let's keep on," she said.

Sansyra looked back to the first dragon, discovered it with its head between its feet. It didn't seem at all troubled. "Did it work?" She spoke softly as she led the horses forward, fearful that her voice would carry far in the vast still quiet.

"I've no way of knowing, yet," Varama answered. "It doesn't seem to register pain or contentment, as I understand it. But the creature clearly has a stomach or the Naor wouldn't feed it. And we just fed it enough atropa to kill forty horses. So assuming it's physiology is not too dissimilar from other vertebrates, we should learn the answer to your question in approximately eight minutes."

"How hard was the dragon to manipulate?

"There was some challenge," Varama admitted. "There's little mind there with which to link; more a series of impulses. You can set one in motion and it moves, almost automatically, as though it has a memorized pattern. I think it would be very challenging to alter that pattern."

Sansyra scanned the ground ahead as well as the walls. In moments they'd stopped near the trough of the next beast, the black one with the thinnest body. She noted its eyes, too, were closed, then slid a quantity of pig meat into the wooden container. The dragon woke with a start and lunged at the meal. Sansyra let out a gasp of surprise and darted back.

Fortunately, the monster seemed only interested in the bloody meat. Soon, it too had downed the poisons, and under Varama's guidance, resumed its slumber.

As they moved on toward the largest of them all, the green, Sansyra felt tension building within her. Each roll of the cart wheel, each hoof clop, she imagined like the sound years made as they swept away.

How much longer before someone grew worried about what they were doing?

"Two baskets for this one," Varama told her as they came to a stop.

Sansyra nodded as she remembered their preparations, but she said nothing. Varama usually only repeated orders to those who seemed unable to keep up with her train of thought, and Sansyra had long since sworn she would prove herself more reliable than that. It was oddly reassuring to note her mentor was nervous too.

This biggest one slept more deeply, and Varama had to force it awake. Still, once it scented the meal it was just as eager as the others, and gobbled up the food.

As they neared the fourth dragon, she felt a stab of remorse, for the torchlight winked upon the dragon's brilliant wing scales. Its appearance shouldn't have mattered, but it troubled her both that they had to slay such a unique specimen and that the Naor were capable of fashioning something with a hint of beauty even if it was likely accidental.

As Sansyra headed to the rear of the cart, she heard the rush of feet behind her and whirled. Her hand went to the place her knife was usually belted, then switched higher when she realized she'd attached it differently on her Naor armor.

A moment later Nereal sprinted up to them and drew to a halt, only a little winded. She sketched a salute to Varama then reported quickly: "A Naor mounted patrol came by. They left, but Iressa believes that they were suspicious."

"And your belief?" Varama said.

"I think her right, Alten. The officer hesitated too long, and they didn't complete a full round before they returned the way they came."

"As though they got to thinking about it and were returning to check in with a higher-up," Sansyra suggested.

"Yes," Nereal agreed.

Almost at the same moment, a deep horn call sounded from the nearby gate tower. Sansyra recognized an alert when she heard one.

So did Varama. "Empty the last basket. Nereal, uncouple the horses. Hurry!"

Sansyra slopped the next-to-last dose of poisoned meat before her favorite dragon. Earlier she'd regretted having to kill it, now she was sorry that they wouldn't have a chance to slay the next one as well. She heard Nereal cursing and stepped away to assist her with a knot as Varama concentrated on spell work.

The horn calls were repeated to the south, and then from somewhere in the second ring. Sansyra knew a stab of fear, for the Naor could pour into this area by the hundreds. Or thousands.

A flash of red light caught her attention from the left, and Sansyra looked up to see the roof of a building aflame on the second ring. A moment later there was a flash of fire from far off in the west.

Varama's backup plan was already underway. Two small additional teams had been deployed with orders to light a barracks building and a Naor stables afire if the Naor blew alert calls during the midst of the dragon mission. Varama had commented that the odds of their escape improved somewhat if there was confusion as to the reason behind any alert calls.

She and Nereal untethered the horses, then, while Sansyra grabbed the cart's hidden shields and javelins, Nereal outfitted them with bridles.

A wordless Varama leapt astride the darker of the two animals. Sansyra handed up a shield and three javelins even as more horn calls rang through the city. Closer by, she heard the whinny of horses and the clash of arms.

Sansyra had ripped off her distracting disguise beard and mustache and climbed onto the back of her horse, urging Nereal to hurry after she'd passed over the second shield and javelins. The squire clambered up and grabbed her about the waist.

Either Varama had a better horse or she was a better horsewoman, for hers surged immediately forward. Sansyra's was fairly unresponsive to heel or reins, which was understandable in a cart horse. Unfortunately, there was no time to be understanding. Reluctantly Sansyra dipped into her small supply of magical energies. She was but a minor weaver, with the ability to cast a handful of spells before exhausting herself. She preferred to reserve all her energies for life-threatening emergencies, such as spears headed straight for her. It annoyed her to have to expend effort to get an untrained animal into useful motion.

She briefly linked her will to that of her mount and set it following its companion. Varama was already several horse lengths ahead, and she was the first through the barrier. A male scream rang through the air and was abruptly silenced.

Just this side of the fence, they passed a lumpy pile that hadn't been here before—the bodies of the Naor sentries, dragged here after the archers had secured their exit. In the road beyond Sansyra spotted a riderless horse cantering away. A Naor warrior impaled upon a javelin crawled feebly after it.

By the light of scattered torches, she saw even more details as they advanced. A dozen warriors charged at them from the right, roused from bed to fight unhelmed and unarmored. Denalia's archers had retreated to the nearby line of houses, from which they launched a devastating volley. The Naor cried out as they fell.

She kicked her horse again after Varama, nearing the archers as they diverted into the lane that was their planned exit. They were only a few lengths along when she spotted a small Naor band, just visible by the glint from helms and spear points.

Varama hefted a javelin as she kicked her animal into gallop. Sansyra saw Varama's throw, and knew momentary disappointment as it arched past the two Naor in front. And then the weapon transfixed a rider behind. He plummeted stonelike from his saddle.

Varama shouted back to her: "Take the one on the left!"

Sansyra used more of her dwindling powers to coax her heavy mount to speed. Two horsemen had galloped past the Naor on foot, and one pitched a spear. Sansyra saw it begin its arc, made a split-second decision, and veered right. She felt the passage of the weapon past her cheek.

Marksmanship had never been Sansyra's great strength. But Nereal was a natural. She gripped Sansyra's shoulder with her off hand, then let loose. Her javelin took the charging Naor in the shoulder.

It stuck in his armor. He rocked in his saddle, then cast it savagely away and pulled his sword, shouting in fury as he closed. Varama was already exchanging sword blows with the man's companion.

Sansyra parried a slash that almost tore the sword from her fingers. Nereal left her second javelin buried in the warrior's thigh, his shout of pain almost drowned out by the squire's exultant war cry.

Then they were past the riders and heading straight on for what must have been two full troops, with two more mounted horsemen and at least four dozen on foot.

Varama donned her other semblance and set her ring to shining. "For Alantris!" she shouted.

But it was not her voice, even if it came from her lips, and as Sansyra came up beside her she saw it was not Varama's image revealed by her azure ring, but that of a dark-haired man with a narrow face. Sansyra had never seen N'lahr in person, but knew his image from the many paintings and statues and the relief upon his tomb. The Naor already gaped, and to ensure they all understood, Varama flourished her blade and cried out theatrically: "I am N'lahr, returned from the dead to drag you down to hell!" And with that her horse curvetted. The alten sent forth a burst of fear, and fully half the Naor soldiers bolted into a nearby alley. Those struck motionless with fear were wide open for the next volley from the archers, who'd run up from the side.

Varama shouted in fury and spurred toward the enemy, sword extended. She galloped one warrior down and sliced another's arm off and then she was into the horsemen.

Sansyra's beast was again slower to answer. Varama was already engaged with one of the mounted officers. The other cast forth a stream of glittering motes into Sansyra's path. She swung up her shield and heard one of the metal things clang against it. Something sharp slashed through the leather of her boot. The horse screamed and Nereal gurgled and suddenly slipped from the saddle.

Years of training kicked in and Sansyra threw herself clear of the collapsing mount. She tumbled as she hit, the air filled with her horse's screams. She staggered to her feet and whipped up her sword, saw the horse struggling to rise. Nereal was slumped on the ground, moving fitfully and with no real purpose, her throat a terrible red gash.

A voice in her head told her to still her movements. It was a very reasonable, commanding voice, and no matter how much Sansyra shook her head and repeated the mantra she'd been taught, throwing up her own meager magical energies to counter, the enemy mage's command grew ever more authoritative. Dully she was aware of others closing, of footfalls, of shouts.

Her lip curled and she showed her teeth, but the voice in her head was telling her to stop the nonsense and she was wondering why she shouldn't.

And then the voice was stilled and Varama was there in her N'lahr semblance and the Naor mage who'd thrown the shining weapons slipped headless from his mount.

"Take his horse!" Varama shouted. And so she did. Iressa and the archers caught up Nereal's limp body and they all stole into the night.

Over the next quarter hour they sometimes pretended to be Naor patrol and sometimes advanced more stealthily around large Naor search parties. Eventually they abandoned their animals, moving over rooftops and through alleys and secret ways until they reached, at long last, the safety of the tunnels.

After a healer had slipped sharp shrapnel from her calf and sewn the wound shut, she sat in Varama's office. She was trying to draw the dragon rather than the image of Nereal she kept seeing as Varama listened to reports. Then she learned that Varama's other forged orders had yielded success: the Naor themselves had delivered armaments to a deadly ambush site and a Naor cavalry patrol had been dispatched beyond the city and promptly vanished, almost surely cut to ribbons by the Alantran cavalry. Other missions had sown additional chaos. Virian, a wiry third ranker, had infiltrated a barracks and slain every soldier on lower bunks while they slept. Other lower rankers had written N'lahr's name in red paint in prominent places that would be seen come dawn.

As important as the donated weapons were, it was the last report, delivered just before dawn by her friend Lemahl, that excited her most. He and a small team of masons and weavers had worked a hole through a secluded spot in the outer wall, and Lemahl had set out to find their allies in the countryside.

With his large, knobby nose and square face, Lemahl wasn't the handsomest of men, but his good spirits were indefatigable. He flashed his winning smile as he entered Varama's office.

"You made contact," Varama said.

"Yes, Alten. And I brought a guest." Lemahl looked to his right and raised his voice. "Enter."

The door opened on the instant and in swaggered a short, darkskinned woman with straight black hair. Like Varama, she wore a khalat and a sapphire ring, but the resemblance ended there, for where Varama's face was rectangular, this woman's was round, and while Varama's nose was long and thin, her counterpart's was short and flat. Varama stared as the newcomer grinned and opened her arms.

She was Enada the Swift, mistress of horses.

"Hail, Alten!" she cried. "I've brought my cavalry. I hear you have some Naor to slay!"

The Hand of the Enemy

Varama stood and politely saluted the shorter woman. Enada laughed that off and stepped around the desk to embrace her comrade, bringing with her the strong odor of horse. Lemahl rocked back on his heels in barely contained excitement.

The blue-skinned alten blinked and half-heartedly patted Enada's back. She herself was never particularly demonstrative and always looked awkward making physical contact.

The horsewoman chuckled as she stepped away, slapping Varama's shoulders. She stared up. "Gods. You look like hell."

Someone else might have been affronted, or made a joke about the horsewoman's appearance in kind, but Varama probed immediately for information. "Why are you here? and who's to command your troops if you're trapped or killed inside the city?"

Enada answered with a shrug. "I came to make sure it was really you. No doubt about that now. Aren't you glad to see me?"

But Varama hadn't received the answer she wanted, so she tried again, hoping a question with greater precision would supply the requested information. Sansyra, long since familiar with Varama's methods, wondered why Enada was so oblivious to them. "Is there someone in charge of your troops?" Varama demanded.

Enada rolled her eyes a little at Sansyra, as though sharing with her audience some private amusement at another's foolishness. It was then Sansyra understood. Enada knew Varama's methods; she just didn't approve of them. "Yes. I've two sixth rankers in charge of them. Now tell me you're glad to see me."

"It's good to see you," Varama said coolly. "How many are with you?"

"I've got enough to make things hellish out there. Those idiot Naor just can't keep up with us. Can you believe they sent a forty-man cavalry patrol after us tonight after we wiped out a hundred-and-fifty-man unit yesterday?" So Enada's force and not just the residual Alantrans had been responsible for the Naor's new reason to fear venture beyond the walls.

"Varama sent them," Sansyra said, for she feared Varama wouldn't explain this herself, and she wanted to remind the intruding alten that Varama was due respect. When Enada's gaze swung around, she continued: "She forged orders to send them out."

Enada laughed. "Well, that sounds about right."

"She also led an attack to poison most of the Naor dragons, tonight. And she forged orders for the Naor to resupply us. It worked, too."

Enada laughed again, her eyes twinkling as she faced her fellow alten. "You're pretty funny for someone with no sense of humor. What are you planning next?"

Once again, though, Varama hadn't received a complete answer, so she repeated herself. "What are your exact numbers?"

Enada relented and divulged the information at last. "I've roughly a thousand."

"Are you expecting more?"

Enada offered empty palms. "I'm not expecting anything. Who knows what will turn up? You're lucky you got me."

Sansyra recognized the fixed look in Varama's eye and knew she was irritated by Enada's informal delivery. "Do you have any word of more reinforcements from Vedessus, or Erymyr? Ekhem?"

The horsewoman shook her head. "I don't know anything about that. You've got a few dozen Alantran cavalry out here with us, a whole bunch of refugees eager to fight, and one alten stabbed up to pieces."

Varama's chin rose ever so slightly—Sansyra noted a slight flare to her nostrils. "Which alten?"

"That cute new one, Rylin. I guess he pulled off some real heroics, to hear the Alantrans tell it. A couple of healers about drained themselves dry trying to save him, but he hasn't woken yet."

The news brought a sharp inhale from Sansyra. Until recently she hadn't had much use for Rylin, and her depth of concern surprised her.

Varama's next query was quick. "Do they think he'll recover?"

Enada roughly shrugged. "They're fussing with him every couple of hours. With that kind of care I guess he's got a fair chance. The Alantrans just about worship him."

"He's been very brave," Sansyra said, then realized that she'd added uncalled-for information, again, and fell silent as Enada stared at her.

The alten's voice grew challenging. "I didn't catch your name, Squire."

"This is Sansyra," Varama said, "my second-in-command."

Until that moment Sansyra had thought herself an adjutant, and blinked a little in surprise.

Enada grunted, nodded once, sharply. "Hail, Squire." She then headed past Lemahl, quietly watching beside Sansyra, and dropped onto the little chair on the wall perpendicular to Varama. She stretched out her mud-caked boots. "I don't have too long. I don't want to risk heading back out through your wall hole come daylight. Your scout here says you're deliberately staying in the city."

"Yes. The Naor are under the misapprehension that this city will be a gateway to their greater ambitions. I intend to convince them that instead it is a death trap designed for them."

Enada bobbed her head. "What do you have in here, a couple hundred people?"

"Less."

"And you're against what, about eight thousand Naor? You expect to stand them in a long line so each of you kill fifty or so?"

"I've a better plan," Varama said simply.

Enada sat forward. "Mysterious as ever, eh? Well, I don't know how we can help you. We've heard that there's a second army of Naor that's supposed to reach Alantris in the next week. We're going to head out tomorrow with the Alantran fighters and lie in wait for them. A few nice ambushes ought to cut them down to size."

"No."

"No?" Enada straightened in her chair. "No?"

"The cavalry here is essential to my plan."

"I don't see how. My people are horse warriors. They're no good on walls."

"Your people need to keep the Naor trapped inside Alantris. Send your scouts to monitor the approach of the second army, but keep the main body of your troops here. You must ensure that no communication or supplies transfer between either force. They cannot be permitted to coordinate their efforts in any way. This will likely cause concern in the oncoming force, and it will almost surely stoke fear among the Naor trapped in Alantris. Further, any foray that leaves the walls of Alantris—and I do mean any—must be destroyed. Your numbers should make that simple."

Enada rubbed her nose and raised her eyebrows thoughtfully, but said nothing. Sansyra wondered why she hesitated to answer, because Varama's reasoning was eminently clear.

"Sure. N'lahr used to say that when you know more about a divided enemy's condition and position than they do they're instantly weaker. But you're still talking about a lot of Naor in these walls."

"I am. But keep in mind that their numbers are not highly trained."

Enada sighed. "That's obvious as soon as you cross swords with them. All right, supposing that we keep the Naor here, what good will all this do when the other Naor army turns up?"

"The other realms should send reinforcements. By the time the Naor arrive you will long since have mastered the land and have prepared conditions to engage their reinforcements."

"You don't expect much, do you?" Enada asked. "There's probably five to ten thousand in the next wave, if I know the Naor."

"We are alleged experts at achieving the impossible."

Listening to the two incredibly capable women talk, hearing the solid confidence in Varama's voice, Sansyra felt a rising sense of hope. Dire as things were, maybe Varama really could get them out of this alive.

The horsewoman chuckled. "All right. Anything else you want me to do? How are we to keep in touch?"

Varama's head swiveled up to the silent squire beside Sansyra. "Lemahl, you're the one who made contact. Is there a place outside where it's possible to signal safely for rendezvous?"

"Yes, Alten." The homely squire knew better than to answer a question from Varama with irrelevant details.

"You and Enada work out the specifics as you take her back."

Someone knocked at the door. Sansyra was about to tell whomever it was to leave be, but Varama answered.

"Enter."

Iressa, her long brunette hair pulled back from her face in a tight bun, opened the door and stepped inside. She was remarkably grave, but she had been ever since their return. She and Nereal had been close. Perhaps, though, it was the news she brought that rendered her so solemn. "The Naor are rounding up prisoners and herding them into the square before the main gate."

Enada sighed. "Reprisals." She faced Varama. "How many of the Alantrans know about these tunnels?

"They're a closely kept secret," Varama replied. "And Aradel worked hard to keep it that way."

"Too bad about her." Enada's tone of voice belied the casual words.

"Yes," Varama said. Sansyra saw just the barest flick of an emotion that might have been grief, then her superior's gaze shifted to her. "Take a small group. Find a vantage point and learn what they're doing. Obtain intelligence about their leaders. Avoid attracting attention."

"Yes, Alten." Sansyra would have liked to have remained behind to rest her injured leg and hear the conclusion of the meeting, but she rose and saluted, first to Varama and then to Enada. She met Lemahl's eyes and his plain face, rough with beard growth, lit with an encouraging smile. She nodded to him then left the room with Iressa.

Confessing she couldn't sleep, Iressa requested to join the mission, and Sansyra acquiesced, asking only Denalia to come along. The young woman knew the city far better than either of them.

Their armor hidden by dark cloaks, they made their way through alleys and across rooftops, thankful that the sky was overcast and shadows long as the sun came up. Sansyra managed to hide her limp.

They saw numerous patrols, but only one passed close, just after they'd retreated into the shadow of a burned-out building. Judging from the predatory gleam in Iressa's eyes, she'd just have soon slain every member of the four-man group, but the trio stuck to the shadows and turned away from the bearded faces that peered into their narrow hiding place.

Eventually the three women worked their way into a house past the edge of the main square. They watched the Naor gathering through the shutters of a second-floor window.

The occupiers had trampled an ornamental flower garden in the middle of the square to assemble a wide wooden platform, one supported on thick wooden pillars. A crowd of Alantrans faced it. Some twenty paces to its left, an immense pyramid of books lay upon the cobblestones. Among the predominantly brown covers were bright reds, oranges, and the occasional yellow or green, which rendered the whole display incongruously festive.

Denalia whispered, her voice cracking in horrified awe. "They must have emptied every library in the lower city."

"Why did they just pile them there?" Iressa asked.

Didn't she understand? "They're going to burn them," Sansyra explained.

"Why?" Iressa's brows knotted.

"Because they're stupid," Denalia hissed, unable to take her eyes from the window.

"Because they want to hurt us," Sansyra said, although that wasn't quite the reason, either. How could she succinctly explain the visceral hatred the Naor felt for learning, and the envy they had for those with the resources and time to devote to study? She sensed there was more to it even than that.

The Naor were out in heavy force. Hundreds of them stood upon the walls or along the edges of the square, hedging in thousands of the cowed Alantran citizenry.

"Where are the rest of our people?" Denalia asked quietly. What she didn't express was the fear that everyone but these were dead.

Surely the Naor hadn't slain that many. Not yet. "Probably still in the slave pens," Sansyra answered. "If the Naor brought them all here in one place, it might be too much for them to handle." She stepped aside so Iressa could look.

Denalia bit her lip. "You don't think they're going to kill all of the people they've brought here, do you?"

"No," Sansyra said, though she hadn't thought of that. Surely not. But there was really no knowing. Iressa stepped away, then sat moodily down on the edge of the empty, unmade child's bed in the loft they occupied.

Sansyra returned to the window as the Naor used spear and sword point to prod a selection of men, women, and children out of the large mass of prisoners.

Their voices were harsh and mocking as they organized the Alantrans they'd selected into ten long lines in front of the larger group, facing the platform. Sansyra gulped as the Naor withdrew to the side, hands on weapon hilts. Gods. Maybe they weren't going to kill all the Alantrans they'd brought here, but just these hundreds. Was that relief she felt that only this mass of people would die rather than the whole? She snarled, furious with the Naor, angry with herself.

The dread uncertainty down there must be unbearable; they could feel it even from their point of relative safety. Denalia's left hand was clenching so tightly it paled. The sounds of small children wailing in fright drifted through the mostly silent square.

Sansyra belatedly stepped away to order that Iressa monitor their exit route, and while her back was turned the loudest of the children suddenly went silent, followed on the moment by a woman's scream. It ended as abruptly as the child's.

"They killed them both," Denalia said in stunned, quiet horror.

Sansyra's mouth had gone dry.

Shortly after she returned to the window, a group of Naor officers used a ladder to climb to the speaking platform. There were five in all: heavy, bearded men in dark armor and cloaks except for one, oddly slimmer and smooth faced, almost surely the woman Rylin had mentioned. The two tallest were clearly guardsmen, their armor trimmed in gold, with two silvered feathers projecting from the height of their helms. One was scarred by weather and battles, his beard laced with gray. The final one wore a burgundy cloak and, unlike the others, stood bare headed. Even though she'd listened to Rylin's briefing, she didn't recognized Koregan at first for a Naor leader, for he looked even younger than he'd been described despite the beard.

The older man stepped forward and raised his hands to the crowd. "Dogs of Alantris, bow before your betters! Bow to your master, the Lord General of Alantris, your conqueror, Koregan, Grandson of King Mazakan, first of all mortals!"

No one knelt. Denalia sucked in a surprised breath as a Naor soldier kicked the legs out from under a young Alantran man. Other soldiers moved down the ranks, spear butting or kicking until a ripple of obeisance ran through those arranged in front of the platform. The large mass of Alantrans beyond hesitantly took their knees as well.

The graybeard raised his arms and clenched his fists, and on the instant, the Naor soldiers let out three guttural chants that rang from the city walls. It reminded Sansyra of the bark of dogs, loud and powerful and intimidating.

The grayhair stepped back, and Koregan lifted his bearded chin. His brighter, booming voice echoed through the square.

"I speak not to you slaves, but to the ones I know are watching!" His head swiveled as he eyed distant buildings. "Those of you who still think we are at war. I tell you now that I have won the war! Those that kneel here, and all their kin, are mine! This city, from wall to wall, belongs to me!"

The graybeard raised a fist and the Naor soldiers let out another mighty shout.

Koregan spoke on.

"I can and will do whatever I want with this city. And I will do whatever I want with these slaves!" He searched the distance, turning his head to left and right, briefly facing their window.

"Gods," Denalia breathed. It did, for a brief moment, seem as though he might be looking right through their slatted shutter and into their eyes.

Koregan faced forward again. "Each time you fight, I will kill my slaves. Today, that number shall be small, for I am a reasonable man, and you might learn from a demonstration of my power. Do not think I will always be so merciful."

Denalia spoke in quiet despair. "He's going to kill all of those in the line, isn't he?"

Sansyra didn't dare answer. She was afraid her companion was right, but didn't want to say it, as if to speak agreement was to breathe life into it.

Koregan stepped nearer the edge of the platform. "These words are for you, slaves. Some of you have useful skills. But don't think that means I care about your lives! When you or the rebels displease me, I'll never hesitate to punish you. You are nothing but cringing rats!"

"I thought they were dogs," Sansyra said quietly.

Neither of her companions laughed; she hadn't expected them to.

He extended his hands, sweeping at the kneeling Alantrans. "Your leaders failed you. They put faith in weak things. How will all these books help you now?" One meaty hand swept toward the mound of texts, and his voice rose. His head lifted at the same moment, to make clear he spoke to his soldiers. "Look at this! Do you know what most of these writings are about?" He paused only briefly. "Love! Texts on love. As though men need to be told how to fuck a woman!"

A ripple of laughter rolled through the Naor.

"Fae are so feeble they have to study up on how it's done!" Koregan said.

Again they laughed, as if Koregan were a great comedian.

Sansyra was positive those couldn't all be love poems. But it wouldn't be the first time Naor lied.

Koregan pointed to the Alantrans. "You stared at clouds and wrote down words when you should have mastered your weapons. What I say are the only words you need bother with! You thought you need only please yourselves? Now you live to please me. And I am not happy."

For the first time, Koregan looked to the grayhair. He nodded, once. The older man signaled to a soldier below.

A trio of Naor stepped forward with burning torches and threw them onto the books. Red and orange flame licked up the beautiful bindings. As the fire spread and smoke rose, Koregan stepped even closer to the edge, shouting at the kneeling figures. His face had reddened. "This is just the start! You will submit, or I will kill all of you boy rutters!"

Denalia quietly remarked to Sansyra: "I thought we were rats."

Koregan stepped back and called to the grayhair. "Pull out every tenth one!"

The old soldier repeated the order.

Naor went down the lines, their counting obvious from their pointing, and dragged every tenth person to the side. As these victims were removed, some stretched hands for them. One weeping woman grabbed at her small child and then was spear butted to the ground.

Once all were separated, Koregan stepped forward, eying the people who'd been removed and forced to one side. He spoke again. "Take every ninth as well!"

Again the Naor soldiers walked the line, counting, and dragged every ninth away. Stifled weeping grew more audible.

Koregan gritted his teeth to the noise. "I had planned on being more merciful, but I'm tired of your whining!" He faced his older advisor, and spoke quietly.

The graybeard stepped forward and let loose a simple command. "Slay them!"

The soldiers advanced not on the gaggle of those separated, but on the longer lines of those kneeling. Some were stabbed from behind with spears. Others were beheaded with swords, or had their throats slit. One enterprising soldier split each head in half with his axe, smiling as he went.

Sansyra saw the blood drain from Denalia's face. She wanted to look away but made herself watch the murders, to remember. Sometimes she scanned the faces of the Naor. A few were grave, but more smiled and laughed, the bloodlust shining in their eyes.

It continued for a very long while. An unbelievable time that Sansyra felt stealing moments from her soul.

When at last the massacre was complete and the soldiers stepped apart, the old soldier addressed them once again.

"You that General Koregan spared, drag the bodies to the fire. If the rest of you are clever, this need be your first and last lesson!"

The three watchers departed. One image in particular stayed with Sansyra—the sight of something popping out of one man's head as he dropped in a spray of blood. As the Naor had laughed she'd realized it was an eye.

They saw far fewer patrols on their way back. Sansyra wondered if the Naor had deliberately scaled down their numbers so witnesses could return to their hiding places and spread word of what they'd seen.

On the outskirts of the temple district, as they neared the edge of the roof, they heard footsteps below. They waited for the threat to pass, and then crept to the edge. They saw the back of four helmeted heads as Naor watchmen walked the empty street.

"Let's get them," Iressa hissed.

Denalia put a hand to her arm as she reached for the edge, as though she meant to drop over on the instant. She hissed: "They'll kill more if you do that! Is that what you want?"

Iressa seemed to wrestle with those words for a while. She stared venomously at the retreating Naor until they turned the corner, then all but slumped in resignation.

Quietly, they returned to the tunnels.

Varama was roused to meet them. Her curling hair was bunched up wildly on her left and flattened on the right, so that she looked absurd. She must have tried lying down after Enada left. Despite the terrible news she bore, or perhaps because of it, Sansyra struggled not to giggle. She knew it would not only be immensely inappropriate, but that it would sound strained and mad.

The alten sat upright at her desk, listening with very little change of expression, firing questions at them as they went. She made no comment upon the tragedy, and seemed especially interested in the distribution of the Naor soldiers. Before long she'd produced paper and set to work on an image that ultimately spread across multiple sheets, sketching what proved a more and more accurate depiction of the surviving buildings around the square. Varama was a skilled artist, if not a truly expressive one, but was phenomenally gifted with matters of scale and extremely precise with measurements. As she worked she occasionally asked the three of them for verification about the height of a house or its proximity to its neighbor.

"And the stage remained?" Varama asked.

"It did," Sansyra said, then explained further: "They were still standing on it when we left."

"It was quite sturdy, Alten," Iressa said. "I don't know why they'd remove it. They'll probably want to shout at more people from it, or speak to their troops."

Varama walked around the drawing to make an adjustment.

Sansyra wondered very much what she was thinking, but it was Denalia who asked. "What are you planning, Alten?"

"I'm judging the best place to locate archers. The next time this happens, we can target the general. Here, or here, I think. Possibly here."

She was so matter-of-fact, even now. So focused. Sansyra's admiration welled up. Varama let nothing cloud her judgment.

"But the Naor won't assemble again without another attack," Denalia objected.

Varama fixed her with a brief, sober look. "We can't stop the killing, but we can put it to our advantage."

"Put the killing to our advantage?" Denalia asked.

"Yes. If we know where the enemy is going to be at a certain time, then we can strike."

Denalia shook her head. "They'd have no reason to assemble so many. Not unless we do something." She spoke quickly. "I mean, they might kill a few, sometimes, but not like today. Not if we don't provoke them."

Varama set down her stylus and turned her full, unwavering attention upon Denalia. To her credit, the Alantran archer didn't flinch.

"The Naor believe us perversions of the proper order," Varama explained. "Slowly, or quickly, they mean to kill us all. There is no middle ground with them that preserves some of us. We must eliminate their power to enact their genocidal ideology if any of us are to survive. Which is why we'll kill Koregan when next he speaks."

Sansyra heard Iressa gasp beside her. She nodded, understanding now what Varama intended, and knowing that the Naor commander's death would set off a scramble for power among his subordinates that would weaken the enemy substantially.

"Do you know how many people they'll kill if we kill *him*?" Denalia asked. "They'll murder thousands! Who are you to make that kind of choice? These are my people, not yours!"

Varama blinked at her, dispassionate. "Alantris is not the city of my birth; I was born in a tiny village in Kanesh. I would defend either with the same conviction, for I am Altenerai, and I am sworn to defend all the people of all our lands."

"It's not the same," Denalia said, shaking her head.

The alten spoke with strained patience. "I will attempt a final time to make the matter clear for you. If we kill Koregan, the remaining Naor will fight each other over succession. They will be weakened; we shall be well positioned to take advantage of mistakes that they make."

Denalia stared as if she had somehow misheard.

"It's likely many of us will perish before the end of this," Varama said. "I assumed that you would wish to be involved in the attack, for you're one of our finest archers. But if you would rather place hope in the Naor being more merciful if Koregan is left alive, you may remain behind."

"Here's a better idea," Denalia said. "Instead of setting our people up to die, why don't we break in and free all the soldiers held in the pens? We can go in force by night and break them out."

Varama spoke over her. "We have one hundred and seven capable of fighting."

"Well, a bunch of the prisoners are soldiers."

"Hundreds of them," Varama agreed.

Denalia pointed to the wall, as if the prisoners were just on the other side of it. "If we give them arms, they'll fight at our side."

Sansyra spoke, trying to sound compassionate and reasonable both. "How will we get all of them into the tunnels, safely? How will we get them out of the city?"

"I'm not talking about getting them into the tunnels or out of the city! I'm talking about freeing them and using them to attack!"

"That is unworkable," Varama said bluntly. "There are more than eight thousand Naor well-organized to slay opposition among their captives. Even if we can succeed in getting to the prisoners, most would die before gaining effective arms or armor, as would their relatives whom they certainly would struggle to leave. We cannot house or feed so many here and our shelter would almost certainly be discovered in the process of moving so many to it." She paused to allow these points to register, then softened her tone. "Perhaps, freeing some would serve as a diversion while the assassination is under way. Now. Consider whether or not you wish to play a part in the attack."

Denalia looked as though she wanted to say more but couldn't figure out what it should be. Varama's eyes flicked over to take in their overall appearance, as if noticing their condition for the first time. "You look terrible. Eat, and rest."

"I don't think I'll be able to do either," Denalia said morosely.

"The odds of our success rise if we're better rested, and well fed."

"I'll take care of myself," Denalia snapped.

"Will you?"

Sansyra winced, wishing Varama would let the matter go.

Denalia's irritation had obviously grown. "I will."

"What are you going to do, Alten?" Sansyra spoke up.

"I need to think."

"You need rest as well," she warned.

"You're correct, but our next actions need to be planned immediately, as well as our counteraction when the Naor seek retribution. I will sleep presently. For now, leave me."

The squires saluted, followed almost grudgingly by Denalia, and then the three women left. Iressa said she wanted to go find a quiet corner and sleep, but she caught Sansyra's eyes and motioned with them toward Denalia, as if to say Sansyra ought to calm her down.

Denalia snapped at Sansyra as the two walked into the dark halls.

"Listen to you. Telling her she needs to take care of herself. Are you always such a foot washer?"

"She needs rest as much or more than the rest of us. She's carrying all of our worries." She put a positive tone in her voice. "She's going to save Alantris."

"Not if she gets all Alantrans killed. What's the point in driving the Naor out if everyone who lived here is dead?"

They had reached the wide chamber they'd dubbed the fountain, although the underground spring was more a wide pool into which water trickled from a small fissure in the rocky wall. It was the largest chamber in the tunnel network, and the squires often retired there to rest beside the water, as the burble proved strangely soothing. The ceiling peaked over much of it at more than fifteen feet high, and that was a relief after walking the warren of tunnels, most of which topped their heads oppressively by only a few inches.

The fountain chamber was empty save for a lone squire sleeping on a pillowed cloak. A dimly flickering lantern hung from a pole driven into the rock beside the wide oval pool, and it cast a dull orange glow across the dark waters.

Sansyra sat down beside the pool's lip, looking down onto the stones revealed in the thin circle illuminated by the lantern light. She really ought to go get some sleep, but she didn't feel like Denalia had the right perspective yet. "Alten Varama's shouldering a lot of responsibility right now."

Denalia kicked off her sandals and sat down on the cool stone beside her. She looked young and sweet, so the bitterness in her voice was all the more jarring. "I bet she didn't bat an eye when Nereal died, did she?"

"I know it affected her." At least she hoped it had. Varama hadn't said much beyond a simple statement as to the unfortunate loss. But that's how she was, and one of the secrets of her success. If she'd been rattled with emotion like the three of them, she'd never have developed her counterplan so swiftly.

Denalia leaned closer, her clean-featured face alive with challenge. "How do you think she'll react if you die?" Denalia didn't wait for an answer. "I think we're all just part of her abstract calculation."

"You didn't see her when she found out Rylin had been badly wounded."

The young woman's critical tone dropped away, and she was instantly concerned and solicitous. "Rylin's wounded? What happened?"

Sansyra had few details. And naturally Denalia wanted them, for she was smitten with him. "He got the people out, but was badly hurt in the process."

"How badly?"

"He hasn't regained consciousness yet." Seeing the mortified expression on her companion's face, Sansyra added quickly: "Healers are seeing to him. They say his chances are good."

She immediately regretted stating the last, because that was what Enada had implied rather than said outright, but gauging Denalia's concern, she decided not to clarify.

"I'll pray for him. He's such a wonderful man. He cares about people. Deeply. You can see it in his eyes."

"So does Varama," Sansyra countered, and then she added: "And she's a lot smarter." She didn't mean to insult Rylin, particularly, but to point out the strength of their commanding officer by comparison.

"You don't like him." Denalia eyed her sharply.

"That's not true. I didn't used to like him. But he's changed."

"Why didn't you like him before?"

She'd thought she'd known Rylin by type—a swaggering man swollen with the sense of his own self worth and certain he was owed the attentions of every pretty face he looked at. Over the last week, though, in the long flight from Darassus, she'd begun to note inklings of what Varama must long since have seen. Even then she'd disbelieved until she saw Rylin's bravery, and the results of his decisive actions. How strange to learn that he'd been worthy of regard all this time. She had never supposed him especially bright, and had even said as much to Varama.

Her mentor had pointed out there were different sorts of intelligence. She'd foolishly imagined Varama had misjudged. Rylin had little talent or interest in science or mathematics, but Sansyra now realized that he thought very quickly on his feet. He was, as some had begun to call him, wily. It might be that he sought his pleasures too readily, but when it was time to stand the line, he'd leapt boldly into place. She wondered, and not for the first time, if she'd been so very wrong, or if she'd been essentially correct and Rylin had risen to his true potential amidst the crisis, tempered in adversity. Might she then expect the same thing from herself? What might she slough off?

She grew conscious of Denalia's consideration. How to explain to the young woman? "He's a good man. I'm just not sure . . ." Ah, she was too tired to say it more eloquently. She gave up and spoke directly. "He always wanted to bed every pretty girl he met."

At Denalia's shocked look, she spoke swiftly before she could counter. "I'm sorry, but it's the truth."

"That's not how he acts."

"Believe me, he's been wondering what you look like naked from the moment he met you."

Denalia's nostrils flared. "The moment he met me he was defending my life. Along with almost fifty others."

"There's no denying his bravery," Sansyra agreed.

"You see the best in Varama, when it may not even be there. And you want to see the worst in him."

"That's not true. I think he's changed."

"I think you're jealous because Varama likes him more than you."

The truth behind that accusation stung. She'd been envious of Varama's sudden reliance upon Rylin for the last little while, but she'd disliked him long before that. If there was any lingering jealousy, it was balanced against her newfound respect.

"I'm right, aren't I." Denalia pointed at her. "You're ready to say I'm blind because I like Rylin. Well, you're blind because you want to cozy up to your commander. I don't know why; it would be like sleeping with a bowl of ice."

"I don't—"

"I'm going to take this up with the other Alantrans, and see what they have to say. Maybe some of the other squires, too. We have the right to question her."

That was enough. She surprised herself by grabbing the younger woman's arm. Denalia struggled to pull free. "Hey!"

"Our chances are slim enough without you stirring up bad feelings. We're at war now. That means we have hard choices. You want the Naor to gradually cull us, or do you want to buck and strain until we throw them off?"

"What if they kill more children? Or babies?"

"That's what the Naor want us to worry about. They're taking advantage of the fact we care about people. You want to be held hostage by that?"

"I don't want more of my people to die."

"None of us do." Sansyra released her arm.

Denalia looked down into the water, then hugged her knees, looking very young. Her voice grew soft. "How will we live with ourselves?"

"Denalia . . ." She sighed, then admitted quietly: "I'm not sure we're going to live at all."

Denalia's soft brown eyes were huge as she looked up at her. She honestly sounded surprised. "I thought you believed Varama was going to win."

"I think she's going to win." Sansyra breathed out slowly, then acknowledged what she'd begun to fear. "I'm just not sure we'll survive to see it."

13

Of Wing and Claw

The distant figures in the cerulean sky looked impossibly small and far away. The kobalin travelling with them were certain that the winged figures were ko'aye, though, and were eager to depart lest they be spotted. Qirok and his followers bowed low to Ortok and then sketched less formal bows to Elenai and Kyrkenall before bounding away. Elenai paid them scant attention, though she wondered if Qirok would rule his brethren when he returned to them.

The land beneath the ko'aye was a long, spindly fragment fashioned of brown rock and black rock and yellow rock and soaring formations of mixed rock; very little that lay before them wasn't rock of some sort. The sun gave up its blazing and the clatter of their horses' hooves echoed into the stillness of that lonely land.

Growing chilly, Elenai shed the head covering provided by her spare shirt and donned her khalat, her eyes more often on the figures far above than the ground before them. The ko'aye had famously excellent sight. "They'll see we're wearing khalats, won't they?" Elenai asked.

"They should." Kyrkenall was hooking his own armored robe closed. "Maybe they'll even see my bow." So saying, he lifted and shook it. Arzhun was nearly as famous as the archer who wielded it, and she expected the keen-eyed ko'aye would have found it just as distinctive-looking as everyone else.

The creatures circled closer. Shielding her eyes, Elenai saw that both were white, although one seemed to have a darker coloration at its feathertips. They will come, she thought, and land before us, and Kyrkenall will have to be very clever.

But the ko'aye flew farther into the distance until they were lost to sight.

Kyrkenall cursed. "I hadn't expected they'd just fly off. I suppose I should have."

"Do you think they'll come back?"

"Maybe. But we'll keep going forward in any case."

"Maybe they're going to go get more to hunt us," Ortok suggested. "It would be a brave battle, if so."

"Let's hope that's not their plan," Elenai said.

"No battles." Kyrkenall's tone brooked no argument. "We need the ko'aye."

"Sometimes battle happens whether you wish it or not," Ortok said.

"It's not going to happen here," Kyrkenall declared obstinately.

Ortok's brow furrowed, but he did not speak. Since they'd arrived at the fragment, his black fur was regrowing, quickly enough that if Elenai looked away for a few minutes and then back there was noticeable change.

Elenai turned to Kyrkenall. "Do you think I should update N'lahr about our progress?"

"Let's wait until we have something more to tell him."

That's what Elenai should have predicted he'd say, and felt stupid now for having asked. She supposed she was growing more and more concerned that they might fail their mission. How then would N'lahr fight the Naor dragons?

By mutual consent, they fell silent.

While the place looked empty and dead, Elenai discovered that small scurrying creatures lived among the boulders, and that low-lying vegetation sheltered in the lee of rock formations. After what she guessed was a half hour, they passed an immense pillar of colored stone resembling an upturned vase and came to a vast plain of waist-high orange grass. Thunder rolled, and a distant raincloud dropped lines of moisture onto the horizon.

"It would be good to eat," Ortok said suddenly. "I am always hungry when I change."

"We might as well," Kyrkenall said. "They know we're here, and there's no way to catch up to them. Besides, it would do the horses good to graze. Let's halt on that rise, so we can see whatever might be coming through the foliage." He pointed to a spot where the grasses thinned on rocky hills.

Once they'd dismounted, Kyrkenall cautioned to keep a close eye on the horses. Elenai had figured that much out. There was no telling what might be lurking out there.

"This seems a stable-enough fragment, and fairly large," Elenai said. "Why hasn't anyone tried to settle here?"

Kyrkenall stepped out of the shadow of a crooked peak and into the sunlight. "We don't know that they haven't, for sure," he said. "But it's too far from the realms to bother with, and too close to the kobalin lands. If that's not enough reason, there were a lot of storms out here even before the shifts got worse. If you settled here you'd have a hard time staying in touch with the central realms."

"It seems pleasant enough. Are there a lot of fragments out here like this?" If there were enough together, a colony might be established.

"Some." He flashed a tired grin at her. "I used to want to go out and see them all. Maybe I will, someday."

She'd never heard anything remotely like that from Kyrkenall before. But then since she'd met him he'd always been chased toward one necessary goal or another. Apart from his quest for Kalandra and his love of theater—or at least the quoting of it—she really had no idea about his aspirations. She rather liked this glimpse of a more curious Kyrkenall and wished she saw more of him.

While Kyrkenall and Ortok used their dwindling charcoal supply to set up a nearly smokeless fire, Elenai sat, downed some wine, and kept her eyes on the horses, belly high in the waving grasses and happily munching. She willed her ring to full power without activating its light, and grew aware of the subtle play of energies around her.

A quick glance with the ring revealed that the grass was thick with smaller signs of life that denoted insects and small mammals. It was said Sartain had fashioned very little out here in the wastelands, so all these animals had to have wandered in through the shifts from other places.

"Well, look at that!" Kyrkenall said behind her, and she scanned the grass for some sign of a slinking feline shape, or, worse, one of the glow-lizards.

"They come back," Ortok said, his mouth full of the tough jerky he chewed.

Elenai looked up to find a trail of long slim creatures with vast wings, high in the sky. A dozen of them dropped slowly until they were only a few hundred feet overhead, where they circled.

Then one plunged straight toward them, claws out. Was it maneuvering for a landing? Or had all of them come back to fight, as Ortok hoped?

Kyrkenall cursed. "Elenai, it's coming for our horses. Do something gentle!"

He might be expecting a lot, she thought. She reached out to touch the hearthstone with her mind, flicked it on, then sent a tendril of purpose soaring through the inner world toward the diving ko'aye.

Her own thoughts brushed the creature's mind and met a torrent of rage. She didn't want to experiment with touching it with hope or joy, which might make it more determined to succeed, so she chose confusion, wondering even as she did if there was a way to promise friendship, or kindness.

Someday, she thought, she'd have to practice her skills with a real tutor and stop relying on the hearthstone's raw force.

The ko'aye pulled out of its dive only twenty feet above, swinging out over the grasslands, shaking its head as if to clear it.

Their horses hadn't cared for the abortive attack; Elenai's mount and the pack horses bolted across the grass. Lyria and Ortok's horse called restively after them. Elenai sent a tendril to calm them, astonished that Ortok's horse, because of its sedate temperament, was more brave than hers and the pack horses, which had years of training. Once the fear subsided in the mounts, she whistled them back, wary of applying too much force against them. Slow and steady was better.

Two other ko'aye swooped down, one seeking the side of the one Elenai had confused. The other, a silvery beast with blue-tipped feathers, flew low overhead, as if to inspect them. Kyrkenall raised his right hand and let his ring shine.

All three ko'aye flapped their wings and rose to rejoin the larger group high above.

Kyrkenall shielded his eyes with one hand as a washed-out sun broke through the clouds.

"Didn't they recognize us as Altenerai?" Elenai said.

"Oh, they recognized us." Kyrkenall frowned. "I think they're a little undecided about what to do. They're flying close enough to communicate." He pointed at the creatures, in tight formation.

"I think they came hunting our horses," Ortok said, as if this weren't staggeringly obvious. "Maybe they wonder if they can eat them. That would make me sad, though horses are delicious. Mine is good for riding."

Kyrkenall shot him a sidelong glance. "You probably don't know this, Ortok, but that's a damned good horse you've got there."

"Is it?"

"Yes. I bet you couldn't find one in another thousand or more that would suit you so well. You should take care of him."

Ortok absorbed this for a moment, then nodded gravely. "I will do that. What makes him good?"

"He's calm, and steady, and walks on without complaint. Like a good warrior ought to do. And he's fearless. Most horses have to be trained to deal with combat, but yours is unafraid."

Ortok grunted.

A latecomer joined the flock of ko'aye and Elenai sensed Kyrkenall's attention sharpen. The winged beasts circled together for a time longer and then the majority flew off to the right. Two continued to circle, slowly. And two others landed on the far end of the nearby ridge, touching down at almost the same moment.

Elenai had never seen a ko'aye at close range, though she'd looked upon paintings and tapestries depicting them. While they were just as noble and beautiful as she'd expected, there was something wild and dangerous to them no art had fully captured. They had been described as winged lizards, but they looked much more to her like long-necked predatory birds, with bright cunning eyes back of their beaks, though they trailed long barbed tails like no bird she had ever seen.

As graceful as they looked in the air, they were somewhat clumsy as they waddled along the rock, their gait growing less cumbersome once they folded their great wings.

The horses cocked their ears forward, attention riveted upon the predators.

Kyrkenall bade Ortok watch the horses and advanced with Elenai for a dialogue.

The two of them climbed ten feet up a steep slope to a shallow, rocky ridge and walked through the cool shadow of a jagged peak nearby. The wind riders raised lizard-like feathered heads on slender necks. With their enormous eyes they appeared wise and alert. One was the white individual with bronze-tipped feathers they'd seen earlier, the other was a brilliant blue, and had a long scar running along the front of its neck. At closer range, both ko'aye looked more spindly than she had first realized. She wondered if they were always this lean.

Kyrkenall bowed formally from the waist and indicated Elenai, who echoed the gesture. "Drusa, it brings me great joy to see you once more. And you as well, Vavesh. This is Elenai Oddsbreaker."

The blue, scarred one bobbed her head. The other regarded them unwinking, then addressed them in a high, clear voice, moving its jaw only a little. Chirrups and clicks were interspersed among the sounds it made, especially hard consonants. "You are not welcome. No more than the kobalin that take our prey."

Kyrkenall showed empty palms. "We come as friends."

The white one answered. "Your people are not our friends."

"I was your friend, Vavesh. Many of us still are."

"Friends hold to their word."

"I am your friend," Kyrkenall declared, forcefully, and addressed the blue one. "You do not need me to declare that with words, Drusa."

"You declared it with deeds." Drusa's voice was more harsh and rasping than her companion's, perhaps owing to the wound that had scarred her. She fluttered her wings and turned her head to Vavesh. "He risked himself to save my mate."

"I fought for more than your mate," Kyrkenall said.

"Which is why we are listening rather than attacking," Vavesh told him. "Some yet think well of you, Black Eye, though they have lost love for your people. But where were you when the Naor sought our nests?" The animal's head rose. "Count the missing, Kyrkenall of the black bow! How many do you see in today's flight? There should be fifty more. But too many fly the red winds!"

Drusa lowered her shovellike head. "You promised that you would help us hunt the Naor in our lands if we hunted them in yours. But after N'lahr commander fell, the Denaven commander brought us the word of your queen, and she told us to be gone. Where were you then?"

Kyrkenall bowed his head briefly. "I mourned my friend, and went wandering. I didn't know what the queen had done until it was too late." He swept a hand toward Elenai. "Elenai slew Denaven. And she and I found that the queen had hidden N'lahr, and that he was not dead. He commands again, and sent us to speak to you."

The heads of both ko'aye snapped up in surprise.

"What word does he bring?" Drusa asked.

"He wishes us to fight again," Vavesh concluded quickly. "You wish to ask more favors, without delivering upon prior promises!" Vavesh's barbed tail twitched into the air and his wings fluttered.

Kyrkenall raised an open hand even as Drusa tilted her head and clucked something toward her companion.

Vavesh shifted, then lowered his tail. "Speak, Kyrkenall."

"I wish to bear the word of my leader to yours."

Vavesh traded a look with Drusa, then they exchanged a series of warbles and clicks that grew more heated, judging by the sway of their necks and the agitation of both sets of wings.

Finally, Vavesh faced them once more. "Wait here." He backed away, then performed an ungainly about-face before lumbering off along the ridge to spread his wings. Elenai was startled once more by how awkward the creatures appeared to be while on the ground. It wasn't until Vavesh beat his wings and launched into the air that his beauty was again apparent, and

Elenai watched his progress with a measure of envy. She might manage sorcery, but she had no power to fly.

Drusa lowered her head until it was level with Kyrkenall's, then cocked it to take him in with one great eye. "It does please me to see you once more," she said. "Though I had put you from my thoughts."

"I never stopped thinking of you," Kyrkenall said gently.

"That is kind. How have you fared?"

Kyrkenall laughed without humor. "I have friends, so I am wealthy."

"Have you a mate?"

"She's lost to me." Kyrkenall managed to hide most of his frustration. "You?"

"I do still. I have hatchlings now. I'd like to take them from this dusty place, for the food is scarce."

"How many do you have?" Kyrkenall asked. "How old are they?"

"Only a year, I think. The seasons pass strangely here and it's hard to mark them. I have two. They do not grow large or quickly in this place. I'm sorry to hear about your mate. Did she fall in battle?"

Kyrkenall waved a hand at the indeterminate distance. "I speak of Kalandra Storm Strider."

Drusa cawed and her head drew up. "Oh, Kyrkenall. This saddens me. Always did I like her. And I thought you two might be mates, and that it was strange to delay it. Did you have younglings?"

"No."

"What happened to her?"

"She wandered into the shifts, trying to find answers that would help us stop the queen. But she never came back. I never knew for certain how she felt about me until she was gone."

"It seems you have borne many sorrows." Drusa's head swung to Elenai. "Is she your new mate?"

"No," Kyrkenall said. Elenai noted no hesitation in his voice. Drusa's unwinking eye stared at her, and she searched for something to say.

"These lands seem beautiful."

Drusa's eye narrowed. "Do you mean a compliment, Altenerai?"

"Yes."

"There is little game here. And the storms come to our borders. And the winds are fierce. And hunter beasts there are, too." It nodded to Ortok, watching them from the bottom of the hill. "And enemies like those, who sometimes seek our eggs. Why do you travel with our enemy?"

"He guided us here," Kyrkenall answered.

Drusa's beak clacked. "I thought you Altenerai warred with kobalin."

"Sometimes we do."

Drusa hooted, and then her head wobbled. "Oh, Kyrkenall. I wish to help you bear this word. But your words will not be trusted. Your people change your habits too often. Sometimes you war with the Naor, who kill your people. Sometimes you make peace with them. Sometimes you war with kobalin, and sometimes they are your companions. Sometimes you fight among yourselves. Might you decide you wish to war with us?"

"Drusa, I trusted you with my life. And I swear that you can trust me with yours." He thumped his chest with emphasis. "I wish to make things right."

"The hunting was fine between us. But what of the rest of your people? It seems there are powerful ones you cannot trust."

"N'lahr is my greatest friend," Kyrkenall said. "I trust him above all others. And he commands us."

"And your queen?"

"He will dethrone our queen," Kyrkenall declared. Hearing it stated so clearly in public for the first time, Elenai couldn't help a sharp breath.

Overhead, Vavesh dropped toward them again, his wings high. In moments, he had landed and, still folding his wings, took his place beside Drusa. There they had a long exchange in their fluting, clacking, birdlike language. Though it continued at length, it did not appear to be as antagonistic as their previous debate.

Finally Vavesh addressed them. "We're on our way to the new homelands. You may follow us, if you wish. But do not imagine that you'll be well received. We know how empty your promises are."

Drusa cut in. "Many agree with Vavesh. But Kyrkenall and Aradel and others are remembered well. And on strength of those memories, you may come with us, in peace."

Vavesh cried out something to that and Drusa said something that ended with a snap of her beak.

Vavesh turned away from them.

Drusa bowed her head. "Follow. It may be a long journey on your horses. Do you need them all? Because they look very fine."

Elenai worried that Kyrkenall might consider cutting some of the animals free, as a peace gesture, but he shook his head.

"I'm sorry, Drusa. They're under our care. They've served us well."

She warbled at him and Elenai suspected that this was Drusa's way of showing amusement.

"Fair enough. Do not dawdle, ground dweller!" And with something that looked an awful lot like a playful look over her shoulder, she turned and started off, waddling until she thrust out her wings, flapped them, and gained the air.

Without another word, Kyrkenall hurried down the hill, shouting at Ortok to gather the charcoal. This they did, using a cloth bag to shield their hands. The kobalin's eyes roved back and forth between them.

"I thought at first they wished to fight," he said. "Did you make friends? Will they join us in battle?"

"I wish it was that simple," Kyrkenall answered. "The situation's a little complicated."

"So your words did not work?"

"We're going to speak with their leaders. And I'll have to do a better job with them than I did just now."

"Use small words," Ortok suggested helpfully. "With many descriptions."

Kyrkenall's answer was a dark grumble.

"I don't think you did too badly," Elenai said.

"Don't get me wrong, I'm thrilled that Drusa's still my friend. But it's the ones like Vavesh I'm going to have to convince. And I'm not sure anything I'm going to say will win him and his like over. Not to mention some who are even more angry."

Most of the ko'aye flew off until they were lost in the distance. Two kept in sight with them across the grassland. Sometimes they seemed to forget that those below couldn't keep up, and then they'd double back and hang in the air currents. This must have bored them, though, for they'd soar ahead and then start the cycle over.

Kyrkenall sat stiffly, his brows drawn. He scanned the horizon from time to time and occasionally pushed back his hair, which the wind continually whipped to his right, but he said nothing.

Elenai waited no longer. She reached out through the inner world and activated N'lahr's hearthstone.

Almost instantly an image overlay the plains on which they rode. She stood upon a forested mountaintop looking down at a distant city. She'd never seen Alantris from this angle, but she recognized it quickly, keying in on the rising levels and the separate walls and the rings of the city's waterways, and the tall, arched length of the ancient aqueducts. Elenai involuntarily sucked in a breath, seeing a badly mended gap in the outer wall, and lines of smoke threading through the sky from multiple points in the lower and upper city.

Alantris had fallen.

Yes, N'lahr told her. And with that single word she also felt his great fury for the lives lost, for the terror brought to so many innocents. For the horrendous waste. It was incongruous to feel such an enormous well of emotion pouring from someone she ordinarily experienced as so impassive.

How bad is it?

Aradel Sky Rider is dead. Thousands have perished. Thousands more will die.

As his sorrow and, surprisingly, guilt rolled over her, he spoke on. *But Varama strikes at them from inside the city, and has slain three of their five dragons. I see ko'aye in the skies above you. Have you made peace?* His query was restrained, but she could feel the urgency of his hope.

I'm not sure we can. They're very angry. No agreement may be possible. Do we still need them if most of the dragons are dead?

She registered his surprise that she should consider that possibility. *Yes. It is not just these, here. The sorcerer Chargan has more and he will arrive within a week. We are vastly outnumbered, Elenai. We must snatch any advantage. What has Kyrkenall told them?*

She relived the moment for him, finishing by telling him they'd speak in audience before a gathering of the ko'aye leaders.

Contact me when you arrive. Maybe I can help.

That could be interesting, she thought, suddenly imagining herself speaking with N'lahr's words. And she saw from his thoughts that's exactly what he intended.

How are you? she asked him. *Are there any more hearthstone incidents? Are you slowing down?*

I've only noticed three of them, which is a decrease, and I wonder if that's because one of the halves is so far away from me.

Do you have a plan? How to fight the Naor? How to free Alantris?

A plan is under way, he said simply. *Enada is here, with cavalry, and she has spoken once with Varama. Our main body of troops is still on the way. We have much to arrange before Chargan reaches us.*

His words were simple; the worry behind them was not. Had he been this concerned about Vedessus? Or was he more worried, now? She didn't articulate the question, quite, but he seemed to hear it anyway. How much of her own thoughts and feelings was she inadvertently revealing?

I am more worried now. The Naor have the city. Their slaughter can continue virtually unopposed. Varama is clever, but they could root out her hiding place. . . .

His stream of thought was interrupted by Tretton, who'd come up on the left to speak about enemy troop movements. Elenai overheard N'lahr politely asking the older alten to wait before he returned his attention to her. *Be alert. We have another traitorous alten. Cerai is leagued with the queen. She recovered a powerful hearthstone that the queen needs to further her own interests.*

Do we know what those interests are?

There was no missing N'lahr's maddened frustration over his inability to do anything about that. He was furious he couldn't halt the queen's machinations, or even learn what she planned. All he broadcast, though, was one word: *No.*

Then: *Cerai abandoned Alantris rather than fighting to save it, and attacked Rylin and Varama. She ensorcelled Aradel's ko'aye and kidnapped her. She has grown very powerful. Be your sharpest if you meet her.*

Elenai thought it unlikely they would, but she bowed her head solemnly. *We will.*

N'lahr glanced at Tretton, waiting impatiently. *I must go. My best to Kyrkenall and Ortok, and to you. Contact me when you speak before the ko'aye.*

Hail, Commander.

Hail, Alten.

At that, she broke contact and quieted the stone. She gathered her thoughts and rode up to Kyrkenall, bearing the tidings.

His jaw tightened at the news of the city's fall and Aradel's death, and his eyes widened in amazement at news of Cerai.

"I can't believe Cerai's working with the queen. She *hated* Denaven."

"Apparently that didn't stop her."

"I'd give a lot to know what they're really up to."

"We already have," she said.

"Aye. And we're little closer to knowing the truth." The archer sighed. "I wish I was there with N'lahr, not here. I'm no good at this kind of thing."

"N'lahr said he'd help, once we started talking."

"And you're sure that the hearthstone isn't hurting him?"

"I'm not sure at all. He says he's having those episodes less." When she'd told Kyrkenall about N'lahr's stone, she'd also informed him of the risks. "He's really worried about the city. He's not entirely sure what to do, and he has only a few days to figure it out, because another huge Naor army is on its way."

"Then we'd best get him these ko'aye," Kyrkenall said.

"Do you know what you're going to say?"

"Aye. At least, I think I do."

"You want to talk it over?"

He didn't look at her. "No. I need to *think* it through. I need to think really, really hard about what I'm going to say without any interruptions." He said the last sharply, as though she made a habit of bothering him, like a nagging shrew.

His tone irked her. "I think I'll go talk with Ortok."

She dropped back beside the kobalin, who'd somehow ended up leading the pack horses.

With his larger horse and larger frame, Ortok rode from a higher vantage point. In the last little while his black fur had almost completely regrown. He was gnawing on what must have been a very tough piece of dry jerky, holding both reins in one dark paw.

"I think you look nice with black fur," she said.

He swallowed, then took another bite and considered her. "Do you wish you had black fur?"

"It had never occurred to me," she answered honestly. "Do you have any control during a storm?"

"Some. The Gods bless our bodies so they change in the challenge times. I control when to grow the fur, and whether it will be black or gray. Can you change the color in your hair?"

"No. And I can't grow it as fast as you, either."

"We kobalin adapt," he said proudly. "You would not live well in the wild places," he added.

"Probably not."

He nodded toward Kyrkenall. "He seems with no cheer. Is there a reason?"

"He's kind of an ass," she decided.

Ortok laughed. "Do you wish to challenge him?"

"No. I don't think I do."

"You should save challenge words until you do, then, so no one will think you rude."

She considered that little kernel of wisdom, then wondered how it was she was so often being schooled in courtesy by a creature who had only slept once in a bed. "What do you say to a leader who's rude?"

"You must decide whether their guidance is worthy of enduring disrespect from them, or whether they should be challenged. But that may not be the way of your people. I have seen. You do not challenge properly. You do not exchange blows or even trade leadership when you win. It is strange."

She didn't know how to explain all the societal niceties and particulars, and wasn't in the mood to try in any case, so she fell silent, fearing for the people of Alantris. The Naor, she remembered, had intended the same thing for her own city, and if not for their desperate efforts, Vedessus now would be a place of horror.

At length they passed a dark little lake before which other ko'aye hunched over the bodies of lanky, long-limbed beasts and tore at their flesh. She didn't get a clear idea of what the prey animals looked like until she saw a distant herd of the green-backed, long-necked creatures watching the carnage. Even when the things bent to graze, a pair of sensory organs remained upright to scan the horizon. She found those eyestalks faintly unsettling.

They continued following their reluctant airborne guides, and the character of the land grew rocky once more. As they headed up a scree-strewn slope, Elenai spotted dozens of ko'aye swooping over the hills ahead. She marveled a little to see so many of the creatures on the wing. Most were of gray and blue hues, but many were dappled with splashes of gold or silver, or splotched with tan and brown.

"This is a bad place to be if they grow angry," Ortok mused. "There are many claws here."

Neither she nor Kyrkenall answered. Deep as they were in ko'aye territory and surrounded by them, Ortok's comment was understatement. Should the ko'aye turn on them, they stood no chance.

Drusa returned and landed fifty yards ahead, saying nothing as she led them through a narrow pass in the hills. Beyond it they could see a vast clear spot in the rocks surrounded on all sides by ledge-studded cliffs. Ko'aye were settling onto both the ledges and a grand collection of natural, narrow rock columns rising three and four stories above the stony ground, arrayed in front of the cliffs.

Drusa paused before descending into the area, looking over one hunched shoulder and raising her voice. "Your kobalin must remain here, with the horses. I am to translate whatever words you bring us. I hope that they are good ones." Drusa then tread downslope toward a clear space before the columns.

Kyrkenall slipped off Lyria and patted her neck while he considered the hostile audience that awaited them. He turned to Elenai and Ortok. "You heard her, Ortok. Can you keep a watch on the horses?"

"What if you do not come back?" Ortok asked. "It shall be hard to avenge you against so many."

Kyrkenall quirked an eyebrow. "Don't bother avenging me." He glanced at Elenai, then down into the gathering. "Just get yourself back to N'lahr and tell him what happened. See if you can get Lyria back alive, too." He gave his mount a final pat. "She's a wonderful horse."

Lyria tossed her head at him, flashing a brown eye.

"I will."

Kyrkenall turned and started away.

Elenai gave a half wave to Ortok, then walked at the archer's side down the slope after Drusa.

"What, no questions?" Kyrkenall asked softly. "No advice?"

Was he trying to needle her into a conflict? Now? "You didn't want any."

He grunted. "Kalandra would have insisted."

"I'm not Kalandra. Did you want me to come up with something? Because this isn't a game. We could have talked about it."

"Yes."

She wasn't sure what that yes was about, but she didn't ask, for they'd come up to Drusa, waiting for them with her gold-brown eyes unwinking. Maybe it was a neutral look. Or maybe she was tense and sad. Elenai couldn't tell how much she was reading into the ko'aye's appearance.

"They will speak first," Drusa said. "I urge profound courtesy. You have few who do not wish you ill, Kyrkenall."

Elenai chose then to reach out to N'lahr's stone. Now she found him drinking from a waterskin. Evening had come to The Fragments, and the sun was half hidden behind a nearby mountain spur.

It's nearly time, she told him.

He called to Gyldara, standing nearby, that he'd need to be undisturbed for a few moments, then retreated to a tent.

Perhaps if you closed your eyes, she told him, *it would be easier for us both.* Seeing both his view and her own was distracting.

Good idea.

They followed Drusa the rest of the way in, crossing through the shadows of the stone pillars where close to two dozen ko'aye perched. To her eyes they looked lean, and strained. The columns they sat upon were only a little thicker than those fronting the great temple of Darassa, but rose to varied heights. The smallest towered easily twenty feet from the ground and the highest almost double that.

Hundreds more of the avians waited along the tiered cliff ledges behind the pillars. This apparently wasn't going to be a conference with leaders alone, but the whole of their adult population. That, she thought, probably didn't bode well.

The ko'aye blinked rarely, and under so many protracted, focused gazes, Elenai wondered if this is how a rabbit felt when watched by hawks.

Some of the ko'aye she supposed for flock leaders preened their feathers. Others clicked and cawed to themselves. The majority, though, continued to watch, and the most golden-hued of these finally gave out a shrill alert that brought the others to quiet, then peered down with lowered brow and gabbled in its high-pitched tongue.

Drusa translated. "You have come without welcome, so the wing guard is uncertain how to greet your coming. He says that you should say your words quickly so that you do not waste much of their time."

"Is that Seneksa?"

Drusa cocked her head a little. "Yes. Do not think that will help you."

Seeing that Kyrkenall readied himself for a bow, Elenai joined him, so that their movement was perfectly synchronized. The archer then threw back his head, and called up to the golden one and the assembled leaders. "My heart soars to see so many of you once more."

Drusa emitted a stream of clicks and tweets and continued to do so as Kyrkenall finished each phrase.

"Some of you have shed blood with me. Some of you know I risked my life at your side, to defend you. I know that your memories are long, and no matter what has happened since, you remember how we slew enemies together. How you protected me from our enemies. How I fended hunters from Seneksa's young."

Elenai sensed N'lahr's approval of that.

After Drusa's translation there was extended conversation among those upon the columns until golden Seneksa silenced them.

A black one called down in a voice so heavily accented with warbles and chirps Elenai had a hard time understanding it. "We remember! But there is much we remember, Kyrkenall!"

Another one shouted down in its own language, which Drusa translated with seeming displeasure. "We remember your betrayal."

Kyrkenall looked undeterred. "Do you remember how we flew against the Naor over the bright fields of Kanesh? Do you recall when Drusa and I landed amidst their numbers to rescue Ekatrin and his mate? How he lived to foster a clutch of hatchlings? I am your friend! My enemies betrayed me, just as they betrayed you! They lied to me, as they lied to you! They told me my brother of the ring was dead! N'lahr, who led us to victories! N'lahr, who counseled with your greatest warriors! Our enemies hid N'lahr away and made peace with the Naor so they could steal what they wished for themselves!"

The ko'aye chattered at this.

Kyrkenall gave them a moment to quiet. "With N'lahr gone my queen put Denaven in charge, and he lied to you! But that speaker of lies has died, and Elenai slew him with her own hand!" Kyrkenall paused to look at her. "N'lahr commands again! He never broke his promise to you, and he means to honor it now that he is free!"

Only a little noise greeted this. Elenai wasn't sure whether to be cheered or concerned by that.

He's doing fairly well, N'lahr observed. *But he needs to get to the point.* Elenai had to agree.

Drusa continued to translate as Kyrkenall spoke with greater confidence. "Even now N'lahr leads a mighty army against the Naor. Already uncounted thousands have been killed by him, with us at his side. If you fly to the battle site you would see no sign of skulls, the Naor prize, but a pyre of dead Naor wide as this clearing!"

The wind riders quieted altogether. They craned their necks.

"We will defeat the Naor! Come fight them with us in The Fragments, and we will help you take back your lands!"

From the right a harsh voice croaked down, "This was promised before."

Elenai swung around to observe a white ko'aye with bronze feather-tips. Vavesh.

Vavesh's head shook slowly on the end of his neck. "It's too late, Kyrkenall. The time has passed."

The ko'aye shrilled at one another then, in disordered cacophony. Elenai waited for a pause, then saw that most of those on the columns were no longer even looking at their human guests, for they were fully absorbed in a vigorous debate.

"What are they saying?" Kyrkenall asked Drusa.

"Some of the young ones want to fight the Naor. Others want to see lands rich with game that elders told of."

"And what do the old ones say?"

"That you lie."

"All of them say that?" Kyrkenall sounded surprised.

Drusa's head bobbed, and she continued sadly: "Some of them say you may not lie but cannot be trusted still. They are curious about Elenai and wonder if she is strong enough to kill Denaven, the Oath Breaker. He was a worker of magics."

"Do you wonder?" Elenai asked.

"No," Drusa answered gravely. "I think that you have done it. Kyrkenall would not say it if not true. And there is an aura of power about you."

There was? She bowed her head in acknowledgment of the compliment, and Drusa returned it minutely.

Seneksa, leader of the ko'aye, had at last quieted his flock, and spoke at length while Drusa translated.

"Kyrkenall, all that you say may be true. Many of us believe that it is so. But who is to say that others will not kill N'lahr again and you will disappear once more?"

"If N'lahr falls," Kyrkenall said, his eyes bright, "I will lead you to your lands myself, and fight the Naor until they're dead or I have perished in the battle. I swear it by the ring that blazes upon my finger."

It was such an impassioned, heartfelt pledge that Elenai sucked in a breath. "I swear as well!"

The archer spoke on. "N'lahr will ask this oath of all who wear the ring, and all they command. But no matter what you decide, you should know that with the Naor on the march, the lands they claim will have few protectors. It seems an excellent time to take back your home."

One ko'aye flew down from its cave and soared past those upon the columns, clacking and chirping and moving its legs in a slashing motion. More outcries arose from the ko'aye, and soon it was clear that another argument was under way.

"What's happening?" Elenai asked Drusa.

"That is Lelaren, the one who wished to attack you earlier. Some are shouting him down for his rudeness, for he is supposed to let his sentinel speak for him, and he said that they are all too pleasant with you. Now others join in . . . it is hard to follow." Drusa fell silent, her head cocking as she listened. Finally Lelaren retreated to the cliff top, where he hunched like a vulture. The tumult calmed, and then a brown one spoke down to Drusa, who relayed its words.

"Your kind is always clever. You want our help, but you have never given anything in return but empty words." At an onrush of noise from the assembled ko'aye, Drusa continued: "Others say that your hearts may be full, but that your heads are empty, to promise things beyond your power. Seneksa says that the Naor are too many and will beat you in the end, no matter what we do."

"What do you think?" Kyrkenall asked.

"Ah, old friend. The truth can hurt. I think that you will fail. But then I think that we will fail. The Naor and the many-legged lizards that shine and the storms of the Shifting Lands shall triumph in the end. Our eyries will be empty and your cities will be strewn with the bleached bones of your people."

Elenai was astonished at the sentiment.

A bleak poet of the ko'aye, N'lahr observed.

"You're not exactly an optimist, are you, Drusa?" Kyrkenall asked. "What can I do to convince them to join with me once more?"

I want you to tell them something, N'lahr said.

She nodded. "Drusa," she said, "I'd like to tell them something. I am linked to N'lahr. He is miles away, facing our enemies, but he speaks through me."

Drusa cocked her head.

Kyrkenall turned a palm over as if to say do what you will.

Drusa had to call the others to settle down and listen. When they had at last, Elenai indicated her willingness to N'lahr.

But he wasn't speaking. She could feel his presence, but he said nothing.

N'lahr? she prompted.

But his mind was unresponsive.

Gods, she realized in near panic, he's having one of the episodes.

Drusa stared at her.

N'lahr?

But the commander didn't answer. She felt him, but the flow of his thoughts had vanished. Of course. The prolonged contact with the stone had brought on another spell. She prayed that it was only a momentary lapse. The safest thing to do was to shut down the stone, and this she did, then closed her eyes and gathered her thoughts.

What might N'lahr have wished to say? Something wise. Something clever. So much for the utility of linking with the commander through the stone. Maybe if she hadn't been relying upon him she would have come up with a line of attack herself. Then she wouldn't have to invent one on the spot. She remembered the vast empty places they'd passed only weeks ago, and came to her decision. Elenai raised her chin and addressed them all, pausing every few sentences so that Drusa could translate.

"We owe you better lands. Until we can help you recover yours, you can share ours. Game in the southern Fragments is plentiful, and there are many high places to roost. You can fly there and claim them any time you like. You need not hunt Naor with us." She paused to let this sink in, and saw Kyrkenall eying her in surprised approval. She studied the ko'aye, hoping the stirrings she saw in their ranks were a positive sign. There might be other suitable lands to offer as well, although she wasn't sure where precisely in the Five Realms, and she reasoned if the ko'aye got to The Fragments and found the Naor, they might not be able to resist fighting them.

She wondered what N'lahr would think of such a promise. Had she gone too far? Even if N'lahr might, as she suspected, find the offer just, honorable, and possibly shrewd, what would the governors say? How would the villages in The Fragments feel about inviting large and fierce predators into nearby lands? She'd just have to trust her instincts and deal with the consequences. She was Altenerai, it was her duty not just to uphold the laws—which certainly included honoring oaths and agreements—but to protect her people and their lands. And the Fragments were apt to be much safer if they included ko'aye as a buffer against the Naor. Alantrans would be foolish to object to the arrival of potential allies, although she thought she'd best clarify an important point. "All we ask is that you keep from people and our herd animals."

The ko'aye began to talk among themselves, then hushed as she raised a hand, understanding she had more. "Right now, the Naor are in The Fragments. But we will drive them away. If you want to help us, we shall drive them faster, but we will succeed, and the skies are yours regardless. There is plenty to eat and enjoy whether you engage or avoid our shared enemy."

The moment Drusa completed speaking upon her behalf, she lowered her hand, and then the ko'aye talked even more vociferously.

"Nicely said," Kyrkenall told her softly.

"N'lahr froze up," she said. "I think the damned stone is hurting him."

"What?" Kyrkenall hissed quietly. His eyes widened. "You mean just now? Or before you spoke?"

"Right before I spoke. I sure hope he likes my offer, because I have no idea what he was going to say."

"I like it," Kyrkenall emphasized, and then to Drusa, watching them, he said, "and we will honor it." To Elenai: "Is he going to be all right?"

"I hope so."

"What is this you talk about?" Drusa asked, her head beside theirs.

"Great sorcery caused troubles for us while Elenai was speaking for N'lahr," Kyrkenall answered.

Drusa's head bobbed. Elenai thought that she might be more concerned about the interchange, but the ko'aye had apparently been listening to the chatter above. "You have convinced some of them that you value us, and you regret the past, and you bring news of help to us,"

Drusa said, then halted. "Seneksa speaks." The animal lifted her head, turning it as the ko'aye settled and their leader, golden Seneksa, spoke alone.

"He says," Drusa told them, "that they have decided. You can stay and rest after your long journey, in honor of the bond we once shared. We were comrades, once."

Kyrkenall spoke quickly. "We are comrades now, if you would have us."

Drusa translated this and then the leader's response. "We do not think so." Behind Seneksa the others squabbled.

Drusa leaned her head toward Kyrkenall and spoke softly. "You should not have interrupted." She then lifted her head once more, and conveyed the leader's final words: "Make no mistake. Some believe you speak the truth. But no one can trust that you have the power to deliver what you promise. You wish us to fight at your side again, and that cannot be. Go now, and rest, and you may leave after a sleeping cycle. Our audience is done."

Seneksa unfurled his wings, beat them once, and then soared skyward. After a moment, the other ko'aye rose with him. Others chirped, and the air was full with not just their feathered bodies, but their calls, so it seemed they were in the world's largest aviary.

Drusa remained grounded beside them. "Come with me. There are low caves you might find comfortable."

A trio of ko'aye flapped overhead, only ten feet above, and the one in the lead let out a piercing cry, slashing the air with one taloned leg in what was clearly a threat.

"I don't recommend staying very long," Drusa said as she turned her shoulder to them.

14

Words from Afar

Drusa led them to a large half-moon opening lower down the cliff face. Elenai eyed it skeptically. They'd still have to scale almost seven feet of sheer gray rock to reach it.

"This should do," Kyrkenall said to Drusa. "Thank you."

The ko'aye bobbed her head. "I think you are troubled. But I think it went better than it might have."

"Drusa," Kyrkenall said frankly, "I need your help with this. The Naor thought N'lahr was dead, and it made them bold. They found huge ko'aye that they ride and use to attack our walls."

"The Naor have captured ko'aye?" Drusa rustled her wings and her eyes burned with inner fire. "How can this be?"

"We don't know," Kyrkenall answered.

"This is a terrible thing," Drusa said, and let out a shrill call. "You should earlier have said this! Are these some of our flock that we thought dead?"

Elenai spoke quickly. "Drusa, I don't think that these are ko'aye like you. And I'm sure that they're not your friends. They're described as far larger, and can destroy walls with their roars."

Drusa's head lowered and she peered at Elenai. "These are strange tidings," she said. "I will bring these words to my friends. There is already much to talk about."

Elenai nodded once in appreciation.

"Tell me, Elenai. Are you mated?"

"No." Why had the ko'aye asked that of her? "It's not really on my priority list right now."

"You must be young. Although you look of an age to be thinking it. Kyrkenall could be your mate, since he has lost his, and you are both warriors of the ring. Also you have clear sight, which he sometimes lacks."

Elenai smirked.

Kyrkenall's response was dry. "We'll take that under advisement."

Drusa returned her attention to him. "I'll talk to some that were more interested in your words. A number were excited by thoughts of better places today. Especially younger ones. You will leave in the morning?"

"Yes. N'lahr needs our help. The battle with Naor in The Fragements must start soon."

"If I have news for you, I will bring it. It was good to be with you once more, Kyrkenall."

"I'm glad of that myself."

They concluded their meeting with a ritual head bob, and then Drusa lowered her neck and turned. Elenai watched her walk farther out and spread her wings, then head to the left and out of sight as she prepared to seek the air.

Kyrkenall turned to her. "Is N'lahr all right now?"

"I don't know. I closed the stone, hoping that might snap him out of it. He'd told me earlier he wasn't having as many of the slowing moments and wondered if it was because he was so far away from the stone."

Kyrkenall cursed. "The only way to find out if he's all right is to use the thing that might be turning him into a statue."

"Do you think I should risk it?"

Kyrkenall hesitated, then shook his head. "No. Not until we have something to tell him."

She nodded at that.

"I'm going to get our bedding and tell Ortok what's going on."

"You're not bringing him in here?"

"First, I'm pretty sure the invite didn't extend to him. Second, someone's got to watch the horses. And third, there's no way that the horses would be comfortable here. Not when the whole place smells like giant horse-eating predators."

It seemed rude to leave their kobalin ally alone with the animals, as though they didn't think him worthy of their company. "Maybe we should stay with Ortok, then."

Kyrkenall's brows rose and he quickly shook his head. "I'll explain later. Why don't you look over our accomodations?" He gestured farewell.

She suspected that he feared insulting the ko'aye by refusing their hospitality.

She willed her ring into life and extended her senses. There seemed nothing but tiny insects living within the cave above, which didn't especially surprise her. She'd hardly expected the ko'aye to keep a pet monster handy for devouring invited guests. There was nothing wrong, though, with being cautious.

She studied the cave entrance, walked beneath its six-foot opening until she found a spot where there was an overhanging lip no longer than her thumb, but wide as her arm. Reaching it would be simple with magic, but she wanted to conserve her own power and resist the temptation to employ her hearthstone. And so she crouched and sprang and caught the ledge with both hands. Elenai knew she didn't have exceptional upper body strength, but she was fit enough to pull herself up, after which she knelt along the rim peering into the darkness both with her sight and the enhanced senses of the ring.

Weak daylight flowed from over the cliff wall and into the cave, illuminating little past the first four feet, enough to show her a curiously smooth floor. To her left and right the ceiling sloped, but there were easily eight feet in the center that permitted her to stand fully upright.

Still willing her ring of office to light, she advanced into the space, discovering that the cave stretched back only twenty feet before sloping sharply down to the floor.

She walked all along the wall, judging quickly that the place was secure, then returned to the entrance and waited for Kyrkenall. He was nowhere in sight.

He was a while coming, and during his absence she reached into her satchel to touch N'lahr's broken hearthstone fragment. What if he was sitting frozen and still in The Fragments right now? The urge to contact him and check on him was almost overwhelming.

But suppose he was fine now, and contacting him would progress the freezing episodes?

She decided to wait, and hope for the best. Just as she might have to do with the ko'aye. She couldn't for the life of her think of anything more she might have said, and wondered if N'lahr had been planning something more clever. Having seen him in action, the answer was probably yes.

She found herself staring at her ring and wondering whether she'd actually thought life would be more rewarding once she wore it. The acclaim and respect she'd so wanted didn't mean as much as she had expected. Instead of joy, she was weighted with responsibility, and worry.

When Kyrkenall returned, he brought a small supply of firewood, as well as both sets of saddlebags. He refused her offer of assistance and, after tossing up the supplies, scrambled to her level with ease.

"How's the cave?" he asked.

"Secure."

"I bet the winds are cold when night comes." He set to erecting a little timber pyramid near the cave opening, occasionally glancing out toward the stone columns and the cliff faces. From where they sat it was impossible to see any of the ko'aye or their ledges, but they heard them calling to one another.

"It always impressed me how quickly they picked up our language," Kyrkenall said as he worked. "I didn't want to insult Ortok any more than you did, but we might have insulted the ko'aye if we hadn't accepted the offer of hospitality."

"I thought it was something like that."

He poured water out of two spare waterskins and into the eelskin bowl he sometimes used to water the horses. "I filled these up at the water hole," he explained. "Thought it might be nice to freshen up a bit."

"It surely would."

Silence settled between them as they washed, until he cleared his throat. "You're a funny mix still."

"What do you mean?"

He gestured to her. "You're all unsure and full of questions, but then you turn up something clever in a flash." He snapped his fingers. "You shouldn't let me treat you like a squire. You earned that ring. Don't act like one, either."

"I still have a lot to learn."

"Don't we all? I think I need to pay more attention to your counsel. There have been enough clues about that all along. Maybe if we'd talked sooner I could've started with that grand gesture you gave them, *then* apologized."

And this, she supposed, was the closest she was going to get to an apology from him. It was the least of her worries. "Do you think Drusa can get through to them?"

Kyrkenall reached back into his saddlebags and pulled out flint and steel before crouching by the tinder he'd spread under the firewood. "All we can do now is hope. We only need a few of them, and if they're swayed by your offer of the skies in The Fragments, enough of them might fly there that the most vengeful will take up the fight. But I can't predict what they'll do. I'm not N'lahr. I don't win every battle."

"You've won every battle I've seen."

He paused in striking, then half looked back at her. "Have I?" He sounded surprised. "Sometimes I think I just stumble along, trying to shake out the answers rather than actually knowing what's there to find." Three quick, precise strikes set a spark into the tinder. He cupped his hands and blew on it and the flame took hold and blossomed along one of the dry bits of firewood.

She shook her head a little at the ease with which he'd accomplished his task.

He reached behind him and brought forth a wine bottle and brandished it. "I brought this in case we had something to celebrate. Like a victory. But I'm declaring it a victory that they didn't just kill us outright. I think some of them wanted to."

Elenai thought some of them still did. "Is that your favorite wine?"

"Don't worry. I brought one for me, too. This is one your father said you liked."

She advanced and knelt beside him, saw to her surprise that it was a long, slim bottle with violet liquid. And despite herself, she was touched that he'd thought ahead on her behalf. "That was decent of you. I don't think we should get drunk, though."

"Who can get drunk on a single bottle of wine?" He saw her look and then laughed. "Are you that much of a lightweight?" He handed her the bottle. "Just take a few sips then. I'm going to start work on our food."

While he cooked, she washed her hands and face and her waist, where the grit bothered her most. Her companion fixed up his favorite road meal of griddle cakes with honey, then quickly roasted two handfuls of nuts before warming up the jerky.

They ate together as dusk crept outside the cave, shadowed by night, and she was glad for the fire, for the temperature was already dropping. And the wine, well, that was a bittersweet reminder of home and her youth and of impossibly long golden evenings that had once stretched on forever.

Kyrkenall moved over to do his own washing, then returned to finish the handful of nuts, staring out past the fire.

It was impossible not to notice how very lovely he was in profile. She wondered whether he was brooding about the ko'aye, or N'lahr, or Kalandra. Or even something else. There was an awful lot he might be troubled about.

"You're staring at me."

Elenai hoped she wasn't blushing. "I was wondering what you were thinking about."

"Too many things to count," he said wearily. He slowly turned his head, the fire catching in his ebon eyes and delineating those faint differences she had only ever noticed in the brightest light. He spoke with gravity, as though he'd made a decision. "But if you must know, at that moment, I was thinking about Rialla."

"Wondering what she meant about jumping left?"

"No," he said softly. "I was thinking about how you were right. I never talk about her. And next to N'lahr, she's probably the best friend I ever had. So maybe telling you about her is overdue."

That was an unexpected surprise, one that she realized she looked forward to. Yet he sat silent for a long while, his lips pursed. Finally she decided to prompt him. "What was she like?"

That did the trick. He answered immediately. "She was quiet and driven. A little like Varama—but you don't know her, do you?"

"Not really."

"She wasn't . . . ordinary. Maybe none of us are, especially in the corps, but she was different even from us." He paused and took a swig from his own wine bottle before resuming. "For instance, she never understood rivalries. You know how naturally they crop up among squires, even when they're friendly ones. At some level we're always competing so that we'll rise to the next level. With her it wasn't even about perfecting her own abilities, although she wanted that, too. She wanted everyone and everything to be better, and never understood when other people took offense to her suggestions. Especially because she was almost always right. That constantly frustrated her. And so did most people. They were mean to her. Even people who were normally very kind. In their defense, her perfectionism could be pretty infuriating, because she never recognized it as a problem. All she knew for sure was that people didn't like her, and so she was always wary of them. And she hated to be touched." His elongated eyeteeth showed in a brief snarl. "Which is why Denaven should have known I was never sleeping with her. Once she was famous and powerful, that hastig suddenly decided he wanted her, and got jealous of me. I was just her friend. And maybe not a very good one."

"What makes you say that?"

He raised an empty hand, as if he planned to offer an example, then lowered it, saying nothing.

"She obviously cared about you a great deal," Elenai said. "She's somehow speaking from beyond to warn you of something that could kill you."

He nodded in agreement but didn't look at her.

"I thought you wanted to tell me about her."

He sighed. "I do." But for once, the archer seemed at a loss for words.

"How did you meet? I guess that's a bad question. You probably met as squires. How did you become friends?"

That seemed to be an acceptable topic for him. His mobile mouth worked silently for a moment before he answered. "You know how rough things can be in the first couple of years when you're squiring. She and I got singled out, a lot. I was sort of probationary for a while because—you'll find this funny—I had some temper issues."

"Did you?"

"I'm sure that's hard to believe. I wasn't winning any popularity contests as a squire, and I never had as a boy, either. I'm not exactly normal looking." He took another drink. "So I understood a little of what Rialla was going through better than the others. She excelled in a lot of fields but was always on the bottom rung because she wasn't very good at interacting with people. You can't be in the Altenerai if you don't know how to be part of a team, or how to read other people to lead them. Anyway, we were both regularly judged as coming up short, and promoted only grudgingly. For a while there, Kalandra was trying to drum me out of the corps."

"Kalandra was?" And yet this was the woman he was mad for?

He smiled at some memory. "I deserved it. I got N'lahr in trouble a few times, too. But you wanted to know about Rialla." He turned up his hands again, as if deciding something was irrelevant. Perhaps small details, for he summarized. "Gradually she came to realize I had her back, and that I wasn't trying to get anything out of it. I don't think the poor thing had ever had a real friend before, and she grew fiercely loyal to me. She even helped me govern my temper with some mental exercises she'd come up with. I lay some of that success at the feet of Asrahn, too, of course. Once I had the ring I learned that he had intervened several times to keep me in the corps. He'd believed that I was improving, you see. And that had a lot to do with Rialla. I figure my friendship with her must be what it's like to have a sister."

Elenai smiled at his ignorance. "My sister and I used to fight constantly."

"Did you? Well, she watched out for me. The first big thing she tried doing with hearthstones was making Lothrun. Did you know that? She took an already-fine blade and worked her magic on it. It's not as fine as Irion, of course, but that's hardly a fair comparison. And the next thing she made? Arzhun." His eyes shifted to his recurved black bow lying near his bedroll. The firelight deepened the lines with which the army of tiny figures were incised into his bow. "She made that for me in a single night, Elenai."

She sucked in a surprised breath. "I never knew that." All squires had heard how the fourth-rank Kyrkenall had bested a powerful kobalin lord in one-on-one combat, then taken his horns, the better to make his great bow. She'd assumed a master bowyer had crafted it over the course of many months.

"All discussions of hearthstone magics were declared highly secret. Which is why all you ever heard about Rialla was her one long, lonely day as an alten. Gods, the works she did just as a squire should stand higher than the deeds of many Altenerai."

"She must have liked you very much."

He nodded. "I kept pushing her. I wanted other people to understand how talented she really was. And maybe . . . maybe I wanted them to see I'd been right to have faith in her. That's what I keep coming back to. I was sure I just had her best interests in mind, but maybe I made her interests about me. Maybe I wasn't much better than Denaven. She was pretty badly messed up after she made Irion. You know about that, right?"

"N'lahr told me she'd been involved in forging it."

"Involved—aye, she was involved all right. Believe it or not, I was friendly with Denaven back then. Things had grown strained with him because Rialla and N'lahr and I had gotten promoted to his rank after disobeying an order he gave us, and then we distinguished ourselves even further. We were going to be made Altenerai and he was still stuck at sixth. I figured maybe it would be a nice gesture if Rialla could make him the next powerful weapon."

"I didn't know she made him one!"

"That's because she ended up giving it to N'lahr instead. Denaven never forgave any of us."

Elenai stared at him in stunned silence as realization dawned. "Wait— Irion was going to be Denaven's?"

"Yes. Except right at the end of forging it Rialla went into some kind of trance and foretold it would always be linked with N'lahr, who would slay Mazakan. She was getting more and more glimpses of the future. Anyway, right after she announced the prophecy she collapsed. She was breathing, but she was very weak and went in and out of consciousness. This all happened in Alantris, as the Naor were marching on the city. You can imagine that Kalandra, who was in command, wasn't real happy with any of us for jeopardizing one of our sorcerers right before the battle. Rialla started to come around, but she wasn't in good enough shape to be sworn to the ring the same day N'lahr and I were."

Elenai had the sense Kyrkenall was leading somewhere with the story, for he was growing more and more tense, but he stilled, breathing deeply. Almost like he readied for a deep dive.

"What happened with Irion wasn't your fault," she said. "Rialla must have been tapped deeply into the hearthstones—"

He cut her off. "So I got royally drunk when I got my ring, but afterward I went to see Rialla. She was still recovering in the Alantran barracks. She was frightened, probably because she was seeing stuff about the future, but I wasn't taking that seriously enough back then. I mean, she had always been so damned perceptive it was eerie, but it was weirder toward the end, and I hadn't quite gotten around to thinking of my friend as a prophetess for the ages. I just remember she was afraid she was going to die. And what use was I? She was baring her soul to me and I was so drunk I couldn't stand upright."

"What did she say?"

He struggled to answer, then spoke with quiet loathing. "She talked about what would happen to several of us but could see herself only as a 'statue in the dark.' She said other stuff, too, but I'll be damned if I can remember any of it. And believe me, I've tried. Two days later she was dead."

Elenai was suddenly aware of the silence about them. The calls of the ko'aye had died, and now there was only the crackling of the fire and wind whistling through the caves.

He seemed finally to have come to a stop, but Elenai had many questions yet. She waited a moment before asking, with respectful softness: "How did she die?"

He answered almost as quietly. "By then we knew that hearthstones were dangerous to use in battle, so we had her using one pretty far back behind our lines. She was altering terrain through the course of the battle. Kalandra had even had the foresight to have a half-dozen weavers protecting Rialla because she'd have to project her energy far from her body. It wasn't enough. Dozens of Naor mages and their students sacrificed themselves to kill her and her protectors. Denaven was one of them. He said no matter what he tried, he couldn't get Rialla back. I think I believe him. Maybe it was the last time I saw honest emotion on his smug face. He thought he was in love with her."

His fists clenched and unclenched once more as he continued. "She was still alive after the battle. She was breathing, but her spirit was gone. I kept hoping maybe she'd make it back, somehow, but . . . a few hours after nightfall she stopped breathing." He grew very quiet, and he had to fight to get the words out as he choked up. "I was holding her hand when I felt her go."

She scooted closer and took his hand in hers. He gripped it tight. He closed his eyes as he fought to control his emotions.

As he turned to meet her gaze she felt her pulse rise. He drew no closer, and his expression seemed neutral. But there was a tension between them, one begging for resolution. Suddenly she wanted, more than anything else, to feel his lips against hers, to press the warmth of his body against her own. He said nothing, but their eyes locked, and she sensed that he wanted the same.

But he released her hand and turned to the fire. "I might have managed better. And now I'm wondering if there's something better I could be doing for Kalandra."

Kalandra, the other missing woman. The one who always seemed to lie between them. She knew Kyrkenall had taken other lovers in the years since Kalandra's disappearance and found herself wondering in irritation why she wasn't good enough.

"There's something between us," the archer admitted, briefly looking up to meet her eyes. "But haven't I screwed up enough relationships already?"

"Shouldn't I help you decide that?"

"Maybe so. But I'm in love with Kalandra. You know that. And just as soon as we get this all settled, I'm going to go find her. You and I can pretend that there's not going to be anything complicated if we bed down, but hopes and realities are two different things."

"You're probably right," she heard herself say. The thought he desired her as well was a pleasant salve to her disappointment. Besides, being involved with Kyrkenall would probably be a terrible idea, and it was the wrong time in her cycle, even if she did have the right herbs.

"Let's turn in, Alten," he said.

As she lay there, her own rationale was fully restored, and she grew wryly amused that Kyrkenall, of all people, had the right of it. As the fire died, she found herself wondering more about how exactly N'lahr and Kyrkenall had become friends, and how Kalandra had gone from wanting to kick Kyrkenall from the corps to falling in love with him. But those were questions for another time, and there were more important things to worry about.

And then, late in the night, Rialla visited her once more.

15

Counsel from the Dead

Elenai sat at a dream fire contemplating an arcing strand of stars scattered across the firmament. Suddenly Rialla was there, stunningly real in her khalat and worn black boots, her high forehead damp with perspiration. Elenai understood, as she had the last time, that all else but the visiting woman was dream.

Rialla's stare pierced her like a sword thrust. And here she'd thought

Kyrkenall's eyes disquieting. No one she'd ever met had a gaze as disconcerting as this. "Have we spoken yet?" Rialla asked.

Elenai had worried that she'd be asked that again, and had prepared an answer. "We've spoken before. In the theater."

Rialla's nod was so small she almost missed seeing it.

Elenai spoke quickly. "I told him he had to go left. But we didn't understand. What did you mean? And are you dead?"

"Probably I am." She didn't sound concerned about it. "Kyrkenall will have to drop, one day soon, upon the flight of the queen. It has to be to the left. It won't look right. But tell him to trust me."

"He trusted you when you were alive. He can scarce talk about you because he misses you so much."

"He is my friend," Rialla said simply. The word "friend" carried more weight and meaning than it did if used in the waking world, conveying the great significance of Rialla's interpretation of the word. It was as if all others were shadows and he alone was real to her. "He will die if he goes right. I don't want him to die," she added. "Right looks better, but it must be left."

"I've told him. I'll warn him again. What did you mean about the world ending?"

"The queen thinks she can control what she's doing. But she won't be able to do so. And if all isn't in exactly the right place, Kyrkenall, N'lahr, you, Naor, kobalin, everything, the world will cease. I've seen it again and again." She sounded now as though she were talking to herself. "All the pieces have to be in the proper places or it doesn't come out right. After the queen opens the last hearthstone, everything is—"

The dream world rocked and faded and she heard her name called from somewhere far off. She tightened her eyes and fought to hold to the fading dream. "Wait!" Elenai cried. "Is there any more you can tell us?"

Rialla shook her head dismissively. "I've little time left."

That in itself was a strange statement—presumably if she was dead, she wouldn't have to worry about time, would she? But if there was little time for either of them, then she should make it count. "Do you know where Kalandra is?"

"If you're where I think you are, right now she's in the stone on the shelf."

And with that answer in her mind, Elenai blinked and woke to the morning. Kyrkenall was shaking her shoulder. "You're a deep sleeper," he said with a grumble.

"Rialla was there." She couldn't keep the snap from her voice as she rose.

He froze. "You're joking. No, you're not." He cursed. "What did she say?"

Outside all was gloom, for true day had not yet arrived in the cave. She heard, faintly, the cries of the ko'aye on the wind.

"She says there will be a time, soon, when it will look like you need to jump to the right, and that's when you should jump left, that otherwise you won't live. Something about being 'upon the flight of the queen.'" She raked hands through her hair and pushed it back, feeling on the floor for her hair tie. "She was telling me more about Kalandra when you woke me."

"Gods. I'm sorry."

She didn't point out that he was mentioning the gods he didn't believe in.

"So does that mean Kalandra's alive?" he asked.

"She's in a stone on a shelf, whatever that means. I assume a hearthstone. She also told me that the queen's going to try to open the hearthstones and it will destroy us all. Oh, and she thinks she's dead, but she said she couldn't talk further because she's running low on time. Which I don't understand at all. And that's all I know. Because you woke me."

Again he cursed, sitting back in quiet contemplation as she finished with her hair. She wanted to ask where he'd relieved himself, because she smelled nothing within the cave confines and wasn't sure where she should freshen up herself, but seeing the confused look on his face, she decided she could hold off finding out for the nonce.

"Do you think that means Kalandra is in a hearthstone, like N'lahr was? That she got trapped by Denaven, too?"

"That might explain why she hasn't contacted anyone."

"So maybe Denaven had her hidden somewhere."

The more she considered that, the less sure she became. "But from what N'lahr said, him getting trapped was an accident."

"Maybe that accident taught them how to do it deliberately."

"Then why didn't they try to catch you that way, or us?"

"Maybe we weren't important enough. I don't suppose Rialla said anything about where this shelf was?"

"She might have if she'd had more time. Look, it's not that I'm not interested in Kalandra, but shouldn't we be more worried about the world getting wiped away?"

"Sure. Let's worry about that," Kyrkenall said coolly. "Any idea how to stop it?"

"It starts when the queen opens the last hearthstone."

"And when will that happen?"

"Sometime soon, I guess." Elenai sighed. "I just don't know enough. If you hadn't woken me—"

"I said I was sorry. Hey— Do you think the reason she's contacting you is because you have her hearthstone?"

"I've wondered about that. Maybe it's because I'm with you, though."

"But maybe a little bit of her is in the hearthstone, somehow. You could try contacting her."

Elenai started to say that she didn't think it worked like that, but what did she know, really, about how the hearthstones worked? "It's certainly worth a try," she admitted. "Maybe I ought to first try to check in with N'lahr. To make sure he's not a frozen statue."

"Assuming that contacting him again won't turn him into one, you mean?"

"Assuming that, yes."

"Why don't you wait until we have something definite to report. If he's still frozen, what can you do? And if he isn't, then you'd be wasting time, because we might have better news to give him a little later."

"All right," she said. Better to not risk contact with him unless it was absolutely necessary, given what had happened last time.

After her morning prayers, they wolfed down a meager breakfast and hurried away, finding a secluded copse of trees to finish their morning routines. The sky had brightened, though the sun was hidden somewhere beyond the cliffs. Overhead, the ko'aye streamed past in knots of ten or more. As the Altenerai neared their horses, a trio of the winged predators watched from on high. With the shadows long and the sun behind them, Elenai couldn't be certain which ones they were. None, however, flew down to speak with them, which explained Kyrkenall's frown.

"I keep thinking that Drusa will report in," he said as they strode on, saddlebags over their shoulders. "It wouldn't be like her to let us leave without saying farewell. Unless last night counted as farewell."

"Maybe she's still convincing them."

Kyrkenall was feeling more pessimistic. "Or maybe they're flying out for the morning hunt and are done with us."

Ortok was where they'd left him at a little hill nestled against a cliffside. The horses were picketed still, munching on the grass while keeping a wary eye on the large hunters swooping overhead. Their ears flicked nervously.

The kobalin looked up from brushing his horse and raised a furry hand in greeting. "Good morning, Altenerai companions. Did the Gods send you messages?"

"Rialla sent us a message," Kyrkenall said. "I just hope she sends more. How about you?"

"I dreamt that I had named this horse, and that I called him Steady-foot, and you praised me for that."

It sounded a ludicrous name to Elenai, but Kyrkenall apparently de-cided against teasing the kobalin. He nodded. "Good enough. You should name the things you value. You'll have to use his name when you're ask-ing him things to do if you want him to know it."

Ortok nodded. "I've seen you do that with your Lyria. I thought deeply on your words, and I resolved to value him as you value yours, for the matter is no longer strange to me."

Kyrkenall clapped one of his massive shoulders.

The kobalin lowered the brush from the white horse now known as Steadyfoot. "Why do you touch me?"

"I meant . . ." Kyrkenall put his hands on his hips. "It's a sign of affec-tion, Ortok. I guess we're becoming friends."

"Are we?"

"Aren't we?" Kyrkenall asked.

Ortok crouched to set the brush into a saddlebag, then scratched his furry chest. "How do you know? Do we shake hands?"

"If you like," Kyrkenall said with a faint smile.

"I did this with N'lahr, but there were words. I don't remember them. Tell me what it is again to be a friend among you."

"It means," Elenai piped in, "that we watch out for each other. That we keep others from trying to do our friends harm, that we share and struggle together. Maybe it means we're a little more patient when we annoy each other, and we listen and try to help when our friends feel poorly."

"It sounds a lot to remember," Ortok said, "although we do some of these things already."

"It is a responsibility," Kyrkenall said gravely. "Maybe some people don't take it as seriously as they should. I like that you do. It speaks well to you being a good friend."

Elenai was perplexed a little by Kyrkenall, especially considering the views he'd espoused about kobalin just a few days earlier. He seemed to change his opinions as the mood struck him. In this instance, at least, she approved, and liked it when Ortok thrust his hand out fully and he and Kyrkenall clasped arms.

"Elenai, too, I think is my friend," Ortok said. "If she agrees."

"I'd be honored," Elenai said, and she found that the powerful arm and its large hand were surprisingly gentle as they enveloped her tiny ones.

"Friends," Ortok said, and Elenai repeated the word. "It's good to have friends," Ortok decided. "I missed the cooking of your little cakes this morning, small archer. If we are friends you must share them always."

"Every morning we travel, if you'd like."

"Will you cook now?"

"Now we need to get moving, I'm afraid. I . . ." Kyrkenall fell silent as a winged form circled down toward the bottom of the hill.

"Pardon me." Kyrkenall hurried down the slope. Elenai nodded to the kobalin and then went after, arriving as Drusa landed gracefully upon her haunches and sat, not bothering to fold her wings.

Kyrkenall paused at the foot of the little hill and bowed at the same time the wind hit the grass, so that they genuflected together. Elenai was just behind him and a moment later in the bow as well.

Drusa inclined her head. Her neck scar was more prominent in the light. "I come to bid you farewell, Kyrkenall."

"Did you talk with the others?"

"I did. There's much talk. Some wish to return to our homelands, some to The Fragments. Others are more cautious. And so we are sending a group to look over the lands. We also want to see these large ko'aye. Some of us remember our reasons to redden our claws upon the Naor."

Elenai felt a thrill of hope, but said nothing, waiting instead for Drusa to finish.

"I will fly with those going to your lands. If I see N'lahr, it may be that we will speak."

"Please do," Kyrkenall said. "If we work together, it will be worse for the Naor."

Drusa let loose with that warbling sound Elenai thought might be laughter. "So Kalandra said! Do you come now, too, to slay Naor?"

"Yes. My greatest pleasure would be to hunt them with you."

"It may be that day will come," Drusa said. "Some of my friends wondered if you would go pray to the Altenerai god, since it is so close."

"The Altenerai god?" Elenai asked.

Drusa cocked her head as they looked back at her in puzzlement. "Are you confused? Do I use the wrong word?"

Kyrkenall's confusion was obvious from his tone. "What are you talking about?"

"There's a barren place in the shifts that the kobalin say is holy. They say an Altenerai god dwells there. Your kobalin should know."

"I'm not sure Ortok does," Kyrkenall said. "He's been away from his people."

Elenai had a sudden memory. "Kyrkenall, do you remember what Qirok said? That if we arrived at the place where the war god dwells we'd gone past the ko'aye lands?"

Kyrkenall nodded. "But that still doesn't make sense. What god are they talking about? Have you been there, Drusa?"

"I speak rarely to the kobalin, for they have nothing important to say. I have flown over the place and seen only bones. But they say there is a god there, and kobalin claim it as a holy place."

"We don't have a god of the Altenerai," Kyrkenall's voice all but shook with excitement.

Not unless you counted Queen Altenera, who had founded the corps. It was just possible that the reverence they gave her could be interpreted by some as worship. But her remains were interred in a crypt on Cemetery Ridge, overlooking Darassus.

Kyrkenall's eyes were bright with hope. "It could be one of the Altenerai," he said. "Maybe a powerful sorceress!"

To Elenai it seemed he leapt to conclusions, but she supposed it was just possible Kalandra was there, trapped in a stone.

"You seem agitated, Kyrkenall," Drusa said. "I didn't mean to upset you."

Ortok had left the horses and was climbing down to join their conversation circle.

"How do I get there?" Kyrkenall asked.

"Go in that direction," Drusa said with a jerk of her head. "I do not know how long to tell you it will take, on your beasts. You will know when you are close because you will see the signs of a kobalin holy place. Rock made into piles." Her eyes narrowed suspiciously as Ortok stopped at Kyrkenall's side.

"Oh, that is a bad idea," Ortok said. "Going to a kobalin holy place invites death."

"It's the war god place Qirok's band was talking about," Kyrkenall said. "Do you know anything about it?"

Ortok shook his head. "Only where it lies, from what Qirok said. But I have never seen it."

"Then that means it became holy while you were on guard, doesn't it? And that means that it almost has to be Kalandra!"

"Going to a holy place is bad," Ortok said. "If you travel there, you will die."

"Why?" Elenai asked.

"Kobalin guard their holy places," he explained. "Even if you think the priests are absent, they know you are there. They kill those not given permission."

Kyrkenall fixed Drusa with an intense stare, and his voice held a hard edge. "How do I find it?"

"You sound wrong, Kyrkenall."

"I must find her, Drusa. You must understand how important that would be."

"I don't think you'll find Kalandra," she answered. "But I will tell you. It's a small fragment past the one we call Kleeshkret, which is a tiny piece with some fruit trees and an orange water area shaped like a youngling's open mouth. There are many little islands near here, but this one is rich with old magics."

"Ortok will guide me."

"If the kobalin says it's dangerous, it probably is." She fixed him with unwinking eyes. "It's a terrible thing to be separated from your mate. If mine were trapped there, I would seek him, so I wish you good fortune." She dipped her head.

Kyrkenall returned the gesture. "Thank you," he said.

Drusa flapped her wings and walked past them into the long grass on a rise, then leapt into the air and soared off.

Kyrkenall spoke to them quietly as he watched her rise. "I know what you're thinking."

Elenai wondered if he did. "Drusa all but promised us at least some of the ko'aye were going to go fight the Naor. We need to get back to N'lahr."

Kyrkenall shook his head. "No. You can go. I swore that the next time I had to choose between Kalandra and the mission I was choosing her."

Probably N'lahr himself wouldn't be able to change his mind this time, even if she decided to risk contact.

"I'm so close now." There was a pleading note in his voice.

It seemed to her that he assumed too much. "How far is it, Ortok?" she asked.

"If Qirok was right, it may be four sleeps."

That was too long. Couldn't Kyrkenall see that? "If we go to this place, we'll arrive too late for the battle. And whatever this is, it's probably not her."

The archer looked at Elenai as though she were foolish. "Do you think the war will end with one battle? If it is Kalandra, we'll have another ally, a powerful one. And we're so close." Seeing the doubt in her eyes, his expression hardened. "I'm going." He faced Ortok. "Can you guide me?"

"I can do that." Ortok turned his furry head. "But what of Elenai? Do friends leave friends behind?"

"Damnit, Elenai," Kyrkenall said. "Don't get between me and—"

"I'm going with you!" she shouted.

"You are?"

"Because the last thing we need is one more lost alten," she said bitterly. "I mean you," she added, in case it wasn't clear. "If you hit a big storm out here you're probably done for."

He might have countered that he had survived them in the past, but he bowed his head in acknowledgment, or thanks, or both.

She started to remind him that N'lahr needed him. That the people of The Fragments needed him. But then she thought once more of all the sacrifices he had made through the years, and the uncounted times he had risked himself for the safety of the realms, and she couldn't find it in her to object anymore. "Enough of this," she said. "Let's get under way."

16

The Next Ride

Rylin came instantly awake. There was no half-fogged state where he swam slowly up to consciousness, or where the waking world was an incessant clamor that drowned out the sound of dreams. His eyes were open and staring at a sloped brown canvas ceiling overhead. A tent. As Rylin sorted through memories for some clue about his location, disjointed images presented themselves. Frantic strangers hunching over him as he tried to speak, two of them women in Alantran head scarves.

Alten Enada peering at him, her round, high-cheekboned face grave. Lasren holding the mouth of a wineskin to his lips, more somber than he'd ever seen. Were any of those real, or were they dreams?

Real. He sat up and winced at a twinge through his midriff. Right. He'd been stabbed solidly. Dreading what he might see, he rolled up the stained white shirt he was wearing—too long to be his—and found a long pink scar along his chest. Unless he'd been out for a very long time, healing magic had been used on him. It would have had to have been.

Come to think of it, there'd been other wounds, and he pulled his shirt to one side and looked at his left upper arm. There wasn't even a scar there. He guessed the weavers had had an easier time with that injury.

From outside he heard voices speaking indistinctly, as if from farther away. There was the smell of horses and grass, and manure, which meant the horses snorting must be picketed unless he's been moved to some village far from where he fell. With a flash he remembered Rurudan's scream as the noble beast had dropped beneath him, and he sighed in despair. It was too much to hope that his horse, too, had somehow survived.

Even as he mourned his favorite mount, the scent of roasting fowl reached him, and his mouth watered without him having any choice in the matter. He ignored the pang from his chest and got moving. His legs shook, but he managed to rise, ducking his head just a little lest he strike it on the canvas narrowing to a point overhead. He made his way to the tent opening on bare feet.

Pushing the flap aside and away from the pole, he looked out on a camp built along a gentle slope. The sky was blue and clear. A breeze caressed the height of grasses without appreciably cooling the warm afternoon air. A field of bedrolls was spread out before him, interspersed with the occasional tent. In the distance, a dozen mounted cavalry rode away. Closer at hand, a number of men wearing baggy pants and loose-sleeved shirts mucked out the long makeshift corral where dozens of horses grazed. Kaneshi, from their clothing and clipped facial hair.

Where was this, and how long had he been out? And what about the city of Alantris? Was he even still in The Fragments? The rolling ground and nearby mountains told him the answer to the last question was yes.

And where was the food? As he peered into the sunlight he ran a hand back through his hair, for the first time wondering how he looked, and then touched the side of his face and found beard stubble.

"Rylin!" said a familiar voice from his right.

It was Lasren, limping toward him in muddy boots. A helmet with a stiff horsehair crest was tucked under one broad arm, and his thinning black hair was swept back from his widow's peak.

Lasren looked at him as though he were seeing a ghost. "I wasn't sure you were ever going to come out of it."

"It's good to see you." Rylin discovered his voice was weak. At least, he thought it was good to see him. Might Lasren be in league with Denaven? If so, Rylin was in no shape to challenge his friend. "Why are you limping? What happened to the Alantrans I was escorting?"

"The Alantrans are fine. I got injured in a fight with a kobalin lord."

"A kobalin lord?" It sounded as though Lasren had encountered his own series of surprises. "What happened?"

"Now that's a story." Lasren paused as if to consider how best to tell it. "Wait a moment." He stepped over to one of the nearby Kaneshi, who was staring. Rylin didn't hear what his friend told him, but the man thrust his pitchfork into the ground and hurried off.

Rylin tensed, wary of Lasren's aims. "What's that about?"

"The commander wanted to be notified the moment you woke up. I'm glad to see you moving. You're a hero now, you know. I go to cover myself in fame and glory, and by the time I see you again you're a living legend!"

He'd never heard Lasren talk quite like this before. "Commander Denaven?" Rylin suggested warily.

"No, Denaven's dead," Lasren said. "It turns out Kyrkenall was innocent. The kobalin was helping protect him, which is how I got hurt."

With that reassurance, Rylin wanted a better sense of what was going on around him. Though he was curious to hear more about Lasren and the kobalin, he was more worried about Varama. "What's happening in Alantris?"

"The Naor are still there. But thanks to the Kaneshi we've got them trapped inside. At night we light extra campfires so they think we've got a much larger army."

"Aren't you in danger from the Naor cavalry?"

"Not anymore. They got crushed between the Kaneshi and a troop of Alantran horse that stayed outside the walls. The Naor haven't dared leave the city again."

The Naor had never been accomplished horse warriors, probably because their own lands tended toward the rocky and steep.

"Those were Alantrans who attacked me, weren't they?" Rylin asked. "With some squires."

"Right. They were sure upset when the 'prisoners' you were escorting started attacking them after you got hurt. And that poor squire who stabbed you is going to be pretty pleased you're finally up. A couple of times over the last few days I think he was close to slitting his own throat."

"I was in disguise," Rylin said. He'd set his ring shining, but in the heat of combat mistakes were simple to make.

"Ah, he'll be fine now," Lasren said, brushing the topic away with a wave. "And boy do the Alantrans love you! Three of their healers completely drained themselves working you over, and one of them is still recovering from it. You were this close to galloping off."

"I owe them my thanks. What about Varama and the squires inside? Any word from them?"

"A little. She's still in there. Apparently the ugly weirdo's running the Naor ragged."

Rylin snarled. "Don't call her that."

Lasren smirked.

"I mean it."

"Sure." Lasren grinned cockily. "You been pounding her or something?"

Cold fury seized him. His hand shot out and grabbed the front of his friend's khalat. Lasren stumbled forward in mute surprise. Rylin's voice shook with rage. "She's worth ten of you, you stupid hastig. You shut your damn mouth!"

Lasren's eyes widened and searched his own, as if seeing something unfamiliar there. Finally, he looked away.

It took Rylin a moment to relax. He lowered his hand and dropped it to his side, flexing his fingers. He felt a little faint as he stepped back.

"I didn't mean anything by it," Lasren said softly.

"An alten should always mean what he says." Rylin's voice was a tense whisper.

Troubled silence lingered for a long moment, and then Lasren spoke on with false cheer. "She managed to kill a bunch of their dragons. We've only ever seen one moving around, and it never flies very far."

Of course Varama had found a way to get to the dragons. He wondered what else she was doing, and wished he was in there helping her, instead of outside listening to Lasren's juvenile ramblings.

"You know, they've even given you a nickname. Well, they're using several, really."

"Who are 'they'?" Rylin asked with only mild interest.

"The Alantrans. Sometimes it's 'Rylin the Valiant' or 'Rylin the Wily' but the one I hear most often is 'Rylin of the Thousand.' I think that's the one that's going to stick. By all accounts you probably saved more than thirteen hundred people, but I guess it gets the point across. It's a pretty good moniker, especially since it's the people you saved who came up with it. Oh, and Elenai's got a sobriquet, too, now. Elenai Oddsbreaker."

Rylin repeated the last under his breath and then shot his friend a searching look.

"She got promoted to the ring. So she's fair game now."

So Elenai got promoted and all Lasren could think about was how that made her a potential bedmate? Rylin had thought him occasionally tiresome before, but shook his head that he would ever have found that kind of chatter amusing. Still, it was nice to hear Elenai had come through, and risen to her potential. Isn't that what Varama had said about him? That he was rising to it?

Suddenly weak, Rylin had to steady himself against the tent pole.

"You look like you're about to collapse. Come on. Sit down."

That sounded a fine idea, so Rylin returned to his tent, conscious now of the smell of sickness. He must have been sweating out a fever.

Inside there was nothing but the bedroll and a bundle of clothes spread over a blanket behind it. There was just enough room for him and Lasren, if they sat on well-pressed grass blades. Apparently he or others had been sitting there a lot recently.

Rylin gratefully drank, a little pleased it was water his friend offered. As weak as he felt, he was pretty sure even a couple of swigs of wine would leave him tipsy. The whole time, Lasren watched him as though he were a rare animal seldom glimpsed in the wild.

"Stop looking at me like that. How long have I been out?"

"Six days."

That was a long time. "And how large is this camp?"

"Not as large as might be nice, but we have about a thousand Kaneshi, some Alantran horsemen, and some advance scouts from Vedessus. The commander and I rode in with them. More are on their way, along with some infantry."

"Vedessus—" Rylin remembered that the Naor had planned to attack it next. "Did the Naor move against Vedessus?"

Lasren laughed. "Aye. And they got themselves killed, along with Mazakan himself."

"Mazakan's dead?" He could scarce credit it. "I thought only Irion could do that."

"Irion did."

"Who was wielding it?"

Lasren's broad, handsome face brightened in a grin. "Funny you should ask."

A trumpet blared outside. It was a call for assembly.

Lasren held up a hand. "I should check on that."

"I'm coming, too." Rylin started to rise with his friend.

"No—get dressed. I'll be right back."

Lasren stooped and hurried from the tent. Rylin frowned after him, jealous of his friend's health. It was only as he looked down that he realized he might not have been as self aware as he'd first assumed. He had only a loincloth under the long shirt.

He rooted through the bundle of clothing, discovering it was his own, for the most part, and laundered. The shirt was different, blue, but proved a decent fit.

By the time Lasren returned, Rylin had poured water from his friend's waterskin to scrub his face, and then donned clothes, stifling most of his groans at the occasional discomfort. He'd also shaken out the blankets and rolled them, and opened the flap to air out the tent.

"You look almost human now," Lasren told him.

Rylin was in little mood for jokes. "Is there a problem out there?"

"No. Just another patrol going out."

"Who's the new commander, anyway?"

A smile lit his friend's features.

"Why are you grinning?"

"Because you won't believe me."

He tried to keep irritation from his voice. "It isn't Kyrkenall, is it?"

"Better."

"You look awfully pleased with yourself. Is it Gyldara?"

"No."

It didn't seem like he'd get it out of Lasren, and he didn't feel like playing games. "Fine."

Lasren still worked to overcome the strained air between them. "Hey, I got to see Enada riding down the Naor. She's a little crazy, but she sure knows what she's doing. I think the Naor may actually be afraid of her, and I didn't think they were afraid of anyone but N'lahr."

"They're still afraid of him," Rylin said. He hadn't missed Lasren struggling to recapture the ease of their old friendship, and he worked to share something the way he might have in the past. It just didn't feel as imortant as it might once have. "I captured a Naor scout, and when I told him I was N'lahr, he nearly crapped his armor. I guess they don't know what he looks like. Later on, at the site of a fight I had with the Naor, I wrote N'lahr's name out in the blood of the dead."

Lasren's laugh was only a little forced. "You're kidding. So they think he's inside the city?"

"They certainly think he's alive. One of the Naor officers claims to have seen him. None of the upper-ranked officers believed her, but I think a lot of the soldiers do. They're so afraid of N'lahr they practically jump at even the mention of his name."

Lasren grinned as a shadow fell just outside the tent. "You have no idea."

As the flap opened, Lasren had a clear view of whoever was out there and hurried to his feet, crouching so as not to hit his head, but saluting as he did so.

"As you were," said a cool voice, and a tall figure in an Altenerai khalat ducked his head and moved under the canvas.

It took a moment for Rylin to understand just who he was looking at, and even then, his jaw dropped. Then he realized it had to be Varama playing a trick with her semblance, and he grinned. Somehow she'd gotten out of the city. "Nice one, Varama."

The N'lahr image she was wearing was far more realistic than Rylin himself might have dreamed up, owing of course to the fact Varama had spent far more time around him. Rylin had met the great general only a few instances as a young squire.

Lasren was unable to hide a snort of astonished laughter.

Varama answered shortly. "I'm not Varama."

"Well, you're not N'lahr," Rylin countered. It wasn't like her to play a trick, but she had long since proved herself unpredictable.

"He is," Lasren said from behind Varama's shoulder.

"I am," said the image, with the hint of a smile.

Rylin stared. In his experience watching Varama wear semblances she inevitably revealed herself, particularly in the way she used her eyes, which never seemed to be entirely focused on the here and now. Either she had been practicing, or someone else was wearing the semblance.

"I'm impressed," Rylin said, "whoever you are. Is this going to be used to frighten the Naor?" He was surprised he hadn't thought of it himself before now.

"Alten Rylin, my death was faked. I was the queen's prisoner in the north. What you see is neither jest nor disguise." The voice was serious but a slight smile played about his eyes.

Only then did the possibility he was looking at the real man reach him. Yes, he'd seen that the body in N'lahr's tomb was a fake, but he was so used to thinking of N'lahr as dead he'd naturally assumed the man continued to be. Especially after Rylin's own recent experiences with impersonation. "Sir?" He put his hand out to help himself rise to attention.

"No." N'lahr, if that's who he really was, sat down across from him on the grass.

Rylin looked over to Lasren.

"It's true, Rylin." His friend was still grinning. "This is no joke. That's him."

Rylin studied the narrow face with the black eyes and pointed chin. He'd never expected to look on it again, alive. Somehow he managed to say something that wasn't entirely bereft of worth. "It's a pleasure to see you again, sir."

"And it's a pleasure to meet you as an alten. The last time we talked you were a third ranker, in Kanesh."

"Yes, sir." He smiled that N'lahr would remember that. He'd been grooming the horses and N'lahr had stopped to ask him how he was faring.

"Are you hungry?" the general asked. "Thirsty?"

"Both, sir." He answered in a daze, still staring.

"Lasren—"

"I'll take care of it, Commander." Lasren put his hand on the tent flap and looked back to his friend. "Sorry, Rylin. I was so happy to see you—I should have made sure you were comfortable . . . anyway, I'll get you something." He limped quickly out of the tent. Rylin heard his booted feet pushing through the grass.

Rylin turned his attention back to the man who should have been dead, gazing in amazement.

"I've been getting that a lot," N'lahr said, with amused exasperation. He calmly uncapped his wineskin and handed it across.

The cool wine was wonderful on his throat. So much for going easy on it. Somehow the wine seemed more necessary in light of the stunning surprise before him. He lowered the skin and returned it. "Thank you, sir. I still can't believe I'm not dreaming. You're a legend. Returned in our hour of need."

"I don't need hero worship. Least of all from you. I need information."

"Yes, sir." Rylin struggled to compose his thoughts. He kept thinking of the dead, like finding Aradel all but drained of blood. He didn't think he was lost in memory for long, but he discovered N'lahr watching him.

The commander was famed for his cool detachment, but when N'lahr spoke, he sounded as if he knew where Rylin had been for the long, last moment. "You can never do as much as you want, can you?"

"No."

"If you've given your all, you have to leave your regrets behind. You've earned the right to let them go."

He nodded, and pulled himself together. He'd gained a lot of important information. He hadn't expected to report it to N'lahr, but that didn't matter. "I discovered a lot, Commander."

N'lahr nodded once. "Go ahead."

Rylin proceeded to tell him all that he'd learned about the Naor officers, the disposition of the troops, and the changes to the city. The general listened intently. He sensed that much of what he said might have been conveyed by some of the squires that had helped escort the Alantrans from Alantris, and other information might be out-of-date, but N'lahr interrupted only occasionally, to request additional details. This reminded him of Varama, in a way, except that N'lahr's intensity couldn't match hers. Even though her questioning sometimes felt like an assault, he knew a sudden pang at the thought of her.

Lasren eventually returned with a platter of dried meat and fruits and some unleavened bread. N'lahr paused in his queries as Rylin started on the food, and then a squire turned up with a request for N'lahr to consult with Enada. N'lahr relayed that he'd be there shortly, and the squire departed.

"I have lots of questions . . ." Rylin said, then faltered. "But I don't want to waste your time."

"If it were vital we'd have heard trumpets. Go ahead."

Rylin hesitated. He imagined a source other than the head of their forces could catch him up on much of it, but there was so much he wanted to know. "What happened to Elenai and Kyrkenall?"

At that, N'lahr actually smiled. "They're both fine. Alten Elenai acquitted herself well and has been awarded the ring. She's on assignment with Kyrkenall right now. She has proven a deft hand with the hearthstones."

"And Commander Denaven's dead?"

"Elenai killed Denaven in a duel."

That seemed only a step lower in credibility than learning N'lahr was still alive. "Elenai did?"

"Yes."

That surpassed all his expectations. He shook his head. "Were there other traitors?"

N'lahr's smile faded. "Not that we know of. Belahn had been deceived into working with them. Cerai, Denaven, K'narr, and Cargen appear to be the only ones. Though four are bad enough. Cerai is especially dangerous."

"Yes, she is." Rylin frowned. "If not for Cerai, the city might have held. She's got a lot to answer for."

"And she will. Later. Right now we must focus on the Naor."

"And the queen, right? Why did she imprison you, and why did Denaven hide the sword?"

"She needed me out of the way to broker an agreement with the Naor about the hearthstones. She wanted their supply. We believe her intention was to subdue me, but the process went awry and the sword was trapped with me in a kind of hearthstone prison. Since the sword couldn't be extricated, a duplicate was hung in the hall, complete with a glamor so it radiated magic."

"So Asrahn noticed it was a fake and they killed him before he could start asking questions." Rylin shook his head in disgust.

"Yes," N'lahr said darkly.

"Are you going to be able to retake Alantris?"

"I'm working on it. But now, I need eyes and ears in Darassus. Someone who can think on his feet and take measured risks and get out alive. I'm sending you."

"Me?"

He must have seen Rylin's doubt, because he explained his reasoning. "Your own report, and those of your squires, provides me with all the assurance I require. You impersonated not just one, but a series of enemy officers, then passed yourself off as one of their staff to attend an enemy meeting, where you learned information you were able to pass on to Varama. You killed two of the men most vital to the maintenance of the dragons. You left the city with more than a thousand men, women, and children who were destined for slave labor and worse. If you can accomplish that among our enemies, then infiltrating a city you know well should be much simpler."

"I don't think it will be simple."

"No. It won't," N'lahr agreed.

"I got lucky," he confessed.

"Sometimes the difference between success and failure lies in knowing when to improvise, and judging when to press your luck. What do you think of Lasren?"

He answered without thinking. "He's my best friend. Well. He used to be."

"We need every alten on the front lines. But I'm loath to send you into Darassus alone. You have to be able to trust whoever I send with you."

Rylin thought about all the spontaneous decisions he'd had to make while in disguise in Alantris, and how often he'd have been handicapped in companionship with another person. And then he thought about Lasren, bluff, hearty, and loud. And capable, Rylin admitted, even through his doubt. He might rise to the occasion. There was no question that Rylin would be safer with Lasren at his side in a direct battle. But moving around behind enemy lines? "I trust him. He's just not very subtle."

"I have you for the subtlety. He's a brave, committed warrior. Are you familiar with the squire Elik?"

He nodded in approval at the thought of the curly-headed, pale-eyed fifth ranker. "He's good." Because of their skill, and intelligence, Elik and Elenai had been two of his favorite squires, but unfortunately he and Varama hadn't been able to find Elik prior to their departure from Darassus. "Why do you ask?"

"He was sent here from Darassus with a small number of reinforcements. He has the most up-to-date details about the city and the standing of various people. If you think he's trustworthy, I'll send him with you."

Rylin nodded. In some ways he considered Elik more dependable than Lasren. "I'll take him. I don't suppose there are any hearthstones?" His mind was already shifting to how he might best run a scouting mission against the capital, and a semblance would be a tremendous asset. He might not have been recognized in Alantris without a khalat, but he was a familiar sight in Darassus.

"Elenai sent most of those we'd recovered along with us. In case some of our weavers could use them before the battle. I don't encourage taking one into Darassus with you. It will make you much easier to find."

"I won't. But I need one to repair a tool Varama made."

"I'll make it available." He eyed him. "In addition to seeking intelligence, I need you to escort the new Alantran governor to the chambers of the Darassan Council. Her testimony about what she witnessed and what she's learned will hold more weight than yours, especially since you've been accused of treachery."

Rylin remembered that Feolia had planned to leave with the refugees for a mountain village, but perhaps she had joined N'lahr's camp.

"Lasren can still freely walk the streets without fear, because he was sent forth with Denaven. He can talk to the councilors about what Denaven actually did. All of this information may be enough to begin a formal inquiry, but the queen is likely to resist, strenuously. And she has the unquestioned backing of the Mage Auxiliary."

"Do you have specific instructions about what you want me to look for?"

"I want you to find out what they're doing with the hearthstones. That is of paramount importance, Rylin." Those dark eyes seemed lit with fury, though the commander's voice changed little. "All the evils she's done owe to her absorption with these hearthstones. She's planning something she is willing to kill for, presumably something that should be stopped."

Rylin nodded acknowledgment.

"All else I leave to your discretion. If you see an opportunity, grasp it. Remember: We need the realms primed to unite against this new Naor invasion. The queen's unlikely to be concerned with that and probably minimizes the threat in her official speech and actions. You may take appropriate steps to remove her, lest she do more terrible damage."

"Appropriate steps?" A chill that had nothing to do with fever spread slowly through him.

"Legal avenues are vastly preferential, Rylin, to ensure the legitimacy of her successors. But consider that if you follow only the writ of law, you might lose the option for both justice and beneficence."

Mind versus heart. He knew the old arguments, for they'd been drilled into him. Seek the truth. Correct wrongs. Harm none if you can. Protect the innocent. Always, first and foremost, protect the innocent. Still. He had to say it out loud to make perfectly clear he understood. "To protect the people I may need to destroy their leader."

"In this case. Yes."

17

Koregan's Fall

Once again Vannek found himself beside the speaking stand in the morning while his brother harangued a crowd. Syrik and his attendants stood close at hand, as well as the tribal kings. Many of the last laughed heartily at Koregan's jests, and so did the guards who ringed the newest crop of Dendressi prisoners, each of whom held the stake they were going to drive into the ground for their own impalement.

Vannek had no love for Dendressi. Since time immemorial they had hoarded the best lands, using treachery and magic to drive back their betters. They were so soft only a handful ever bothered to train with weapons, and they celebrated pointless and decadent arts.

Yet he abhorred his brother's plan for retribution. This was not how a wise ruler treated slaves needed for work. And there was much work to accomplish in this city, starting with crops that needed planting and tending. From prisoners they'd learned that there were at least two Altenerai within the city, and more than a hundred of their warriors-in-training. Vannek had reminded Koregan that the fighting Dendressi were a mighty warrior clan, and not to be confused with the Alantrans themselves. Bloody demonstrations would not cow them, only make them more determined.

But Koregan had laughed and called him a woman, claiming that he would strike so much fear into the fae slaves that they themselves would turn on the Altenerai rather than suffer more torment.

More concerning yet, Koregan seemed to really be enjoying the attention, and strutted, rubbing the end of his beard. He was likening the stakes to phalluses both men and women fae enjoyed . . . when he took an arrow through the mouth.

It didn't fall alone. Five rained in and struck the Naor general. Another missed, and one hit Rolk's hand as the grizzled general leapt to shield him.

It was too late. Vannek's brother had already been fatally hit, and dropped gagging on the stage as though he'd swallowed too large a piece of meat and not a wickedly barbed arrow. To make matters even more final his death throws sent him rolling off the edge of the platform, and he landed on his head. Probably the whole city heard his neck crack.

Syrik grabbed Vannek's arm. "General! The arrows came from there!"

A bugle call of alarm rang from a distant corner of the city.

Vannek whipped into action while the tribal kings yelled to themselves or searched the skies. He called to the king of the Swift Hooves. "Tozhok, take your men and head north! Syrik, come with me! "

With his mage and bodyguard he raced for his horse even as an additional flurry of arrows winged toward the stage.

"How is it we didn't see the arrows sooner, like now?" Vannek demanded as he grabbed the reins from a slave and hurried into the saddle.

"They were shielded from sight," Syrik said beside him.

"You guess, or you know?"

Syrik spoke softly as he looked up at him. "I saw them coming in."

Something in the mage's tone alerted him. "You *let* them?"

Now Syrik sounded defensive. "I saw their target," he said quietly but insistently. "You needed him eliminated."

At some level Vannek had always known his brother would have to die. He'd just never imagined it would happen so soon. He dropped his voice as the attendants drew within earshot. "Now might not have been the best time."

"It was the perfect time. You leapt immediately into the lead. Now we need only find the assassins. Or at least one." Syrik climbed onto his own horse, a shaggy-maned white.

"Easier said than done."

"Not so hard. I see through the eyes of my apprentices and slaves, and I had them stationed about the square. We want to veer left."

His guards cried out for Vannek to hang back as he and Syrik led the way on horses. He ignored them as they headed into the abandoned blocks of buildings, scanning the rooftops for archers. Before long they arrived at a block of second-story homes. Syrik diverted through a narrow lane and up a side street. "They'll be heading this way. For that house."

By all rights he should already have arrested his mage and chief advisor. But that would hardly help his own standing, and he would lose his most capable follower. He didn't mind that Syrik had allowed the death as much as he minded the mage hadn't asked. On the other hand, a good subordinate had to be given rein to act on their initiative.

They arrived at the side of a wooden one-story building that had been painted green, and Syrik shouted again that this was the one. Vannek vaulted to stand in his saddle as they drew close, then leapt to the coping and pulled himself up.

"Follow the general, fools!" Syrik cried to their foot soldiers.

Vannek climbed up a slanted gable and on to a second story over the back half of the home. Once there he was shocked to find a Red Feather archer on the other end of the roof with a nocked arrow aimed his way. Vannek took a knee and whipped up a knife as the arrow sailed over his shoulder. The bowman collapsed as Vannek's weapon buried itself hilt-deep in his throat.

His mother had set him to practicing with a knife since he was a small girl.

Three more of the Dendressi leapt over from the nearest house, each of them disguised as Red Feather archers. Vannek smiled in satisfaction. Syrik had perfectly anticipated their movements.

He dueled briefly with the first before he drove a blade through armored chest. By then two of Vannek's guards were up and fighting the second Red Feather, who killed one and wounded the other before Syrik climbed up to drive a spear through the imposter. The third Dendressi wove past, dashing for the ledge and a jump for the next house over.

As the nearest guard readied to pitch a javelin, Vannek knocked the weapon aside. "Catch him alive!"

Syrik stepped up beside him, extending a hand as the last false Red Feather put a foot on the edge, then froze. Was the enemy soldier hesitating?

Vannek saw Syrik's strained expression, his bared teeth, and understood he worked a spell. Vannek dashed over to grab the immovable soldier's arm. He thought it strange the man's limb was hairless. It wasn't until he twisted the warrior back from the edge that he saw her face and realized it wasn't a young man, but a fresh-faced woman, her eyes rolling in hate. Vannek grabbed his second knife and shoved it to the Dendressi throat. "Yield!"

His soldier came up from behind and grabbed the woman's other arm. Now would come answers, at long last, and as he pulled the knife free he smiled wolfishly.

And then the arrow slammed straight through the woman's neck, coming in one side and going out the other with a splash of blood.

Vannek instinctively released the arm and dropped. Blood fountained, but the woman remained in place, dying from the wicked injury, but unable to fall with Syrik's spell holding her in place.

Crouched, Vannek spun, and saw a figure on a distant rooftop shaking his bow. A dark-haired man in a blue khalat. N'lahr. Vannek had never heard that the swordsman was so fine an archer.

The alten dropped away.

Vannek, cursing, climbed to his feet even as Syrik released the body and let it fall to the rooftop. He trudged to stand before Vannek.

"They shot their own rather than risk her capture." There was no missing the approving note in Syrik's voice.

Vannek looked down at the young woman, wondering who she had been. What it must be like to be able to choose your role in society without having to worry about your gender. But there were more important matters. "That was N'lahr. Again. He's in the city."

Syrik looked doubtful. "N'lahr is no bowman. And that archer used sorcery."

"You can also tell me N'lahr's dead, but I keep seeing him alive."

"It could be someone pretending to be him. There was definitely spell-work in that arrowshot. I felt it as it touched my magic holding that girl in place."

"It's N'lahr." Even as he insisted it, Vannek wondered if he was being too sure.

Syrik decided not to press the point. "Whoever it is, he's formidable. And now it's completely up to you to stop him, General. You acted swiftly and issued orders, which were obeyed without hesitation. Now you can return, with your brother avenged and these archers as the proof." He nudged the woman with his booted foot. "But you'd best act fast before your so-called allies maneuver themselves into position. You may need to carry out some examples."

"They're fools! Rather than fighting among ourselves we need to focus on the Dendressi here. They're far more cunning than we've been led to believe."

"You can tell the tribal kings that and waste your breath, or you can get them in line."

"I'll get them in line."

"Spoken like the new ruler of Alantris," Syrik said with a smile.

18

———

Final Plans

Sansyra and Varama's strike team could spare little thought to success and failure in their mission as they raced for their warrens. This time pursuit followed so closely they were forced to collapse a tunnel behind them.

By the time they had advanced the long way to the central halls reports had arrived from sentinels posted at key watch points. Word of the Naor reprisals spread quickly through the ranks of the Resistance, and as the officers filed into Varama's little office, Sansyra was surprised by how many faces were twisted by anger rather than grief. The countenance of the archer, Tevrik, was downright belligerent.

From behind her desk, Varama addressed the eight of them with little preamble.

"Early reports suggest that the kings are already scrabbling over city resources. Their rule is fragmented as they struggle to find a new leader. A runner reports that Lemahl's distraction succeeded beyond expectations. He freed several hundred able-bodied men and women, who overpowered Naor at a sally gate and won freedom outside."

"Meanwhile thousands are dead," Tevrik interrupted. Like all of the men of the Resistance, he'd let his beard grow, lending his sharp-chinned face a savage cast. "Thousands more are being tortured. Our women are being raped. You call that success?"

Varama's eyes were cold. "Ask leave to speak, Tevrik, before you interrupt your superior."

Tevrik visibly mastered himself as Iressa put a calming hand on his armored shoulder. He gave the barest of head bows and then addressed Varama with icy courtesy. "With your leave, Alten, I would like to speak."

"You may do so when I finish." Her voice betrayed no resentment but brooked no opposition.

Tevrik's teeth showed in his beard.

Varama's gaze shifted from him to her staff. "We achieved our goal and returned alive."

Sansyra heard someone mutter softly to this, though she couldn't understand the words.

"Some of our comrades did not survive to return with us—"

"And you shot one of them," Tevrik said.

Varama's mouth set firmly. "If you do not intend to follow the chain of command, then you may leave my service."

"Are you even going to hold a memorial for Denalia and the others?" Tevrik demanded.

"We will honor all of the dead, as well as the sacrifices of the living in due course. But we have no time for luxuries."

"Luxuries?" a burly Alantran soldier asked.

"When we've so much to do that even sleep is rare, yes, time to mourn is a luxury." Varama put a snap in her voice. "Listen well, for I despise repetition. By my calculations, reinforcements should arrive from Erymyr and Ekhem before the Naor reinforcements, as these have been delayed. Before they are here we need to so weaken and divide our enemy inside the city that they are rife for destruction by the forces beyond the wall. Now, who would like to speak?"

Tevrik said nothing, so Iressa asked quietly, "Do we know for certain that our reinforcements are on their way, Alten?" She wore her squire armor and tabard, her dark hair braided tightly.

"I can predict with reasonable certainty, given our mutual defense pact. If Arappa has withstood their own attack they may well send aid themselves."

"Alten." The third ranker, Virian, haggard and worn, tentatively raised his hand, then lowered it as Varama shifted her gaze to him.

"Speak," she said.

"What if Ekhem and Erymyr only send help to Arappa? Not us?"

While she waited for Varama to speak, Sansyra appraised her fellow officers. The three Alantrans, she decided, were the most angry. But the squires were confused, worried, weary, and even frightened. Only after looking at all of them did she ask herself how she felt, discovering she didn't know. It was as though she had been closed off from her own emotions.

"Unlikely, but this is war," Varama said bluntly. "We cannot guess the future but we can calculate likelihoods. We must prepare based upon the information we have so that we may act when opportunities present themselves." She looked away from Virian and addressed them all. "I know you mourn. Every loss is a bitter blow, and not just because we treasured their company. But you must not let yourselves be ruled by emotions. If we are divided, then the Naor win. And I will do my utmost to keep that from happening. Now you must rest and gather strength. Soon, very soon, there will be more that we must do." Her gaze shifted to Tevrik. "Is there more you wished to say?"

His answer was short and gruff. "No."

Varama nodded once. "Dismissed."

Sansyra thought that Varama's speech had given the squires heart, at least, and even assuaged some of the Alantrans. Tevrik still fumed, but he exited with the rest. Sansyra remained, closing the door behind them.

Varama, still standing behind her desk, arched an eyebrow at her. "Is there something you require, Sansyra?"

"I thought you might need assistance."

"No. Thank you."

Sansyra hesitated, wanting to offer some comfort to her commanding officer. "I thought you handled that situation well, sir. It could have gone very badly."

"The compliment is appreciated."

"Are you sure there's nothing you need?"

"Is there something that *you* need, Squire?"

Yes, Sansyra thought, though she found she could not speak. She wanted to be told that they were making a difference. She wanted reassurance that all would be well. She didn't ask for what Varama could not give. She wanted companionship, but her closest friend Renahra had been slain by the queen on the long exodus from Erymyr, and Lemahl had left the walls in the company of the prisoners he'd freed. Who could say if he might return, or if he had even survived?

"No, Alten," Sansyra said at last.

"I need some time alone. Take some for yourself. I'll have need for you soon enough."

"Yes, Alten."

"Dismissed."

Varama was true to her word, as always. Sansyra had eaten more from their rapidly depleting stores, then grabbed a nap before her commanding officer requested a briefing on the aerial project. With the sewing complete, the team had shifted to construction of lightweight platforms, which were proving more troublesome even than manipulating the thin fabric. Most of the men and women assigned this task chafed that they weren't deployed in the raiding parties. Sansyra had told them of Varama's experiments, but they couldn't quite envision the outcome.

Only a month ago, Sansyra had stood with her mentor on the bluffs east of Golden Darassus as the fifth iteration of Varama's heated balloon had risen into the air. Her mentor had thought it might be used as a signaling device, or, if they solved some nagging issues, even to take people aloft.

Now Varama intended the balloons for an entirely different purpose.

After updating her superior about that team's progress as well as the state of their supplies and other matters, an exhausted Sansyra sat in the dirt at the foot of the ladder nearest the hidden exit from the city Lemahl and his assistants had created.

She gnawed on a strand of jerky with all the texture of shoe leather. It was terrible, but it gave her something to contemplate apart from Denalia's death, and Lemahl's absence.

Try as she might, she couldn't hold onto the emotional distance that had plagued her after their retreat.

Only a few short days ago, she'd been looking on this entire experience as an adventure, a delay that would keep her at Varama's side for a while longer. She sneered at her naïveté. She understood now that the longer they lasted here the better were the chances they'd be discovered. It was only a matter of time before someone slipped up, or left a track, or was spotted when they thought they were being cautious. This place was a death trap, mostly of Varama's design, but not just for the Naor.

She sat back against the wall near the sentry, thinking she'd remain awake, then was jarred back to consciousness by the clank of booted feet on the ladder at her back. The two sentries with her waited with ready spears, focused on the descender as Sansyra climbed to her feet and steadied herself against the wall beside the ladder.

She needn't have worried. As the boots came down the ladder, it was clear they were those of a squire. Finally, Lemahl dropped down the last two rungs, returning a salute from the cautious sentries. His plain face broke into a warm smile as he caught sight of Sansyra, who held off hugging him in front of the Alantran soldiers, lest they get the wrong idea. Instead, she took both his arms and clasped them tight, and he grinned at her through his beard.

"You look happy." Was he overjoyed simply at sight of her? If so, that was a new development, and one she wasn't sure how to assay.

Lemahl chuckled at her. "I have good news."

That was a relief. "What kind of good news?"

He glanced at the two sentries, scruffy with their beard growth. "You won't believe me." He searched her face, and his own expression fell. "What's happened? Did you kill Koregan? I thought for sure you had; the Naor were out in force."

"He's dead. We lost Denalia." She glanced over at the sentries.

Lemahl let out a slow sigh. "I'm sorry to hear that. Come on, I've got to report."

They started down the hall, leaving the sentries at their station.

"I didn't realize you two were close," Lemahl said.

"I didn't realize we were, either," Sansyra admitted. "Maybe we weren't. But she was brave and good, and she's dead. Varama had to shoot her," she added.

He looked at her sharply.

"Denalia was surrounded and weaponless."

"That's terrible."

That was an understatement. So was her acknowledgment. "Yes." Sansyra let out a long slow sigh that did nothing to relax her. "She shouldn't be dead. None of this should be happening. I can't believe . . ." She grew conscious of Lemahl's concerned look, and pulled herself together. There'd been a panicked edge to her words, hadn't there? "It's useless to complain about fairness, I know. She's just one more loss we can't afford. I don't know how much longer we can do this. The Naor aren't stupid. They found one of our tunnels. We collapsed it, but sooner or later they'll find a way in."

"We may not have to hold out for too much longer," Lemahl said with great confidence. A smile levered at the corner of his mouth again.

Even in times like these, his good nature was irrepressible. "You really must have good news."

"I do."

"Can you say?"

"I'll tell Alten Varama. You can hear then."

She walked at his side, quietly pleased to see someone so happy. It occurred to her that she hadn't actually known happiness for a long while, except in small ways—if the momentary thrill of returning alive could be considered small.

While she'd napped earlier her dream had been rich with stone sculptures and fountains; strange and beautiful painted beasts that smiled and sprayed water. Maybe the dream had been inspired in part by Lemahl, who came from a family of stonemasons. Like many of Varama's preferred squires, he had an artistic bent, and his sketchbook was full of little doodles of faces in stone.

It wouldn't be a bad thing, she thought, to design fountains. She had enough of a grasp of the fundamentals that would be necessary to get them running, and she could certainly design their outer look. In concert with some stonemasons, she might make a go of it, and bring a little pleasure to whomever looked at them. They'd stand for long years after she was gone. And that was a better testament to a life, she thought, then a lonely statue in the Hall of Heroes and a dry list of battles where she'd spilled blood and witnessed comrades fall.

Looking at the confident Lemahl, she wondered if he might want to join her, startled at the idea that she might be considering him as more than a business partner. Well, why not? She was one rank higher, but that wouldn't matter at all if they both left the service. He was a good man, brave and resourceful and cheerful. He'd be fine company. She eyed him, thinking that while he wasn't especially handsome, she had always liked his smile and the way he made the best of bad moments.

She reached out and patted his shoulder, then he grinned at her once more.

"We'll get through this," he promised her. "You'll see."

They found Varama in her little office, the half circles under her eyes darker blue than ever, even though the eyes themselves were fever bright. Sansyra idly wondered if the machinery within the alten's mind would keep turning long after the body itself failed.

Lemahl kept grinning confidently even during his salute. At Varama's command to report, he filled them in about the success of the mission. The escaped soldiers had been received by Enada's troops. "And they have reinforcements," he said. "Close to two thousand foot soldiers, a mixed company from Arappa and Erymyr! It's even better news, Alten. The Ery-myrans were sent to help at a Naor siege of Vedessus, but they weren't even needed, because the Naor army at Vedessus was wiped out! Including Mazakan!"

Sansyra felt relief wash through her at that. Gods, it was nice to know the Naor weren't unstoppable. And this meant that Varama's prepara-tions had left them as well positioned as she had hoped.

Varama didn't smile, but her slow nod spoke volumes. "Who com-mands the allied forces?"

"Here's the unbelievable part," Lemahl said, and looked over to grin at Sansyra before he continued. "N'lahr's alive! I met him. It's really him, Alten. He's in command!"

Sansyra stared in disbelief before turning to take in Varama's reaction. She had occasionally seen Varama surprised, so she knew what that looked like. All the woman did now was tilt her head and nod, as though she'd expected something of the kind. How could she possibly have known?

Varama let this titanic revelation pass without further comment. "Did you report our situation to him?"

Lemahl looked a little deflated by his superior's response, but gamely pulled himself together. "Yes."

"And did he have ideas?"

"He did," Lemahl said. "But he wished to speak to you directly. "

"I see. So we've a difficulty to surmount."

"Can you be sure it's really him?" Sansyra asked Lemahl. "Couldn't it be a trick?"

Her friend spoke with certainty. "It was him."

Varama apparently agreed. "The trick was his faked death. Did he divulge where he'd been?"

"There wasn't a lot of time," Lemahl admitted, "but he mentioned that Alten Kyrkenall and Alten Elenai had freed him."

"Alten Elenai?" Sansyra repeated. Had she heard that right?

Lemahl nodded quickly. "Yes, N'lahr himself saw her rise to the ring."

Just a few weeks ago, Elenai had been a fifth ranker in line with her for N'lahr's parade. Dead N'lahr's parade. Now N'lahr wasn't dead, and Elenai had jumped straight on past sixth rank and gotten herself a ring. And found a hero of legend. Some people had all the luck. Sansyra was puzzled and a little ashamed to recognize envy, particularly curious since she was starting to be certain she didn't want that ring. She often found Elenai's relentless drive a little irritating, though she'd liked her well enough and certainly respected her dedication. She knew she should be pleased for her.

Varama was speaking. "I'll be interested in all the details later, Lemahl, but stay focused. Did N'lahr suggest a means for communication?"

"He gave me one, Alten." Lemahl presented a cloth bundle pulled from a belt pouch.

"And what will I find when I unwrap that?" Varama said without accepting it.

"It's a hearthstone shard. N'lahr says he's linked to it. And here's another he said you'd put to good use." Lemahl fumbled with his pouch and produced a second cloth-wrapped parcel as Varama grunted appreciatively.

"N'lahr's no mage," Sansyra said.

Lemahl nodded, as though he'd said something similar, then hefted the smaller bundle. "He says he's linked to this one because of the way he was imprisoned. He wants to talk to you through it at your earliest opportunity. It's actually very dangerous for him and if it gets into enemy hands, well . . ."

"Place them both here." Varama patted the little table in front of her and Lemahl stepped forward.

The alten carefully lifted the wrappings away to expose two crystals, one with a sheer side as though it had been cut precisely in half while the rest was as irregular and compellingly beautiful as it's neighbor, albeit a different hue. Sansyra knew on the instant they were hearthstones. She had assisted Varama with her own secret hearthstone back in Darassus, and even without slipping into the inner world, to her eyes the cut one looked a little duller.

"Interesting," Varama said, finally, but showed no inclination to touch either.

"Do you think it's a trick?" Sansyra asked.

"No," Varama admitted. "But as I open this peculiar shard I want you to monitor the situation. Tap it for energies so you don't drain your own power, but don't touch the other one yet. I want to keep that one closed. If there's a Naor mage working spells somewhere close they might be able to sense even this damaged one once open. Watch for tendrils of intent. Warn me immediately if you sense them."

"Yes, Alten."

Varama looked over to Lemahl. "Thank you, Lemahl. You've done well. Seek rest and food. Sansyra, are you ready?"

Sansyra was weary, but she nodded her assent. If Varama could force herself forward through her exhaustion, then so could she. She raised a hand in farewell to Lemahl and knew a profound sense of loss as he slipped through the door and closed it behind him. She'd only just gotten him back, and now he was leaving.

Varama had already turned her full attention upon the stone.

Sansyra opened her sight to the inner world and considered the cut shard as Varama activated it. It radiated at best a tenth of the power she'd detected from the one Varama used to work or the one next to it. Perhaps that owed to its smaller size.

She reached out with her will and made tenuous contact with the stone's exterior. Instead of being energized she merely felt . . . normal. This shattered stone at the least seemed to bolster her so that spell work didn't drain her. It just wasn't revitalizing her in any way, as a hearthstone usually would. And that was a shame, because she could really stand a boost.

Once rooted to the hearthstone, she looked outward, rather than inward. Such was the intent when watching for magical intrusions. She'd practiced being alert for them while Varama had worked with her hearthstone in Darassus. Until two week ago, she'd always looked on it as merely an exercise. She understood now that Varama had expected someone might be watching her one day when she was using them, whether it be Naor mages, or someone loyal to the queen.

She couldn't help but be aware of Varama's own consciousness, now reaching deep within the stone. She deliberately kept apart from her mentor's thoughts, yet sensed her, as she might hear the vibration of a lute string gently touched. And momentarily that string shook violently.

Varama was in contact with another mind, and speaking with it.

Varama sent: *It's good to speak with you again. I had hoped you might yet live, but I feared you were in custody of the Naor.*

The responding mind, which Varama seemed to have already accepted as N'lahr's, obviously had no sorcerous instruction, for his emotions bled all over his communication, along with the occasional stray thought.

As he communicated his reply, Sansyra sensed a mix of concern and relief as well as a worry that the Naor might listen in.

Well met, Varama. I hear you're stirring up the Naor.

In contrast, Varama's response was utterly controlled, revealing only what she willed. *How are we in contact? Is there a sorcerer on the other side, aiding you?*

Sansyra certainly didn't sense another sorcerer, but then she didn't sense the stone's connection to N'lahr, either.

It's just me. There was an accident seven years ago and one of the side effects is my connection with this stone. With this came a torrent of powerful feelings of betrayal, fear for self and others, anger, helplessness, confusion, even some shame.

You took a risk having it sent into the city. Unless you have become skilled with magics you're in great danger if the Naor get hold of this. They could use it to attack you directly and from afar.

There was a grim humor in his thoughts. *You'll have to ensure that doesn't happen. As for the risk, this was the one certain way of speaking freely with you.*

Partly he had been worried that this hearthstone wouldn't work; he had wondered whether he might still receive contact when the other half was with someone else. Someone he'd sent far away.

I have my second-in-command listening in. N'lahr, this is Squire Sansyra.

Sansyra focused her words, although she knew her own excitement and even a measure of shyness was conveyed. *It's an honor to meet you, sir.* She still had a hard time imagining this was real.

He wished to speak of other things, but was striving not to grow impatient: *Thank you.* He did not say that Varama's faith spoke well of her, but his thoughts intimated it. *Now we must make plans.*

Of course, Varama replied. *Sansyra will monitor for us. I'll appraise you of our situation and we'll decide how best to achieve our goals.*

As Sansyra listened in over the next few minutes, she grew to understand that Varama spoke to someone she recognized as an intellectual equal. She'd never heard her do so before, and that in itself was interesting enough.

So far as she knew, N'lahr had none of Varama's artistic or mathematic gifts. She did not expect that he contemplated trajectories, or bottled gasses, or plotted the course of stars, nor that he analyzed metallic compositions. On the surface, he had none of the same interests. And yet as they spoke it was with shared direction and purpose. Varama never had to backtrack and explain herself, and she never once questioned whether N'lahr understood her. On his part, he spoke concisely but with great precision. When talking to other people, Varama almost always poked and prodded for more information. N'lahr seemed to provide her with exactly what she required.

In part, she thought, the success of their conversation might have risen from their long familiarity with one another. Yet Sansyra sensed it was more than this, that he wasn't moderating his communication because of Varama's idiosyncrasies. This was how he usually talked. In their own way, each was a genius, and freed from the constraints required by conversation with ordinary mortals, the exchange of their ideas was swift and certain, though sometimes a little hard to follow.

Sansyra realized that the strong emotions leaking through N'lahr's dialogue were only accessible because of the unique circumstance for this form of communication. He sometimes seemed a bit chagrined by the obvious spillage of feelings he normally kept under tight rein, but was undaunted by them. This was a form of bravery she hadn't before considered, and Sansyra found herself honored to be listening in.

Soon each had laid bare the strengths and weaknesses of their positions, and what each proposed doing about them. As Varama laid out her plan, Sansyra couldn't help expressing some silent shock at its audacity, and felt N'lahr's admiration as well. Varama had laid the groundwork for a moment like this from the very start.

How much additional preparation time will you require? N'lahr asked, a question laced with concern.

We can be ready by dusk three nights from now.

That pushes things very close. Tretton reports that an advance force from Chargan's army is four days southeast of the city. His worry for the city was palpable.

You have a plan to deal with them?

For now, we monitor, but I'll lay an ambush at Trenellis pass to slow them. His anxiety switched to how many under his command he might lose in such a maneuver.

Does the queen know you are alive and free?

She is likely to have learned by now. That is a talk for another time. It's dangerous for me to use the stone for any longer.

Very well. Be alert for exalts.

Of course.

They were so matter-of-fact here. It would have been easy to dismiss both as emotionless if Sansyra wasn't sensing a steady murmur of apprehension from N'lahr's side of the communication.

Signal me tomorrow night with an update.

May the fates smile in your favor.

They bade each other a bloodless farewell, although N'lahr's fond feeling toward Varama swelled over them. As the contact ended and Varama set the stone aside, Sansyra wondered if the alten had experienced reciprocal feelings toward N'lahr. Had it pleased her to speak with someone at the same level as herself?

There was certainly no knowing from her expression.

Someone else might have stopped to compare opinions about what they had just experienced, but Varama had no need for that. "We've much to do. But we should rest before we begin preparations for the final push. See that I'm awake by four bells."

Sansyra saluted. "Sleep well, Alten."

"And you."

She left the office for the cool, dim hallway. She was both surprised and pleased to find Lemahl lounging outside.

"How did that go?" he asked as he pushed off the wall.

"Better. I think. Aren't you hungry?"

"I grabbed some food while you were in there. Should I let you get to sleep?"

"I'm not sure if I could, right away. It might be nice to talk for a while."

They made their way to the fountain, finding the cavern area completely deserted, the lantern dim. They sat down in silence, and she was acutely aware of his presence in a way she hadn't been before.

"Pretty amazing about N'lahr being back, isn't it?" Lemahl asked. "I couldn't believe Varama already knew he was alive. Did you know?"

Sansyra shook her head, no. Varama's thorough grasp of information often eluded her and she had no idea how to convey the privileged view she'd just gotten of a now living legend. She was still a bit stunned by it.

"Things have been hard," Lemahl said, "but we've come through so far. And think where you'll be when this is all over. You might even vault right past the sixth circle and on up to the ring, like Elenai did."

"I don't know about that."

"You don't think you deserve it?"

"Maybe." She sighed. She'd never tried explaining her feelings about advancement. "What did you think it would be like when you joined the corps?"

He scratched at the black beard on his chin. He looked a lot more mature with it; less like an overgrown boy. It somehow balanced out his nose a little as well. "Back then, Alten Varama promised me a chance to hone my skills and talents. She said it would be hard work, but that in her workshops I'd be exposed to exciting experiments and techniques. And she was right."

She'd almost forgotten that he was one of those rare ones Varama had directly encouraged to try out for the great games. She did that, occasionally, with young people of great artistic accomplishment, emphasizing they'd need to work hard in martial fields but they could also learn a variety of the highest skills no one else was studying.

Varama tended to mentor those with an experimental or artistic bent, but Sansyra had come under her tutelage by being transferred in at third rank. "Sometimes I think I've gotten too far. Everyone kept telling me that I had enough talent I ought to join the squires, so I tried out for the regional games, and the next thing I knew I'd qualified for the corps. So here I've been, Sansyra the squire. After the first year or two I decided I'd leave at the third or fourth rank."

"But you stayed," Lemahl said with a grin.

"Not because I'm after the ring, though," she said. "I know that's why you're supposed to stay on to fifth rank. I could have left and become a guard captain or agency chief or something, but I just didn't want to stop learning. I don't think there's anywhere else in all the realms where I'd get a chance to have been exposed to all the things Varama has shown me." She sighed, and confessed the truth. "I think I want to be an engineer. Maybe I can help reshape Alantris when this is all over."

"Perhaps," Lemahl said with great seriousness, "you should stay on and become a great alten."

She shook her head. "Then I'll be the one who gets stuck choosing who gets sent on terrible missions, or whether I need to weigh the death of hundreds, or thousands, against the success of a plan. I might be the one who has to shoot a friend." Her eyes were filling with tears. Stupid. She wiped them.

"This kind of thing isn't going to happen again," Lemahl said. "No other alten has ever had to make these kinds of choices."

"Maybe not these specific ones, but there have been terrible ones all along. You know that. Right from the time Queen Altenera picked out the hundred warriors to stand the ridge at Rinner's Gorge. Only seven came back."

Lemahl nodded. He knew the history. He'd had to pass all those exams as a first ranker, just like her. And then he spoke slowly, and wisely, as if channeling one of the great Altenerai they'd both learned about. "There will always be hard times, and hard choices. When they happen, we need people of sound judgment to see us through. People who've been tried by adversity, who know what's come before, and what mistakes other leaders have made, so they won't repeat them. People like you."

It seemed as though something inside her melted a little as he said that, and as he looked up to meet her eyes, he reached to wipe a tear from her cheek, and she shivered just a little at the electricity of that touch.

"I'm proud to serve with you," he said. "And I would proudly follow you. You're calm and capable and deadly. Isn't it said that some of the best leaders are the ones who aren't desperate to seek command?"

"I think I should like to kiss you," she said slowly.

"You outrank me." At least he didn't seem surprised. Just cautious.

"Yes." She reached out and squeezed his hands. "You're right. Some other time. When we're both promoted, or when I'm out and you're an alten, riding through some square where I'm building a fountain in the middle of Alantris. On your way to glory."

He laughed. "Is that what you want to do? Build fountains?"

"You could sculpt them."

"Maybe I could. How about you decide whether or not you'll quit the corps when we're out of all this, and things are normal again."

She fought off another break of tears. "You know nothing's ever going to be normal again, don't you?"

He spoke with great reluctance. "Yes."

They sat in companionable silence, and she wondered if he might dare to flaunt the traditions and kiss her anyway, or if she should, but neither of them broke the strictures and she was mostly glad of that. Mostly. "Maybe an intimate relationship is forbidden between us," she said. "But there's no harm in two friends holding one another in a time like this, is there?"

He didn't answer immediately and she wondered if she'd pushed too far.

"No," he said finally. "No, I don't suppose there is. Not between friends. And a time like this." He put his arm around her and she leaned her head against his thick shoulder. And it felt comfortable and safe there, and even if he smelled a little, that long sweet moment was the best she'd known since before they'd left Darassus, and because of it, when they left the cavern for their separate sleeping rolls, she didn't feel quite so lonely.

19

Sealed with a Kiss

This time when the blood formed above the trough in the barn, the chair Chargan occupied was better aligned with Syrik's wooden stool, so that he actually seemed to sit upon it.

Outwardly circumstances were much the same as the last time Vannek had spoken to his brother: the old barn, the reek of blood and horse flesh and the fear of the animals. The labored breath of Syrik, hard at work maintaining the spell.

As Vannek had guessed, Chargan hadn't been especially moved by news of their younger brother's death. He was more worried about Vannek holding onto power. For none of the tribal kings would trust him as well.

"Killing his assassins isn't enough," Chargan said. "You need to root out the Resistance and crush them."

If it were a simple matter, Vannek would already have done that. "That's one of my top priorities."

"One of them?" Chargan said archly.

"Holding to power is the first. Kaneshi cavalry are here now. Sometimes N'lahr is within the city, and sometimes without. None of our own cavalry patrols return—"

Chargan cut him off. "You have thousands upon thousands of soldiers!"

"Not even a tenth of them are horsemen. And none of them are as good as the Kaneshi. They have us pinned. If we go out, they cut us down."

"I'm not diverting."

Vannek felt close to losing his temper, and held it just barely in check. "This is folly, Chargan! Come relieve us, here, and the city and The Fragments will be ours forever. They can't stand against your dragons."

"They could have stood against yours, if you hadn't allowed the fae to poison them!"

Chargan wasted time with arguments that led nowhere. Vannek looked over his shoulder to Syrik, eyes wide, powerful chest heaving, hands taut with fingers splayed, as if invisible threads hung from them. The spell's complex nature was already taxing him. "Those were Koregan's arrange-ments, not mine. How can you even think to conquer Darassus? The sup-ply line will close behind you!" The more Vannek had thought about his brother's plan, the more foolish it seemed. "Yours is a relief force, not a full-fledged army. Even if you take Darassus you cannot hold it!"

Chargan's bloodred lips parted to show bloodred teeth in a ghoulish smile. "I never planned to hold it, sister-brother. I will smash its walls. I will tear down its monuments and trample its fields. I will behead their queen and burn their people. They will be broken for generations, and their remaining lands will retreat unto themselves."

Vannek was astonished by the passion in his brother's delivery.

"You want me to come help you in Alantris?" Chargan asked. "The steps I take will cripple the fae so thoroughly they will abandon The Frag-ments, and the rest of their separated lands will pay tribute to keep us at bay! We can ultimately take whatever we want from them! All you have to do is hold an impregnable city with a vast army supplied by immense storehouses. Soon the Dendressi will retreat forever!"

Vannek recognized the strategy behind what his brother said. He re-called lessons from their own father, who taught them that daring action often yielded success because so many others lacked the vision and espe-cially the courage. Probably wide-ranging Kaneshi scouts had detected Chargan's army advancing through The Fragments via the southeastern passes, and they might have been told from captured soldiers that Char-gan brought reinforcements to Alantris, as Chargan had planned with the kings. Only Vannek knew he planned to move straight on for Erymyr. By all accounts, the Dendressi had nearly emptied their central realm to rein-force Arappa and The Fragments, so if there ever was a chance to deliver one swift deadly blow against Darassus, this might be the time.

And if Chargan proved right, his hold on power would be unassail-able. If. Vannek needed more. "I need a powerful victory to solidify my position. Lend me some of your dragons."

Chargan's red brow clouded. "Because I have bounteous numbers of them, and am overflowing with well-trained men to command them."

"Give me two."

"For what purpose?"

"I will send out one of the clans. They're eager to fight. And when the Dendressi ride out to assault them, I'll unleash the dragons in a massed attack."

Behind her, Syrik began to gulp air, as though he was nearing the end of a long run. Chargan had to have heard it, though he fell silent in consideration.

"Your plan has merit. Especially if I send the dragons at night, when the fae may not see them coming."

Yes, Vannek thought. Finally his brother was seeing reason.

"I will send you one," Chargan said after another moment.

"One?"

"Yes. One of my two most powerful, piloted by my greatest dragon lord. You will then have three. Use them judiciously. Now, that is all we can say. Our Syrik is almost spent."

"I don't have two—one of them is still ailing from the poison!"

Chargan scowled, his displeased expression reminding him suddenly of their dread grandfather. "Make yourself worthy, sister-brother."

Vannek sneered at that oft used insult.

Chargan continued. "Earn your place. Even two dragons, striking from different directions, should lay waste to mere ground forces. Lure them out near dusk, then send the dragons sweeping over. Now let me be. Expect the dragon in the next few hours. Let him rest through the day."

Vannek was attempting to mask his displeasure and mime some thanks when the spell failed and his brother disintegrated into a rain of blood.

There was a clattering noise behind and he whirled to see that Syrik had fallen against a stall door and lay with his back against the wood, his legs sprawled across the floor.

Vannek hurried to his side and bent down.

The muscular mage breathed raggedly. His eyelids fluttered as his eyes rolled, as though he couldn't quite fasten upon anything.

"I'll call your attendants." It was improper to show much concern over an underling, but Vannek's tense tone unmasked his worry

"Wait." Syrik said weakly. "We must talk."

Vannek clasped one of Syrik's powerful arms, pleased by the strength he felt there even as he was repelled by his own attraction. He helped the sorcerer to sit upright and then stepped back.

Syrik watched him as his breath gradually slowed and Vannek stood looking down and hating that he found the man so distracting.

"He takes too great a chance," Syrik managed finally, "and you know it." He breathed in and out a few times then spoke with more ease. "If he came here, we would be unstoppable."

"He's not coming here. So it's pointless to talk of it. And your words are treasonous." Vannek put his hand to knife hilt and crouched beside him. "He trained you. You know he'll not be swayed and I'll not give you reason to take me down for his aims."

Syrik's deep brown eyes swam with hurt. "Chargan may think I serve him. And we would be right to tread carefully in his presence. But I think the fae stones have warped him. He's grown overly confident in his power. You are the one who deserves to rule. If you can hold Alantris, the clans will follow you. I know it. No one trusts a sorcerer."

"So says the sorcerer."

"I did not ask to be one," Syrik said fiercely. He pulled himself fully upright and seemed to consider standing. Then he met Vannek's eyes. "You know you can trust me. I see it in your gaze."

"You see too much."

"No, I see the truth. I see how you still feel. I feel the same. I am yours until the end."

Vannek's hand tightened on his knife hilt even as his heart raced and his skin warmed. "Don't say that!"

Syrik refused to look away. "I don't care what you call yourself. Don't you see? If you hold Alantris, you can be whatever you want. We can be whatever we want."

His eyes held, and then there was a split second when Vannek wasn't sure if he would drive the knife into the fool's neck.

Instead he pressed his lips to Syrik's. The shared hunger was so great that it left Vannek breathless and he wished to lose himself completely in the man's embrace. His fingers tore into Syrik's dark hair even as his own pressed against Vannek's back so that their bodies grew ever tighter. He straddled the mage, felt the press of his desire against his thighs and moaned a little for want of him.

Then he forced himself back and away, sitting on his haunches just beyond Syrik's bootheels. They stared at each other wonderingly, and from the mage's dazed, predatory look, Vannek knew his cousin longed to throw himself forward and resume their embrace. More than anything, Vannek wished the same. But such a coupling would destroy everything he'd managed to achieve.

He forced himself to stand, hand on knife hilt. "I will hold this broken city," he said, pleased that his voice sounded stong. "I'm placing you in charge of the dragons. Find out exactly how they work. See that the injured one is healed faster. I think Chargan's dragon lords lack imagination."

"Yes," Syrik said, and gulped. "What clan are you using to draw the Dendressi?"

"The Snowbird," Vannek said. "With any luck, Tarjezhan will get killed." The Snowbird king was ever eager for combat, a troublemaker who was quick to critique his rivals and even quicker to flatter his betters.

"And if he comes back a victor?"

"Few like him, and if he does win, it will only make them more jealous. Besides, it will be the dragons who win this conflict."

"It will be you who wins this conflict," Syrik said, and dusted himself off as he climbed to his feet.

Vannek nodded, not daring to speak further, and then turned and strode for the door, lest he meet the mage's eyes again.

20

The God in the Wastes

Silent and still were the wastelands beyond the realm of the ko'aye. Tiny islands of reality lay every few miles, and to a one they were empty of anything but sand-scoured blue rock. The nearby shifts reflected their appearance completely, so that for hours on end the only sound Elenai heard was the clop of hooves on stone.

Kyrkenall seemed uninterested in talking. Though he'd said nothing, Elenai recognized that he feared his course of action meant he was failing N'lahr, Kalandra, or both. Maybe even the present company, despite which he pushed them and their animals to their limits.

Of the three of them, only Ortok made much noise, from time to time mumbling a tuneless chant about the lands and the hardy kobalin who lived within them. Elenai had asked him if he thought he might find an army in this direction, but he'd looked doubtful, saying only that an army might find them if they violated a holy place.

Eventually, evening came to the inhospitable run of fragments and splinters, and with it a chill wind that brought sound at last, as though the emptiness itself were given voice, or that all those who'd been lost in this vast beyond were crying out for warmth and company.

Ortok called them to a halt as they finally came upon an area they recognized from Drusa's description: a rocky embankment with a little pool of orange water, twisted yellow trees, and scrubby gray grass. Kyrkenall asked Elenai to picket the horses while he started a fire.

The night fell, starless and cold. There was only the blackness, and the mottled corpse of the moon, hanging overhead at the wrong angle. By its light she saw Kyrkenall's breath as he spoke. His voice was low and somber, as befitted the haunted landscape. She could barely make out his words at first.

"In the halls of Kantolus' central palace there's this painting I visit." He didn't look at either of them; the fire flickered under a particularly fierce blast of wind. Kyrkenall shrugged his cloak higher on his shoulders. "It's mostly black, and sort of . . . representational? Anyway, there are dozens of white ghostly figures streaming away from the viewers, heading deeper into the painting. Every one of them is straining after this floating globe of light that wafts a few feet away from and in front of each, until the lead figures are lost in the distance. I've never seen anything so lonely. They don't seem to notice each other, or the fact that someone else's light is within closer reach. They're just after their own." He looked out into the night. "The painting's titled *Chasing the Dream*. I wouldn't be surprised to spot some ghostly figures chasing light spheres in that landscape out there."

"You're afraid that's what we're doing," Elenai guessed.

"Aye. Maybe that's what I've been doing for a long while. If I hadn't been hunting for Kalandra, I might have kept a better eye on the Naor, don't you think? I got too wrapped up in my own troubles. Maybe that's what most of us do, our whole lives long. Probably out of sight in that darkness is the cliff we'll finally fall over."

"Bah," Ortok said. "We have joys together, and we will have more. And when we fall, we shall tell our tales to the Gods, and if they are pleased, they will laugh, and send us back in new bodies so we can bring back more stories."

She liked his spirit, although, in this cheerless place, it was easier to atune with Kyrkenall's mood than his. Ortok, whose concept of time would forever remain hazy, appeared oblivious to the pressure she and Kyrkenall felt. And it was clear that guilt ate at the archer as well. She felt for him, wondering how she might have chosen in similar circumstances. Would she have raced desperately out on the chance her lost love might finally be recovered? Or would she have turned back to aid her best friend? Either choice would have twisted her up inside.

"There is something I wonder," Ortok said. "How does an alten find a mate? Is there a ceremony? Or a dance of some kind? Do you trade the heads of your fiercest enemies, or present one another with succulent flesh from animals you hunted?"

Kyrkenall actually laughed. "Not usually. Sometimes there are dances."

"How did you fall in love with Kalandra?" Elenai asked. "You once told me she tried to get you kicked out of the corps."

"When I was a squire, aye. I wasn't good about following orders. And Kalandra went by the book." Kyrkenall flashed a lopsided smile. "She didn't have much use for me until the fourth rank, and she came around mostly because she was fond of Rialla and approved of N'lahr and they both stuck by me. But I still didn't think she liked me much. It was Rialla who brought us together, in the end." Elenai would have thought that he'd smile at that memory, but Kyrkenall grew darkly sober. "Everyone mourned her, of course, but Kalandra and I knew her best, and we found solace in each other's arms. Rialla was Kalandra's squire," he added for Ortok's benefit.

"Is that when you danced?" Ortok asked.

Kyrkenall's head shook slowly from side to side. All humor seemed to have left him. "Maybe we should have. Maybe there should have been a grander declaration. We were friends who sometimes bedded together, and I lied to myself and said it wasn't much more than that, even though I knew it was. And we were in the middle of the war. We tried not to talk about the future."

Elenai smiled sadly.

"And then she was gone, and I couldn't find her to tell her what I should have, all that time, and I didn't know . . ." His hand rose as if he physically reached for a word. Finally he got it out: ". . . until that image of her told me she'd been feeling the same way."

Elenai considered saying many things, and dismissed them all.

"You know," Kyrkenall said, meeting Elenai's eyes, "it was her who got me reading Selana. I used to think her poetry was as old-fashioned as you do."

"Ah, Selana!" Ortok said with relish. "The great writer of poems and stories."

Elenai blinked in astonishment that the kobalin knew her work, until he spoke on.

"In the evenings when I kept Kalandra company, she told me many of Selana's words. They were fine. Sometimes Kalandra would act the part for me, and tell me lines to say in response. What a wonderful thing that was! I was once saying the lines of mighty Alvor of the Black Axe as he readied to smite his enemies!" Ortok sighed wistfully. "I should very much like to see that whole play. Kalandra told me she would take me to see one in Darassus, someday, when the war was all over. But now there is another war, and she is not here."

"I'll take you to my father's playhouse in Vedessus," Elenai said, astonished she could offer such a thing without consideration. The ancient city had been stunned to hear of a kobalin walking their streets. What would they think of one sitting in the audience beside them? She decided she didn't care. "He runs the greatest theater in the realm."

Ortok smiled widely. "Oh, that I would like very much."

"That," said Kyrkenall, "is something I'd like to see." Whether he meant the play, or Ortok watching one, wasn't clear. Probably he meant both.

"It would be fine for us to see it with Kalandra," Ortok suggested.

"Yes," the archer agreed quietly. "Yes, it would." He reached out with a sturdy branch and stirred their little fire.

Before she turned in, Elenai contemplated the hearthstone once more, her back to the blaze and her companions, reaching into it for some sign of Rialla herself. But she had no greater luck finding her this evening than she had the last. There was power there, of course, fascinating power, and she shut the thing down before she lost herself in its contemplation, disgusted with how hard it was to resist the lure.

"No luck?" Kyrkenall asked.

"I just don't think she's there. We'll have to wait for a dream."

"I promise not to shake you awake," Kyrkenall said.

"I appreciate that. But you'd better wake me, because time presses."

"Aye." Kyrkenall sighed.

Elenai wrapped the hearthstone and restored it to her satchel, then withdrew a smaller parcel, well aware of Kyrkenall's regard. She might easily have worked the magics without holding N'lahr's stone before her, but somehow taking it from the cloth and considering its physical presence felt right and proper. It was like the ritual moment of lighting candles before giving thanks. Soon she was looking down at the smooth side of the crystal, a clean slice made by the great sword Irion.

"He'll know if the ko'aye are going to help him if they drop by to visit," Kyrkenall said.

"He'll want to know where we are," she said. "And we can see if he's well."

Kyrkenall frowned, then turned up a hand. "I'm worried about him, too."

"I won't be long about it," she said, sounding calm and wishing she felt it.

She turned the stone over in her hands, drew a deep breath, and opened it.

And she looked through N'lahr's eyes. He was upon a small incline somewhere in The Fragments, in evening. The sun was at his back, and a thousand enemies lay before him. To his left a rank of spearmen held fast against a press of sword-bearing Naor warriors. She gasped, for N'lahr leapt in amongst them, reaping a bloody harvest with Irion, his breath in time with his motions, almost like a meditation. And even as he slipped past a thrust and sliced down through an armored shoulder and the muscle beneath she heard the flow of his thoughts and knew the plan for this battle—how N'lahr's force had pretended to retreat, luring a band of Naor after them. While the enemy outnumbered them, the Naor fought uphill, facing into the sun. The Vedessi spearmen had but to hold here, using the ground to bolster their right flank while a mixed group of foot soldiers from Vedessus and Darassus held the left. It would be a close thing, with the Naor numbers in the thousands—what force was this?

The Snowbird clan.

That was all N'lahr had time to explain. She heard the blare of Kaneshi trumpets and understood from N'lahr's thoughts that this was Enada's cavalry striking the Naor force from the rear. If the foot soldiers could hold just a little longer the Naor would be smashed between them and the cavalry.

This was no time to communicate with the commander. Bad enough to distract him in the midst of combat, worse to render him stunned or senseless.

She was readying to shut down the stone when the pain lanced through every muscle in her body. She cried out even as N'lahr writhed, his sword uplifted for a death strike he couldn't deliver.

You sought to aid him? The voice in her head asked, and she recognized it for Chargan, though she'd only heard it once before. Somehow the blood mage was interrupting her contact.

You may watch him die.

A howling Naor warrior came at the commander and slung his sword for his chest. N'lahr struggled to turn, failed, and she felt the impact against her own body as he went stumbling, felt the air leave his lungs as he tripped backward over a body. His side hurt, but the famed khalat had protected him.

That will not guard him for long. I sought in vain for him until your stone led the way!

As a bearded face loomed over N'lahr, Elenai flipped on the hearthstone at her side and added its power to her own; she sent energies hurtling through the connection to the gloating sorcerer, somewhere far outside the battle. She reflected her own pain at him, felt him recoil.

N'lahr moved, but slowly, oh so slowly, and the large Naor towered over him, his chain shirt dangling. His sword rose and teeth gleamed in a wicked grin through his heavy brown beard.

Elenai shouted out, dimly aware that Kyrkenall's hand was on her shoulder.

And then another figure interposed herself before N'lahr—someone in a khalat and dark boots, and the Naor fell backward. N'lahr struggled to sit up, the pain fading, and through his eyes Elenai saw her friend Gyldara facing away from the commander, blood streaked sword in one hand, throwing axe in the other. "Hold the line!" she shouted hoarsely to a group of spearmen. "Hold the line!"

A dark winged shape dropped from the sky, a long tail swinging behind it. N'lahr called out to hold fire until his command, and Elenai knew from his thoughts that this, too, had been anticipated, that he had readied a counter for the dragons, so long as they dared fly low.

And then Chargan's assault resumed, and the spell he sent against Elenai flattened her. Her mouth worked silently, like a fish ashore, for the air itself had been drained from her lungs. She gasped for air and could not pull it in until she rooted herself deeply in the stone.

She longed to fight back, even as Chargan readied new energies. But then the commander climbed to his feet and she remembered he was the battleground. Sooner or later Chargan would return his attack to N'lahr. And so she shut down the commander's stone, then her own. She hoped that would be enough to keep the Naor sorcerer away from him.

All was dark and still and the moon was crooked overhead. As the pain faded, she realized Kyrkenall was with her, hand to her shoulder, his eyes sharp with worry. Ortok loomed behind him, looking confused.

She slowly pushed herself up from the rocky ground where she'd landed. Her head hurt, probably because she'd bumped it when she was thrown back.

Kyrkenall was asking what had happened and whether she was all right. He'd been asking it repeatedly.

"The Naor blood mage," she said, surprised at how weary her own voice was. She looked up at the archer. "He used N'lahr's stone to attack him and me both. And he's far stronger than I would have imagined."

"What about N'lahr?"

"I think Chargan could only attack him because the stone was active.

So I shut it down." What kind of power did the man command, to reach through the distance to attack two of them at once, in different places? And with her wielding a hearthstone? She gulped.

"N'lahr was in the midst of a big battle in The Fragments. I think they were winning, but it was a close thing, and there was at least one dragon readying to attack. Maybe two. I didn't get a chance to tell N'lahr anything."

"Was Chargan there?"

"Not right in front of him. It's hard to know where. He must have been monitoring the situation with his magics, looking for some advantage, and sensed the sorcerous opening to N'lahr." She pushed to her feet, looking down at N'lahr's pale stone, its faceted sides reflecting the flickering red fire from a dozen angles.

"I should be there," she said quietly. "We should be there." She looked up at Kyrkenall and saw the worry stamped on his face. He stepped away and began to pace, as was his habit when he was truly vexed.

Chargan was a frightening foe. She had grown too used to the idea that her hearthstone use would see her through any challenge. But what was that power in comparison to whatever source Chargan wielded? She'd have to start thinking more tactically and stop relying on power alone.

A fine idea. Now how to apply it? She wasn't sure.

Kyrkenall stopped in front of her. "We're so close now." There was a pleading note to his voice. "If the ko'aye get there, he'll be all right, don't you think?"

She spoke honestly. "I don't know, Kyrkenall."

The archer cursed and stepped away.

He took first watch that night. The chill deepened, but they let the fire die, for they had little wood left. The sun was slow in coming at dawn, and a wordless Kyrkenall gestured Ortok to lead.

A silent Elenai accompanied him, wrapped in both cloak and blanket, hunching in her saddle as she rode and thankful for the warmth of the horse against her legs. Their breaths streamed away in curious little curls.

After midday they hit a little run of land with scintillant skies where long-limbed grazers with oblong heads munched spiraling blue-violet grass. They let their horses eat for a while before mounting up once more. Near evening a storm blew up and cast everything in shadow, changing a few features nearby but requiring little effort to withstand. Elenai was pleased when the raindrops proved oddly warm.

The following two days were drier, but similar in the rising sense that they spent time they did not have wandering the wastes.

The next day they reached a land lined with hundreds of white and yellow objects, carefully spaced a few strides apart. It wasn't until they drew near that Kyrkenall pointed them out for what they were: skulls.

The nearest were those of horses and oddly proportioned humanoids that were almost certainly kobalin. There were some of other large animals she couldn't identify, and those of humans as well, though with the skin rotted away there was no knowing if they were Naor or her own people.

"We are very close to a place of power," Ortok said. "And you should not be here."

"I don't see anyone here to stop us," Kyrkenall said.

Their kobalin companion's reply was ominous. "They will know."

"So are these people and creatures that tried to come close and were killed?" Elenai asked.

"No. Each visitor brings a sign of their reverence." Ortok pulled on his reins to guide Steadyfoot around the skull of some large horned animal.

A few miles after they crossed over the grim border, the skies lightened almost to white and the breeze that rolled over them was cool and laden with moisture, as though it had traveled from some warm, rainy place. Ahead loomed a low hillock upon which a small rounded building rose. The gentle slope was riddled with boulders and detritus.

"This is what we called the Round Stone Home, though none we knew made a home of it, for it was strange. But look now." Ortok's voice grew uncharacteristically soft. "A veritable place of numbers."

Kyrkenall's response was almost a whisper. "Upward of sixty."

Elenai didn't understand what he meant until they drew a little closer and she saw that the slope wasn't decorated with any kind of rocks, but the remains of kobalin. In the strange light, she hadn't seen them clearly, nor the long rusted axes, spears, and swords that lay beside them.

"It looks as though they approached the slope from the easiest side, first." Kyrkenall rode slowly around the hillock. The place had appeared gentle from a distance, but Elenai saw now that all but one side was steep and scattered with small, red-thorned bushes. Even there, around the side of the building, were some skeletons, suggesting that some determined kobalin had climbed around or through the obstacles to meet their death. The majority, though, lay along a single route, the ramp that led to the building.

"What killed them?"

"The god," Ortok said with grim certainty.

Elenai's eyes drifted up to where the god presumably dwelt, a small temple with circular portico, supported by gray stone pillars. It was reminiscent of the temple they'd found in Kalandra's stronghold, though much smaller. While there was luxuriant grass upon the summit of this hill, much like there had been around that other temple, only two or three good strides across the grass would take you from temple to hill edge.

"It's hard to imagine anyone living here," she said. Elenai resisted the inclination to seek with the hearthstone, relieved by her own willpower, peering only with aid of her Altenerai ring.

And she sensed no life before them, apart from the tiny creature in the soil. But then she wasn't yet close enough to sense anything within the temple. As they finished their circle and closed again on the ramp, she detected something at its height.

Elenai felt the hairs rise along the back of her neck and arms. "An Altenerai ring," she said. But why would it be lying outside the building? And how could such a small building sustain someone in any case? Could it possibly stock enough food and water to keep one person alive for what must be years? Might someone somehow be hidden out of reach of her ring's senses, or hidden inside a gem? Might that explain it?

Kyrkenall climbed down from Lyria and led the way up the path, arrow nocked. Elenai followed suit, scanning the kobalin bodies. Scraps of clothing still rotted upon some of them, and little bits of rusted armor. Great knotted bones littered the grass, and long rusted weapons lay beside them. Some of the bodies rested upon their side, and a few upon their stomach, but many looked as if they'd been blown on their backs by a mighty force. Spell work.

"This was a brave battle," Ortok mused behind her.

"Kalandra?" Kyrkenall called as he drew close to the top of the slope. He scanned the shadows of the portico.

There was no answer.

Kyrkenall advanced into that portico, froze, then, very slowly, dropped to one knee, head bowed. Elenai didn't see the form lying with its back against the pillar until she reached his side.

The body had lain there for a long time. Yet there was no missing the Altenerai khalat, its colors little faded. The pant fabric had rotted away, but some boot leather still wrapped skeletal feet. And a sword lay across the breast, where it had once been clasped by the dying hand since desiccated. A ring circled one weathered fingerbone.

"Hail, Commander," Kyrkenall said softly.

"Is that Renik?" Elenai asked quietly. She looked down at the eyeless, heat-mummified features. Wavy black hair flecked with gray still clung to the dried, skeletal head.

"Aye." Kyrkenall was silent for a long time.

"I don't understand," Elenai said. "I thought they said a god dwelt here." Unless, maybe, he'd left a recording of himself? He didn't appear to have any other belongings.

"Of course the kobalin would think him a god," Kyrkenall said. "Look at him. He took on almost seventy-five kobalin, and almost half were lords—did you see the size of those bodies? Can you imagine? They must have come up in waves and somehow he took them all."

"But they left him here," Elenai said. "Don't the kobalin take the heads of their defeated enemies?"

"They must not have defeated him," Ortok said. He had crept up quietly behind them. "If no living warrior delivered his death blow, then no one had claim to him, and they would let him lie. And they would honor him. And who would not come to pay respects to such a warrior as this, and to ask for his blessing in war things? It is all clear to me now. He is the one even N'lahr reveres."

"He was the greatest of us," Kyrkenall said, his voice ever so soft.

Elenai had never met Renik, nor even seen him in the flesh, but her eyes welled with tears as she thought of this lone man standing off so many. And she knelt with Kyrkenall. "Hail, Commander."

Kyrkenall's voice took on that reflective quality he often used while speaking verse, absent the usual playful note. This time he was deadly serious. "Here was flesh and blood, yet here there rests a grace divine. I would that he yet lived. We shall not see a one like him again, even should our lives stretch on and endless." He faltered, then directly addressed the corpse. "You were the torch by which we sought the path. You lived the principal by word and deed. You were the model we all strove to meet." His voice fell to a whisper. "When you were with us, it was easier, somehow, to rise above our own weakness."

Elenai wasn't able to place the quote. "What's that from?"

"That's me. Just now. Would that I had more." His words came out in a snarl. "Would that the queen hadn't wasted the life of this brave man. He didn't need to die out here. Alone. Honored only by his enemies." He continued to stare down at his old commanding officer as Elenai climbed to her feet.

Reverently, Kyrkenall slipped the ring from the skeletal hand, then placed it with infinite care in one of his smallest belt pouches.

Elenai gently touched the archer on the shoulder. "Let's see what he was guarding."

The temple itself was a round room no more than twelve fair paces across. It had but a single opening. There was no light within, nor wall sconces to hang lanterns had they wished them, so she and Kyrkenall both willed their rings to light. There came an answering glitter from hundreds of mosaic floor and wall tiles inset with sparkling motes. At chest level all about the wall were empty recesses. Elenai counted thirty of them.

"What do you think those are for?" Kyrkenall asked. "Busts of the gods?"

"I think they were for hearthstones," Elenai said. They were just about the ideal size. "Or maybe those stones that Kalandra was talking about. The remembrance stones."

"So where are they?"

"A good question."

"Maybe they're in some kind of protected spot," Kyrkenall said, "and we have to find a trigger to release them."

"Or maybe Renik wasn't protecting them, he just got caught here at the wrong moment. Maybe they were gone when he showed up."

"Or maybe the kobalin took them," Kyrkenall suggested.

"Would they disturb the temple of a god?" Elenai asked.

He nodded shortly and then threw up a hand to stop her before she walked any farther. "I'm an idiot," he whispered, and bent low to the ground, ring shining. She could tell he searched at random until he halted for a brief moment and bent even lower, before pressing on in a straight line for one of the empty recesses.

"What is it?"

"Tracks in the dust. They're dusty themselves," he said, "but they're more recent."

"Renik's tracks?" Maybe he'd taken the hearthstones out and someone had stolen them from him.

"No. Boots, though. Smaller. I think a woman was here, looking around."

"Kalandra?" Elenai asked.

"I don't think some random woman could make it here, do you? We've walked over some of the tracks," Kyrkenall said as he moved on. "It seems pretty clear that whoever this was went to each alcove. So she was collecting the stones."

Elenai fought down a surge of excitement. "So she was here, and got away."

"It seems so."

"Friends," Ortok called from outside, "I have bad news."

It was only then Elenai noticed he hadn't entered the space with them. He lingered in the open air just beyond the portico, not daring to set foot within the temple.

Elenai was first through, and there was little need for Ortok's arm to point downslope, for she saw figures charging toward them across the plains as a great green lightning bolt split the whitened sky behind. She'd seen enough large groups of warriors now to guess troop strengths. At least four hundred were closing on them.

"Mount up." There was a curiously cold calm to Kyrkenall's voice.

Elenai needed no urging and was soon in the saddle. Kyrkenall was about to start down slope, then caught sight of Ortok, still looking into the distance.

"As weary as our horses are, we're going to have a hard time staying ahead of them," Kyrkenall said.

"You go," the kobalin said. "I will stay."

"They'll kill you," Elenai objected.

He turned and met her eyes. "I hear the fear in your voice and know that it is for me. But you need not worry. Kobalin are not forbidden from this place. And they will stop to speak with me. It will give you some space. Go. Take Steadyfoot with you."

"Don't make this sacrifice, Ortok," Kyrkenall said. "There's no need."

Ortok showed his teeth. "I make no sacrifice. N'lahr wanted me to find an army. Well. There one is. I will challenge its leader, and then I will take them to fight Naor. It is a simple thing."

Maybe it seemed simple to Ortok, but Elenai shot a nervous glance to the lithe archer. How could the kobalin even know who led the oncoming horde? It could be a greater warrior than he. Might well be, given how many kobalin followed him.

"Then we'll stay," she said.

He quickly shook his furry head. "No. You are not welcome here."

"But we have every right to pay respects to a fallen alten."

"He died on our lands, and has been honored by us. Not you. Maybe later this can be done. Not now. Go, friends. If I live, I will fight again at your side. Think well of me, and share my name with those you meet."

Elenai could only stare in astonishment and sorrow. She had seen Ortok challenge and win before, but it had never occurred to her he would leave so soon.

Kyrkenall put hand to chest in salute and addressed him solemnly. "Hail, Ortok. Win glory. I hope to see you again."

Elenai, wordless, repeated the gesture. As Ortok returned it Kyrkenall was already headed down slope, guiding Steadyfoot by a line. She followed, leading the pack horses, surprised at how much closer the kobalin were already.

Kyrkenall pushed Lyria into a weary canter and circled around the hill before riding off in a straight line. Elenai followed.

She glanced over her shoulder. The hill blotted out sight of their pursuers and the temple blocked sight of Ortok.

She knew she should have been more worried about the kobalin pursuit, but it was the sudden absence of Ortok that disturbed her most. She realized that she never should have supposed he would permanently be in their life, and reminded herself that in the end he was pledged to kill N'lahr or die trying. It was inevitable that he leave them, eventually.

And yet she couldn't help thinking of a moment from Selana's play, *The Fall of Myralon*. She'd often thought Selana stiff and old-fashioned, but that moment in the third act—when the aging queen discovered her young grandson dead upon the stairs—it had remarkable power. She thought of it now, of the woman separated suddenly from the person in whom she had invested hope and love and time, killed not by assassins but by a tumble down steps. Elenai could no longer remember the full lines, but recalled how the queen had cradled the child, complaining that the Gods might at least have warned her his fair days were almost through.

It wasn't that she equated the queen's love for her grandson with her affection for Ortok, but her sudden understanding that time with Ortok was finite paralleled the queen's lament.

Now they rode toward dark hills in a dark land under benighted skies.

It was easy enough to guess Kyrkenall's plan—ride for the hills, lose their pursuers there, find a way to double back.

She glanced again over her shoulder and this time saw warriors to either side of the hill. The sky, splashed again by lightning, limned them so that she glimpsed their strange hulking outlines and mismatched horns. Those weren't Naor helms, but the horns of kobalin. And she couldn't be sure but . . . she looked back once more to confirm.

"I don't think they're following," she shouted up to Kyrkenall.

He called back to her, his voice shaking as Lyria's tired hooves pounded over the black soil. "Ortok's challenge will hold them in place."

She knew that she would see nothing that might tell her their friend's fate as she looked back, but she couldn't help doing so. Ortok might even now be fighting for his life. Or standing victorious. He might be dead.

Less than a mile separated them but he might as well be realms away, or a hundred years apart. What was the difference, she thought darkly, between a memory from a few moments ago, or yesterday, or from decades past? None of them were real, anymore. They were equally gone, every single one, no matter when they'd transpired.

Kyrkenall and Elenai slowed their horses, lest they run them to ruin, but they moved on, and the hills resolved themselves into dark, ruddy shapes. Kyrkenall guided them into a low pass.

Just beyond it, horsemen were waiting.

There were six in all, bareheaded, each a fine figure of a man in their late twenties, their musculature obvious even under loose blue shirts. They wore a uniform of sorts—matching short-sleeved tunics, dark kilts over which a sword belt hung, and strap sandals.

Though imposing, there wasn't anything immediately challenging in their presentation. The foremost bowed his head respectfully, then pressed a closed fist over his heart. He addressed them in a warm alto. "We bring you greeting. Our lady extends her invitation and welcome to you. You are to accompany us to meet her."

"Who are you?" Kyrkenall asked. "Where do you want us to go? And who's your lady?"

"I am Sorak, speaker with the Shift Dwellers. I am here to take you to the lands of our lady, the Alten Cerai, Goddess of the Shifts. Come. She is eager to speak with you."

24

Last Words

Someone sat on the bed. Vannek awoke in darkness, and on the moment his hand was under the pillow and around the knife hilt. He smelled horses, and sweat, and beer, and knew it was someone heavy from the impact of him sitting on the mattress. And then Vannek had twisted on the lantern, and he saw the craggy, scarred face of graying Rolk. The older man was half-turned and looking toward the knife Vannek leveled.

Rolk looked away from the knife tip and met Vannek's eyes, then spoke as though they were already in the midst of a conversation. "The problem with your father wasn't that he lacked bravery, or smarts. It was that he was too busy fighting to make enough children. And when he did, it was always with the wrong women. So we got Chargan, spawn of a Dendressi doxy. We got Koregan, spoiled son of a pampered mother. And we got you."

Vannek sat up, but didn't put the knife away. He wasn't yet sure how he would play this. It had already been a long day, and a bleak one, and he'd only managed to fall asleep in the last hour. It had required all of his cunning to keep the kings in line after they learned that not just the whole of the Snowbird clan but two of their three dragons were lost. Only the recovering one was left them. He'd spun the failed attack as emblematic of the problems of impulsive leadership under Tarjezhan and perhaps placing too much faith in magic, and he thought it had worked. He'd thought, too, that Rolk was convinced. Yet here he was. Was this a challenge?

Vannek wavered for a moment and decided that threatening would only sound weak. So would retreat. He kept his knife still as his voice, and pretended to be part of the same conversation. "That means there's a problem with me?"

Rolk gestured to Vannek's breasts, unbound and visible through his night shirt. "The obvious ones."

The mattress creaked as Rolk shifted heavy thighs. "Your father was your grandfather's favorite. And mine. The best of his whole brood." Rolk had assumed an easy familiarity, as though they were old friends around the campfire, or he some kindly uncle. "We hoped the line might breed true, through him." His scarred face twisted. "Maybe we could have whipped Koregan into shape. He had mettle. Chargan's too clever for his own good, and he's a mage. No one will take a half-breed for a king." Suddenly Rolk's eyes were sharp, and seemed to suck in the light, as though they were the only thing in the room giving it off, except for teeth, now bared. "That leaves you. And right now, you're hanging by a thread."

"That sounds like a threat."

"Learn to hear truth. Your grandfather sent me with Koregan to be his voice. He's gone now, and so's Koregan. So who should I serve? Ostensibly you're next in line."

"I am next in line. I've already taken command."

"You've told people you're in command. That doesn't mean you are. Since you're a woman."

"I'm a man now."

"Are you? If I tore your clothes off I'd find what I'd see under any woman's garments." His smile wasn't at all warm. "I could take you and make you squeal."

Vannek fought down the anger, and indignation, and strove to sound coldly competent. "You'd die first."

Rolk leaned infinitesimally closer. "I'm stronger than you." He frowned, suddenly uncaring, and dismissed Vannek with a twist of his lip. "But I want a woman who smells like sweet things, like a tasty dessert. And you do your best to smell like a man. I also want a woman who knows how to bed a man, and I don't guess you ever have. Or at least not enough to count. Have you been bedding Syrik?"

Vannek felt a flush rise on his cheeks, and involuntarily his hand tightened on his knife hilt. He then lost control and voiced a threat. "I can have you killed."

Rolk's response was instantaneous. "It's the other way round."

He hated that Rolk had angered him into sounding foolish, and glared as the old warrior continued. "I see the way he follows you. I see the way your back stiffens when he does, and by the Three it is bloody priceless. You haven't had him, have you?"

He's trying to bait you, he told himself, and forced calm

"In a way," Rolk said, "I feel sorry for you. If you'd been my daughter I'd have married you to one of the Red Feather chieftains. They take care of their women, and they raise strong sons. You could have been happy. Instead—*pfft*. Your grandfather's had you playing this foolish game for the last four years."

"I'm not your daughter. And the past is gone. I'm in charge now. I assume you have some reason for this intrusion. Although I don't appreciate your approach, I note your candor. Truth is good."

Rolk said nothing.

"So let's start over," Vannek said slowly. "You tell me your point, and I'll decide what I wish to do with it. You think I'm hanging by a thread."

Rolk's voice had been faintly mocking before. Now he was in dead earnest. "I know you're hanging by a thread because the kings already plot who'll run the city then you're disposed of. When will Chargan be here?"

Amongst other talents, Vannek had become a gifted liar. "Within five days."

"Still so long? Here are the things in your favor. Koregan looked weak because after he won the city, the rebels kept giving him trouble, and then they killed him. Now people say the only reason he won the city is because of Chargan's dragons and his father's army. They're probably right. And here you are in contrast, the personal slayer of his assassin within a quarter hour."

Vannek didn't correct him. It had been Syrik's idea to spread word that the Dendressi Vannek had slain was the one who'd fired Koregan's death arrow.

"You're still a woman. Now normally that would make you pointless, but the rank and file are more loyal to you than their own kings. They saw you were the first one through when the wall went down. They love that you avenged your brother. And they're superstitious about the magic they were told made you a man, and the fact the god-king's blood fills your veins. Their strutting little kings can't compare with that if you sing it right."

"How shall I sing? With your words?"

"Don't spurn offers of help, girl."

He pretended the insult didn't affect him. "I don't think your offer comes free."

Rolk grinned without mirth. "Wisely said. Hear me out, and judge the worth of my advice."

"Before we talk price?"

"My price is that you keep me at your side. I think you see the worth of that. I'm legitimacy. I was with your grandfather; having me eases the transition for you. You must have a child, several children, to cement your hold."

"I will have no children."

"Exactly. I will provide the children. I have three grandchildren of the right age. We'll find some woman to claim that they were hers, and how you bedded her with your man parts and how bloody stunning you were. Like a stallion, with a cock as long as my arm."

"No one will believe that."

He snorted. "You don't know how stupid people are. Maybe the kings and chieftains won't believe, but the people will. You'll be safe."

"Until your grandchildren come of age."

"That's the future. Right now you may not last the week, and you worry for twenty years later?"

If he had learned one thing from his father, it was to think further than other men, but he nodded as if Rolk made complete sense, knowing the while that Rolk would use him only so long as it was convenient, and until Rolk's family was entwined completely into the power structure of the empire. Like a vine that grew so gradually about your throat that you wouldn't notice until you were choking to death.

"Fair enough," Vannek said. "But I want only intelligent, capable children."

"Of course."

"And your advice?"

"Stop keeping out of the way. It's worked to your advantage so far. You have mystique, and whenever you're visible, you're seen doing something competent. But now you have to be seen leading."

Vannek thought he was already doing that.

Rolk spoke on. "Fortify your alliances with the kings already kindly disposed to you. And the mages. Your Syrik has been good about keeping that connection open. Circulate among the troops and the junior officers. Be there at odd times of day—the worst shifts. Like the middle of the night. They'll see that you're tough and aren't sitting back pampered like the rest of their officers."

"That's why you're here at night."

"Yes. And to get your attention. But mostly because you've no time to waste. In a half hour your last dragon lord is going to begin his rounds. Head out and make his rounds with him, then cycle through the sentries."

"Is that an order, or a suggestion?"

"It's a suggestion. If you don't take it, though, you're worthless." Rolk stood and stepped away from the bed. "I don't think you're completely worthless. So I'm going to wait outside these quarters for a few minutes. I'll assume you'll meet me out there. If you're not out in a quarter hour then I know you're stupid and I'll go to Stilkar."

"Stilkar's a craven weasel."

"Maybe so. But he knows it, and values good counsel. Of all your warlords, he's the one most likely to be a firm ally."

Vannek nodded slowly. "Very well. Leave my chambers, and you will see what you shall see."

Rolk's seamed face revealed a little curiosity. He bowed stiffly, showing both formality and a little age, then shut the door behind him.

Vannek stared at the closed portal for a long moment, sorting through observations and conditions and possibilities. Though completely aware of his feelings, he divorced himself from them all, the better to reach wise conclusions. This, too, was something his father had attempted to instill within them all.

Dressing was no great feat. He did this quickly, as he had done uncounted hundreds of times. He was no woman, to linger at the mirror.

If he'd cared about Rolk's approval he would have been disappointed,
for he greeted Vannek's emergence with no obvious pleasure. Vannek considered the two sentries waiting outside the door, knowing that these two
had allowed the old general within his chambers without first alerting
him. They were traitors, or lacked judgment. In either case he would remove them from his service.

Vannek himself led the way down the stairs.

"I think you should move into the citadel at the earliest opportunity,"
Rolk said quietly.

"I'm told it's still not secure. There's talk of hidden tunnels."

"We'll fill the place with soldiers," Rolk countered. "Your brother was
wary of occupying it. You will boldly do so. Or at least claim to. Instead
you can be visiting with the troops all over the city at odd times, and sleep
wherever you happen to be."

"Sounds unsecure."

"Or maybe more secure, if the enemy can't predict your movements."
Well reasoned.

The new young dragon lord was already dressed in finery, including a
feathered helmet, when they walked up to the row of houses that housed
him and the remaining mages under his tutelage. Apparently he was fas-
tidious about his appearance, possibly to distract from his otherwise lack-
ing physical attributes.

"You want to round with me?" The mage sounded suspicious.

"The general thinks that his predecessor was not in close enough communication with important assets, like yourself," Rolk said.

"I want to see how everything works," Vannek said shortly. He didn't
need Rolk to translate for him.

"Oh, of course." The man couldn't hold back a self-satisfied smile.

Rolk addressed him once more. "You should be honored. General
Vannek's beginning with you because you're one of the most vital members of his command."

The young mage shined a little at that, and Vannek nodded. He'd been
about to say something similar. To demonstrate competence and interest,
he kept the young man busy with questions as they left the grounds for
the checkpoint into the new dragon security area. Syrik, now overall commander of the dragon and its mages, had located it to a smaller and better
defensible position, a large empty rectangle. It had once been some kind
of fae marketplace accessible from multiple streets. Syrik had ordered all

the homes upon the block but those ringing the marketplace dismantled so that there was no way to approach the place unseen. All but a single entry point between two stone houses was blocked off.

Vannek looked directly at the four soldiers manning the checkpoint as they walked up, for his brother had never paid enough attention to the rank and file unless they were sucking up to him. The lantern light was dim in the passage, and all four of the soldiers stood away from the fire rather than beside it. Was that so that they'd be less convenient targets? Maybe they were being overcautious.

The four men came to attention on either side of the dark entryway, saluting as Vannek and Rolk and the mage came up and drew even. The mage was still gabbling when the first guard shoved a knife into his chest; Vannek had been watching the mage's face, so he happened to see the blood spurt forcefully from the murderous attack. The second blow caught the mage in his back.

Rolk was likewise fending off a slice and Vannek drew his sword and turned a thrust more by instinct than plan.

The Resistance again! How had they gotten in so far?

Rolk let out a choked roar and one figure stumbled past Vannek, blood spraying from a nearly severed leg. The attacker collapsed with a hissing scream.

The light showed Vannek the square face of another attacker with a long bulbous nose. Vannek thought to himself that the attacker's beard wasn't quite long enough to pass for a Naor soldier, which was probably the real reason they'd hidden in the darkness.

"It's the general!" A woman's voice cried this warning, and it came from the figure behind the big-nosed man with the short beard.

Vannek worried about being flanked, was dimly conscious that Rolk, bellowing like a wounded eshlack, fought for his life against a fourth. The old man staggered on a wounded knee, effectively spoiling attack from another rebel on Vannek's left; Rolk bumped into Short Beard.

And this put Vannek's assailant off balance. It was the tiniest opening, but for a practiced swordsman, it was all Vannek required. He swung for his throat.

But Short Beard was no easy mark. He slid back so that Vannek's sword only clipped his chin. Blood sprayed, but it was hardly a mortal wound.

A horn blast sounded. Someone must have heard the commotion and raised the alarm.

"Retreat," the woman warrior ordered, and it was only then Vannek realized with a jolt of envy that she was in command.

Vannek drove at Short Beard, beat his sword down, then stuck him in the thigh with her blade point. It was a debilitating wound but not, she thought, a killing one. Maybe this time they'd have a prisoner.

The man fell, groaning. Rolk had driven his small hand axe through the fourth rebel's chest. There was the sound of running footfalls from outside.

The woman rebel cried out a name, Lemahl, as if it was ripped from her, then nimbly leapt past Vannek's slice and dashed past him into darkness.

Vannek saw guards running toward them at last, but Vannek shouted and pointed at the woman dashing diagonally away. "After her, fools! Catch her alive!"

The soldiers swung away and followed the rebel into the darkness.

Rolk limped over to the wounded man, lying now on his side, and stared down before putting his foot to him and kicking him over. He bent down by the limp body.

The old man cursed. "He's bled out."

"Nonsense. I didn't hit an artery."

"No, fool, he jammed his knife into his own throat."

Rolk didn't see his death coming; Vannek drove his own blade into the side of his neck, just above an old nick on the graybeard's shoulder armor. Rolk gasped and the hand clamped up toward the weapon, bloodying his fingers on the edge as Vannek withdrew it. Rolk slumped, but kicked at Vannek as he stepped away.

"It was all good advice," he told the old man as he died. "And I'll take it. Except for the part where I'm beholden to you. I am no man's lackey. And if you're so fond of your grandchildren, I'll send them after you, on the pyres."

He wasn't sure that Rolk heard the last, because he'd stopped moving. It didn't matter.

Vannek bent down and wiped his blade on the sleeve of the dead rebel. He stared into unseeing blue eyes fixed forever in proud defiance, then sheathed his weapon and stepped from the dark corridor to join in the search for the surviving assassin.

22

Gathering in the Dark

S ansyra would have expected to be racked with grief, but after insensate rage it was numbness that overwhelmed her. All during the long, difficult return journey to their hiding place, and the terrible report, Sansyra doggedly carried out her duties. It was almost as though she was one step removed from herself, a dispassionate observer watching her body work. She was even able to rest, although she hardly felt connected or refreshed after she woke in the afternoon. When Varama asked if she would guard while contacting N'lahr, she agreed without reservation.

The two altens swiftly compared states of readiness. N'lahr couldn't help revealing apprehension when he learned noises had been heard outside one of the tunnel entrances deeper in the city. The Naor had begun to probe another access point so Varama had once again collapsed the entire tunnel. It would take the Naor a very long time to clear that obstacle.

From N'lahr they learned additional details about last night's significant Naor defeat outside the walls, including a summarized description of Alten Gyldara's battle with a wounded Naor dragon.

Once the two Altenerai had traded information, N'lahr changed subjects. He'd gotten a little better at masking his feelings, but there was no missing the concern in his tone. *How's morale?*

Varama's answer was blunt. *It's low. We've lost almost all of my original lead officers, and nine warriors. The Alantrans shift constantly between anger and despair, for their city is being destroyed and their people suffer and they feel that our actions are futile.*

It was worse than that, Sansyra thought, and was a little ashamed that Varama noticed and wove it into her conversation.

Sansyra is correct in that some feel our actions actually exacerbate the Naor depradations. At least one of the Alantrans blames me for slaying Denalia, although if she had been captured alive she would have suffered terrible anguish and may have been forced to reveal our position besides.

Will they follow your plans? N'lahr's simple words belied the serious edge behind them.

By contrast, Varama was coolly controlled. *They need follow me this one last time. The plans will see us through. There is nothing more that can be done.*

You are wrong, for once. Speak to them, Varama. Tell them you're aware of their suffering. Let them know that you've suffered, too, for some will be too self-involved to realize how well you conceal your reactions.

That sounds like what Renik would have said. Sansyra thought she detected an echo of some ancient loss there, different from grief in a way she didn't fully understand. And then Varama's feelings were opaque once more. Sansyra struggled to keep her speculations to herself, but couldn't help wondering a host of things that she had never before suspected.

N'lahr was briefly pleased. *If I sound like the Commander,* N'lahr communicated, *then that's all the more reason to heed my advice.*

I shall take it under consideration.

Following that pronouncement, the surprises were complete, and the two touched briefly upon their timetable before concluding their conversation. Varama shut down the stone and sat for a time staring into space. Sansyra wondered if she was expected simply to depart, but held still in the chair across from her superior.

Finally the alten met her eyes.

"All of us have had our hurts," she said. "I believe it often surprises the young that their elders have a number of tragedies in their accumulated experiences. But I think the old often forget how painful wounds can be while fresh. I couldn't help but notice yours, Sansyra. How is *your* morale?"

In attempting to put her own thoughts into perspective, Sansyra's discipline faltered, and before she knew it, she'd begun to cry. This shamed her, and she struggled to put an apology together as she kept her face low to minimize its scrutibility.

"Dialogue is a poor salve to many hurts," Varama observed sadly.

Sansyra fought to master her feelings, and to curtail regret, and to put aside those last comforting moments with Lemahl, with her head upon his shoulder. She wanted another memory like that, and not to constantly see him fall, hand tightly gripped to the hilt at his side. She'd known what he would do if he couldn't rise and follow.

"And it's generally more devastating to watch death take those who are dear, or those depending on you," Varama added, "than to brave a deadly direct assault."

"How do you find the strength to go forward?" Sansyra managed to say softly.

Varama looked away before answering, her gaze directed at something beyond the wall. "Renik once said that when there is no avenue of retreat, and you cannot hold your ground, the only choice is to advance."

That hadn't helped. "I'm tired of advancing," Sansyra admitted quietly. "I want to be somewhere where people's lives don't hang on every choice we make, and to be someone who doesn't have to make those choices."

Varama faced her. Her overbright eyes held a fierce look in an otherwise haggard mein. "We're fighting so that other people, and maybe even ourselves, might reach that place."

"That's what you should tell the others." Sansyra wiped at her eyes. She'd finally managed to regain control.

Varama eyed her coolly. "I suspect that they've heard enough from me already."

"No, Alten. I think you need to talk to them as you've talked to me. They've seen your strength. Sometimes people need to see your weakness as well. It lets them know you're . . . human. That you're able to see things as they do."

Varama smiled faintly. "I am all too human, Sansyra, and also weary of the choices to be made here." She regarded Sansyra quietly for a time, then addressed her courteously. "It's time we both rested. Your counsel is appreciated. You're dismissed."

"Yes, Alten." Sansyra rose. "Thank you," she said, but to that Varama only nodded distractedly. She left the alten there and returned to the welcome oblivion of sleep. That afternoon, those who remained met in the cavern with its wide pool. Sansyra tried not to dwell on their diminished numbers. The squires and soldiers were drawn up in formation, by rank. In the last days they had blended freely, united in their struggle, and their loss.

Varama faced them and told them to stand at ease. Her eyes were dark rimmed and deeply lined, as they had been for days, but for once her hair was properly brushed. Her khalat was clean and her boots, if not quite shining, held a dull luster that reflected torchlight. Sansyra felt a pang, sensing something in Varama's gaze that was lost and fragile and bewildered before the door slammed shut again. What, she wondered, might Varama say to allay their worries?

The alten spoke in her high, clear voice, thinner with fatigue. "If I've asked much of you, it is in part because there was no one else to ask. We few were in this place, at this time. None of us wanted bloodshed, but the enemy brought it, and they are resolute in their aim." She paused and let her regard roam over them. "They mean simply to end us—body, mind, and soul. They end us not only at the points of their weapons, through their depraved degradations, and in the fires of their wanton destruction, but by ending the freedoms that we usually take for granted; that so long as it harm none, we may choose our vocation, our loves, our dwelling places, even our customs. These freedoms are defined in our laws and define us to friend and enemy alike.

"Those of you who pledged, like me, to the Altenerai Corps, swore not only to defend these laws, but to shield the people who practice them, unto your dying breath. And those soldiers of Alantris who stand with us vowed to defend their city and their homeland with their lives.

"Those vows have been bravely kept at great cost. We have been united in our efforts to weaken the enemy, and we have succeeded beyond hope. That so many have perished to reach this point is a bitter measure, but like the taste of hard liquor, let that give you fire. For we have come to the decisive moment. Everything hinges on the actions we take tonight. If we falter, all those who have given their lives will have died in vain."

Sansyra felt a lump form in her throat.

"But if we triumph, the enemy will be driven from our sight, and our people will live, free once more. This night we must let loose the beast of war, red handed and merciless. And if this be our numbered day, we must rejoice, that we fall in so noble a struggle."

There was a rustle behind her as one soldier came to attention and saluted, and then the remaining Alantrans followed. Quickly, Sansyra called the squires to attention and presented her own salute, and she felt rather than saw the outpouring of emotion from the squires with her.

She would have liked, so much, if that shared humanity had somehow pierced the strange bubble that surrounded her commanding officer and provided comfort to the person within, she who was ever befuddled by the imperfect resolve of those around her.

Instead Varama gave only the slightest of nods, and ordered them to their stations. Men and women filed past. The alten, though, beckoned her close, and they stepped to the pool, under the shadow of a single lantern.

"That was nicely said, Alten," Sansyra offered. At Varama's blank look, it occurred to her that Varama was already thinking beyond the speech. The compliment passed over the alten with an eye blink as her officer got to the point.

"I want you to have this." Varama pulled her hand from her pouch, opened her fingers, and revealed a semblance stone. Sansyra felt a little dejected at the sight of it. She looked up at her mentor's face. Did she expect her to take on the semblance of an alten as she and her troops secured the gate?

"I know your own magical stores are scant. You can tap this not as a way to disguise yourself, but as a source of energy to power your weaving. It's like a limited hearthstone."

"Don't you need it?"

"I have Belahn's old stone, the one N'lahr sent, and I will tap it well this night. Take the semblance. Drain it dry. It might make the difference."

"I will. Thank you." The gesture touched Sansyra deeply, for it was tantamount to a deep embrace.

Varama continued, "It's vital you win your gate and hold it. This should be an assignment for an alten, but you're nearly there—"

"I'm not sure I want the ring," Sansayra blurted out in confession.

Varama looked startled at last, then quickly recovered. "That's your prerogative, and something about which we should speak at a later time. Assuming we have one."

Sansyra nodded but didn't interrupt further.

"Whatever happens from here, I wish you to know that I appreciate your aid. Yours was a challenging role. I told you the numbers needed for a task, and it was you who had to pick the names. And often it was you who saw them fall." Briefly Varama's invisible veil slipped and Sansyra glimpsed a hint of anguish.

It was gone so swiftly she might have imagined it. "Thank you," Varama said, for once meeting Sansyra's eyes with something approaching warmth.

"It is my pleasure, and honor, to serve you, Alten. There is none with whom I would rather work."

"That is kind," Varama said, and it might be that just this once she actually registered the compliment, for she hesitated a brief moment before continuing. "I've wished for years we could outfit the higher-ranked squires in better armor, because too often we have to send you into places where we'd go ourselves, and without so fine a protection."

There was no way around that, owing to expense and lengthy preparation of the fibers used to fashion khalats, and the slow growth of the trees from which they were processed. "That's how it's always been. You know we couldn't have gotten to this moment without you, Alten. Please be careful. We may need you yet."

"I will do what must be done. Just as you will. Now we'd best be on our way."

So saying, Varama stepped past. Sansyra followed, and they headed forth to free the city or die in the trying.

23

The Fire in the Sky

Vannek hadn't drawn in the new road. He could have, if he'd wanted the map to reflect the current situation, but he'd left the huge sheet of paper unmarred. Mostly this was because he thought his brother Koregan's plan to build a road straight through the midst of the city stupid, and he meant to restore the preexisting roadway with its better defenses shortly.

But part of his hesitation lay behind a reluctance to alter what was a stunning piece of work. He knew the dangerous allure of the soft arts, and how the Dendressi corrupted and weakened their society by encouraging a reverence for pointless, pretty things. This map, though, wasn't useless. Some unknown artist had drawn out an immense lovingly detailed image of the entire city, noting each and every dwelling, road, waterway, and change in elevation. Even the teeth in the walls were minutely delineated.

He had bade Syrik pin the masterwork drawing very carefully to the wall. The mage had suggested the map be placed upon the conference table, but Vannek knew it would be ruined by the kings that gathered, even if he agreed with Syrik's assessment that they'd prefer to be closer to the drawing.

He wished Syrik was here, at his side. But with the death of the last dragon lord under his command, there was only one junior mage tutored in their use, and so she had ordered Syrik to find a way to master control of the animal himself, lest the final beast be rendered completely useless.

With Vannek instead were two scarred, grim brutes from his newly swelled corps of personal guard; most of Rolk's followers were furious to learn of his demise and duly impressed with Vannek's swift slaying of the old man's assassin, so had pledged their swords. Nearly everyone seated at the table in the high white room was a similar somber, scarred man.

As night fell that evening, Vannek had gathered the nine highest kings of his expeditionary force. He hadn't bothered serving a dinner first—that's what Koregan would have done. It wouldn't have impressed any of these suspicious men, just given time and a forum to test their veiled insults.

Now they waited at the table, silently watching. Probably they hoped he would suggest a policy they could deride, or a tactic they could question, seeking only to prove themselves to one another.

Outside, the sun had set. The two lanterns hung from the chandelier glowed low by prearrangement, and the two suspended above the map brought out a florid hue in the parchment. Vannek preferred the dim conditions; it was less obvious then that he looked like a woman. There was nothing he could do about his voice, save to speak with gruff directness.

He slashed out his hand toward the paper. "Our enemy left us an exacting map of our new home. Until now we've but crouched here, like a dog." He pointed to the main gatehouse and quarter of the outer ring, and the raised second ring, with the manor house they occupied.

"We claim to hold the city, but we brawl over the bones we've already chewed. We own the Dendressi and yet we cower in their walls." He said the last with a snarl and drove his fist into an open palm.

"What do you suggest?" This question came from velvet-voiced Kavnat, the deceptively casual master of the Shakni people, famed for their fierce axemen. "Please don't tell me you want to send our men out on foot to attack the Dendressi horsefolk. We saw what happened yesterday. We must be patient."

There were a few chuckles and a smirk or two, but others around the table weren't willing to give Kavnat even that small amount of support. They waited for their own line of attack.

Vannek had anticipated Kavnat's response would come from someone. "Patience. Old men plead for patience. What I lack is bold warriors who are *im*patient. It is high time we truly made this city ours! We are careless with its riches. We trample the grain fields. Our men piss in the canals that water the crops, and throw filth into the wells. Soon they'll be unfit for anything. My brother kept us from the great temples and their wealth, thinking we needed Chargan to secure them from curses. We are Naor! We have wrestled life from lands with little more than rock and sand! It is time to act!" Vannek jabbed a finger toward a point just off-center of the map. "I will occupy the citadel tomorrow. From there I will rule. Who is brave enough to master the temples?"

"My people will see to the temples," young Stilkar said. "I do not fear."

"That's because you're stupid," Kavnat said, to a laugh from those nearest.

But Trelk, Red Feather chieftain, thrust up his hand. "I will see to the farm lands."

Kavnat sneered at Vannek. "And you want me for the river, I suppose? What power is that?"

"The power is in pleasing me through serving me well," Vannek said, and didn't wait for the reaction. "He who controls the water has a hand in both our food, and our defenses. But perhaps that is too much for you, Kavnat."

"I'll take the north ring," Mazhrel volunteered quickly.

That was too large an area for one man. Vannek shook his head and pointed to one portion on the northern area of the map. "You can take this region from the gate to the fruit groves."

He didn't mind the smile creeping over his face. It was working even better than he'd suspected. They were suddenly eager for his favor, for he'd demonstrated his power to distribute wealth. They would quarrel among themselves to set their own regions prospering, rather than unite against him.

Kavnat seemed suddenly to realize he'd best get involved and was shouting for attention about the southern pasture just when there came a loud knock at the door.

"Wait," Vannek ordered, and pointed to one of his sentries, who stepped out, closing the door behind him before conferring with a concerned-looking messenger.

"I wish to pledge a location," Kavnat shouted, but others called as well.

"Wait!" Vannek snapped, and the door came open and the sentry waved him over.

He walked into the hall, shut the door behind him, and gave his sentry his best "this had better be good" look. The sentry merely nodded to the messenger, so Vannek looked to him. "Report."

The youth spoke quickly. "There are fires, floating in the sky. Above the city."

Vannek struggled to attach meaning to the words, then realized that even if he didn't fully understand, the Resistance must be up to some kind of attack. Wordless, he reentered the room. One of the kings must have already spotted something, for they were all crowded about the windows.

Vannek pushed his way through. Night had fallen, and the sky was hung with strands of clouds through which pockets of stars shone coldly down. From his vantage point on the second tier of the city, Vannek looked across the wide first circle of Alantris, glimpsing the fields and towering arches of the old aqueducts, the streets and the clusters of buildings, the canals in their stone channels, the gardens that sprouted seemingly every-where, and the distant city wall. The invasion entry point was out of sight to the left, along with the dragon landing field.

Between clouds and ground, some forty yards to his right and at most a half mile out, a flame hung in the sky. He felt a chill as he realized it drifted closer by the heartbeat. Behind it, advancing over the abandoned expanse of an arena that was built along the edge of the second tier, were a score of additional sky flames.

While the kings muttered worriedly about sorcery, Vannek noted that something above each of the fires blotted the lighter shape of clouds. Each flame was suspended beneath some *thing* that drifted in the darkness. Might their enemies have conjured beasts of their own? Magic was surely involved, for the flames traveled against the wind.

An alert horn call sounded from the north, and seconds later another rang from deeper in the city.

"They're trying to distract us with multiple fronts again," Vannek declared.

The kings talked excitedly among themselves, ignoring him. One pointed to the stadium watchtower. It sat sheer on the side of the cliff look-ing down upon both the lower ring of the city and the stadium grounds. A lone figure stood upon its battlement performing grand sweeping gestures with his arms, as though he encouraged the wind. Upon his hand was a glowing blue ring.

"It's N'lahr!" Kavnat cried.

"Yes," Vannek said, though he wondered if it was true. Kavnat seemed less frightened than eager.

The closest flame veered to the right and slid toward the slate-roofed stables across the street. One of the kings gasped and jabbed a finger at the inverted vaselike shape revealed by the flames suddenly eating it. Then the object crashed down in orange agony on the roof, which instantly blazed into life.

Vannek swore. His brother Koregan had allowed the chieftains and kings to lair in the city's government buildings, perched here in a cluster.

Fiery doom could shortly engulf all their wooden command buildings. Another flame already sank toward the mansion where Kavnat had set his headquarters. Nearer still, the flames dropped beside a trio of headless statues and began consuming the homes on either side of the street.

Vannek grabbed Trelk's arm and shouted at him to organize his men in bucket brigades. He called the cavalry commander close. "Ride like the demons are on you to secure the gates!"

"The gates?" Kavnat scoffed. The cavalry commander was already running for the door.

Kavnat wasn't usually this stupid. "They'll try to draw us to internal problems while they assault from outside!"

Kavnat's brows rose in surprise, and for a brief moment he looked on Vannek as though he were an equal. "The clever bastards. All right. I'm going to go kill N'lahr," he vowed.

Almost surely that alten was a lure, for she knew Altenerai could move with secrecy and had no need of letting their rings shine, even when they practiced sorcery. But he'd be damned if he'd let Kavnat take command. "Good—come with me."

The stables were an inferno. A small band of attendants had managed to pull a few animals free, but the rest whinnied frantically from within the fiery death trap.

While Kavnat complained that there were no saddles, Vannek's chief bodyguard helped calm a stone-white stallion. Vannek thought the animal ready enough to mount, yet waited for his honor guard to join him, watching the twenty men of Kavnat's squad as their troublesome leader climbed onto his own horse and kicked it forward. His men raced off at his side.

Only then did Vannek mount, crying for his men to hurry. He had no intention of catching up to Kavnat, though. If there was a trap he'd let the king find it.

The Altenerai amphitheater was carved into the cliffside, the seats descending toward the long field where knee-high grass rose. A wall curved along the rim; beyond it was the fifty-foot drop to the first ring below.

The tower where the alten had stood rose on the far end of the stadium, built along the curve of the wall, just in front of a row of outbuildings. Vannek saw no sign of the alten atop the tower, and visibility was simple, for the fire to their rear stained the clouds with crimson and lit the sky like sunset.

Kavnat advanced his horse at a trot, his men running along beside. "Come on, boys! We're going to go kill the king of the Altenerai!" His men shouted enthusiastically, and Vannek wished more of her people showed such spirit at mention of N'lahr.

As Kavnat drew within twenty paces of the tower, his horse screamed in pain and then reared. Five of his warriors faltered, and two leapt back, one hopping on his foot. Kavnat dropped from his mount rather than hanging on to be thrown. It galloped awkwardly into the darkness, one leg stiff.

"Watch your footing!" Kavnat cried. "They've scattered spikes!"

As he and his men picked their way carefully toward the tower, constantly glancing down, Vannek held his men behind, waiting for the inevitable. And it came. A pair of figures popped up along the tower battlement. Each held a bow.

"There are only two!" Kavnat screamed. "Charge them!"

As Kavnat shouted, an arrow found him and he dropped with a shaft buried in his face. Two of the soldiers fell to their knees to check on him and the rest charged the tower door.

Vannek got a faint whiff of oil as he drew close to the point where Kavnat had encountered spikes. He urged his soldiers to ready spears.

The archers sent a few more shafts, then dropped from sight. Four of Kavnat's men were taking turns banging into the sturdy door with their shoulders. Another had reached the tower's side and called for his companion to scale his back to try for a low, deep-set window. Others simply milled around, staring upward, fingering their axes.

"The Dendressi archers are going to return at any moment," Vannek said to his men. "I want you three to aim at the archer on the right, you others for the one on the left."

His soldiers nodded their assent. The battlements were just barely in range.

The archers stepped back into view and Vannek's men cast their spears. Both archers dropped. One cried out.

And then someone else fired from the second-floor window. This arrow was aflame and it seemed unlikely to hit anything or anyone, for it passed over the heads of Kavnat's men, and it was well clear of Vannek's soldiers.

When it struck the ground, flame erupted and flared out through the grasses to left and right.

Vannek's horse pitched in terror. He fumbled to grab its neck as fire blinded his view. He dug fingers into the stallion's mane, realizing the Altenerai had spread oil along the ground, cursing himself for failing to realize the import of the smell. He nearly lost his seat as his mount spun and bolted free.

His men ran, but they were in the midst of the flames. Their long pants caught fire, and they screamed in pain and fear. They ran as far as they could, then fell writhing in the burning grass.

Vannek slid down from the fear-maddened horse just clear of the inferno, his nose wrinkling from the smell of searing flesh. Then he saw the fire hadn't finished with him. It had caught in the dry grasses beyond the oil-soaked area and a wave of flames roared toward him.

He sprinted for the stone wall along the rim. The pressure of the flame was like a huge hand against his back. It felt as though the armor was melting to him.

He reached the stones and heaved himself up.

This section of the wall wasn't intended as a battlement, and was only two feet in width. Beyond was a drop to a dark canal. If Vannek hadn't known it for water he might have thought it a road at the cliff's base.

He looked back toward the tower, and saw figures there outlined against the battlement. They were lifting bows. Some were firing into the flames, presumably at those few targets left alive.

His anger rose higher than his fear. He would find a way to take down those arrogant Dendressi. Rather than retreating, and taking an arrow to the back, he decided to advance upon the tower, jogging along the wall with its perilous drop on his left. He was an old hand with heights, for he'd often climbed tall trees when he'd been a young girl.

The first arrow struck against his breastplate. An unpleasant surprise. There was smoke, too, but it was blowing parallel to him, rather than across, and the closer he got to the tower, the less there'd be to conceal him.

His helm he'd left behind in the council chambers, so he lifted an armored arm to shield his face.

The next arrow caught him near the wrist. It didn't penetrate, but the impact slammed his own fist into his cheek. His step faltered and he leaned left . . . promptly sliding from the wall.

The instant between falling and registering the impact coming seemed an eternity. The wind rushed up at him and he lifted his legs. He hit the water canted forward, first with his feet, then his arms, then his face, the force nearly stunning him.

The canal was dark and cool, but proved not especially deep, for he quickly struck its bottom with his booted feet and, panicking, he kicked off, rising to find the surface despite his armor. Rather than fight his way out and expose himself to archery, he let the current push him along, managing to stay above the surface some of the time by holding to the rough stone on the side of the canal. His chest plate and greaves kept trying to drag him under despite constant and vigorous kicking and he soon grew alarmed. How could he possibly hold on to the sides and unbuckle the armor?

So he pushed himself along, thinking himself already too tired to attempt scaling the canal side.

Then, by the blessings of the Three, he arrived at a set of stairs cut into the side of the wall, presumably for maintenance.

Coughing, he started forward, and found himself on his feet halfway up the steps, sodden, and stared apprehensively back toward the tower. No one watched. Smoke laced the red sky. The shouts of men and clash of arms drifted on the night. He heard the whinny of horses, as well.

Thoroughly soaked, he staggered away from the canal, then, at the sound of hoofbeats, pressed himself flat against a stone wall. The horse clopped closer, accompanied by another peculiar sound, as though something was sliding along behind it.

His mind alive with images of a great Dendressi serpent, he peered out, only to discover a brown mount, head bent with exhaustion, dragging a dead Naor king whose broken leg was caught in its stirrup. Trelk.

The Three had blessed him again. One more blessing, then, this night, Vannek thought, and then would come a run of bad luck. For now, though, he would take the horse and rally the city.

He caught his breath, steeled himself, and started forward.

24

The Last Dragon

The snarling faces were half-lit by bloodred lanterns that stained everything crimson. Sansyra and Iressa pushed across the battlement into the gate tower, and then Sansyra was hurtling down the stairs. She'd dropped the spear and managed with a Naor sword, notched and gore-streaked. The heavy wooden shield she'd snatched up splintered when she smashed a Naor head with it.

Somehow, though, she reached the lower level and the wheel, and she turned it, ignoring the sound of carnage above. From outside came the thunder of hooves. She didn't know if they were Naor reinforcements or the Kaneshi cavalry riding out of the darkness until she ran up the stairs to the second level. There, a wounded Iressa sagged against the wall while another squire bound her shoulder. Out on the wall, Virian was waving and grinning, a terrible red gash livid on his cheek, two arrows protruding from his left arm.

Kaneshi riders, distinctive in their cloaks and pointed, burnished helms, surged through the gate and hurried into the city.

"We did it!" Virian shouted, exultant.

Somehow, in fact, they had achieved the objective, no matter that their deception had failed against the most important of the two gate towers. The Naor guards had slammed home the barrier and their group had to fight their way up the right tower, along the battlement over the gate, and on across and down to the wheel that withdrew the gate bar.

Now, like a good commander, she considered her forces. A quick count told her that four from her attack team were dead and another three wounded. So might it go throughout the assault.

Varama had assured her that it wasn't about numbers, but control, and that they would win a series of smaller battles if they controlled the ground and the momentum. All that was likely true, but in the capital buildings of Alantris Varama might even now be breathing her last. The alten had struck at the heart of the enemy command, daring a close approach so she could use sorcery to guide her amazing flying weapons toward the best targets. She'd split the rest of the troops out to open the gate and liberate the two largest groups of prisoners herself.

Varama had worried that the civilians could be burned up as fires spread, and Sansyra now saw her concerns had been justified, for flame roared all along the second rim and points of the third. Buildings were silhouetted by the writhing red blossoms of fire, and the scent of burning wood and smoke filled her nostrils. In saving the people of Alantris, she saw with sober consideration, they might well have delivered the city itself a mortal wound.

Sansyra appointed her soldiers to sentry points, lest the Naor try to attack along the battlement, then listened to the thunder of the horse troops advancing below.

That was when she spotted the dragon.

She knew it was her favorite. The other had been artfully slain in the recent battle when N'lahr offered a tempting group of spearmen upon a ridge. Camouflaged spear catapults had killed one sent from the Naor sorcerer, and crippled the other, which Alten Gyldara had finished almost single-handedly.

Only the smaller one with the shining wings remained. Though it had imbibed some of the poisons, the Naor had painstakingly saved it, and tonight it was in the air, circling over the second ring, and the tower from where Alten Varama had launched her assault.

The dragon was searching, and with chill foreboding Sansyra thought she knew what it was after. Varama. She hurried to Iressa, whose features were streaked with dirt and someone else's blood. The third ranker watched from the battlement with grim satisfaction as their horse soldiers continued streaming into the city.

"The gate is ours," Sansyra said. "See that it holds. Foot troops are supposed to reinforce us after the cavalry gets through."

Iressa's slim, arched brows climbed her forehead. "Where are you going?"

"Dragon hunting," she said.

Iressa raised a cry of indignation, but Sansyra was already turning down the stairs and soon hurried from the tower. In the adjacent stables she found a half dozen sturdy Naor ponies, and a beautiful spirited gray. She worked quickly to saddle him while the hoofbeats shook the ground outside.

She heard a hoarse masculine voice shouting orders and the tramp of feet, and wondered if that was N'lahr, commanding foot troops. She was curious to meet him in person and ordinarily would have been fascinated by the idea, but now had only thoughts for Varama. The longer her preparations took, the more danger the alten faced from that dragon. And so she chafed when she had to adjust the bit, and cursed aloud when she discovered there was only one spear on hand and that it was a little short.

She would have to make that spear count, then. Just as she'd learned Gyldara had done with a single axe.

She emerged into a crowd of hundreds of Vedessi foot soldiers, and some shouted in alarm as they saw a mounted figure enter their midst from the darkness. She paused so that they might register her as a squire and not a threat, and maneuvered around a band of pikemen.

She debated calling for them to follow, and then heard someone shouting at her.

"Squire!"

The call came from behind, and she knew it was directed at her, but she moved on as though she hadn't heard, and soon she was past and guiding her animal swiftly around other troops.

Before long she had a clear view down a wide lane that led south, where she saw a knot of Naor swordsmen tussling with a unit of pikemen. A second group of Vedessi hurried forward to reinforce the first.

She continued east where she could see the whole of the arena upon the cliffside, outlined in flickering red and orange. Second-story buildings were so well illuminated she could pick out individual bricks, though lower levels were but dull shapes wrapped in shadow.

She came upon a large lane slanting up to a gated wall around the second level. Kaneshi cavalry charged it, undeterred by fierce resistance from Naor on the walls, flinging spears and casting arrows. The Kaneshi archers sat well back, launching arrow after arrow against the ramparts while spearmen galloped forward, the tails of their long protective coats flying behind them. They aimed low, rather than high, thrusting their spears into the great double doors. Three separate parties of them rode and cast spears, losing three or four soldiers with every charge.

On the fourth attack she recognized Enada herself leading a dozen to the doors. The cover fire from the Kaneshi bowmen seemed to treble.

Rather than casting spears like those before her, Enada leapt nimbly from her horse, caught an embedded spear, and pulled herself up. Other riders followed behind her, leaping to the spears and clambering up like the weapons were irregular ladder rungs.

Enada took the lead, not climbing so much as hopping from one to the other, quickly ascending. The bowmen lessened their cover fire as she drew within a few feet of the top, and then she leapt the merlon, three of her soldiers coming almost immediately after.

Awestruck, Sansyra watched the figures dashing along the battlement height, wondering if she herself might ever be so competent. It dawned on her then that there was no good way through to the tower, nor that she could reach it in any kind of timely manner. By the time she got there, Varama would likely be gone.

She had acted rashly, and now she sat ahorse alone in an occupied city when at the very least she should be holding her post. Smarter would have been to insert herself into the command structure and lead some of the troops to battle. She knew the city far better than the Vedessi and could help guide them. She looked down at her single short spear and sneered at herself. Certainly a brave alten might fight a dragon, but Gyldara, she knew, had faced an injured animal and had an army behind her.

She frowned at her own foolishness, and wondered if it was adrenaline that had sent her hither, or some kind of unconscious craving for glory. At some level, she realized she still wanted to be a hero, childish as that notion seemed. It was heroic enough to have taken that gate. With that way open, the allied forces were advancing through a city bereft of leaders and overwhelmed by multiple distractions. Varama's plan was bringing victory, just as she'd told Denalia.

Wherever Varama was now, she would doubtless tell Sansyra to retreat to the lines. She was turning to do so when she heard the drum of hoofbeats.

She spotted a figure on a horse between two lanes and wondered if it was fate that had delivered her here. For something about the way the rider carried himself reminded her of the Naor general. The woman, Vannek.

She swung the little gray around and kicked into pursuit.

Following onto the wide Avenue of White, she caught a glimpse of the rider in silhouette as she looked over her shoulder. Even in that poor lighting Sansyra recognized her beardless quarry.

Sansyra spurred her mount harder, and galloped after. Vannek, too, kicked her beast into gallop, but the animal struggled. In the shadow of a great fountain, Vannek's horse stumbled and pitched its rider out of the saddle.

Sansyra grinned fiercely. Only a few hundred yards lay between them, and she thought for a moment the Naor might be dead, but Vannek pushed herself to her feet, looked over her shoulder, and stumbled into a run toward the great oval pool around Alvor's Oak.

Somehow the little park was still mostly unscathed. The beautiful tree that Alvor himself was said to have planted soared up from its platform in the midst of the pool. Incongruously, no matter the distant screams and the red fire reflected from dark clouds, stone animals hidden about the tree still spouted water into the basin that circled at their feet. The Naor, who lived in drab lands, might have appreciated the simple, natural elegance of this garden. Or it might be that they simply hadn't gotten around to destroying it yet.

As Asrahn had taught her, Sansyra considered the land over which she was about to fight for advantageous positions. And as Varama had taught her she calculated how best to use the resources at hand. She had a horse she didn't know well. Her sword. A short spear. A knife.

And the semblance stone. Now, she thought, was the time, and she tapped it to reach out for energy with tendrils of her magic. As Vannek turned to launch a spear Sansyra touched the threads of its trajectory and sent it twirling off course.

She pitched her own spear, using her magics to propel it to increased speed. Vannek spun away, but the cast caught her in the back and she plunged into the fountain. Whether or not the weapon had pierced she couldn't see, not amid the splash of Vannek's fall.

Sansyra drew her blade and guided the gray on. It hesitated at the lip of the pool before gamely leaping the verge and splashing into the fountain.

Vannek rose with sword in hand. Sansyra leaned out to slash, but the Naor general dived beneath the blow. Sansyra kept on, putting the tree between her and her foe. She kicked the gray into a canter then grabbed a low hanging branch to lift her off out of the Naor's sight.

As the horse continued its noisy progress, Sansyra swung hand over hand to the raised middle of the pool and the stone path that circled the oak, then dropped silently beside the life-sized wolf spitting water from its maw. She ran along the inner curve of the poolstones as the horse continued splashing around.

The distraction got her very close to Vannek. The Naor stood with her back exposed. She wore complicated armor of interworked metal plates, and there was no sign of the wound Sansyra had hoped for. The javelin point wouldn't have easily pierced armor so fine.

She must have given herself away. Vannek whirled. Sansyra saw the gleam of her teeth. The Naor general's hand whipped up and Sansyra felt something thud into her armor near her collar. A gleaming object plunged into the water nearby and she understood that the Naor had thrown a second knife. A few finger spans higher and it would have caught her throat.

Sansyra flung herself forward.

Vannek met her blade a fraction of a moment too slow, but blocked the blow. Sansyra could tell by the way she parried that Vannek was already winded. She looked half spent. Yet the Naor met each strike with determination. Soon both warriors breathed heavily, and Vannek forced Sansyra back. Their feet kicked up shining beads of water.

Vannek seemed to find her second wind and advanced with a vengeance. The squire's arms ached, and one of her calves cramped. She'd had only a brief respite after the battle for the gate. Her breath came in great gasps and her head pounded. Sweat streamed from the line of her helm and into her eyes, stinging them.

Afraid that if she didn't act now she was done for, she tapped the semblance stone. She felt its energy drizzle as she stole the last of its power, waited for Vannek to swing, leaned back, then plunged in, willing speed into her motion.

Time seemed slowed. Vannek's eyes widened as with the last of her magical power Sansyra came in with astonishing speed, aiming a vital blow.

Vannek lowered her head instinctually, trying to shield her neck and twisting away, so the strike that would have taken her in the throat slid along the side of her lowering head and tore into her ear, sending a large bloody flap flying.

The Naor gasped, tried to steady herself with a backward step, and lost balance to crash to her knees. Her sword dropped into the water.

Sansyra was quick to follow, her sword point low. "Yield!"

Vannek's pain-wracked face turned and met her eyes even as the woman reached sideways into the water for her blade. Blood flowed down the left side of her face.

"Yield!" Sansyra was astonished by the way her voice rang off the stone, how dry it was, how hoarse she sounded, how it hurt a little to speak at such volume.

From behind came a rush of wind. Little wavelets rose in the water. And Vannek's expression brightened as she caught sight of something to Sansyra's rear.

Every instinct told Sansyra she needed to move, now, that she had to get out of the way, that she was wide open for whatever was happening at her back. She stepped right, so that the tree was behind her, and Vannek lay at her left hand.

She stole a glance away and found the dragon with the shining wings. It carried two riders, and its fanged mouth was open. One of the two men riding it cried out in a hoarse voice to get down.

She knew the warning was meant for Vannek, but Sansyra threw herself into the basin beyond the tree.

The sound was but mildly dulled by the water, and she felt it strike not just her ears but set her chest vibrating, and her limbs shook. It felt as though every bone in her body had been struck at once.

There was a resounding crack and she felt the ground shift beneath her even as the stone rim of the pool crumbled. All sound seemed to have departed, leaving nothing but a ringing noise in its wake.

She sensed rather than heard the fall of the great tree behind her, and somehow managed to drunkenly crawl to one side in the swiftly draining pool as a titanic limb slammed down across it. The main portion of the branch missed braining her by a few finger spans. Smaller branches scratched her face and one struck her helmet and twisted her head, painfully.

Still deaf, she dragged herself away. Aching terribly, she struggled to pull free the helm. She blinked in an attempt to clear her spinning vision. On shaking limbs she pulled herself up by the branch, seeking her enemy, certain Vannek would come leaping over at any moment.

But she saw instead that the Naor general was climbing into a saddle upon the dragon, already flapping its wings.

No. Gods damnit, no.

She searched frantically for a weapon. After all that had gone so very wrong, the Gods smiled at last, because within an arm's reach was the spear that had rebounded from Vannek.

Her hand tightened around it as the dragon beat its wings and turned away, plodding into the lane. There at last, only a few blocks off, were some Kaneshi cavalry officers. Why couldn't they be closer?

It was up to her to stop the general. Sansyra rose, legs quivering beneath her, and hefted the spear. It was a foot shorter than those she normally used. Through blurring vision she saw the beast gaining speed, and she stumbled after.

There might be no more energy within the stone, but there was her own magic, feeble as it was. She emptied her mind of all but form and motion, her weary feet finding the right position, advancing after the quickly receding dragon. No strike against that beast was liable to harm it, but there was the broad back of the man supporting the general. With any luck, he was its pilot.

Her arm rose with little conscious thought, and she felt limb and weapon wobbling. It didn't matter. She took two more steps and flung, and then threw all her energy behind the spear. It was almost as if her consciousness left her at the same moment the weapon passed from her fingers. Partly she was rooted to her fragile form, reverberating still with the blast from the dragon's maw. And partly she was behind the spear, shaping its course through the air, whittling away the thread of friction and gravity that strove to pull it down, massaging the wind in just the proper way.

She felt it strike the broad neck of the man, and then Sansyra's bond with the spear was shattered. As he dropped away from the beast, limp as a sack of potatoes, she dizzied and sank to a knee. She caught a last look of Vannek's face screwed up in anguish, half turned in the saddle to reach for the falling man, and then the dragon was up, and Sansyra was down.

She lay there on the paving stones, a few small steps from the ruined pool and the downed tree, staring weakly at the stars and wondering which way the dragon might go, or if it might swing back around to finish her off. She wished she felt more satisfaction at killing the Naor dragon rider, but it seemed not to have mattered much, for the dragon soared on. Maybe the other figure was the actual pilot.

A moment passed, and then another, and it occurred to her that the thunderous drum in her temple had stopped. She wished to feel for the pulse in her neck, as she'd been taught, but her arms didn't seem to work. I'm dying, she thought, and wondered why she didn't care so much. Was that fatalism, or mere exhaustion? Had she drained herself too thoroughly with her own magic, or was this an aftereffect of the dragon's attack? Maybe it was both.

The last thing she heard was the clatter of approaching hoofbeats on cobblestone. The last thing she saw was the reddened clouds, flickering a little, and she wondered why destruction was sometimes just as beautiful as creation.

25

Darassus Awaits

He had raged that the pilot turn and have the dragon kill the squire, but the man confessed he barely knew the means for controlling the beast, let alone any sort of clever maneuvers. Syrik had told him their only purpose was to get Vannek out of the city safely and rendezvous with Chargan's army. Syrik was gone now, but the pilot meant to follow his last orders, and no amount of threatening would get him to change course. The coward was determined to take Vannek to safety. The general debated holding a knife to him and forcing him down, and then he looked below and saw the Dendressi sweeping through the city with their ally, fire. He'd have never guessed that they would destroy their city rather than give it over.

Alantris was lost to him. And so was Syrik.

Tears flowed, but the rage plugged Vannek's throat. He shook but made no sound.

As they climbed into the cool night sky, the tears streamed away, and he gripped tight to the saddle as he turned, watching the ever smaller figures lit by fire. His ear throbbed, as if someone struck him over and over again in the side of the head. It didn't matter.

If he'd had just a little longer, he could have ruled that city properly. The failure wasn't his, but his stupid brother's. It was the fault of Chargan, for if he had come to the city, no amount of fae cleverness could have toppled them.

He tried to tell himself that he was weak for feeling this way, that Syrik had probably been a toy of Chargan's. But, he didn't believe it. Syrik had always liked him. Vannek. Even as all other allegiances became those of station and power, the mage's affection had been true. It had been tempered by lust, a lust that should have shamed him, but it had been real. Syrik was the closest thing to a friend that Vannek had known. In the future there might be other advisors, and other mages, but there could be no other whose bond stretched so far back in time.

A warrior, his father had taught him, must practice making his heart a stone.

This grew easier over the course of their flight, for it felt as though that transformation was underway already. All feeling seemed to leach out. The problem was that all care leached away with it.

It took long hours before they saw Chargan's encampment, in a little east-west valley in the very southern section of The Fragments, fairly close to the border with Erymyr itself.

It seemed a smaller army than he'd supposed. Perhaps that was because there were few campfires. Under the starlight he guessed there could only be a few thousand men at most.

"Did you see that, General?"

The reedy-voiced pilot had said very little over their journey, but there was a note of caution as they circled down and he pointed.

"What is it?" Vannek's voice was gruff, dry. He realized how very thirsty he was.

"Those hills are moving."

Vannek started to say that the mage was an idiot, but then he, too, saw that one of the many similarly sized hills on the landscape crept slowly forward. Even as he peered the hill drew to a stop and he wondered if he'd imagined it.

They flew on toward a cluster of tents. Below lay the prostrate forms of seven dragons. Seven. With those beasts they could have held Alantris for the ages!

Guards ran up the moment they approached the ground, and stood warily at attention as Vannek dropped from the saddle; they appeared unsure whether he was friend or enemy.

The pilot's voice cracked as he barked at them behind her. "At attention for General Vannek!"

The delivery might have been less than desired, but the reaction was pleasing. The five guards formed themselves into a long line, spears upright at their shoulders. Vannek strode past them without meeting their eyes. He realized he ought to praise the pilot, but he hated the pilot almost as much as he hated the dragon and the guards and the camp. He wished all of them were gone, that he himself was far away from all this nonsense. He would very much like to be somewhere where he didn't have to gird for more battles and shout more orders and sit down across from his odious brother and listen to more of his grandiose schemes.

Somewhere with Syrik.

But it was with Chargan that he found himself. Chargan, who ushered him into a tent after Vannek had gruffly accepted a healer's care and refused the offer of a bath. His brother pointed him to a cushioned chair under the high canvas ceiling, where a pretty Dendressi slave presented a platter with wine and bread and various cheeses and dried fruits.

Chargan didn't look as ridiculous as he probably should have. He wore soldier's gear from the Blue Fire clan. Fit and stocky, his beard closely trimmed, he even looked a soldier, although he'd left off his breastplate. He bade the servants leave and sat down on a matched chair across from Vannek, the table with refreshments between them. A perfumed lamp stood on a camp table to their right, and an actual bed, with a frame and mattress and sheets, sat tucked in a corner to the left. From its size, Vannek strongly expected Chargan did not sleep alone, and wondered if the Dendressi woman would be there tonight.

"You should be careful whom you go to bed with. You might not make it to morning."

"You sound terrible." Chargan handed over the wine. "And you look terrible. Is that any way to greet me?"

The wine was strong and cool and it felt good on his throat. The sharp taste was like a kick to his senses. He wiped his mouth with the back of a hand and set down the goblet with a clunk. "How do you think I should greet you?"

"You should be impressed at my speed. Did you see how far I've come? How close I am to the heart of the Drendressi holdings? Did you see my dragons?"

"You haven't asked what I'm doing here."

Chargan pushed dirt out from beneath his fingernails and flicked it onto the rug.

Vannek suddenly noticed his brother traveled not just with a bed, but with an actual rug. The front legs of his chair were even standing on it.

"I judge by your quiet that it's very bad news. Were you deposed? Which of our petty little kings did it?"

"The Dendressi did it."

Chargan's eyes flipped up at him. "Are you saying that the city has fallen to the fae?"

"Yes."

Chargan took a long, slow breath, glared at her, then let out a disgusted sigh. "I suppose it won't matter in a few more days. There can't be more than a handful of soldiers left within Darassus. There's also the new group of mages, but I don't think they can move mountains like I can." Chargan smiled.

Had he taken leave of his senses? "You're still going through with it? If we turn back now, we can surprise the Dendressi—"

"No!" Chargan smashed a fist into his palm. "I will destroy Darassus!" He leaned forward, eyes gleaming. "I've built monsters of titanic power. Our army may be small, but with my creatures, Darassus will fall before us! I've fashioned great magics that will not only see us through the shifts between, but most of the way through the realm itself, without detection."

"For what?" she demanded. "The invasion has failed, unless you turn back now. Use your . . . spells of transport to take us back to Alantris! We could take it back and hold it."

Chargan's lips curled. "I've been very patient with you, and your limitations. And your failures. Whereas I have nothing but success behind me. You were once a useful ally to me but . . ." He snapped his fingers. "What are you now? I assume your own forces are dead or dying in Alantris. What do you have to bring me? Is it strength in arms? Because there are many warriors at my call who are stronger than you, and at least as skilled. Is it loyalty? I have thousands who would lay down their life on my order. Tell me, brother"—he said this last with a sneer—"are you of such use to me that I should tolerate your insults?"

Vannek felt his own face flush, knew his jaw tightened, and for some reason that made his bandaged ear throb. But all anger swiftly drained away as would water from a bucket full of holes. Why should he care when it was so patently obvious that nothing here was very important? He sank back in his chair. "You might as well just kill me," he said wearily.

He stared at a sagging spot in the canvas ceiling.

Chargan was quiet for a long time, and then broke into a low chuckle. At first it sounded forced, but after he reached across the table to slap Vannek's knee and he flinched, the mirth sounded genuine.

"I wouldn't kill you!" he said. "You're the only one left who's not afraid of me! Grandfather always said you needed a trusted few who knew you from when you were human. You and me, we have to stick together. Because we're going to rule as gods!"

26

The Alantran Road

The shortest route between The Fragments and Erymyr lay along the Alantran Road, which extended from Alantris to the Shifting Lands at the closest point to Erymyr. Rylin and his small party made good use of the outposts stretching west from the city, stopping to exchange their animals for fresh ones every fifteen to twenty miles so they could press on at speed. All of the staff they met were desperate for news, but their group had little additional information to share.

They spent their first evening at a way station, and after they dined and shared news with the small staff, Rylin, Lasren, and Elik adjourned to the square roof of the station's two-story signal tower which commanded a nice view and offered cool evening breezes. Governor Feolia eventually retired to one of the clean, tiny rooms below.

A few wooden slatted benches were set against the walls of the tower, and the staff had loaned them the same cushions they used when posted up top awaiting signals. A bronze mirror used as sun telegraph rose from the tower's center, along with a raised stone platform by which less complex but urgent signals might be sent by night. No signals had come from Alantris since the night of the invasion, although they had been passed along through the working stations east of the city in the days since.

The way station stood by necessity on a hilltop and was therefore exposed to a chill wind as the night settled in. Still, it was lovely there above the countryside, with the forested Kelistrin Mountains under moonlight a few miles north and the more rounded Mervil Range farther south. The stars gleamed in the firmament. Those in The Fragments were the same Rylin had grown up watching in Erymyr, and as he and his companions sat in the darkness, he picked out familiar constellations as though they were old friends. There was The Lantern, and The Lost Queen, and, almost directly overhead, The Winking Cat, with its one bright blue eye and the flickering white one and its long, long tail hanging down onto The Stairsteps.

Lasren had brought up a wine bottle, and he passed it over to Rylin. Though not really thirsty, he took a pull and handed it off to Elik, wishing this brief moment of silence might extend for a little longer. But there were important matters to discuss. Wide-shouldered Lasren looked at him expectantly. Elik passed back the bottle and scratched his head, fingers shaking his curly brown hair.

Rylin cleared his throat and launched into a detailed talk about what he and Varama had found, and how the queen had attacked and killed squires on the way out from Erymyr. And he emphasized that they were walking into enemy territory. "I know that may be difficult to contemplate," he said, "because these are Erymyrans. We have to practice deception among them. Especially me, but you may have to do your share of misdirection as well. Perhaps even outright lying."

Neither man looked especially comfortable with that.

"You can stick mostly to the truth. You really are coming to return the shield and ring of Decrin to places of honor, and to escort Governor Feolia to speak with the council, and one of the things she's going to be doing is pleading for assistance for The Fragments. No one but the councilors need to know that she's going to present a letter from N'lahr."

"What should I say if they ask me about Denaven and N'lahr and everything?" Lasren asked.

"I'd keep silent about that until you speak to the councilors. So far as we know, none of the Erymyrans have learned what's happened to Denaven yet. Once behind closed doors, you can bear witness to all that you've seen."

Elik shifted, looked uncomfortably at him, then blurted out a question. "Sir, if you don't mind me asking, what will you be doing?"

"The squire's got a point," Lasren said. "Are you ever going to tell us why you're traveling in disguise?"

Rylin wished he could, and slowly, sadly, shook his head no. "If something goes wrong, and you're captured, and I'm not . . ." He shrugged rather than finish the sentence.

"You're saying the exalts could use magic to force the answer out of us," Lasren said.

"Yes."

"Even with the ring?" Lasren looked down at one big hand and the darkened gem upon his finger.

"Maybe. But they'd probably relieve you of it first." On that dire note, he turned to Elik. "The commander told me you were sent from Darassus to Alantris with a message and a small force of soldiers."

"Yes, sir." Elik frowned thoughtfully. "Exalt Thelar's been placed in command of the Altenerai. He's the one who sent me."

"Thelar?" Rylin repeated the name in disbelief. Thin-skinned, humorless, and priggish, Thelar had clashed with Rylin as they rose together through the squire ranks, until Thelar had jumped over to the Mage Auxiliary. Rylin hadn't been at all sorry about his departure. When he'd last seen him, Thelar had been lying in the hall of the Mage Auxiliary with a broken limb. Varama's doing as she and Rylin made off with a cache of hearthstones and compelling evidence of the queen's treachery.

"How's his arm?"

"I wasn't aware there was anything wrong with it," Elik replied, and Rylin felt foolish. The exalt would have been healed immediately by some of the finest mages in the realms.

"Forget about the arm. Thelar sent you? What were his instructions?"

"Yes, sir. The Alantrans had sent a plea for help because the Naor were invading—well, you know that part. Thelar told me to request volunteers from different units, as swiftly as possible, then to depart without fanfare."

"How many men did you take?" Rylin asked.

"I ended up with twenty-five."

"So Alantris asked for help, and he sent twenty-five people?" Rylin was aghast.

Elik looked troubled. "I think he wanted to send more and was angry he couldn't."

"He told you that?"

"No, sir. I could just tell how upset he was. And the queen's official note was only a few lines, saying that she regretted she had no troops at her disposal to send. I got the sense Exalt Thelar wasn't supposed to send as many as he did."

That suggested Thelar might actually be taking his job seriously, which Rylin decided shouldn't have surprised him, because Thelar took everything seriously. "I've gotten off subject. What I was wanting was a status report on the city. What are we riding into?"

Rylin had known the studious younger man for years, for he'd come up through the ranks in good order and Rylin had marked his progress. He'd seen Elik chagrined on the practice field when he'd failed, and elated when he'd succeeded. He'd seen his eyebrows knitted in concentration, and he'd seen him laughing when he relaxed with his fellow squires.

But he'd never, ever seen him so consistently somber. Elik had apparently long anticipated the question, for he answered without hesitation. "When I left, the queen was as quiet as ever. But the exalts were far more visible."

"How many exalts are there?

"Less than two dozen, all told. But there are aspirants as well, probably forty or so."

"Aspirants?" Lasren asked.

"That's what they're calling their squires now. They travel in groups. They're almost always in pairs. Keep in mind that the Exalted have nominal command over the city guard, since they've taken over command of the Altenerai."

"How many squires are in the city?" Rylin asked. "And where are their loyalties?"

"There's just over thirty of us, predominantly first and second rankers. Most are confused but a lot of us were upset we didn't go with you and Varama."

"Why couldn't they?" Lasren asked.

"Some were off duty, or on patrol, or standing watch," Rylin explained. "She got everyone she could."

"I was in charge of the lower gate that evening." Elik sounded disappointed.

"If you'd come with us, you'd probably be trapped in Alantris right now. Or have died on the way when the queen attacked. Like Renahra."

Elik's eyes widened at mention of his fellow fifth ranker, then he nodded once, in grim resolve.

Rylin brought him back to the subject with another question. "So are the squires loyal to the exalts, or the Altenerai?"

"A lot of them are skeptical, but they can't talk about it. They were told Kyrkenall and Elenai were traitors. I knew Elenai couldn't be a traitor but thought maybe she'd gotten involved in something she didn't understand. It's when I heard the exalts saying *you* had joined forces with the cabal I was certain they lied."

Rylin was a little touched by the younger man's regard of him.

Lasren looked over to Rylin. "A bunch of second and first rankers aren't going to be that much help against dozens of trained mages."

He was missing the point. "I'm worried that they might stand against us," Rylin said. "I don't want them harmed. But we should be working to avoid any kind of conflict in any case. The enemy's too powerful. Are there any Altenerai in the city?"

"No, sir."

Rylin was puzzled by that. "Cerai isn't there?"

"No."

"Hasn't she appeared? Riding a ko'aye?"

"No, sir."

"That would have been hard to miss," Lasren said.

Rylin agreed, although he supposed it was just possible Cerai might have turned up late at night, with magics to conceal her. But if she hadn't ever returned to Darassus, what would she have done with the keystone? And if she hadn't planned to give the stone to Queen Leonara, then why had she kidnapped Lelanc and abandoned Alantris to the Naor? "Cerai is a problem for another time. What about the people? Any idea what they think about all of this?"

"Opinions vary. I get the sense that they're suspicious of the exalts. And there have been little jokes about the queen for a while now, about how she's lost in her own fog. People are apprehensive about her. A lot of them are skeptical that any of the Altenerai are traitors."

Rylin couldn't think of anything else to ask, although he was certain Varama would have come up with much more.

Lasren sighed and sat back in disgust. "I sure never saw any of this coming. It's still hard to believe Denaven was lying to us all that time."

"There've been a lot of terrible surprises," Rylin said. "And we may see more. That's for the future, though. Right now we'd best turn in." He rose, clapping a hand on the squire's shoulder.

Lasren reached out for his arm. "Rylin. Stay a moment."

Rylin hesitated, then nodded to the squire. "Go on. We'll be down soon."

Elik saluted and departed, with a backward glance before he headed down. Rylin felt a little guilty to be sending him off apart from them, but turned to his friend, who patted the cushion beside him.

Rylin took the seat as Lasren pulled on the wine. After, his friend held the bottle by the neck, beside his leg, until he found his voice. Lasren partly turned his head, and tried to sound casual. "Remember when we used to dream of being Altenerai?"

"I remember." Rylin nodded with a mixture of amusement and sorrow. "We weren't the only ones."

Lasren looked up. "But from our class, only you and me and Gyldara made it."

"I think a couple of others could have, if they'd stayed with it." He didn't mention Tesra, or Vatahn, a redhead who'd mustered out at the fourth rank after falling in love with a book binder.

"That's just it—they didn't want it like we did. Gods, but I wanted to be a hero. Get the ring. The khalat. The glory. The girls." Lasren grinned and looked briefly like the man Rylin remembered. "I wanted songs to be sung for me. I wanted to hold the gate, like Herahn, or even go down in a blaze of glory, like Kyrikin. I mean, once I was older." He met Rylin's eyes. "I held the line, against the Naor, with Kyrkenall the Eyeless and N'lahr himself. I wanted but wasn't sure I'd ever see a day like that."

"You've more than proven yourself," Rylin assured him.

Lasren sat back against the bench. "Have I? All this time I thought I knew what a hero was, and maybe I didn't have a clue."

Rylin thought this introspection refreshing. "A hero stands with his friends," he said.

Lasren didn't respond to that. "N'lahr and Elenai—they're the ones who saved Vedessus. Me, I was just along for the ride. Oh, I fought well, but the Naor were coming to kill us. It was fight or die. That might have taken heart, but we're supposed to be more than warriors, aren't we? We're supposed to see with heart and mind. You did."

"I was just as fooled as you were," Rylin reminded him. "It was Varama who opened my eyes."

"Is she the one who told you to lead those people to freedom under the very eyes of their enemies? Rylin of the Thousand. That's the stuff of heroes." Lasren raised the bottle in silent toast. Rylin searched his friend's eyes, expecting to find jealousy there, but seeing only honest admiration, touched with grief. And then his friend asked the question he'd probably kept Rylin for. "Would I have done so well had our places been traded?"

Once, Rylin might have offered an easy platitude. And then, more recently, he might have dismissed the notion that Lasren was capable of growth and tried to change the subject. Neither was the right response. "We have different strengths," Rylin said at last. "Only a few days ago, Varama was consoling me when I realized I couldn't be as clever as she was. Ever. I'll never be as fine an archer or swordsman as Kyrkenall. And we'll never track as well as Tretton, or ride as well as Enada. But we are siblings of the ring. Maybe we were too busy dreaming rather than seeing, but our eyes are open now. We just have to know our strengths, and use them when they're needed. That's what I've done. And that's what you've done, and will continue to do."

Lasren spoke softly, with another sidelong look. "What I said about Varama the other day . . . I wasn't thinking. You were in some tight places together, weren't you?"

"Yes."

"So you have her back. I get that. I guess that's how I always wanted it to be between us." He was deadly serious again. "I don't know what you're really doing, and I guess I'm not supposed to know but . . . if you need help, I mean to come through for you. The two of us, together—I figure we'd be pretty unstoppable."

"I'm glad you're along," Rylin said, and meant it. "If I need help I know that you'll be there." He'd recently been doubting, but his faith in his friend had been restored. "Now let's get some sleep." He rose. Together, the two of them headed down.

It was a good two days before they arrived at the road's terminus, at the closest crossing points between The Fragments and Erymyr. A small village with two inns and stables prospered on The Fragments side of the border. While Lasren and Elik traded horses and stocked up on supplies, Rylin and the governor walked to the settlement edge and contemplated the storm churning on the border.

Feolia stared at the of roiling mass of clouds, now black, now charcoal gray, hiding the entire horizon ahead of them from the ground on up. "I'm afraid that's the end of it, then," she said. "There's no crossing today."

Rylin wasn't ready to give up. "Not necessarily." He slipped into the inner world and tentatively probed the storm. He found whirling currents advancing and rotating and moving past one another like a maddened line of dancers. What he was most concerned with was their unnatural predictability. The wind was strong, the currents flowing in a consistent way.

"We should cross now," Rylin said.

"Young man, I appreciate your haste. I do. But I'm not in a hurry to kill myself."

"The storm's steady," Rylin said. "But the landforms are still solid beneath it. I think I can get us past. "

"Anything can happen in the Shifting Lands," Feolia said. "That solidity may not last at all."

"And the entire storm may worsen if the queen wants it," Rylin said. "That storm is deliberately strengthened."

"You really think she's that powerful?"

"I think she and a small army of mages with hearthstones could be that powerful, and desperate to hold back the Naor. Or possibly us. That's why we can't wait for things to get better. They won't, and they could get worse. We have to chance it. Lasren and I have rings to keep us safe, and I have magic to make things safer for all of us."

Feolia regarded him as if she had caught sight of a madman. "How fine a mage are you? There's almost a four-hour ride through there, and that's in the best conditions. And all you have to protect us is a couple of Altenerai rings. I was always given to understand their protection didn't extend much farther than the alten and her immediate belongings."

Technically, they had three rings, for Decrin's was borne in one of Rylin's pouches. He wore his own on a thin necklace tucked under his shirt. "We're going to have to double up in the saddle, lead the other horses, and trust to luck."

"Luck," Feolia huffed. "When I was a little girl there used to be a great stone archway right here." She pointed into the storm. "It was generations old. And the actual border didn't start for another hundred feet. The storms in the last years just blew it away."

"Yes," Rylin agreed, "the storms have worsened and the borders have crumbled."

She sighed. "My point is that if a storm can do that to ancient stone, it will have no problem with us."

"If you want to wait behind—"

The lines about her face deepened into crevasses as she frowned at him. "I'm no coward, young man."

"I didn't mean—"

"That's exactly what you were implying. I just don't intend to die owing to stupidity."

"If you die, it will be my fault."

Her look suggested that this was precisely the sort of stupidity she meant. Maybe he deserved that. He turned away from her as Lasren and Elik arrived with fresh horses. Rylin explained his plan to both men while they sat down with full wineskins and dried rations.

Lasren's reaction wasn't that different from the governor's. "If that's what we're doing, why did you have me request four extra horses?"

"For when we get through."

Lasren smiled crookedly. "You say that with such certainty. Maybe we should spare a couple of horses instead of killing them along with us. Take pity on them, like."

Rylin glanced at Elik, wondering if he understood Lasren was joking. The squire did his best to look at ease.

Lasren took a swig from his wineskin, addressed his friend more seriously. "You're sure about this?"

"I'm sure."

Lasren looked over to Elik. "I don't think you ought to make this journey an order for our squire."

"The alten raises a good point," Rylin said to Elik. "This is strictly a volunteer—"

The bright-eyed squire cut him off. "I'm going with you. Sir," he added quickly.

Less than a quarter hour later, Rylin led them into the storm. Governor Feolia sat behind him, one hand about his waist, the other grasping the line tied to two of the spare mounts. Riding a few paces to his right was Lasren, with Elik as passenger, holding the lines to their extra horses.

None of the animals looked any happier to head into the rolling clouds than Rylin himself felt; their ears were erect and they snorted in concern.

Visibility was limited to less than a few feet. What little Rylin saw was normal grassland.

The wind, though, was wild, and the older woman clung to him. His horse strained to move forward. He could just make out a vague shape moving in the gloom to his right and saw Lasren's ring winking.

It was a long, slow process. The nervous mounts walked ever forward at the urging of their riders. Rylin's, at least, was little troubled by the extra weight. Lasren had chosen a sturdy gelding, and so far as Rylin could tell, the animal was bearing up well.

He felt the governor jerk to one side.

She had to shout into his ear to be heard over the storm. "The horses slipped away from me."

The wind stole his curse. He turned, but there was no sign of the spare mounts now, lost somewhere behind them. He felt the land contours rippling before the transformation spread. Dark water stretched away on their left, and a wall of palms stood on their right, shaken by the roaring wind. Beneath their horses' hooves the grass rippled away into red sand.

The low-lying fog had vanished, although storm clouds hung above the white-capped ocean, which thundered against distant rocks. Rylin looked through the inner world and studied the land around them, saw that it all but vibrated with incipient violence. More alterations could follow, and might well wreak life-threatening changes.

"Hang on," Rylin cried. "Lasren, fall in behind me!"

He reached into his ring, remembering that first day it had been given him, and the impatient tutelage Denaven had provided as he woke it to his service. "Someday," the commander had said, "this ring may save your life, so listen well."

He touched the threads of its power to himself and the governor, then stretched out with his own magic to assist Lasren in the same. All who were given the ring could learn to manipulate it, but mages naturally had a greater advantage. Varama had told him hearthstones were a far more effective ward during shift storms, and he supposed having a great weaver would be a tremendous asset as well.

But he had neither Varama nor a hearthstone.

When the ocean rose up from its bed in a great curling claw he threw up a mystic shield and the waters rebounded. When the ocean fell away into a glowing void that threw forth blue sparks, he conjured a wind to sweep them off.

Under rumbling skies the land shifted again, and they rode a rolling, empty country populated only by towering trees with massive boles and drooping branches that swayed contrary to the wind. Swirling dust intermittently obscured their vision.

He guided them on, keeping to the clear spaces. He heard the storm growling in the distance, its strength centered somewhere else, and he prayed silently it would remain that way.

It did, and so for an hour they had to contend only with the occasionally sandy soil and the eager tendrils of the unwholesome things that weren't real trees. After one cast up a wriggling root to grasp at them, Rylin gave them an even wider berth.

Eventually these, too, fell away and they traveled a dark land under dark skies. A half moon rose. Rylin stretched out with his senses, feeling that they were close to Erymyr.

He found something else. A presence, enormous and distant.

The thing's awareness fixed upon them, as if Rylin's scrutiny had drawn its attention. He felt its fascination, and its ravenous hunger, and pulled swiftly away.

"Lasren," Rylin called, "something's out there. We need to push for it. I think Ermyr's close!" Rylin turned his head to the governor. "Hold on tight!" The moment he felt her fingers dig into his side he kicked the horse into a gallop.

From behind there was a change in the air. The wind wailed.

He'd never had the magical reserves of the great weavers. He had only a finite amount of power, and he used it now to feel ahead. Faintly, as if seen through fog at great distance, he brushed the outline of Erymyr, its solidity pulling to him. His ring enabled him to sense the life force of Lasren, Elik, their horse, and the riderless mounts they led. And he sensed a vast cloud that was much more than a lack of life energy gaining upon them all.

He willed his ring to full power and brought all his energy into contemplation of the solidity of them and their horses. Lasren had the wisdom to ride nearly stirrup to stirrup, his own ring shining its brightest, and Rylin stretched his magics to bolster him and Elik.

Behind them a storm cloud filled the heavens. Their amorphous pursuer reached toward them with a tendril of will, a brush of nightmare cold and lust. It pressed against them, a cloud given will and purpose. This was no bracing fog, but an entity that fought against the very bonds that held them together. Rylin knew that if he relinquished concentration they would dissolve like sugared candies in a bowl of water.

Teeth gritted, he forced home the coherence of the bonds of their existence, and the multitude of threads that composed them all. He touched the energy centers of the four remaining mounts, lent them strength, soothed the threads that composed their straining muscles.

On the instant, he felt his own mount leap ahead, Lasren's horse lagging only a heartbeat behind.

The entity swam after, a vast tower of hungry will. Despite all his efforts, Rylin grew colder, and colder still. His grip weakened. His concentration ebbed until all he could sense was the blue light about his ring. Dimly he was aware of a vast cloud bank that loomed before them and kicked his mount into further speed. They galloped into the shifting fog as the creature reached down, greedily—

And then they were in sunlight, upon the grass. The wind howled behind them, and Rylin thought he heard the thing's anguished, frustrated roar as a rising moan. Still shaking with cold, he turned in his saddle, alert for a looming pseudopod of cloud or energy or whatever it had been, exactly.

Praise the gods, nothing of the sort emerged from the wall of storm clouds rising skyward behind them.

Fatigue grasping at him, he examined his companions. The governor slowly released her hold. At his side, Lasren and Elik took in their surroundings, wide-eyed. The four horses neighed nervously to one another.

This looked to be an balmy Erymyran evening, although Rylin didn't

recognize their point of entry. Probably he'd gotten off course by diverting around so many of those terrible trees. The skies beyond the border
were clear but hazy, a washed-out blue. The air itself was still and a little
humid, despite which he continued to shiver.

"How about lighting a fire?" he suggested to Lasren. He just managed
to slip down from his horse. He'd planned to check the roan over, but he
discovered his legs really couldn't hold him up.

Nor, it proved, could his arm completely arrest his fall.

His companions hurried to him, pushed food and wine on him, and
eventually set camp with a fire roaring.

Rylin chafed at his weakness and the delay it necessitated. He could
only nod as the other three voiced speculation that there'd been a monster
in the shifts, and shake his head when they asked him what it really was.
Something hungry. He was thankful he hadn't seen it.

After nearly an hour, he started to feel human once more, although
he could probably have gone straight to sleep. Lasren had slipped off to
scout. Elik kept watch, and Feolia sat beside him.

"A little harder going than you expected, was it?" she asked, not un-
kindly.

"A little."

She chuckled. "Well, you said you'd get us through, and you did."

"That may have been the easy part." His thoughts had turned toward
the challenges that still lay before them. "Do you know what you're going
to say to the Darassi counselors?"

"Yes. After I tell them about what happened in Alantris, I'll tell them
about N'lahr. And I'll move on from there. Probably to his letter."

Rylin nearly had the text of the commander's letter memorized. It had
been a little strange reading his own accomplishments described through
someone else's eyes. The extent of luck involved in Rylin's activities had
been glossed over; everything had been presented as if planned with great
foresight.

Rylin took another swig from his own wineskin, wishing that he had
some of Varama's energy-fortifying juices. He wished even more that she
was here, with him. Her own situation seemed even more impossible than
his. He brought his thoughts to what Feolia had last said. "Probably?" he
asked.

The old woman adjusted the forehead line of her scarf. "I know how
to read a crowd, young man. I'll play them as best I can. What I don't
know is what their mood will be."

"Nervous," Rylin answered. "They're always nervous. It doesn't matter that they're the safest realm in our alliance. They're deathly afraid of the Naor."

"You sound awfully critical for someone who grew up in Erymyr."

He shrugged. "You saw what the Naor did to The Fragments. What they've done again and again. The Erymyrans have a right to be nervous. Just not more nervous than your people, or the Kaneshi. Maybe they fear battle more because they've so rarely experienced it."

Elik called up to them from the nearby hillock. "Alten Lasren's on his way back," he said, even as Rylin heard the hoofbeats of his approach.

As Lasren drew to a stop on his black he turned his mount to face southeast. "A patrol spotted me. They're riding this way."

"Do you think them hostile?" Feolia asked.

"I'm just being cautious," Lasren replied. "But we ought to stand ready. There's six of them."

"Squires?" Elik asked.

"Yes," Lasren said. "And an exalt's leading them."

27

Among the Missing

As Elenai looked over the lightly armed horsemen facing them, she realized she should have been more skeptical with her assumptions when they'd found Renik's body. Kyrkenall had gone right on thinking that the woman's tracks near the dead man were Kalandra's. Now, given that the leader of these warriors, Sorak, had proclaimed they would escort them to the "Goddess" Cerai, it seemed more likely that the traitorous alten had been the one exploring past Renik. And while that hadn't been an obvious deduction, Kyrkenall had been too quick to believe his own hypothesis and Elenai hadn't questioned it.

Kyrkenall sat silent upon Lyria's saddle. Sorak waited patiently, certainly unaware of the sudden violence the archer could unleash against his enemies. The remaining five soldiers were spread out behind their leader almost indifferently. They were all well-built men in sleeveless shirts, armed with swords that none reached for, astride mounts of brown and gray that none seemed ready to kick forward into battle. If this were an ambush, it was the least aggressive in history.

Finally Kyrkenall asked, with careless directness, "Suppose we don't want to talk with Cerai?"

The question puzzled Sorak. The handsome young soldier's brows wrinkled in confusion, as if he had never once considered the thought someone wouldn't want to speak with his ruler.

Elenai glanced at the man's companions and discovered them still waiting dispassionately. She worked to stretch tired muscles without revealing her intent, for she more than halfway expected Kyrkenall to launch into deadly action, pulling her along with him.

"If you did not wish to talk with her," Sorak said finally, "why did you come?"

"That's a good question, Sorak," Kyrkenall said, although he didn't answer it. "Does Cerai know we're here?"

"Yes. She called for us to show you the way to her."

Kyrkenall exchanged glances with Elenai, who realized that he was as confused as she. Yes, they'd been told Cerai was a traitor working with the queen. But this didn't feel like a threat.

"Did she say what she wanted?" Kyrkenall asked.

"She wanted to speak with you. Don't you want to speak with her?" Sorak's voice rose in confusion.

Elenai saw no evidence of threat on Sorak's face, or on the chiseled visages of any of his companions, merely earnest curiosity. There was something almost childlike in the sincerity of their consternation.

Kyrkenall mulled over an answer for a little while longer, and then relaxed. "You know what, Sorak, I think I do. Why don't you show us the way."

"I will." Sorak turned his horse and started forward. Elenai assumed that the others would ride at their sides, or behind them, but they merely fell in after Sorak, leaving Elenai and Kyrkenall to trail as they wished. The two Altenerai followed after, along a winding trail into the dusty hills. Behind them they heard a distant crack of thunder. Ahead, the light was dim under darkened skies, but the storm seemed uninclined to follow.

"We need to be get back," Elenai said. "The commander—"

"I know," Kyrkenall said, quietly but sharply. "But don't you think this begs looking into?"

"What if we're riding into a trap?" she asked.

"Here's what I'm thinking. We couldn't safely turn back without a wide diversion." He glanced at their escort, many horselengths ahead.

"I'm pretty sure we could take those guys, but what would that get us? They seem like innocents, too, so killing them didn't feel right. They're sort of odd, but I really don't think they have orders to take us prisoner."

"What if they take us some place where we'll be even more outnumbered?"

"What if pastries grow on trees?"

She frowned at him. "You know the one's more likely than the other."

"By a damned sight," he agreed, "but our options are low, and I think we ought to play along. Let's talk with Cerai."

She couldn't help being curious herself, but she thought his reasoning sloppy. "N'lahr warned us that she's gotten very powerful."

"So have you."

"I appreciate the compliment, but I just got beaten by a godforsaken Naor sorcerer a few days back. And Cerai has been studying hearthstones a lot longer than me."

Kyrkenall arched an eyebrow as he turned in his saddle to look at her. His horse Lyria snorted, too, as though she were a little disgusted. "We'll just do what we do best. Improvise."

She almost commented that was always his plan, but fell silent.

Before very long they had rounded two more hills, after which the land rose. And then they topped a rise and its character changed entirely. Low, tree-topped knolls surrounded them. The temperature warmed, and the thick-limbed trees were heavy with the creamy gold fruit known as sunberries, farmed just north of Erymyr's Storm Coast.

Elenai stretched out with her inner sight and felt for the borders, discovering they had just crossed from the shifts into a true landscape that extended for many miles in a roughly oval pattern.

Their escorts glanced back, but kept on across the hilly terrain. Elenai caught up to ride beside Kyrkenall.

"Did you know a fragment this nice was out here?"

"From here on out this is all new." She half expected him to be brooding, but he actually seemed to be in good spirits. "I've been thinking. You and I have a bad habit of coming up with the answers to questions we weren't asking."

"What are you talking about?"

He raised one hand, index finger aloft like he was ticking the first point on a list. "We went to find N'lahr's sword and we found N'lahr." His second finger joined the first. "We went to find Kalandra and we found a Naor invasion." He looked over at her and raised a third finger. "We went after the ko'aye and we found Renik's resting place. And then

I thought we'd found Kalandra's whereabouts, but it turns out we've discovered Cerai's hidden kingdom."

"Wait—this is a hidden kingdom?"

"It kind of looks like it, doesn't it? A private little fragment out here. And apparently she knew about Renik but didn't tell anyone."

Elenai realized that must be true. "All you've really said about her is that she hates Denaven. N'lahr says she's a powerful mage. What else can you tell me? Cerai Far Treader, right?"

"Well earned. She's always been the one to report about the fringes. She came to the ring a little before Renik, so she's older, but not as old as Asrahn or Tretton, obviously. I always felt like I understood her better than the others, because she was a little bit like me."

That was surprising. So far as she knew, no one else had ever made the comparison between the flamboyant archer and the secretive mage. "Is she?"

"I thought so. Remember how I told you I wanted to go out there and see all the different little fragments and splinters? Cerai's done that. She loves the distant places and had no problem being gone for weeks or months at a time on some errand for the crown. She's very quiet, but sharp, and she has a wicked sense of humor."

"Anything else?"

"She could be a bit obsessive, but we all have our little quirks. Especially Altenerai."

"You seem well disposed toward her."

"She helped sponsor me to the ring." He eyed her. "Don't get me wrong, Elenai, I'll have my guard up. But there are generally two sides to every story."

"Sure." Elenai didn't hide the skepticism in her response. "What about this business of these men of hers thinking she's a goddess?"

He had an interesting answer. "I don't guess there's anything against deification in the oath, but if you're busy out here setting yourself up as a ruler it's kind of hard to bring justice to the people you're sworn to defend, isn't it?"

"An excellent point. One to remember."

"Heart and mind, Elenai, heart and mind."

He was repeating one of the lessons their instructors worked so hard to instill in their charges, to judge each challenge both with reason and emotion, so that you weren't convinced into folly by reacting without thinking, and so that you didn't apply laws so rigorously that you failed to apply compassion. Even if the admonition were appropriate for this particular instance, she resented his chiding manner. "Remember when you told me not to act like a squire?"

"Yes," he answered cautiously.

"Don't treat me like one."

He grunted and fell silent.

The escort led them over the next rise and down onto a dirt road stretching long and straight through the fragment, past long fields of cultivated wheat and vegetables and arbors of trees. Dozens of men garbed in white tunics worked those fields, weeding and harvesting the produce into wheelbarrows.

To a one they looked broad shouldered and powerful. They glanced up with dull curiosity as the riders passed. They were universally strong jawed and handsome, curiously similar in appearance, with dark hair and eyes.

"I guess she prefers a certain type," Kyrkenall said.

To Elenai it rather looked like she was building her own personal army. These men did the work of farmers, but they didn't especially look like the men she'd known whose habit was to till the soil. She wondered where they'd come from. Surely they weren't Naor. Maybe their origin point was one of those unallied fragments beyond Erymyr.

The road curved around one of the hills, past a trail that led to a village of tidy square brown-shingled homes. More of the handsome men walked along the row of identical cottages. "Where are the women?" she asked. "The children?"

"Or the elderly, for that matter?" Kyrkenall asked.

Maybe they were all inside the village huts.

The road rounded another hill, and they looked suddenly upon a fortress built of brown stone. It had been fashioned from smooth rock, a hexagon of four stories with battlements. A tower stood at the juncture of every wall.

The riders led them through a grand black gate standing open before an arch cut into the front of the fortress.

"No seams," Kyrkenall sounded troubled.

For a moment she puzzled over his meaning, and then realized he was right. None of the walls were built of separate bricks or stones, nor did they seem to have been covered over. They were simply there, one immobile, solid piece, as if willed into being.

"Hearthstone work," Elenai whispered.

"She was always talented," Kyrkenall said, still taking in the height of the walls. "But this is beyond anything I knew she could do." He looked over to Elenai. "This is Rialla-level magic. Maybe even better."

"I'm not feeling reassured," she said. "In case you were wondering."

They passed under the cool dark archway of stone, a tunnel through the building. The clop of the horses' hooves echoed in the enclosed space.

They emerged in an open courtyard where a large fountain jetted water into the pool at its feet. Bright multihued fish swam there.

They left their horses under the care of four of their escort, then, still preceded by Sorak and one of his companions, walked over a rounded stone pathway amidst lush grasses until they reached the back wall of a courtyard and a wood door carved with winding vines. Sorak opened it for them. "I will lead you to a place of refreshment. It has many waters."

That struck Elenai as a very kobalin-like statement, and with a pang she wondered how Ortok was, and whether he was even still alive.

The walls of the spacious hallway beyond the door were strangely barren. It was staggering to believe that Cerai had really built all of this with the aid of hearthstones, yet there was no other conclusion to be drawn, for all of the stone was mortarless. It had not been shaped by an army of craftsmen laboring carefully for long years, but by a single woman who'd lifted it into existence from the surrounding bedrock. The level of control that had taken impressed, intimidated, and alarmed her.

Sorak turned to the last of his companions. "Report to the goddess."

As the man hurried down the hall, Sorak started up a stairway winding into one of the nearby walls. Kyrkenall and Elenai followed him.

"So," Kyrkenall asked Sorak, "where are you from?"

"I am from here."

"Always? Is this where you're from, originally?"

"I think so."

"And how long have you lived here?"

"A while now."

The answers were nearly meaningless, but they were delivered without any guile, as if Sorak's evasiveness wasn't deliberate.

They left the stairwell for a long walkway overlooking a garden four stories below. The sun streamed in without hindrance, for the garden had no roof; there appeared to be a higher walkway running along the battlements.

Elenai stayed close to the hall's stone railing, studying the trees and plants. These, too, were arranged in rows, and she realized she was looking upon a variety of flora found in Erymyr. Stranger yet was a long line of lifelike statues of various fauna, from tiny birds to cats to dogs and horses, as if Cerai had commissioned the works and hadn't yet decorated the building with them. They had been painted with stunning detail. But who could have designed such beautiful pieces? Were some of these strange men artists and artisans? If so, they possessed amazing talent.

The wall reached the tower at the junction with the next section of the hexagonal wall, and they passed a window overlooking the road they'd come in on. She glanced briefly at the distant hills, thick with fruit-bearing trees, then stopped with Sorak, who gestured into a doorless chamber with a long row of simple frame beds and straw mattresses.

"You can have any of these beds. There's a room through there." Sorak pointed to a dark opening in the wall. "It is where you can bring water and make water. I will carry cooked food to you, and then the goddess will wish to speak with you."

Even as Elenai wondered again at the man's peculiar speech patterns, he turned and started to leave. "Sorak, wait."

He paused.

"What was that chamber we passed through, with all of the plants and the statues of animals?"

"That is the Erymyran storage section."

"What does that mean?"

He blinked, as if her meaning wasn't clear, either.

"Storage for what?" she asked. "Why is everything in there from Erymyr?"

"That is the storage section for Erymyr," Sorak repeated.

"What's it for?" Kyrkenall asked.

"For safekeeping after the big storm."

Apparently there was never going to be an answer from him that didn't provoke more questions. "What big storm?" Elenai asked.

"There's a big storm that will be and the goddess makes samples in storage to rebuild after. I was told to bring you food by the goddess as soon as you were here, unless some of you were injured. I should do that."

And with that said, he departed. Elenai listened to the sound of his retreating footsteps. "Who bothers to say that food is cooked?"

"He sounds kobalin," Kyrkenall said, "from his name to his speech patterns. It's the damnedest thing."

"Do kobalin ever adopt human children?"

He mulled that over for a long moment. "I suppose it's possible. You're thinking he was raised away from humans. I get the sense all of these people would sound like that if we spoke to them, though. Our entire escort acted just like him." Kyrkenall glanced longingly at the dark archway through which water had been promised, then back at the doorway they'd come in through. "I'm going to take a look around."

Travel worn and weary as she was, Elenai nodded agreement, then comforted herself with a gulp from her waterskin. She replaced it and followed him, speaking quietly. "Maybe this isn't all just her doing. Maybe this is what the queen's planning, and this is all the result of the Mage Auxiliary exalts."

"Whatever it is, it's impressive and concerning."

A left turn would have taken them back to the Erymyran section, which is probably why Kyrkenall headed right, past a series of open archways leading to additional empty bedrooms. When they emerged from the tower at last, passing through another arch, the wall funneled them into the next side of the hexagon. Once more they walked through a wide space, looking down from a balcony onto long rows of plants and statues of creatures from the realm of Ekhem. There were marsh grasses and painted figures of gangly sea walkers with their nobbed knees and blue feathers and long necks, a stand of curving palms with drooping saw-edged leaves, and countless bushes and smaller trees festooned with different brilliant flowers.

Elenai leaned against the balcony and stared long and hard at those statues. Even from four stories up their realism astonished her. It seemed as though each feather had been carved with incredible skill and then painted by a greater master than she had ever seen. The thought came to her as she opened her eyes to the inner world, and beheld the magical threads that bound them all in place. "These aren't statues. Cerai has frozen them."

Kyrkenall frowned. "They're not locked in a hearthstone," he said. He must have been thinking of N'lahr.

"Neither were the people Belahn froze. Sorak said Cerai was making preparations for a storm. If we keep going down this hall, I bet we'd find an area like this from every single realm. The building's a hexagon, just like the Altenerai table. Five sides, one dedicated to each realm, and then one side for administration. In this case, that includes living quarters."

Realization had been dawning over Kyrkenall's features as she spoke. He cursed softly. "But how could a shift storm build up enough power to damage everything beyond a realm's borders?"

"I don't know, but these aren't just creatures from near the borders. It looks like she's trying to preserve any living thing she can lay hands on."

"She must be expecting a pretty big storm." Kyrkenall stepped up beside

Elenai and looked down upon the wide, open space, every foot of which was crammed with frozen, lifelike statues, and living plants.

"There aren't any people," Elenai remarked.

"I wouldn't expect her to save people like that. It'd be a little crazy, wouldn't it?"

"Isn't this a little crazy?" Elenai encompassed the surrounding walls with a wave of her hand.

"Maybe it's brilliant," Kyrkenall countered. "What if she really is trying to help protect and preserve everything?"

"If she wanted to protect and preserve Alantris, she wouldn't have abandoned it to the Naor. Maybe she doesn't care about the people, just the creatures. Maybe this is what the queen's been up to all along. Cerai's out here keeping tabs on this preservation project because Queen Leonara and the exalts know some deadly storm is coming. One that threatens nearly everything. One that they need the hearthstones to stop."

Kyrkenall raked back his hair, pensive but silent.

"The queen's good at keeping secrets far from Darassus. Like N'lahr and his sword," Elenai prompted.

"First off, that's not what Leonara told Belahn. He said the queen had shown him a goddess who was going to come and save us all. And I don't think he was talking about Cerai."

That was true enough. Elenai remembered the gist of Belahn's words, and how the hearthstones were a kind of shattered altar to a goddess, whose voice he had heard through the munificence of the queen. But then Belahn had been crazy, driven mad by complete absorption with a hearthstone, his once-powerful frame shrunken to nearly nothing because he had been subsisting solely on the energy he absorbed from the artifact.

"Second," Kyrkenall continued, "this place doesn't feel lived-in at all. I get the sense it's just Cerai here, along with her weird little army. If this really was the queen's project there'd be some exalts here."

"Maybe they're just away. Or maybe they're all talking with Cerai right now, deciding what to do with us."

Kyrkenall stilled and eyed her balefully. "You're getting really good at suggesting the worst."

"We're getting really good at finding it."

He chuckled. "'Fear not the coming man but news he brings'," Kyrkenall said, from his staged manner and meter clearly referencing something.

She couldn't place the quote. "Selana?"

"Tsk tsk. And you the daughter of a Vedessi playhouse manager. That's by the only great Vedessi playwright, Tolahn. When the prince is waiting for the messenger with news about his father's army? After he learned about the assassin?"

She flushed a little. Of course. "I'm afraid I was focused on the here and now."

"My point is that we're just speculating, but we're going to know when we talk with Cerai. Soon. And whatever we learn I bet we're not going to like it."

"That seems a pretty safe wager."

"Come on. Let's go confirm your theory." He pushed away from the rail and they were starting for the other hall when they heard a footfall behind them.

They turned and saw Sorak walking toward them. The lines upon his brow cleared as he approached.

"Ah! I was confused when you were not in the place I saw you last. The food is waiting for you in the room I left you in."

"Thanks, Sorak," Kyrkenall said.

"The goddess says to offer apology, but that she has been delayed. She says to make yourselves comfortable and that she can speak to you in the morning."

"Where is she now?"

"She found an emergency, and had to leave," Sorak said.

Elenai wasn't sure what to do with that information, and glanced over to Kyrkenall, who seemed unperturbed. She started to tell Sorak that they really needed to be going, but realized that they and their horses were spent. "I guess it would be nice to grab an actual bath, and sleep in a real bed for a change. But Cerai has to know we're in a hurry. Can you tell her that?"

"I cannot speak to her until she returns."

Kyrkenall thumbed over his shoulder. "Say, Sorak, if I keep moving around the building, will I find a bunch of animals and plants and things from Arappa and Kanesh and The Fragments?"

"Yes."

"That saves me some walking," Kyrkenall observed quietly to Elenai, then faced Sorak again. "Are there any exalts around here?"

Sorak stared at him, befuddled. "What is an exalt?"

"They wear clothes like us," Elenai said, "but they have red decorative lines along the seams."

"And they're assholes," Kyrkenall added, which only seemed to confuse Sorak further.

"There aren't any of those exalts here," he said at last.

"Have there ever been any here?"

"Not that I have seen."

"How about the queen?" Kyrkenall asked.

"I have never seen a queen here. Are you hungry? You should come to the food."

"You know what, Sorak, I think we will. Lead the way."

Sorak looked pleased, almost smiling before he turned. Kyrkenall and Elenai trailed after.

"Do you think he's telling the truth?" she asked softly.

"Don't you?"

"Yes."

"I get the sense he'll tell us the truth about anything we ask." He raised his voice. "Hey, Sorak!"

Their host stopped and turned to face them.

"The food's not poisoned with anything, is it?"

Once more the man looked confused, as if he had to process the information. "You are guests," he said finally. "Under protection. No harm will be given you here."

"What if we want to leave?"

Sorak frowned. "The goddess said she wished to speak with you. She might be angry if you leave before she speaks with you."

"I suppose that's true. Very well." Kyrkenall gestured for the man to precede him. "Lead on, Sorak! We are in your hands."

Their repast consisted mostly of fruits and vegetables, though there was a spread prepared from some mix of mashed lentils. There was sunberry juice rather than wine, which proved a little cloying. Best of all were the long slim loafs of bread, perfectly baked and quite flavorful, crisp on the outside and soft in the middle.

By the time they'd finished, sunlight was sinking below the tree-clad hills. Elenai was surprised by that, because some little fragments like this didn't have any sun at all, much less one that set, but this sun looked and behaved very much like the one she saw in the realms.

After the meal, Kyrkenall availed himself of the baths, expressing delight that there was a pump that brought water.

Though the water proved ice cold, Elenai immersed herself in it once Kyrkenall had left. She hadn't felt so clean since they'd departed Vedessus

There were towels and soap as well, and even fresh undergarments, though they proved a little large. Both she and Kyrkenall scrubbed out most of their dirty clothing and hung it to dry. They'd packed light, and even her third shirt had seen use after so many days.

Kyrkenall spoke softly as he spread out the sheets Sorak brought them. "In the morning, if this takes too long, we may need to start improvising."

"Should we take watches?"

He arched an eyebrow at her. "Given her resources, if Cerai wanted to cause us trouble, I think she'd already have done it. Let's get a full night's sleep for once, and see what the morning brings."

The morning brought a ko'aye.

28

An Unexpected Guest

E lenai woke to a hand on her shoulder, in the still hours before sunrise. "You're not having an important dream, are you?" Kyrkenall asked softly.

"It would be a little late now if I was," she said, a little dazed. "But no, still none. What's going on?"

"Time for a little stroll. Shall we?"

The man's energy levels were mythic. She wanted to tell him to go back to bed, but she rose, trying not to grumble. No matter the speed with which she dressed, Kyrkenall paced back and forth along the aisleway, clearly impatient to be on his way.

"I think I heard a ko'aye," he said, although from his manner he might as well have told her to hurry.

Elenai was still struggling into her boots. For some reason the soft bed seemed to have made things worse, for she was suddenly aware of aches and pains she hadn't noticed when she'd wakened from sleeping on the ground. "Ko'aye?"

"I heard a couple of calls. You slept right through it."

"Do you ever sleep?" She sighed.

But in another moment she was standing and buckling on her sword belt.

"Will your ring on," he said quietly, "but set the light so it won't shine."

"All right." During one of their overnights he'd finally gotten around to explaining how to use the ring that way, admitting that it had taken him a few years to remember when to use it to his advantage.

A ghostly sliver of moonlight shone through the open window and illuminated the lithe archer as he crept to the doorway. He paused briefly, then moved through, and she just caught him waving her on to follow.

Halfway expecting that they'd encounter Sorak or one of his similar fellows, she used the power of the ring to sense the way before them, and discovered that they were alone in the hallway.

Moving quickly but quietly, Kyrkenall led them into the dark stairwell. Here he paused briefly, and Elenai checked with her ring herself, thinking he must be doing the same, and found nothing. Useful though it might be, the ring didn't have a particularly long range. If someone were trailing them twenty-five paces back, they'd not know it. She wondered why she wasn't sensing the threads of possibility that had earned her the Oddsbreaker moniker, and decided it must be because she wasn't in any immediate danger. That seemed to be the only time she grew aware of branching futures, although it wasn't entirely dependable even in those circumstances.

Kyrkenall headed upstairs rather than down, looking back only when Elenai inadvertently scuffed the toe of her boot on one of the steps. He paused long enough that she imagined him glaring, and then they arrived at the upper landing.

Here there was a door, and Kyrkenall briefly activated his ring at low strength, playing the blue light over the surface. They discovered it of solid wood similar to oak, and still smelling of the dark stain it had been treated with. The archer quietly slipped the thick bar aside, dimmed his light, and ever-so-carefully opened the door.

She wished to ask why they'd come this way, but given the measures he'd taken to remain quiet she reluctantly followed suit.

After the profound darkness of the stairwell, the moonlight upon the battlement left her feeling exposed. Kyrkenall waited on the threshold, scanning the area, hesitating only briefly as he looked overhead. Then he advanced.

She crept after. The battlement proved almost as wide as the hallways below, with a chest-high wall on the inner side, and crenelated battlement on the outer. Four warriors might easily have walked abreast. Kyrkenall seemed determined to remain on point, and so she followed, senses extended through her ring, her view alternating to left and right, and straight ahead, where the tip of Kyrkenall's great bow, Arzhun, curved out past its shoulder holster and higher than his head.

All was quiet but a cool breeze that rattled the trees on nearby hilltops, bringing with it the sweet scent of sunberries. It was only after they advanced a few paces farther that Elenai thought to look up, and realized what had caught her companion's attention when he first emerged.

In her nighttime travels through the realms and shifts, she had seen the moon high, low, in different phases, and entirely absent, and sometimes strangely twisted. Never had she seen it twinned. Here in this strange fragment the silver moon was low upon the horizon and mostly full. Higher and more distant, a second moon hung, waning and red, with a slim gold ring. A strange and beautiful sight.

They walked fifteen paces before she sensed something ahead. Kyrkenall had already slowed. Without looking back to her, he'd raised a warning hand even as he quietly slipped Arzhun from his holster and nocked an arrow.

Elenai reached forth with the ring and sensed . . . something. Life was there, yes. But it seemed somehow wrong. It was, she realized, like that restraint cast about the life-forms in Cerai's holding areas.

In only a few more paces, she saw a creature crouched in the midst of the battlement. Kyrkenall advanced upon it, bow ready, though the string wasn't taut.

As they drew closer, the creature seemed uninclined to move. Elenai suspected that it couldn't.

"Here's the ko'aye," Kyrkenall said quietly as he drew up beside it.

"It's frozen," Elenai told him.

She saw Kyrkenall look to right and left, and then he knelt, activating his ring light.

Its glow reflected eerily from two black eyes shining only a handspan above the floor. The ko'aye's body seemed a hunched mass from which clawed feet were thrust, and it took a moment for her to understand what she took as a misshapen cloak on its back were two wings folded in upon themselves, partly hiding a saddle. The head perched atop its long neck was narrow, somewhere between that of a bird's and a lizard's, with projecting beak.

Under Kyrkenall's ring light, the feathers mostly looked different shades of blue.

Tentatively Elenai put a hand toward it, encountering the same kind of resistance field she'd found about the people Belahn had been "protecting." Once she was a thumbspan away, she couldn't get any closer, no matter how much harder she pressed.

"This is Lelanc," Kyrkenall said quietly, turning off his ring before he rose. "Aradel's friend."

"N'lahr said Cerai had kidnapped her from Alantris. What's she doing here on the battlement?"

"One guess," Kyrkenall said. "Cerai's been traveling. She got back only recently, and I heard the landing."

"And then Cerai put her like this?"

"I think so."

"That doesn't seem very kind," Elenai said. Surely Cerai should have let the creature drink and eat. But then if Lelanc was an unwilling servant, this was a far simpler way to keep her prisoner than placing her in chains somewhere.

"Can you free her?" Kyrkenall asked.

"I can try. But shouldn't we talk with Cerai, first?"

"We know she stole Lelanc. And it seems pretty clear that she's keeping her prisoner. And we need every ally we can get. Even one ko'aye could help N'lahr against the dragons."

"Yes," Elenai said slowly, a little puzzled that Kyrkenall couldn't see the larger issue. "I agree with all of that. But isn't freeing Lelanc liable to anger Cerai? And didn't you just say that we needed every ally we could get? Shouldn't we talk to Cerai first?"

"Never ask permission before you act rightly," Kyrkenall remonstrated. "Lelanc shouldn't be a prisoner. And we may not get another chance to free her."

Still doubtful, Elenai used the ring to study the magical net woven about the ko'aye. Viewing the magical holds Cerai had made last night, she'd sensed they were different than those she'd seen in Wyndyss. This one, too, proved less powerful than Belahn's work because that strength was unnecessary. Where his spell had been thorough and, she now saw, coarse, Cerai's was refined, minimal, accomplishing the same end by slowing the creature's life force to a near standstill without lancing through every inch of its body.

All the energy seemed knotted to a single point at the base of Lelanc's neck.

"Well?" Kyrkenall asked.

"I'll have to turn on the hearthstone."

"So go ahead."

He was sounding more and more irritable, and she was growing tired of it. "First, I'm not sure this is a good idea. Second, if I turn on the hearthstone, Cerai might sense it."

"And third?" Kyrkenall said. "Because it sounds like you were going to say a third."

She shook her head, though he was right. Almost she'd told him she was growing more and more concerned about wielding the artifact. "Nothing." And feeling the shame of that, she threw caution to the winds and reached with threads of intent to the hearthstone in her pack.

The instant she opened it, the crystal all but enthralled her, even without reaching into its depths. She gasped, her lips tilting into a smile despite herself, and resisted that seductive downward draw, taking only just enough energy to touch the very heart of that knot about Lelanc's neck.

The net collapsed upon itself, though Elenai still sensed it quiescent and gathered about the animal's neck. Elenai turned down the stone, vastly relieved that she'd avoided its temptations.

Lelanc's head rose sharply, her eyes still unwinking. Her wings sent a feathery gust at them as they unfurled, and Elenai and Kyrkenall stepped back. The animal let out a cry of anger that rent the night.

"So much for stealth," Kyrkenall said.

That's what we get for doing it your way, Elenai thought.

Lelanc's head lowered and her brows drew down over dark eyes. "Who are you?" she demanded. Her voice was high and harsh.

"Lelanc, it's me. Kyrkenall. We've freed you."

The creature's eyes narrowed and its neck extended toward the archer. Then its head drew back and its eyes widened. "Drusa's friend, Kyrkenall? How came you here?"

"We were looking for Kalandra."

Elenai briefly wondered how he expected this ko'aye to know an alten, then remembered Kalandra was the one who'd brokered the original agreement between the ko'aye and the Altenerai.

Lelanc certainly seemed to recognize her name. "I do not think she is in this place. There are none but the traitor Cerai and her people."

Kyrkenall gestured to Elenai. "This is Elenai Oddsbreaker. Her magic set you free."

The creature bowed her head in gratitude. "I thank you, Oddsbreaker."

"Why is Cerai keeping you prisoner?" Elenai asked.

"So she may use me to go where she wills. She stole my mind!" Lelanc's beak opened and she let out a cry of rage. "She makes me go where she wishes! She took me from Alantris and my battle brother, Rylin. I wished to stay! We would have slain the Naor together!"

"You've really got to quiet down," Kyrkenall said.

"It's a little late for that, isn't it?" Elenai asked him.

The ko'aye was ranting and paid heed to neither of them. "She said she did not kill him, but he lay unmoving! I saw the walls fall and the Naor charging in!"

"Rylin lived," Elenai said, trying to soothe the agitated creature. "He's wounded, but he's still alive."

Those eyes, great pools of darkness, turned upon her. "Did she tell you that? She is a maker of lies, Oddsbreaker. She lied to Varama, and to Rylin. She tells me now that if she lets me go, I will perish, for all the lands to the distant places will be ripped apart."

"That," a woman's voice called from behind them, "is no lie!"

Beside her, Kyrkenall whirled, arrow ready. Lelanc growled from deep within her throat and clawed at the bricks, her wings stirring with menace.

Only then did Elenai sense anyone approaching through the ring, for the woman and her companions had just entered its radius. As she herself turned, she saw the trio. Sorak and another of the well-formed men walked behind, his companion bearing a lantern. Leading them, at the point of the triangle, was a tall woman with dark hair cascading past the collar of her blue khalat.

She walked with complete confidence, and though Elenai could see little of her face with the light behind her, her smile was in the sound of her words. "Kyrkenall. You've always had terrible timing."

Lelanc let out a harsh cry, then screeched, her voice so distorted with trills and clicks and whistles it was barely coherent. "Betrayer! Mind stealer! Egg-thief!" This last must have been the most dire insult of all, because it was the loudest. The ko'aye leapt forward. Elenai ducked, Lelanc's wing beats stirring her hair.

The creature landed on her back legs, her front claws stretched forth, her wings fanning the air.

And then, quite suddenly, Lelanc sank back on her haunches, lowered her front legs, and folded in her wings as her neck dropped. The immense blast of magical energies that brought this brushed Elenai's ring, and she felt the invigorating presence of a hearthstone flower open in the moment before the stasis net once more enveloped the ko'aye.

As quickly as it had begun, the attack was finished and Cerai's hearthstone closed. And the vibrant being who had momentarily wakened to strike with vengeance was once again an immobile prisoner, for all intents and purposes, a statue.

Lelanc's attack had blocked Elenai's view of Cerai's activity. It might be that there had been nothing to see, for Cerai was visible once more and she seemed not to have moved in the slightest. Still silhouetted by the light, she stood with arms relaxed and loose.

It didn't matter that she herself had cautioned against freeing the ko'aye, Elenai now knew rage at the way the noble creature had so contemptuously been rendered helpless, her legitimate grievances silenced by smug authority.

"Let her go," she said, her voice steely.

"Aye," Kyrkenall echoed. He wasn't pointing his arrow directly at Cerai, but it could be brought into line in a heartbeat.

"If I let her go, she's going to fly off to her doom. She's impossible to reason with."

"For some reason she doesn't trust you," Elenai said.

"You're awfully rude to someone who's provided you with food and shelter." Cerai sounded disappointed, as a mother might with a child playing at the table when dinner guests were present. "I'm not your enemy, Alten. Perhaps you should hear me out before doing anything rash, and judge with all the facts rather than feeling."

"We need Lelanc's help, Cerai," Kyrkenall said. "To fight the Naor beasts."

"You really don't need to worry about the Naor," Cerai said. "I've tried explaining it to Lelanc, but she refuses to listen. I have cared for her with healing magics, and provided food and water, but she will not trust me. Maybe she'll listen if you explain it. But for now, for my safety, and hers, I'd prefer to keep her as she is. Do you understand?"

Kyrkenall lowered his bow, then slid his arrow back into its quiver. He pushed Arzhun back into its holster, accomplishing the last with practiced ease.

Elenai feigned relaxing, though her senses were still stretched taut. She disliked Cerai intensely and distrusted her, but the older woman's powers seemed likely to dwarf her own.

"I'd planned to talk with you after sunrise," Cerai said. "It's been a very long night for me. But seeing as how we're all awake and you two are bristling, let's just get it over with. Come along, then." With that, she turned on her heel and advanced past Sorak and his companions. Those two followed obediently and Kyrkenall went after. Elenai spared another look to Lelanc, sitting with eyes frozen in fury, and her own anger flared once more. *I will free you,* she vowed.

Cerai said nothing to them during the long walk back. Speaking with her would have been inconvenient given that she remained fifteen feet or more ahead of them even once they were descending the long flights of stairs.

When they reached the bottom of the stairwell, they passed through a series of short corridors, arriving at last at a spacious room with a large fireplace. Bright woven rugs were cast over the dark granite floors, between groups of plushly cushioned furniture arranged in conversational groups. A wide bookcase stuffed with volumes sat near a window.

As Sorak and the other servants lit lanterns, Elenai realized the sound of falling water she'd heard originated from a decorative cascade two spear lengths wide spattering down the wall opposite the fireplace and into a little channel that flowed into a circular pool between the furniture. Little fish, frightened of the human shadows, flashed silver as they darted from one side of the pool to the other.

Elenai saw Cerai's face in full at last, fastening upon the lovely features: the slim nose; the bright eyes burning with intelligence; the dark, full lips twisted most of the way into a mocking smile. Her collar was unhooked, baring her throat down to her clavicle.

She dominated the room. It wasn't that she was physically the most beautiful woman Elenai had ever seen, although she certainly compared, it was that she projected something more than confidence, more even than charm. It was, Elenai decided, a kind of regal dignity that most rulers only aspired toward. She wondered if it were magical.

"Welcome, Altenerai," their host said, her hand pressed in salute. As the lanterns showed their full glow at last, Cerai was revealed as older than she first appeared. Her face had age lines and the occasional wrinkle. Elenai tried and failed to remember her true age, but thought that she did not appear nearly as old as she should.

She and Kyrkenall returned the salute and answered as one. "Hail."

The archer stepped around the rim of the pool and offered his hand to the enchantress. They clasped arms below the elbow, his dusky fingers at contrast with her pale ones.

"You are even more beautiful than I remember," Kyrkenall told her.

"Thank you for noticing. And you are as lovely as I recall." She then took in Elenai. "Congratulations on your elevation," she said. "I'm sorry, I don't recall your name."

"Elenai," Kyrkenall said. "Elenai Dartaan, known as Elenai Oddsbreaker."

"A sobriquet already?" Cerai's expression was both curious and faintly amused.

Elenai found the older woman's grip firm as she clasped her arm and stepped away.

"N'lahr gave it to her a few weeks ago," Kyrkenall explained.

Cerai's look grew sharp; gone was a hint of playfulness. Kyrkenall had caught her off guard.

"You're not joking."

"No," Kyrkenall assured her. "Did you know where he was?"

"I'd assumed he was in his tomb."

"So had most of us."

Cerai's lips twisted thoughtfully. "It looks as though you have more to tell me than I thought. Please. Sit." Cerai indicated the overstuffed couch at a right angle to the chair into which she sank, and motioned the servants away.

Kyrkenall removed Arzhun and leaned the bow and its quiver against the couch, unbuckled his sword belt, carefully propped Lothrun beside the great black bow, and then took the offered seat. After a moment, Elenai followed his example.

Cerai paused at the sound of footsteps. A trio of male servants arrived bearing platters with bread, smoking meats, and cheeses, and additional goblets and wine. A fourth followed with small wooden tables, which he deposited near Cerai, Elenai, and Kyrkenall before bowing and departing. The others then placed the items that they carried and all but the one who'd brought the wine bottles left on the instant. The sweet scent of warm ham was umistakable and very pleasant. Until that moment Elenai hadn't realized she was hungry.

"Is there anything else you need?" The lead servant asked.

"Not currently. Wait over there in case one of us requires something."

"Of course." He bowed and then retreated to stand near the fireplace.

Cerai shook her head, with the air of long-suffering patience. "You should try the bread. They've gotten a lot better at baking."

"They're kobalin, aren't they," Elenai said. "You've changed them somehow."

Cerai smiled the way one would with a very clever pet. "Very good. Kobalin are naturally sensitive to magic, so I use them to ferret out the hearthstones. And some I alter for my own purposes."

Elenai hid her dismay. She'd really hoped for a different answer. "How do you do it? Shaping living beings is—should be—impossible. Even the most basic kinds of healing take years to master—"

"I'm a quick study. And I've grown used to hearthstones."

That was hardly illuminating. "So you've been spending a lot of time out here experimenting," Elenai said. "I'm not at all clear on how that helps the realms."

Cerai looked to the archer, speaking as though Elenai weren't there. "She's so critical, Kyrkenall. You can trust me, you know."

"I'm not sure who I can trust anymore," Kyrkenall said. "N'lahr. Elenai. Probably Varama and Tretton and Gyldara. Maybe Enada."

"That's a short list. I think you can probably depend upon Decrin, too."

"Decrin's dead."

Cerai's face fell. "How did he die?"

"I slew him," Kyrkenall said grimly.

At Cerai's stunned stare, Elenai interjected: "Decrin had been tricked by Denaven into fighting us."

"Ah. And Kyrkenall then killed Denaven, I hope?"

"Elenai managed that."

Cerai arched an eyebrow at Elenai, her head rising at the same moment, as if her respect notched a mark higher. "So where was N'lahr all this time?"

"Denaven and the queen had him as a statue, like the ones you have here."

"Really." Her brow furrowed. "I didn't think they knew how to do that."

Kyrkenall answered. "I don't believe it was intentional."

"Curious. So. You really didn't know I was here?"

"No. I'd heard you were on long patrol, keeping an eye on the Naor and steering clear of Darassus and Denaven."

"Like you?" she asked.

"It looks like you've been mostly here. Unless you built all this in a day."

Cerai's smile was highly satisfied. "I have become something of a miracle worker, but I didn't manage this in a day. Please—eat. I've just finished a light meal," she said, lifting a goblet, "but as soon as I was alerted that you were awake, I ordered my people into the kitchens."

"Perhaps later," Kyrkenall said. "We've a lot of questions."

"I imagine you do." Cerai put the goblet to her lips and sipped. "First, though, why don't you tell me what you're doing here?"

"We came for help."

"For Lelanc?"

"We didn't know Lelanc was here. The realms have been invaded by several Naor armies. N'lahr sent us to find the ko'aye, and we heard rumors of an alten out here. I thought it might be Kalandra. But it turns out it was the commander, whom the kobalin have been worshiping as a god." Kyrkenall's tone grew accusatory. "You knew the commander's body was there, and you just left him to rot, with his ring and everything?"

Cerai laughed. "*That's* what you want to talk about?"

"It's a start. A lot of us would have liked to have known what happened to him. And you know we're low on rings."

"I think the kobalin had the right idea. Let a man like that lie." She raised her goblet in salute. "Ring and all."

"You think maybe you should have run that past the rest of the Altenerai?"

"If I told anyone else, they would have headed out here. And Denaven and the queen would have learned what I was doing. I couldn't have that."

"What *are* you doing?" Elenai asked. Because it certainly didn't seem as though Cerai was keeping to her oath.

Cerai hadn't missed the skepticism in her voice. "Are you judging before you have the facts, Alten?"

"I haven't judged yet. But I've seen the way you treated Lelanc. And I know you abandoned Alantris."

"You've obviously spent a whole lot less time protecting the realms than you have practicing with hearthstones," Kyrkenall said.

Cerai set down the goblet and crossed one slim booted leg over the other. She rested one hand upon each chair arm, looking very much like a queen upon her throne. "Well. I thought my hard work might save the realms. It's too late for that, but I'm the only one who'll be able to restore some semblance of their previous appearance."

The woman spoke with such matter-of-fact surety that Elenai felt a chill. "From the storm your kobalin told us about?"

"Yes. It's going to wipe out nearly everything. That's the reason I'm preserving Lelanc, frustrating as she is. The queen's grand experiment is going to begin any day now. And we'll be lucky if there's a single realm left by the time she's through."

"So the queen's going to summon a storm?" Elenai asked, doubtful.

"No. That's not what she's planning to do. But she's so obsessed that she won't listen to reason or see where her actions will lead."

Kyrkenall took the reins, sounding remarkably composed. "You've clearly been sharpening your claws here, Cerai. If the queen's about to do something stupid, why haven't you challenged her?"

"I might have, earlier. But I tried too long to reason with her. Once I realized just how dangerous she really was, it was too late. I have finite skills. I can't risk myself, or I risk losing all that's at stake. I have followers for menial tasks, and an army to fend off the curious, but as you've seen, that army isn't capable of a great deal of independent thought. The queen, on the other hand, has many more hearthstones and a whole cadre of people trained to use them. Until recently she also had Denaven, and the entire Altenerai Corps."

"You could have come to Altenerai you could be sure of," Kyrkenall suggested. "Like me."

"Oh, Kyrkenall, I've always liked you. But you're hardly dependable."

"All right then, but over the years you might have spoken to Aradel, or Varama, or Decrin, or Tretton. Even Enada."

"Aradel's dead now, and Varama is probably dead, too. Pity, that. She was very clever. And I imagine poor Rylin died with her. I really wanted to take him along with me, but he was just too heavy."

"You'll be happy to know that Varama lives. And Rylin does as well, although he was gravely wounded."

Cerai's head tilted. "That wasn't so very long ago. How could you possibly know the details and be here?"

"A little bit of magery."

Cerai's gaze instantly swung upon Elenai. It wasn't cold, exactly, but it was searching. Elenai knew then that she'd been reappraised, reclassified perhaps from curiosity to potential threat.

"And the city?" Cerai asked.

"Thousands are dead, and the Naor are in control. Thousands more will die." Kyrkenall gestured to the surrounding stone. "We could use your help. And your army, to turn them back."

"Don't you mean to accuse me of treachery?" Cerai asked. There was a purring, catlike quality to the query.

"Do you want me to accuse you of treachery?"

She sighed. "It's too late to risk ourselves with anything related to what they're doing. But I would welcome your help."

"You need *our* help?" Elenai asked.

"I'll need assistance once the repairs start. I didn't want to involve anyone sooner because I didn't want any hands dropping ingredients in the stew pot. I'm the head chef. I know exactly what I'm doing."

"We still don't know what the queen's up to," Elenai said. As Cerai reached over and broke open a crispy hunk of bread, she resisted the impulse to reach out and join her.

"The queen thinks she's going to bring eternal blessings to the realms by restoring a lost goddess for us all to worship."

"We've been hearing a little about her," Kyrkenall said.

"How much do you know?"

"Belahn told us that the hearthstones were a kind of altar to this goddess, and that the queen was going to call her back."

"So Belahn talked to you about it?"

"He was dying," Kyrkenall said.

"My. The bodies are piling up." Cerai paused to swallow, then brushed crumbs from her hands. "He didn't quite get the details right, but he had the gist of it. The queen's convinced those idiots she's surrounded herself with that you can reconstruct the being whose imprint is threaded through the hearthstones, simply by stacking them in the right shape and activating all of them at once. Do you know what's going to happen when that much power is streaming out in the same place?"

"I'm guessing it's not good," Kyrkenall said.

"That's an understatement. She's going to loose an immense amount of destructive power. We're almost surely looking at dissolution of all but the realm centers. Maybe even those."

"How do you know it won't work?" Elenai asked.

"Because I know how the Goddess was destroyed in the first place." Once again Cerai looked pleased with herself. "There's nothing left but the energy. And once our idiot queen releases it . . ." She shook her head with dramatic regret.

"Why is Leonara so obsessed with this?" Kyrkenall asked.

"She thinks she holds the secret keys to paradise, Kyrkenall, so that none of those little problems like Naor and kobalin, and storms, and decaying borders will ever plague us again. Just one god controlling all, through her loyal queen."

Elenai had any number of questions, but she was still struggling to absorb the information.

"So there really is, or was, a Goddess like this?" Kyrkenall asked.

Cerai shrugged slim shoulders. "The founders thought of her as one. A god of our gods, if you will."

"And what happened to this goddess?" Kyrkenall asked.

Elenai had begun to suspect the answer.

"Our gods got together and killed her. And her loyal adherent, Sartain." Cerai smiled. "That paints things a different color, doesn't it? It turns out the betrayer was the only loyal one."

Elenai opened her mouth to inquire further, but Cerai cut her off.

"Why don't I just summarize. That will save a lot of time, because it does seem that you've missed some details. The queen began hunting hearthstones after she chanced upon a memory stone left by none other than Sartain. The Gods we know and love and worship were all busy outdoing each other with their creations, but Sartain and the Goddess got tired of it. Our revered Gods ambushed her and Sartain and defeated them. The battle's survivors decided to scatter her hearthstones all over the realms so that no one person would have access to all the power in one place." Cerai paused to crunch delicately into another hunk of bread and Elenai watched enviously.

"You can join in anytime you like," Cerai said.

Elenai shook her head.

"Suit yourself. Now, the hearthstones have an added benefit. They create points of solidity, wherever they are. By scattering them around the realms the founders actually solidified our borders. And some small fragments and splinters came into being that wouldn't normally have existed because they coalesced around stones that had been left in the Shifting Lands. When the queen started retrieving them, she upset everything. Altering the borders changes the energy patterns in the shifts. That's part of the reason the storms have grown so much more volatile and frequent lately."

"Part of the reason?" Kyrkenall asked.

"Well, we have an inherently unstable system. These little islands of creation that the founders made weren't really designed for permanence. They're like unfinished sketches. They'd be more secure if they weren't poised always on the brink of chaos."

"That explains a lot, actually," Kyrkenall said. "Although we'd suspected some of it."

Elenai finally found her voice. "Why hasn't the queen acted before now? Was it because she didn't have enough hearthstones?"

"In part. They also have to be assembled in just the right way, which is painstaking. She still doesn't have them all, but she thinks it's close enough. For the longest time she was desperate to present the Goddess with what Leonara called the keystone—sort of a master design of the realms—so that the Goddess would grant her immediate permission to restore the original plan. But I liberated that stone. I thought it might slow her down, but it doesn't seem to have done so."

"We need to stop her before she opens those assembled hearthstones," Kyrkenall said.

"I think I've explained why that's impossible."

"Nothing's impossible. N'lahr just defeated an entire Naor army, and Mazakan, with a herd of eshlack. We can stop the queen. Maybe all this problem needs is the right arrow."

"That's a brave sentiment, Kyrkenall. But you've only a few days, at best. And besides, the Naor are nearly to the walls of Darassus right now, with an army that's going to smash it flat. Even if you stop the queen you can't save Darassus."

"What?" Kyrkenall demanded.

"The Naor have a sorcerer of their own, and he's been playing with hearthstones and blood magic. I would have stopped him but it would have taken time and energy I simply didn't have."

"You don't even sound like you care," Elenai said.

"I've resigned myself to the destruction of Darassus some time ago. It's happening in a different way, but . . ." She shrugged.

"How do you know all this?" Kyrkenall asked. "Where did this army come from?"

"I can monitor things through my own small collection of hearthstones." Elenai was tiring of her matter-of-fact tone. "Monitor how?"

"There's so much I can show you." Cerai might have been striving to sound kind, but the result was condescending. She was more genuine as she swung her attention to Kyrkenall. "Look. I understand your first instincts. Really, I do. And if you want to go charging off, you can. I won't stop you. But there's no way that you'll reach Darassus in time to make any difference."

"Can you tell what's happened to N'lahr, and what's going on in Alantris?" Kyrkenall asked.

"I didn't even know he was alive," Cerai reminded them. "And the Naor already destroyed the walls of Alantris and took the city. None of it matters. It's all going to be destroyed anyway and it's not worth dashing about to try and do anything. I see you don't believe me."

"It's not that we don't believe you," Elenai said. "It's that we disagree. You may be unwilling to fulfill your oath, but we're up to the challenge."

She seemed finally to have disrupted the older woman's equanimity. Cerai glared. "I've spent the last five years of my life finding a way to fix the problem the queen's brewing. You can't even conceive the time and effort and sacrifice it's taken."

"Whose sacrifice?" Elenai asked.

A contemptuous frown crossed Cerai's features, and she shifted her attention to Kyrkenall. "There will be a lot of work to do. I'll need the assistance of other mages, as well, to put things right." She nodded to Elenai without really looking at her. "We'll have to rebuild almost entirely from scratch. Fortunately, the keystone contains the original plans. It will be a tremendous aid. Why don't you stay, and help me?"

"That's the real reason you didn't want help before, isn't it?" Elenai asked. She didn't wait for an answer. "You're looking forward to this. You get to remake the world yourself, maybe with a few improvements."

Cerai laughed. "Look what I've done here! Imagine what I can do with even more energies!"

"Isn't that exactly what the queen thinks?"

"The queen wants to turn power over to a greater being. I mean to take the reins myself."

"I think we're going to have to pass," Kyrkenall said. "Although we'll be happy to help rebuild if we can't stop the queen."

Maybe he'd be happy. Maybe, though, he was just trying to stay on her good side, and Elenai was the one betraying her temper. Elenai looked sidelong at Kyrkenall, realized his road was the safer one, and wondered when it was that they'd switched roles.

"It sounds as though Darassus needs us," Kyrkenall continued, and Elenai kept silent.

"You won't make it in time. The best you can hope for is to end up killed by the Naor. More likely you'll be separated into component pieces by a storm. And I won't be able to put you back together, even if I know you well."

She sounded disappointed in the last, like someone did when they'd been drafting a poem that hadn't turned out. Elenai suspected that she must have tried to put people back together. She wondered how far she'd gotten.

"Elenai's kept us together through some pretty terrible storms."

"Has she? Well, the thing about riding through the storms is that you have somewhere to go. If everything's blasted into pieces, there are no points of safety." Cerai turned full attention on her. "If you're as good as Kyrkenall says, then I'll be even happier to have your help if you can find your way back here. Take a stone so you can center yourself. And if you're really determined to go try, you'd best get moving."

"Is there anything more you can tell us?" Elenai asked.

"The amount of interesting things I could tell you would fill your days."

"I'm taking Lelanc," Elenai said.

Cerai stared at her, then laughed at Kyrkenall. "She's so subtle. Is she your lover, Kyrkenall?"

"No," Elenai answered, sounding more resolute than she intended.

"My. I didn't mean to touch a nerve." Cerai waved grandly. "Go ahead. Take the creature. I was going to use her as a model to restore ko'aye, but maybe I'll just design something better." She stood, and spoke to the transformed kobalin waiting patiently near the fireside. "I need more supplies packed, two satchels full. The same as I took with me. Have their horses brought out."

"Yes, Goddess." The servant bowed his head and hurried away.

"They insist," she said slyly to Elenai's disapproving look.

Elenai was about to ask how hard Cerai had worked at getting them to call her something else, but her ring lit. At first she thought their host must be working some attack, but Cerai's brows wrinkled in dismay to discover her own ring shining. Kyrkenall's was alight as well, and he was already standing with his sheath in one hand, Lothrun half drawn.

A woman had shimmered into being across the pool from them. The color of her khalat and dark hair were washed out, but beneath her high forehead her eyes were bright points like miniature suns.

"Rialla," Kyrkenall whispered in stunned amazement.

Elenai looked to Cerai to see if this were some trick of hers, but the older woman's aplomb was fully shattered.

"Can you hear me, Kyrkenall?" Rialla's lips moved, but Elenai didn't hear her words, only the echo of them within her mind.

"I hear you," Kyrkenall said, and then he risked a look over to Cerai, who had climbed to her feet in rapt absorption. "How is this being done? Are you trapped somewhere? Like N'lahr?"

"I think I am dead in your now," Rialla answered, and, curiously, brought a hand to her face. "Time's short."

"This isn't some trick of yours?" Kyrkenall demanded of Cerai, a harsh edge to his voice.

"No," Cerai answered, still astonished. "I swear by the ring. How—"

Rialla's attention swung to Cerai. "There is something I must do. Meet me in your fortress courtyard."

"What are you going to do?" Cerai demanded.

"We have to get them all to Darassus," Rialla said impatiently. "I can show you a way to open a portal, and you must watch, because you will do it again yourself."

One of Cerai's eyebrows peaked. She must have liked the sound of that, for she looked very curious.

"You're the one with my hearthstone," Rialla said to Elenai, her eyes like sharp metal points.

"Yes. And you've been warning me about Kyrkenall."

"I have?"

"About him having to jump left."

Rialla frowned. "I'll have to look into that." She sounded irritated.

"The jump hasn't happened yet," Elenai said, wishing the strange woman would finally provide some clarity and details. "I really wish you'd give us more information so we know what to look for."

"If I said it's important, it is. But right now I can't tell you, because I don't know of it yet." Rialla was making even less sense than she had in the dreams. "You must get the ko'aye," she insisted, an edge to her voice. "Everything has to be in just the right position at the right time or it will have all been for nothing."

Elenai hesitated, looking to Kyrkenall, who still stared, disbelieving, then to Cerai. None of this sounded quite right, but if Cerai were tricking them she was choosing an odd way to go about it.

Besides, Elenai reminded herself, she had wanted to free Lelanc in any case.

"Right," she said. "I'll meet you in the courtyard."

"Speed's of the essence."

Elenai sprinted from the room and into the stairwell, taking the steps two at a time.

29

Homecoming

Rylin looked out to see a half-dozen troops riding at them over the lush green grass. They wore helms, and blue tabards over their cuirasses, and their horses were a mix of whites and browns. Though none raised weapons, they radiated a sense of menace.

Lasren willed his ring to light and raised it high.

Rylin hoped that signal would still mean something, and told Elik to mount up. "I'm just a common soldier, remember," he said.

With an apologetic look, the squire climbed onto the animal.

The patrol slowed, then drew to a halt only a few horselengths off.

They arranged themselves in a semicircle behind their leader, a dark-haired woman in an Altenerai khalat with red piping. An exalt. A native of the Storm Coast, she had narrow eyes and coppery-brown skin.

"Hail, Alten," she said to Lasren.

"Hail, Exalt," he replied.

Rylin felt the regard of the exalt and companions shift to each of them. One was a second-rank squire he'd help train, but the man didn't recognize him through his disguise. He'd temporarily deactivated his ring as well.

Lasren nodded at his companions. "This is Governor Feolia of The Fragments, and our assistants."

The exalt wasn't interested in getting to know any of them. "Your passage was detected," she said. "And the presence of two rings. Where's the other alten?"

"The other alten is dead," Lasren said.

"In the shifts?"

"Killed in battle against the Naor," Lasren said. "Decrin died defending Vedessus, and I'm bringing his ring back."

The exalt was unphased. "And you activated it?"

Lasren edged his horse closer and looked down on the woman, using his bulk to his advantage. "If you sensed my rings then you sensed the storm, and know my reason for using both. And didn't you hear me? A hero of the realm is dead. Decrin of the Shining Shield has fallen." Lasren's indignance certainly seemed genuine as he swung to take in the riders. "What's wrong with you? Vedessus is saved but Alantris has fallen. You two—give over your horses."

The news had caused consternation among the squires, several of whom brought their hands to their hearts in salute.

The exalt frowned. "I'm sorry, Alten. But I'm supposed to question all who come through the barrier. The fact that you didn't come through on the usual path suggests you may have been attempting to cross through undetected."

"We lost our way in the storm and barely made it through." Lasren's anger was genuine. "We lost two of our horses and some *thing* came this close to eating us! Before that we risked our lives fighting Naor and you want to quiz us? Who the fuck do you think you are?"

"I am Exalt Narissa. And I take my duty seriously."

Feolia stepped forward. "Then do your duty and help us to Darassus, dear," she said. "We must get word to the councilors and press for help. More of my people are dying every hour."

Narissa stared at her, fell silent.

"We need fresh horses," Lasren repeated.

Finally, Narissa nodded and raised her hand, then pointed at four of her followers, calling them by name. "Trade them your mounts."

Rylin wanted to ask more information, but thought the less attention he drew to himself the better. He instead hung close to the governor, as though he were her personal guard. In moments, he was trading out saddlebags with the beak-nosed second-rank squire and assisting Feolia into the saddle. Lasren led them off in a canter.

Soon enough they came to the Great Eastern Way. Like the Alantran Road, it stretched from the border to the capital, with convenient way stations even better supplied than those in The Fragments, for each maintained a small serving staff and a generous supply of extra mounts. None, though, had erected signal towers.

They were still weary from the storm, but they pressed on through the evening, stopping finally at a small village. They didn't interact beyond answering a few anxious inquiries about the "rumors" of Naor incursions—their answers excited greater concern. Up before dawn, they rode through the little farming communities of the Erymyran countryside, trading for fresh animals at way stations every few hours and leaving better informed disquiet in their wake. As evening fell they passed twisting Lake Dahrial, where fishing boats plied the placid waters. If they'd diverted a half day farther south, Rylin could have visited his brother and nieces.

But there was no time for diversions. After nightfall, they grabbed sleep at a way station and then rose before sunrise to resume their trek. The old governor looked each morning little better after rest than before, but always insisted she was ready.

By midday the golden domes of Darassus gleamed upon the horizon. Rylin's heart lightened at sight of the great city, but for the first time his contemplation of the capital was bittersweet. Home to lawgivers, poets, sculptors, and playwrights, it was also site of a festering conspiracy that threatened to destroy the Allied Realms. Was he, then, a lance to the boil? Or were he and his companions merely bugs to be squashed beneath the boots of the more powerful?

They passed the long stretches of fields where wheat and barley grew, and the riverfront fish farms. Closer in were the famed orchards with their apples, little more than buds now. In coming months they would grow to glistening yellow fruits that were perhaps the original reason the city was known as Golden Darassus.

When they had moved beyond the eastern bluffs and their ancient fortifications, they spotted the great bronze statue of Darassa herself overtopping the walls, head downcast, the very image of a weary soldier. The old fortifications that defined the city limits were made of fine-cut gray stone with rounded parapets rising at hundred-foot intervals. Here in the east and at the south the walls looked a formidable barrier. Out of sight to the north, though, much of the wall had long since been removed and, despite some efforts in the last war, it had never been fully reconstructed. It would be hard to come upon the north wall unseen, it was true, for there was no easy access to the city save from the south. But Darassus would not long hold out against a siege-sized army.

The south gate was open, as usual, and the first- and second-rank squires who manned it gamboled almost like puppies at sight of an alten. One of them called out in delight: "Welcome back, Alten Lasren!"

"What news from the outer realms, Alten?" a helmed guard officer called down from above.

"Vedessus repelled the Naor," Lasren replied. "But Alantris has fallen. Our forces fight now to free it."

The soldiers and squires called for more information, question piling on question without waiting for answer, but Lasren shook his head. "I'm sorry. We bear urgent news, but must share it with the council first." He urged his horse into the city, and the rest of them followed.

Beyond the gate lay the wide cobblestone streets and the stone buildings of the old city, with the six-story statue of Darassa at least partly visible most anywhere. Some named her the weeping warrior, for she stood with shoulders slumped, head bowed, one hand over her eyes. A sword dangled limply from one hand, balanced against a rock where she rested one sandaled foot.

Never before had Rylin understood just how ably the sculptor had captured that terrible sorrow and fatigue after combat.

There was no other statue in all the realms quite like it, and Darassans liked to claim it had been modeled after the goddess herself, rather than from distant memory. Rylin wasn't as sure, but it was demonstrable proof that Erymyr had outshone all other realms in artistry from the days of the Grandmothers.

They passed the great square where the colossus loomed, riding past merchants selling spring tunics and restaurants doing a brisk lunchtime trade. A woman with harp engaged a crowd, including many children, singing the age-old tale of M'gahn and his ride down the river Idris, and the listeners clapped along. They were the only folk who didn't look up nervously or quiet their conversations when they caught sight of Lasren's uniform.

As their group made their way through the streets of the old city, they passed a town crier reminding folk to gather at the stadium by three bells for an announcement from the queen. Lasren looked as though he wished to stop and ask for more details, but Rylin urged him forward. They could lean what that was about when they reached the Hall of Ancestors. A large gathering would likely distract the attention of exalts and aspirants and might well prove advantageous. He just hoped the event itself wasn't something to worry over.

Eventually, they crossed the Idris, flowing through the city in its stone channel, and arrived before the second great square of the city, around which almost all the important government buildings sat, including the Hall of Ancestors, where the judges and counselors held court. The palace was a few blocks farther on. Leaving their weary horses with stable girls outside the square, they started up the worn black granite stairs and under embellished mosaic archways. More vendors waited beneath the portico, their goods uniquely tailored to suit visitors and travelers. The scent of sizzling lamb set Rylin's stomach growling, and Lasren grinned at him as they passed a young woman with a dazzling smile working the cook pot.

"I wouldn't mind a little of either," Lasren remarked as they passed.

Other merchants offered bottled wine, wineskins, and even garments and jewelry for visitors who thought they needed to improve their appearance before presenting themselves to the council. Rylin saw the governor's eyes track past some lovely cloaks and was afraid for a moment she might stop to haggle. Her own garments were threadbare and soiled, apart from her scarf. Before they reached the outskirts of Darassus she'd traded her nondescript traveling scarf for a new embroidered blue one, now wound about her head and concealing her hair.

They made their way to the central fountain and halted before it. By ancient decree all visitors there drank free, although it was customary to tip the waterboys a few small coins. The boys saw both to the maintenance of the water and the cleaning of the tin cups into which they poured, drawn with a ceremonial pitcher. A sheltered building to one side offered toilet facilities they each gratefully visited. After Elik refreshed himself, Rylin sent him into the colonnaded, three-story building beyond to learn the whereabouts of the high counselor.

This stop would be their last respite, and Rylin drew out the moment, savoring the stone sculpture of the ancient lawgiver, said to be a grand daughter of Darassa herself, immortalized in stone at the fountain's center. He found himself cherishing the care with which the forgotten sculptor had lavished on the lawgiver's face, so that the matron seemed both intelligent and gentle, suggested by the lines of care about her mouth.

Against one hip she rested a tablet onto which were inscribed the laws of passage. In her other hand she held a pitcher by its graceful, curving arm, identical in appearance to that used by the waterboys, and from it poured a constant clear, sparkling stream into the oval pool beneath, then immediately taking on a deep blue aspect, owing to the lapis tiles lining the basin. Rylin breathed in the pure, clean, moist air and smiled wistfully that this joy was so fleeting.

He felt Lasren at his side, along with his impatience, but swung his attention to the fretted arches above the second-story windows of the Hall of Ancestors, admiring the tiny heroic images there. How is it he had never paid them any heed before? Lasren, he knew, wished to confer, and yet he delayed. When he acknowledged him, the rest of their lives would launch forward. Lasren took the cue and went to speak with Feolia, who'd just emerged from the bathrooms.

Rylin lingered in the shade of an enormous plane tree until Elik stepped around the side of the fountain and stopped before him.

He saw the younger man's hand rise automatically to salute before Elik remembered Rylin was in disguise. Elik's blue eyes sought his self consciously as he stepped closer. "I've found the High Advisor," he said. There was an unvoiced "sir" in the announcement. "He was with the defense council, but I've told him an urgent report's come in from the field and an alten wants to speak to him alone."

Lasren spoke up from just behind, Feolia at his side. "Excellent."

"Maybe, sir," Elik said, turning to include them all. "But Exalt Thelar's with him and extremely curious."

Rylin bit back a curse.

"Comm . . . Exalt Thelar demanded answers from me," Elik went on. "I told him I was under orders only to report to the counselor, and he wasn't very happy about it."

"He's liable to be unhappy about a lot of things, going forward," Rylin said. He sat the cup on the fountain's side. "Did you find out what the queen's calling everyone together for?"

"No one's entirely certain," Elik confessed. "But rumor has it she's going to reveal some big secret to the populace, and the exalts are closely involved. They've overseen the transportation of boxes to the stadium for the last few days."

Rylin frowned, then decided that was a mystery for another time. Right now they needed to get Feolia into the counselors. He faced Lasren directly at last. "Thelar's going to try to pull rank on you."

"I know."

"Don't let him. And don't tell him anything about Commander N'lahr or the political situation—"

"I know," Lasren said pointedly. He dropped his voice and stepped closer. "Trust me, all right? I can handle this. If we have to, I'll take him down."

Rylin nodded, hoping Lasren could actually best the mage in a fight.

Lasren clapped him on the shoulder. "Good luck to you, whatever it is you're off for."

"You too." Rylin wanted to say more, deciding against further advice or anything mawkish, then clasped his old friend tightly about the forearm as Lasren returned the gesture. He saw something fragile and unfamiliar in his friend's gaze and almost told him that he would make the right choices, when the moment came. Instead, he simply squeezed his arm reassuringly and nodded, once. A thin smile touched Lasren's lips.

On impulse Rylin clasped Elik's arm as well, and the squire returned the grip with sincere affection.

"Good luck," Elik said, his eyes level, and Rylin saw that the younger man was more worried for him even than Lasren. Perhaps he guessed Rylin's mission might be the more dangerous.

"And to you," Rylin said, and then turned to Feolia, bowing her scarf wrapped head to him.

"Thank you for seeing us through," she said. "Do take care of yourself, young man."

"Thank you, Governor. I hope to see you soon."

"May the Gods light your way." She made the sign of the four in the air above her chest before turning from him. Rylin watched them for only a moment and then returned to the stable for his horse.

Though his disguise was fairly convincing, a kaneshi cavalry soldier wasn't exactly the best character for seeking admittance into the inner city. Rylin had only managed to restore a little power to his semblance in N'lahr's camp. He'd watched Varama charge one only once, and he'd apparently missed something. By his own estimate, he had somewhere between a half hour and a quarter hour of power within the stone, and it was likely the lesser amount.

And so he kept to his current disguise until he was very close to the palace grounds. He stopped in at a tiny roadside chapel to Darassa, erected beside a rock where she had blessed the masons laying the foundation of the inner wall. No pilgrims worshiped within, so he slipped out of the Kaneshi robe he'd been wearing and into the Altenerai khalat he'd carried in a saddlebag. He felt a momentary contentment as he tightened the belt, then centered himself and activated the semblance stone.

When he left the building he wore Thelar's image, and soon presented himself to a lowly first ranker standing sentry at a sally gate.

His first inclination had been to return to the exalt archive to search for information, but he'd had long days to reconsider his plan of action. And so he headed first for the Altenerai wing of the palace.

He was dismayed to find a lowly first ranker on duty on the front steps as well, something that would never have happened before the current crisis. First rankers might get posted to watch from walls, but they were never assigned to protect buildings. Though Elik had reported the scarcity of squires, seeing the evidence of their low numbers came as an unwelcome surprise.

He returned the squire's salute and passed into the building without a word, striding for the commander's offices. A third ranker sat at the outer desk, idly scribbling on a parchment. The young man looked up, startled, and struggled to his feet to snap a salute.

Rylin pretended not to see the artistic doodles decorating the paper. "At ease. I'm not to be disturbed."

"Yes, Commander."

It still needled him that Thelar, of all people, had been appointed commanding officer of the Altenerai. Inside, he closed the door and deactivated the semblance.

There was only one change to the room since he'd used it while overseeing Altenerai funeral arrangements—a bust of Asrahn sat on a plinth to the left of the door. That was new, and he wondered who had authorized its placement. It certainly hadn't been here when he'd been working from the office after Denaven left to hunt Kyrkenall.

This was almost certainly Thelar's doing. Strange that someone so clearly at odds with what the Altenerai stood for should still harbor affection for the old Master of Squires. Unless Thelar was putting on appearances. But no, if Thelar was capable of putting on appearances he wouldn't always look as if he'd been tricked into drinking vinegar. Back in their squire days, Thelar hadn't even permitted a joke about Asrahn to take place behind the old man's back, and there were certainly some to make, as there were with any stern instructor. Upon reflection, he grudgingly gave young Thelar credit for that, at least.

Rylin put aside any further ruminations, stepped to the wall, and put his ring to the little concave pattern beneath the relief of Queen Altenera with raised sword. He heard a click, and then the entire two-foot-square panel swung wide.

A variety of treasures lay upon the shelves within, among them the original editions of the corps commandments, the most recent strategic analysis of the strengths and weaknesses of the realms, and an ancient copy of Altenera's memoirs, lovingly illustrated by Herahn himself. But on a lower shelf sat a wooden box covered with stunning scrollwork and carvings. Its front piece depicted the founding Altenerai, all eleven. Rylin breathed out once, in contemplation of those noble figures in their old-fashioned cloaks, then gently removed the lid.

Inside were the three remaining spare rings. According to the logs, one had belonged to Asrahn, and had been found in the Idris. Was Denaven suggesting Asrahn's ring had been separated from his body? He supposed listing the ring as being discovered in the water was technically true even if it had still graced the dead finger of the Master of Squires, but this was an unusual way to note it.

Additionally, the box held five sacred sapphires removed from their housings, cradled within an inner velvet-lined niche. Rylin warred with himself as he stared down at them. He'd carried Decrin's ring from The Fragments and for a brief moment he contemplated abandoning his plan and simply placing it with these and restoring them to their proper place. Together with Decrin's, these were the last of the unassigned rings, and the last "spares" handed down from the days of Queen Altenera and the first few generations of champions of the realm. He'd thrilled to the exploits of the Altenerai since he was a young man, but few as much as that first circle, flawed though they were. Did he have the right to abscond with these tools and risk their destruction? Altenera herself had probably handled each of these rings, and perhaps the sapphires as well.

Yes, he thought. Yes, he did. He had left the hearthstone he'd used to charge the semblance with Commander N'lahr, lest he be revealed by carrying it with him. Without a hearthstone of his own, if someone were to use one against him, the surest bulwark was an Altenerai ring. A single one hadn't had the strength to hold back an attack, though it had slowed even Cerai, wielding multiple stones. One tiny ring. If he faced a similar assault from another hearthstone-armed attacker, he would be better prepared.

He knew he should hurry, but he took each one from the box and placed it gingerly upon the old dark wood of the desk, then the sapphires beside them. He shut the box, slid it back into the safe, then gently pushed it closed until he heard the click. He recalled the relatively simple steps Denaven had shown him, knowing it was a process created by the great Herahn himself. With his own ring shining, he reached forth with his will and activated the quiescent power within every single one. He couldn't think of a time in history when an alten had wakened a ring for himself, much less used more than one.

But he tied the threads of those rings to his own magics, one by one, and then did the same thing to the sapphires, only to deactivate them. It wouldn't do to wander around with all of them active and shining, but with them all linked, they would be at his command in an instant as surely as his own ring.

With care, he placed them within his belt pouches.

And then he hesitated as he caught sight of Asrahn's noble features looking out at him beside the door. Rylin carried the future of the corps with him, in a very real way.

No, he seemed to imagine the old Master of Squires say, the future of the corps lay with the squires coming up. These were their tools, and he risked much to carry them all together. But then the corps, and the city itself, was at stake. This was a step Rylin had to take.

Before departing, he gave thought to the squire sitting at the desk outside, and how he might unobtrusively gain information from him. While he easily knew the sixth and fifth rankers by name, and probably all of the fourth, there were considerably more of the lower ranks, and the man's name escaped him, which might be a problem, given that Thelar had probably picked him for this post.

Rylin reactivated the semblance stone and his Thelar disguise, left the room, and paused before the desk. The squire, a long-limbed fellow with a shock of thick yellow hair, eyed him through wide brown eyes and failed in his attempt to not look apprehensive. Rylin noted that the sheet with doodles had disappeared. Once again the squire made to rise.

Rylin signaled him to keep his seat then adopted an approximation of Thelar's clipped tones. "You seem burdened with spare time today, Squire."

The unfortunate man wasn't sure how to respond to that. He tried not to make a show of gulping, and his eyes fixed upon Rylin's as a hare watches the predator about to attack.

"Why don't you order your thoughts and provide me with a security assessment. Assume that I've just ridden in from a long patrol. Advise me on the state of the city's defenses."

"Yes, sir." The squire hesitated only a moment. "The walls remain the same as ever. Wide-ranging patrols watch all approaches upon Darassus. The exalts have used magic to carefully monitor these approaches, especially in light of the recent Naor attacks."

What did he mean by that? "What sort of attacks? Be specific."

"The invasions of The Fragments and Arappa."

"If you were in my boots, what would you be most worried about at this particular instance?"

The younger man looked up at him warily, as if he were attempting to judge how angry his superior would be with the truth. "Well, sir, given that we're aware that the Naor are invading both Arappa and The Fragments, I feel that we ought to direct resources to the city's walls."

"Yes. And I sense that you wish to offer more suggestions?"

"Yes, sir." The squire was warming to the topic. "I don't actually know what it is that the queen's going to be saying in the stadium this afternoon, so perhaps it's necessary to pull back our patrols to have all of the exalts there. But the security arrangements around her appearance are taking resources away from our borders at a bad time. And the exalts . . ." He stopped without finishing the thought.

Now that sounded interesting. "Go on."

"Yes, sir." The young man's squared jaw revealed an undercurrent of anger. "I don't understand why there's so much secrecy over whatever's been transported to the stadium. I assume it's going to be revealed when Queen Leonara speaks, or it wouldn't be moved there from the Exalt wing. But why not brief the squires about what's happening? We're traditionally responsible for the security of the realms."

Hearthstones, he realized. She was moving hearthstones. But why? "I see. So you don't like the security arrangements of the transfer?"

"It seems as though you've planned it well, sir—"

"I don't want a compliment. I want an analysis."

"Yes, sir. I think it would have been safer, whatever it is, if there were more squires deployed. I know the exalts can keep a watch for any disguised enemies, but we can provide physical security against unforeseen threats."

"How many disguised enemies do you think there are?"

"At least two." The squire eyed him as if considering that he might be one.

Rylin didn't think it likely this third ranker had any magical talent, though. He was darkly amused the exalts would be so troubled after he and Varama had infiltrated the Hall of Exalts under disguise that they remained alert for their return. He decided to prod for further information with a Thelar-like question. "You don't think the exalts are a good enough martial resource?"

That changed the squire's focus. Perhaps he suddenly remembered that it was Thelar who trained exalts. "It's just . . . they may be more magically focused, sir." He grew more certain he was in the right, and spoke on. "No offense, but I know it's true. The squires are loyal to the queen, I know it. She should trust them."

"Are they loyal to the queen, or the realms? The realms come first."

"Yes, sir."

"Before all things, you must remember that you are the shepherd of the lands, not a sentinel of the queen."

For the first time, the squire seemed to appraise him, personally, rather than him as a superior officer. Probably Thelar had never said anything like this to him before.

"Yes, sir."

"The queen may change, but the realms endure." Rylin knew he was saying too much, and that he no longer sounded like Thelar, but he sensed an opportunity to impact the squire's understanding of the corps' principles.

The younger man answered. "Yes, sir."

"Carry on."

The city's population could be packed into the stadium, which was designed to seat tens of thousands of locals and visitors for the annual Altenerai games. But why would the queen be gathering there, with the hearthstones, unless it was to reveal their power to the Darassans? Rylin couldn't imagine the point, and suspected he must be missing some key piece of information.

Immediately stricken with a strong sense of foreboding, he debated going to the stadium himself, but it occurred to him that with the palace nearly empty of exalts and squires he might be better served with a look around the queen's rooms at this time.

Course chosen, he headed past the squire deep into the recesses of the Altenerai wing, and stopped at the display case where the replica of Irion should have hung. The glass broken by Kyrkenall had been repaired, but someone had removed the fake. Rylin frowned at the thought and saw, in the reflection, Thelar frowning back at him. It was a reminder of how little time he had remaining on the semblance. He touched it through the inner world and realized he had less than a few minutes.

He'd been foolish to waste any of them with that squire.

He strode past the entryway into the famed hexagonal meeting room of the Altenerai, just managing not to stop to salute the ancient statue of Queen Altenera, and moved on toward the central section of the palace. A grand hallway lay directly ahead, leading to the throne room, but he turned instead up a smaller flight of dark granite stairs he'd only used once, when he'd been invited to a less formal receiving room upon being awarded his ring.

Beyond the stairs lay the reception area, and beyond it another open hall, and a series of doors. A second-rank squire stood guard outside one set of double doors, just to the left of a shaft of bright blue light shining through a stained-glass half-moon window.

Rylin stopped in front of the young woman and returned her salute.

"The queen's not in, sir."

"I know that." Rylin snapped in what he thought was the best imitation of Thelar he'd yet managed. "She sent me back to retrieve some important materials."

"Yes, sir. Sorry, sir."

He was still debating what he'd do if the squire challenged him further when the young woman simply moved aside. Rylin opened one of the double doors and went through, dropping the semblance and closing the portal behind him.

Beyond was a small sitting room. Apart from the ornate furniture beside marble top tables, there were walls with red leatherbound books, and a large window overlooking a courtyard. He was fairly sure that the double doors to the right would lead to a bedroom. The single door on the left, though—

It was an empty office, one furnished with a quartet of sumptuous chairs and an elaborately carved white desk and many bookshelves. For all that there were a multitude of storage places, the room was disorganized. Papers were stacked on nearly every surface, and scrolls were piled high both in their own cubbies and atop books. A second door faced the desk. He stepped to it quickly, saw the key set into its lock, and tested it gingerly to confirm it secure.

Turning, he used his Altenerai ring to sense the powers within the room, keeping its radius tight.

He immediately detected multiple energy sources, and found a shelf just below eye level given over to a long row of small crystalline marbles of different shades, each smaller than a hearthstone. At one end sat a long, rough-cut emerald a little smaller than the palm of his hand. And beside it lay an Altenerai ring.

He picked up the ring and turned it over in his hand, wondering as to its purpose here. Altenerai had a hard time walking away from their rings, even if they left the corps. Retired Altenerai often wore them unto their deaths, only afterward having relatives or friends return them.

While a variety of Altenerai had been lost in battle or vanished over the centuries, only a handful of rings were unrecovered in recent years. He wasn't sure what had become of Cargen's or K'narr's—though they were likely in Kyrkenall's possession, since he'd killed them and their sapphires hadn't been in the storage box. Probably one of those was now Elenai's. Two others were likely in the trophy rooms of the Naor who had killed their wearers. An additional two had simply disappeared with their owners. This particular ring was more likely to have belonged to one of the latter pair. But was this ring Renik's, or Kalandra's? It looked smaller than his own, but just to be certain he attempted to slip it onto his finger.

It didn't fit. He'd heard an awful lot about Renik over the years, and he'd never heard anyone mention he had delicate fingers.

Likely, then, this was Kalandra's ring. Why was it here, rather than with the others, unless the queen had been involved in her disappearance? Almost certainly she was dead, probably at the hand of the exalts. He felt his mouth tighten.

He ran his eyes around the familiar lines of the oath inscribed along the rim about the sapphire, wondering about the ring's history. Denaven had told him his ring's lineage when it had been bestowed upon him, and he knew it had come from Lahnik, and Sergahn before him. It had once been worn by Ceria Silverhand. Kalandra's ring surely had an equally grand heritage.

He used the power of his own ring to light hers, and threaded it in with his already powerful collection. Rylin realized he was carrying more sapphires than there'd been Altenerai in a single place in a long, long time.

He reverently pocketed the ring, then sensed again for nearby life force, finding no one but himself and the guard within range.

Rylin turned his attention to the stones, each of which radiated a faint magical dweomer. Were they tools, or weapons? There'd be no way to know without time spent in careful examination. Reluctantly, he turned away and looked over the piles of paper.

The majority proved to be extremely detailed topographical maps. Here was a coastline with a river delta, here a mountainous landscape with tiny trees where two rivers joined. There were pages and pages of these maps, some of which were filled with cramped handwriting that provided additional information to an absurd degree—the precise scale of a slope, the elevation of a ridge, the depth of a river. After a few moments, he stopped trying to make sense of them and set them aside, shifting his attention to the material on Leonara's desk, most of which sat in a single stack.

The queen was often followed by a secretary to whom she dictated, but he'd seen the queen's hand on several documents over the years and this looked like it might be hers.

He lifted the top paper, and his first assumption that it was a letter was quickly dispelled. It wasn't addressed to anyone, unless you counted that opening line, where Leonara made clear she was speaking to the people of Darassus. He sifted through the parchment beneath with interest, discovering that he held pages from the rough draft of a speech. He read quickly, growing both confused and a little frightened as he did so.

The queen planned to usher in a new age which would be presided over by one lone, benevolent goddess, which she herself would bring forth from lost artifacts her retainers had risked their lives to recover. Hearthstones, he thought bitterly, though the queen didn't call them by name.

Who exactly that godddes was she must have addressed in sections that weren't there, for the speech stopped in mid-sentence at the bottom of one page. The dozens beneath it were taken up with the composition of a prayer to the new godddess.

Rylin read, and then skimmed ten pages of permutations on the prayer before leaving off, understanding he'd find only relentless adjustments of glowing adjectives and lines of praise. He lowered the papers, shaking his head in bewilderment and alarm. So this is what the queen and the exalts had been working toward? This is what they planned to share with the people of Darassus this afternoon? It staggered his imagination.

The neglect of the realms, the lying, the betrayals, the murders—all of it apparently stretched to the queen's unshaking belief in the return of her lost goddess, for whom the queen had written "sacrifices have been made, necessary for a better world." None of those losses, she planned to declare, truly mattered in the ultimate glory that would be shared with all.

To Rylin's way of thinking, those sacrifices mattered more than anything else. Even if there was some unknown goddess ready to fill their lives with bounty, the queen's moral deficiencies and religious zealotry rendered her unfit for any kind of decision, much less one so monumental. She didn't have the right to summon a god without the consent of her people. She didn't have the right to choose for everyone a radically changed world that would alter every life in ways she couldn't possibly anticipate.

Rylin dropped the papers on the desk. He'd round up Lasren and

Elik and all the squires and guards and head to the amphitheater. He'd wait while the queen said her piece, so her madness was made obvious to all, then arrest her, probably without much outcry from anyone but the exalts.

His ring alerted him to a person nearing his proximity. He stilled, putting all his concentration into it, and realized two people had just moved into the adjoining room and appeared to be walking toward him.

He stepped quickly to the locked door, twisted the key to open it, listening to the sound of footfalls draw closer. He wasn't sure where this door led, but he didn't sense anyone beyond, and he heard a hand on the other knob.

He activated Thelar's image with his semblance, opened the door a narrow distance, and slid through, closing it quietly behind him. He emerged upon a landing flanked by two closed doors, one on his left, the other to his right, with a huge mosaic of galloping horses at sunset between them. A white granite stairwell stretched down from the landing to the palace hall.

A pair of exalts strode confidently up the steps. To the rear was a tall, brown-haired man. In the lead climbed the corps commander, Synahla, she of the striking violet eyes. Her pretty throat was bared, the top hooks of her khalat undone so that he glimpsed a ruby pendant resting upon a silver chain above the swell of her breasts. A dozen or more squires, including the third ranker he'd spoken with outside the Altenerai offices, waited at the foot of the stairs.

As surprised as he was to see her, just outside of the range of his ring, she appeared not in the least bit startled to see him, although she paused halfway up.

He advanced onto the landing, for he sensed the people behind him drawing near, just as he now sensed a pair of people moving through that room on the other side of the landing.

"You might as well drop your disguise, Rylin." Synahla's smug, honeyed alto rang from the granite. "You're practicing your last deception. The queen's dealt with your allies and the traitorous council."

He felt himself go cold, thinking of the squires he'd fled Darassus with transformed into hunks of crystal. For the briefest moment, he questioned that Queen Leonara would dare do that once more, to Lasren, to Elik, to members of the council. And then he realized that she would stop at nothing. And at close range it might be that Lasren's ring would not have held back her attack.

Behind him he heard both sets of doors opening, and stepped to the edge of the stairs to look down on Synahla. He understood that he'd been herded by someone who knew just how far the sensitivity of the rings extended. Now two separate pairs of combatants were at his rear.

He dropped his semblance and set the ring on his hand alight.

Synahla smiled in satisfaction. Below her the squires gasped in surprise and disappointment. They hadn't wanted the exalt commander's accusations to be true, he realized. That he had revealed himself walking hallowed halls in disguise was clear evidence to all who watched that he had failed to honor the spirit of his own oath.

She had engineered this moment with great cleverness. Those squires might have had doubts about what they'd been told by exalts, but now they could see a traitor in the ranks of the Altenerai. They would not already have determined, as he had, that the queen and the exalts were enemies who had murdered the innocent. They could not yet know this was war, and in war he had practiced trickery to prevail against evils.

"I see you've grown a beard. Another attempt at disguise?"

"How did you know where I was?" He didn't really care; he wanted a moment to further assess the situation.

She laughed at him. "How could we not? You were watched from the moment the four of you entered the city. Naturally you were followed, and when a Kaneshi horseman changed himself into an exalt I was immediately alerted."

"Very well organized," he said.

"Not really. You were merely careless. Now shut down your ring, and unbuckle your sword belt. You are surrounded, and outmatched."

Theater, he decided. These words weren't for him so much as those who watched. "Surrounded," he said, feeling those behind him hesitating ten feet out. "But not outmatched."

She laughed at him. "I thought you arrogant when I first met you. You tricked your way into the Hall of Exalts then, spying for your traitorous masters, attacked us, and stole our hard-won hearthstones. It didn't matter to you that men and women had died for those stones. That the safety of the realms depended upon them."

Again she spoke for her audience, not Rylin. She might mean to evoke a response from him for which she had readied a counter. How best not to play?

"If you seek a traitor," he said, "look to your own ranks."

"Is that all you have to say to excuse your actions?"

He drew his sword in a flash of steel and set his footing. Behind him he felt his opponents reach for their own weapons. One had begun manipulating a thread in the inner world.

"You will die a fool, Rylin," Synahla told him.

What better response could there be to that than the one seared across his soul? "When comes my numbered day," he said, "I will meet it smiling."

Was that an intake of breath from that blond third ranker below? Perhaps Synahla hadn't expected Rylin to invoke the oath.

Why, then, did she still look so satisfied? Those full lips parted. "There's no more need to lie. We have you caught. Your only chance is to tell the truth, Rylin."

Her spell struck him as she spoke, and his brows rose in surprise that she should wield so great a magic while concentrating upon something else. Her sorcery was backed by all the power of a hearthstone shard she carried at her side.

"Tell them, Rylin." Her smile grew. "Tell them how you conspired against the queen and the exalts. How you have stolen and lied and allied with murderers. Confess, and surrender, and beg for mercy."

He knew the pressure of her suggestion only as a voice shouting from a distant room, no matter the intense force of the spell, for it struck the protective energies of his ring, which was linked to all those rings and sapphires he carried. One by one their powers lit within his pouches. And for the first time he saw her smile waver, witnessed surprise dawn and then envelop her face and lift her eyebrows.

"No," he cried, voice ringing with confidence. "I shall tell them how the exalts murdered noble Asrahn and framed Kyrkenall for the crime!" His voice rose. "I shall tell them how the queen lied about N'lahr's death and imprisoned him!"

The squires shifted in confusion. He felt Synahla's power strain against the defensive web of his shield, saw anger light those eyes, knew that she drew more power from her hearthstone shard.

And while she fought to break him, he spoke on to the audience she herself had gathered: "The queen murdered innocent squires as they slept, and brokered peace with the Naor for the sake of her accursed hearthstones!"

"Take him," she shouted.

"Come for me," he cried. "Who dies first?"

He did not expect to live. There were six arrayed against him. Three were mages, and they lingered in the back while their exalt companions came at him from left rear, right rear, and front. The weavers wove masterful spells meant to daze or blind that had all the effect of a gentle breeze, so easily did he shrug them off.

Those weapons bearers to his rear were closer, and one, a dark-haired woman, had flung a knife before her charge. This Rylin crossed with the tip of his sword and sent clanging into a distant wall.

He advanced against a tall black-haired man, now trying to slow so he and the knife thrower would reach him at the same moment. He felt an influence spell from Synahla brush past him, then slashed under black hair's guard and struck his leg below his exalt's coat. Fools, to be thinking only of tournament sword rules.

The exalt shouted in pain and went down as the leg collapsed. Rylin pivoted before the exalt warrior on the stairs caught him from behind, one sword-bearer on either side now. The exalt knife thrower was a few steps closer. Rylin brought his sword in line and beat her back with a series of savage cuts. He raised his blade to lock hers as she lifted it for a head strike, paused a heartbeat as the man behind him closed, then ducked and spun to the right.

The warrior's sword swept through the point where Rylin's head had been only moments before and sliced deep into the woman's face. Rylin felt the spray of blood, heard her gurgle and the man's gasp of horror. The mages tried a new spell as he pivoted, but they still hadn't worked out why their influence wasn't effective.

The male exalt struggled to pull his sword from his mangled, scream-ing ally. Someone more experienced would have released the weapon and backed off.

Rylin finished the spin by cracking his pommel into the back of the man's head. He heard a sickening crunch and felt something give. As both exalts tottered and fell, he leapt toward the closer mage behind.

A broad, dark-bearded fellow with a white shirt with laced sleeves, he wore no armor. He raised a round, decorative shield in a desperate effort to ward the incoming attack. His eyes were wide with fear.

Rylin grabbed the shield's rim in one hand and forced it down. Rather than releasing it, the mage leaned in, fighting to lift it, and soon found it bashed into his own face when Rylin released it suddenly. He dropped cold, nose spewing blood over his beautiful shirt.

Snatching the shield from the wounded weaver, Rylin turned to con-front his remaining opponents.

Synahla had arrived at the topmost stair, her eyes alive with fury. The other mage had withdrawn to the far door. Rylin's four downed oppo-nents were mostly still, save for the man he'd struck in the leg, who'd crawled to one side and was frantically calling to the mage by the door for help.

That man, likewise in a white uniform shirt, ignored black hair's plea, and sent a spell against Rylin. He felt the touch of dizziness, as though he'd spun too fast, but this ebbed, and he advanced toward Synahla with his reddened blade before him.

He sensed Synahla had reached deep into her own stone. Gone was her subtlety when she threw her next spell. She leaned into it, hands extended. To those watching below it might have looked as if she simply held out her palms. Through the rings, though, Rylin perceived a coruscating whirl of bright energies, a line of magic threaded from her shard and into the combined shield of his Altenerai rings.

This magery hit him hard. The hair on the back of his neck stood upright, and even under the sleeves of his armored khalat the chill raised his arm hairs. For the first time, the power of the rings flickered under the assault. He stepped forward, but it was like walking into a gale wind. He advanced another step but could go no farther.

He faced Synahla two sword lengths out, saw her gritting her teeth, and comprehended that while he could not reach her, she couldn't reach him, either. Whatever the other mage attempted seemed ineffectual.

Synahla redoubled her efforts, and he winced as shocking blue energy sparkled before his eyes, straining against his protective barrier. Worse, the mage behind him had found courage. He heard a blade being drawn and his ring senses informed him the mage crept closer.

He considered and dismissed the notion of using Synahla's own hearthstone energies against her. She knew that tool far better than he. No, Asrahn had told him that sorcerers in combat often made a vital mistake.

In their intense mental concentration, they forgot to consider the physical.

He lifted the shield and lobbed it.

The exalt commander's eyes widened as the shield slammed into her just above her belt buckle. That in itself was at best a mild discomfort, but the sudden intrusion into her own personal space wrenched a cry of surprise and disrupted her spellwork.

Free now from the blistering attack, Rylin lunged and thrust his blade through the opening in Synahla's khalat, where her necklace hung. The blow pierced flesh and broke bone. He ripped the weapon from her body and Synahla's hands clutched at the jagged wound left above her pendant. She staggered as her life blood poured from the injury and down over the faceted ruby.

He spun to face the attack of the man behind him. He heard Synahla's death rattle and collapse even as he swept the attacker's knife strike aside with the shield in his off hand and slammed his temple with his sword guard. The man groaned, staggered on wobbly legs, and sank to the floor.

Panting, Rylin turned to contemplate the field of battle, verifying his opponents were dead or out of the fight. Elik had reported that there were somewhere close to two dozen exalts, and he himself had downed four, along with two of some forty aspirants. While he had survived the battle, he hoped he wouldn't have to tangle with the rest in similar circustances.

He stepped to Synahla's body. He wiped his blade upon her pant leg, and found the side pocket where she kept her hearthstone. It proved a dull ruby shard as long as his finger. He considered it briefly before he closed its power and slipped it into one of his belt pouches. He relieved her body of the ruby pendant as well, almost certainly a magical enhancement of some kind, and stepped to the head of the stair to look down at the squires. They stared back at him with rounded eyes.

They had but watched through the whole struggle and he had no idea where their loyalties might lie.

"Our enemies are revealed," he said as he descended. "The queen and her exalts plan to use accumulated artifacts to summon an unknown goddess that they think will usher a new age of power, and they've broken every ethic to further their secret plan. They've cut a path of treachery and deception, murder and betrayal that has damaged our nation to its core." He stopped two-thirds of the way down and sheathed his sword. "They mean to force us into their version of a better world. I mean to fight to preserve and truly better the one we have. Will you stand with me, or stand aside?"

They looked back and forth at one another, and at him. And then the blond third ranker he'd met earlier stepped forward. "We stand with you."

The others nodded assent, and a dark-skinned woman said: "We will strike as one."

He nodded, pleased at the sentiment, and rattled off his orders. One he sent running for a healer. Others he dispatched to retrieve the old-fashioned binders from storage. He searched for and confiscated all the prisoners' magical tools while five stood guard, then left those five with the healers tending the restrained injured. The exalts and aspirants would be relocated to holding cells once their wounds were stabilized.

He led the remaining awed squires to the armory to equip for battle, and ordered them to fan quickly through the city and quietly spread word to all their brothers and sisters: prepare for action and meet them at the stadium. Any they found who were already geared for duty were to join them in spreading the message. He posted the stunned third ranker in charge of the armory, providing more exacting instructions, as well as a thumbnail account of the events. He was to share them with all who reported in, and lead them to the amphitheater when the crowd assembled there, to await for Rylin's signal.

Rylin departed to scout ahead, not bothering this time with the nearly drained semblance. He wanted to preserve it for emergencies.

The sentry he'd met outside the palace was one of those who'd gathered at the foot of the stairs, so the only one waiting outside for him was his horse. The animal whickered nervously as Rylin drew to the hitching post, and he reflected ruefully on Rurudan's calmness. He wished, again, that the faithful gelding had survived.

As he undid the reins, a man jogged from the shadow of the Altenerai stables. Rylin put his hand to his hilt, then saw that it was Elik, who drew panting to a stop and threw up a salute.

Rylin smiled in relief to see him. "I thought you and Lasren were dead."

Elik's tense expression didn't ease. He breathed in heavily. "Lasren *is* dead, sir."

Rylin stilled, thinking of his friend's hearty laugh, his solid presence. He hadn't had a chance to truly consider his absence, and with its certain confirmation a spark inside him dimmed. It was as though he listened to someone else speaking. "How did he die?"

"The queen." Elik let out a breath and then succinctly rattled off a report: "Three councilors listened to the governor and Lasren testify about what happened, and they looked over N'lahr's letter. They called all the councilors present for a conference. Dozens of them. Somehow the queen got wind of it."

"Thelar," Rylin said. "Was Thelar still with you?"

"No. He left after he overheard our report."

"Lasren let him leave?" How could his friend have been so stupid? "Thelar must have headed straight back to the queen!"

Elik shook his head. "I don't know, sir. He looked pretty shaken. I think he believed us."

"Even if he believed you, if he went to the queen—" Rylin pulled himself together. Lasren had allowed one last ill-considered choice. But this was no time to dwell on it. "Finish your report. The queen turned up . . ."

"Yes, sir. She tried, briefly, to win us over, telling everyone there was far more to the story, and that they needed to trust her. But all the councilors looked uncertain and a couple grew pretty challenging, and that's when she cried out she didn't need to waste any more time. It was just like you said about the squires she killed. A few at a time, she turned them into lumps of crystal. It was more horrible than I'd imagined."

The squire paused, dilated pupils and streaming sweat communicating more threat response than a simple run from Hall of Ancesters would produce. "Lasren used his ring to protect as many of us as he could, and backed toward the rear door. But only the governor and one councilor and I got out. Alten Lasren's just . . . frozen there in the doorway. He was already crumbling a little."

Rylin felt tears welling, and thrust up his chin, wiping his eyes. Now was not the time to mourn. He faced the squire.

"I've sent word for all the squires to gear up at the armory. I'm placing them under your command now. Relieve the third ranker I left in charge. Make sure they're ready to support as I deal with whatever the queen is doing at the stadium. It's going to be very dangerous."

"You can't face her, sir. She went through the councilors' spells and swords and even a ring's shielding. You'll be no better off than Lasren."

"I have other safeguards." He forced a smile. "I want you to use your best judgment. Lead them to the stadium and await my signal. But if the queen overwhelms me, flee. Preserve what's left of the corps to fight another day."

The fifth ranker frowned.

"This is no time for last stands. I'm not acting until I can reasonably succeed in saving our people and you shouldn't either. Remember that Lasren sacrificed himself so that *you* might live." He paused, breathed out before grief overcame him. "Your most important duty is to protect the lives of the men and women under you. You must protect every one you can. Heart and mind. Do you understand?"

"Yes, sir."

"Where are Governor Feolia and the councilor?"

"The survivors fled to speak to councilors who weren't there, and any city leaders—and anyone else who will listen."

"Good luck to them." He climbed into the saddle.

"May the gods go with you," Elik said solemnly.

"And with you. Treat Darassus as enemy territory. Stay alert. Trust no exalts."

"Yes, sir."

They exchanged a final salute. He didn't look back at the palace as he rode away.

He reached one of the sally gates in the inner wall and let himself out. No guards remained to close it behind him, and he realized he didn't especially care.

Lasren was dead.

While he'd grown to find his friend a little juvenile, he missed him already, and not just because they'd been comrades for more than a decade. He'd glimpsed what Lasren might have become. The man had never lacked courage, and he had strength and stamina and skill. He'd been finding his way to wisdom.

He'd perished upholding his oath and defending those under his protection. Rylin hoped that had been consolation to him at the end.

It was little solace to Rylin, who felt all the more alone as he guided his mount into the nearly empty streets. Darassus looked as deserted as he himself felt. The vendors had rolled their carts away, and the children were absent from the parks. Most stores were shuttered. A few city criers still wandered the streets, reminding Darassans of the queen's address.

It seemed most of the Darassan citizens were already on their way. They did not expect that the queen was a tyrant who had cast aside the rule of law, a liar who murdered anyone who proved inconvenient. If he'd had any humor left, he might have laughed to think how he'd once questioned if he truly had the right to kill her. Now it was his duty.

30

Strike as One

Rylin found a mass of people streaming from the west gate and out into fields that girdled the amphitheater. Once through the gate, he kicked his horse into a canter around the clogged thoroughfare and on toward the rear of the stadium where few but important visitors from other realms entered. Its oval walls rose toward the gray skies, pennants flapping with colors and symbols from not just the realms but the cities within them. Banners draped above the entrances, promising joyful news.

The venue was primarily intended for the yearly games where competitors who'd excelled at the trials throughout the realms competed for a place in the Altenerai Corps. Other competitions used it throughout the year, but none that filled it so thoroughly.

As he rode to the guest entrance, he heard the noise of the restless masses beyond, thousands talking amongst themselves, presumably curious about what the queen intended with this unprecedented gathering. There was a festive excitement in the air.

The city guards on duty at the back entrance let him through without question, for he briefly wore the semblance of the black-haired exalt he'd fought on the palace landing. He nodded when their eyes fell upon him then stepped into the cool shadows of the stadium's hallways and into the darkness. He hurried up back stairs, conscious of the low rumble of the crowd, then stepped into a narrow hallway, empty and lit only intermittently with lanterns.

Having watched the squire tryouts at the stadium as a boy, applied at the games, and then supervised them from backstage as an upper-level squire, he was familiar with the layout of the place. There were dozens of dressing areas and several fine suites set aside for visiting dignitaries. If the queen was going to address the people within the hour, she was probably there already in one of the three largest suites, having her hair brushed, adjusting her dress, practicing her speech, and so forth.

He saw a trio of white-shirted young men and women in the hall ahead—he now knew them as aspirants—and re-donned his semblance to wordlessly return their salutes. Fortunately, they didn't seem familiars of the person he imitated, and they didn't tarry to converse with him. Almost he asked if they knew the location of the queen, but he decided against it. He had no idea how this person he imitated actually sounded.

The semblance was all but spent, now. He was checking its supply as he neared a narrow service stair. At the same time he heard the scuff of boot heels descending he sensed he had but moments of energy left.

Thelar stepped out of the stairwell. Behind him was a gaggle of aspirants and another exalt.

Rylin couldn't help that his lip instinctively curled, which might have been why Thelar looked startled when he met his gaze. The hooked nose turned straight at him as Thelar's eyes widened farther, and Rylin knew then the man had recognized him even through the semblance.

Yet Thelar stepped forward, calling to him in a friendly manner: "Meraht! Just who I wanted to see!" Rylin flinched as Thelar put a hand to his arm and guided him toward a dressing room door. His own hand was to his sword hilt, but Thelar called over his shoulder to his companions. "I'll be along shortly."

And then the exalt had thrown open the door, and with a significant look to Rylin, entered before him.

Rylin walked warily after, searching right and left in the little dressing area for ambushers. He saw a couch and desk and one lantern with guttering candle. A woman's dress lay across the back of a lone chair, beside discarded footgear and a small travel kit.

Rylin kicked the door shut, keeping his hands free.

"What are you doing here?" Thelar hissed. "You're going to get yourself killed."

Rylin's semblance dropped. Apparently mages skilled enough could see right through the thing once they knew what its effects were like. He stared at Thelar, ready to slay, and yet . . . this wasn't the reception he'd expected.

"I am not your enemy, Rylin," Thelar said softly, and raised two empty hands.

"No?" He couldn't stop the tremble of fury in his voice, though he spoke softly. "So you're not the one who fled to tell the queen about the meeting with the councilors?"

"I . . ." Thelar searched his eyes and found no compassion there. "What's happened?"

"Did you tell her?"

"I demanded she tell me if any of it was true. She killed them, didn't she?"

"She murdered most of the councilors. She killed Lasren." He waited for Thelar to challenge him so he could cut him down.

But his old enemy refused satisfaction. In all the years he'd known the man, Thelar had carried himself with smug self-assurance. This halting, troubled creature seemed a pale shadow. "I've tried to plead with her ever since I learned The Fragments were under attack. She keeps saying that it will all be fine in the end, that the pain is transitory . . ." Thelar looked up at him. Even through Rylin's anger, he saw that the man's eyes were anguished. "That all would be made right in the end. When I asked her why N'lahr had been imprisoned, she said it was because she needed the Naor hearthstones, and that they'd threatened to destroy them. She expected I'd understand."

"You're saying you're suddenly filled with remorse?" Rylin didn't believe it.

"It's not sudden," he snapped, finally sounding like the arrogant, bitter hastig he'd always been.

"It seems sudden to me."

"You always thought you were better than the rest of us," the exalt said with a sneer. "So quick to judge. But you never felt the Goddess. She's there, inside the hearthstones. Queen Leonara taught me how to find her pulse."

"The queen's insane. You should know that by now." He saw Thelar looking at him in doubt. "Why am I even bothering with you?"

Thelar gritted his teeth and started for his own sword. Then his shoulders slumped. "Maybe I should just let you kill me," he said softly.

Silence had grown as a presence in that room, a shield between them. Rylin heard the thud of a multitude of distant feet as more made their way into the seats above. "Why did you place that bust of Asrahn in the office?" he asked.

Thelar's answer sounded a little like his usual self, for his reply, though subdued, implied his listener was an idiot to miss the obvious. "To honor him."

"Did you know that Alten Cargen and an exalt killed Asrahn?"

The answer was strained. "It was M'lahna. And no. Not until I heard the governor read Commander N'lahr's letter. I'm still not sure I believe it."

"You must," Rylin said slowly, "or you wouldn't have pulled me in here."

"There have been little things, all along," Thelar said bitterly. "I was so certain, once I felt the Goddess, that the queen had the right of it. That we had to act in secret. But I've started to see what the secrets have wrought. The signs have been there, and I kept pretending I didn't see them." His voice trailed off and his expression soured. "You've always hated me," he snapped. "You look like you're just waiting for an excuse."

Rylin's first thought was to confirm that, but there seemed no point. "I'm really waiting for something else," he said.

Thelar looked the faintest bit curious. "And what's that?"

"First tell me why you pulled me in here rather than exposing me."

"I'm trying to figure out what to do," Thelar admitted. "After the queen raced out of here I tried talking to Tesra, but she's one of the ones Synahla altered."

"Altered how?"

"She won't believe any bad news about the queen, or her plans. She used to question more than I did."

Rylin had come pretty close to being manipulated by Synahla himself. He hoped Tesra's transformation wasn't permanent. But this wasn't the time to worry about that. "Do you know what your queen did to the squires after Varama and I fled?" Rylin waited only briefly before answering his own question. "Every morning we'd wake up and find a couple more of them dead. Turned to bits of crystal while they slept. That's what she did to Lasren and the councilors."

Thelar groaned as if he himself had taken a blow. "What are you waiting for?" he asked softly. "Get it over with."

"I'm waiting," he said, slowly, uncomfortable with both his words and his sentiment, "to see if you're an ally. They're in short supply."

"An ally for what?" Thelar looked up cautiously.

"I've got to stop her."

"By yourself? Even with me it's impossible. Do you know how powerful she is?"

"I have an inkling."

"You have no idea."

"I'm going to let the queen say her piece so everyone can hear how crazy she sounds, and then when she finishes I'm going to arrest her."

"It's not possible," Thelar repeated. "She's surrounded by exalts."

"She has to be stopped."

Thelar breathed out through his teeth, then spoke slowly. "After she shares her prayer, the queen's going to start opening the stones. Even with the exalts and the aspirants it's going to take a while, and a lot of focus. I suppose that might be time to try something."

"When she has all of those stones open?" Rylin asked.

"That will be too late. I mean right as she starts."

He wished Varama was with him. She would know what to do. "Are there any other exalts you can talk sense into? What about those twins you had me fight?"

"Meria and M'vai? I don't know. I've occasionally heard some of the exalts express doubts, but I don't think you ought to expect them to help you arrest the queen."

"I don't think she's really going to allow me to arrest her," Rylin said, wondering if his newfound ally would balk at more severe action.

"I know."

"And you'll back me?"

Thelar hesitated, then nodded, his eyes bleak. "Yes. How bad was it in Alantris, really? Do you think the people have a chance?"

Never, in all the years he'd known Thelar, had he seen him so open. So vulnerable. He knew the truth would hurt, but he shared it. "It's bad. Varama's in there making things difficult for the Naor but a lot of people are dead, and more are probably going to die. You have family there, don't you?"

His voice was heavy with anger and regret. "All of my family's in Alantris, Rylin."

"I'm sorry," he said, and meant it.

He reached into a belt pouch without giving himself time to question his decision, and came out with his hand closed around the object he'd found inside. "I went by the Altenerai offices. I linked all the rings and took them with me. Synahla couldn't break through when she attacked, even with a hearthstone shard."

"What happened to her? Oh."

Rylin nodded.

"You held off a hearthstone shard with linked rings? That's pretty clever."

"The rings won't shield us from a concentrated attack, but if we can strike fast . . ." He hesitated to use the famous Altenerai battle cry, then decided it fit, perfectly. ". . . if we strike as one, we may get past their defenses." Rylin opened his hand to reveal an Altenerai ring. One he thought would fit. Probably Asrahn's. "You should wear this."

Thelar looked down at the ring in the palm of Rylin's hand, then back up. He was clearly startled.

To blunt the delicacy of the moment, Rylin spoke casually. "It's linked to the same network of rings. As long as we're within a few feet of each other I think we'll both be protected by all of them."

Thelar, too, pretended this was only the acceptance of a tool, and not the borrowing of a sacred symbol from a guardian order in which he'd once fervently sought membership. Probably, at some level, he still desired it. He spoke with quiet dignity. "Thank you, Rylin. I'll guard it well, and strive to prove worthy of its heritage." He eyed the ring reverently as he lifted it from Rylin, then slipped it onto the ring finger of his right hand.

Rylin made sure he didn't sound critical as he spoke. "Do those ruby rings you exalts wear do anything?"

"They're similar. Honestly, they're not as good. Synahla was working on improving them. But I'll link my ruby to your defensive screen. Every little bit helps." He cleared his throat. "I shouldn't have cheated against you."

"What?"

"In the duel. With the twins," Thelar added, seeing Rylin's blank look. "Oh. "

"You were just so cocky. Like you owned the world and were set on kicking me out of it."

He supposed he had been. That entire moment felt like it had happened to another man.

"But I acted without honor, and, worse, set a bad example for my charges. It's bothered me ever since."

"Whatever lay between us is behind," Rylin said. "We can only succeed if we stand as one."

From somewhere far away trumpets sounded. Both men stilled as the fanfare continued, and then musicians struck up a tune. Not, Rylin noticed, anything Altenerai related, as was usually heard within the space, but something new. She'd probably commissioned it recently.

"Come on." Thelar rose. "I think we can monitor best from one of the boxes. All the exalts and aspirants will be in the stage wings, or up there with her."

"Won't they be wondering where you are?"

"They're probably wondering where Synahla is, too. But don't the actors always say that the curtain must rise regardless?"

Rylin nodded. He thought he probably knew the arena at least as well as his new ally, but allowed Thelar to precede him through the narrow back hallways. They paused as someone ran down an intersecting corridor bearing a tightly wound scroll, then preceded around a corner and slipped into a small audience box. As they did so, applause echoed through the stadium, louder than a thunderstorm, and Rylin looked out on a sea of heads, young and old. He recalled that venue's capacity was almost fifty thousand, to accommodate visitors from out of town coming to the games. The static population of the city was somewhere in the thirty thousands, and it looked to him like most of them were there.

The far end of the stadium had been closed off by a huge black curtain, so that the remaining three quarters of arena had good views of a raised platform extending out from the curtain: a stage.

The queen had stepped onto center stage as the musicians retreated to the wings with their trumpets and drums. She was garbed in a flowing green gown with wide sleeves, and her long hair was bound high in a swirling emerald tiara. She looked vibrant and crisp and slim and lovely, waving regally to the assembled cheering crowd. Behind her in two long half-circle lines were the exalts, and white-shirted aspirants. The huge curtain backed them all.

As the queen raised her hands for silence, Rylin kept to the shadows of the box so as not to draw attention to himself. Thelar did the same.

The crowd quieted, and the queen spoke, her voice confident, even joyful, magically amplified. The opening words were almost identical to those he'd read in her chambers.

"My people, I am grateful for your love and support. I know that there are some among you who have wondered about my long absence from public life. I regret that I have had to be apart from you for so very long. I want you to know that I would never have made such choices if I had not had good reason. It was my love for you that kept me closeted away."

She paused, then continued in a more serious tone. "We are under grave threat from many quarters, you see. My loyal exalts have risked their lives to put a permanent end to those threats, and many have died for their efforts, and their glory has been unknown, for it had to be done in secret, lest you be alarmed about the dangers on every hand."

Only "the exalts," Rylin noted, knowing that Altenerai had fought and died for the accursed stones as well. And some who'd been sent after them had never returned, like Renik.

Murmurs rose from the crowd, but she raised a hand and they stilled. "You needn't worry! A time of prosperity lies before us. We are shortly to walk the streets of paradise." She encompassed the crowd with her hands. "Yes, my people, paradise lies before us all. The true goddess is nearly here. With the aid of magical artifacts my loyal exalts have recovered, we shall summon a new age."

The queen continued. "There shall be no more war. Old age and death will no longer await us, and those lost to us will live again!" She beamed at this, perhaps expecting applause. The audience only looked back blankly, confused or even alarmed. The queen pressed on. "The Naor, the kobalin, and terrible predators from The Shifting Lands will no longer threaten us, for we shall be one with the great goddess, who will finally oversee our realms as was meant from time immemorial."

Low talk spread through the stands. Rylin saw heads turning and even those who weren't asking those nearby what was underway traded looks of consternation.

"Is this the sort of thing she used to say to you?" Rylin asked his companion.

"Yes. But I swear to you, Rylin. You can feel the presence of the Goddess in the stones and when you do this all makes more sense."

The queen spoke on. "What I am doing will not be easy, and it comes at great personal risk to myself and my most loyal allies. But I do it for you. Behold, the one true goddess!" She pointed with both hands to the stage rear.

The curtains parted, creaking faintly and swaying as they were drawn by hidden stagehands, and then Rylin and the people of Darassus looked upon the Goddess.

He muttered in unconscious awe. "By all that's holy."

He had thought the statue of Darassa, or of the lawgiver, were masterworks. Here, though, stood a forty-foot statue of beauty undreamt, a woman beyond parallel formed all of shining crystal, composed of hundreds of colors. She was slim and muscular and impossibly perfect. She stood with head turned off-center, her hands raised in a warding gesture, one well-formed calf twisting as she rotated. She was supported in part by scaffolding, but so lovely was she in all those blending streams of colors that Rylin scarce noticed.

The crowd let out a variety of sounds that registered as a collective gasp.

It was only as Rylin looked more closely that he saw there were gaps in the structure. Her nose had a few chips missing. A wedge was absent from her right hand, and there were various smaller holes and divots across her body.

The queen turned and beamed at her audience, and they clapped appreciatively, if a little hesitantly.

Only then did Rylin begin to feel misgivings. "She's certainly beautiful."

"You've felt the beauty of the hearthstones, haven't you?" Thelar asked him. His question was challenging.

He hadn't known quite what to expect and he realized now he'd been a fool not to ask what he might see. Somehow it had never occurred to him the hearthstones might actually piece together *this* way. Or that being in the presence of them all would evoke such warmth, even when they were inactive. He cursed. If he himself was feeling drawn to the thing, what must the crowd be thinking?

"We should have tried to stop her before," Rylin said to Thelar. "Why didn't you tell me they'd react like this?"

"I've never been near her this assembled," Thelar admitted. "I didn't know."

A trumpet blast sounded from the nearby walls, a high, clear call. Rylin knew it instantly for a summons to arms. The queen froze, puzzled, and her head rose, as though she could see through the upper rank of stands. He wondered if her powers allowed her even that.

Many in the crowd might have no better idea of a trumpet fanfare versus a signal, but there were enough who'd served or paid attention that shouts of alarm spread through them. Someone backstage shouted that Naor were almost within sight of the city.

Surely that was paranoia. How could the Naor have gotten so close to Darassus without word having spread beforehand?

Thelar turned to face him. "What do you think we should do?"

"I think we'd better finish this while her attention's diverted." Earlier he had assumed the Darassans would side with him. Now he understood that his actions might earn him their enmity. He worried, too, that Thelar's resolve would falter.

The exalt slid with him from the booth and together they hurried to the backstage stairs, where they discovered a frightened young guardsman in the midst of reporting to one of the red-haired twins Rylin had dueled in the exalt practice yard. Today she wore a stiff new khalat with red piping, and as she turned he saw the mole on her lip and recognized her as M'vai.

"The scouts have gotten a good look at them. They're riding immense black beasts," the guard reported, panting. "And there are huge ko'aye things flying above them!"

"How far out are they?" M'vai demanded.

"Less than a half hour."

"How did they get so far with no one seeing them?" M'vai asked. She sounded as though she meant to find the person responsible and bring them up on charges. She caught sight of Thelar and Rylin for the first time and her eyes widened. "Where have you been? Why is *he* with you?"

"What are their numbers?" Rylin asked the guard.

The soldier replied quickly. "There's one huge ko'aye closing on the city now. Our scouts spotted six more. There are dozens of the huge animals carrying standards. They're gigantic, sir," he said in dread. "Monstrous. Each is longer than a house and crowded with Naor troops. The earth shakes when they move. Cavalry follow in their wake."

Rylin spoke quickly. "The first priority's getting these people safely out of the arena and behind the inner walls. I have squires standing ready—signal an alert and put them on that. Until the people are secure keep the guards solely devoted to the gates and walls."

"Yes, sir." The soldier saluted and hurried off.

Rylin turned to M'vai and found her staring warily.

There were more important things to worry about. Rylin peered past her and saw scaffolding, and a giant crystal leg, and the ranks of exalts and aspirants. He couldn't see the queen, but he heard her working to quell the growing fear of the crowd, some of whom were already rising from their seats.

"The Naor pose no lasting threat!" the queen shouted.

Any remote chance of calm was shattered the moment a huge black-winged shape appeared in the air above the stadium. The crowd gasped almost as one, and then screamed as the beast circled, dived, and roared.

The sound of its attack was drowned out by the rumble of falling stone as a back section of the amphitheater collapsed upon itself. Screams of terror were replaced by screams of pain. An arch toppled sideways through the upper stands, smashing all it reached and sending stone shrapnel flying. A cloud of dust plumed and the dragon arrowed through it and banked even as Rylin raced forth, calling the exalts to attack. The wooden platform supporting the statue and its presenters vibrated under Rylin's bootheels with each crash of masonry. He saw the queen's look of surprise as he and Thelar drew close. She didn't look so much like a queen as an actor who'd suddenly forgotten her lines.

The beast roared once more and sent another section of wall to ruin, along with hundreds of innocents crushed by the falling stone. And then it vanished beyond the side of the stadium once more.

The smell of blood was borne up on the wind with the white dust of crumbled stone. The air rang with the cries of the injured and bereaved and frightened, and the pound of feet as people fled for multiple exits.

Rylin turned to the ranks of sorcerers. "Exalts! Aspirants! It's going to come back! Ready for its return!" He saw dozens of confused and anxious people, many of whom looked familiar, and some of whom he knew, like Tesra and Meria, M'vai's twin.

"I will wake the Goddess," the queen declared, her voice nearly lost in the sounds of her panicked people. She spoke then with greater force. "We will waken the Goddess together, and all will be well!"

"No," Rylin cried, turning on her. "Use the hearthstones," he urged, "but we're summoning no goddess today. Not without consultation from the council and the people of Erymyr!"

"He's right, Majesty," Thelar urged. "Let's just focus on repelling the Naor."

She glowered. For a brief moment it looked as though she meant to say something, for her lips worked. Then she threw back her flowing green sleeves and sent blue white tendrils of energy rippling at them.

Rylin heard Thelar's sharp intake of breath beside him and felt the sorceries like a physical force. The sapphire on his hand lit and with it all those linked to it blazed to life. The spell slid to either side of them both, striking the wooden floor, which shifted on the instant to that terrible crystalline substance.

Rylin's face went ashen as he understood what she'd tried to do to them, what she yet attempted as she shouted and sent more power.

Even knowing she meant to kill him, he knew regret when he leapt with his knife.

He grasped one of her slim shoulders and delivered the perfect killing blow, the blade sliding up under her ribs and driving toward her heart.

She staggered and goggled as she leaned into him, and he was sickened by how much this death was like a loving embrace. He saw astonishing little blood as he pulled free and stepped back.

The queen looked down at the injury, then up at him, and he saw madness in her eyes, along with the glittering energy of the hearthstones. She should have been dead, or dying. Instead, she slapped at him, and while no strike landed, the air hit like a physical force. The rings couldn't shield him from a hurricane wind, and he tumbled backward through the air, on past the scaffolding and the impossibly beautiful statue of the Goddess until the wall dividing field from seating arrested his flight.

As he painfully struck the stone, bright points of light trailed before his eyes, and he struggled to refind the breath that had been knocked out of his body. The screams of the crowd trebled, by which he guessed the dragon had renewed its assault.

He raised his head and called out feebly to Thelar, fearful the queen would kill him with the linked rings out of protective range, but the queen was distracted. This time the dragon aimed straight for the stage.

A handful of mages were whipping energy at the monster, not knowing to target the men who rode it. He saw the dragon's massive maw open, and then the creature roared.

The queen cried out and threw up a vast, glittering screen of energy. By accident or design it not only shielded the people on the stage, but most of her precious goddess, and Rylin wondered why she hadn't done something similar to protect the crowd.

As great as her spell was, it still wasn't large enough to protect the whole of the statue. The end of the left elbow was blown free, along with parts of the face, and hearthstones rained down across the back of the stage. The floorboards rumbled under him as the immense statue swayed in its scaffolding. He staggered to his feet.

At the same moment something happened to the dragon. Just as it was pulling up from its dive white energies streamed out from the broken points of the statue and slammed into the monster.

A lattice work of crystal erupted across the dragon's head and swept up across its shoulders. It dropped, wings beating furiously as it struggled not to plummet. What looked like a fine sheet of alabaster lay across the monster's snout and down the length of its spine. The effect struck the Naor pilot and the three mounted behind them, coating them in what looked like ivory shards. They froze in mid-motion, though the dragon's tail, unencumbered, still twitched.

The dragon struck the un-peopled back area of the arena, above Rylin's head, with the sound of thunder, shaking the stage and the damaged statue once more. The queen screamed in fury, somehow louder than the background pandemonium. The citizens were still in flight for the exits, although some made their way to tend the wounded, and others cradled the dead, inconsolable with grief.

The queen cared only for her goddess, shouting for help. She should have long since dropped dead from that well-placed knife wound, and he could only assume Leonara's intense connection to the hearthstones somehow sustained her.

He wondered what he might do, as his senses settled in. He tested his battered limbs by putting hand to his sword and sitting up. He hurt in many areas, but nothing seemed to be broken. He supposed he'd try to find out if the queen could keep weaving once her head was lopped off.

He searched for sign of his lone ally, thinking to find him dead, and discovered Thelar and a small group of exalts bending all their magical energy to keep an exitway out of the stadium from crumbling. Great jagged lines riddled the front of its decorative arch. Only their sorcery held it upright as hundreds fled beneath.

Right—he couldn't call them from that. He turned for the queen himself.

That's when he saw what the queen and the mages wrought: a distortion in the air behind the statue, almost as though he stared at salt flats at midday in the height of summer. That distortion multiplied, spread, and suddenly ripped open to encompass the queen, the statue, and her followers, and would have reached Rylin if he hadn't dived away.

Groaning from yet another roll, he picked himself up and saw that beyond that wavering outline an entirely different landscape was superimposed upon the stage, a twilight land stained in crimson by a setting sun.

That landscape faded like morning mist, taking the queen and her statue and some scattered hearthstones with it. He glimpsed a bewildered Tesra caught at the spell's edge, as if she were uncertain she wished to go, and then the dark-haired exalt faded with all the rest of the queen's mad followers. The stage was empty.

31

Joining Forces

Elenai found Lelanc where she'd last seen her upon the battlement, under the twinned moons. It had somehow seemed easier to release the ko'aye the first time, but then she hadn't been in quite as much of a hurry.

Lelanc awoke and reared, wings wide, ready to throw herself into the attack. She let out an ear-splitting battle cry and searched the walkways and stone embrasure for enemies.

"Where is Cerai?" Lelanc demanded. "Where has she fled?"

Elenai had thought about what she'd say as she'd pounded up the stairs. "There's a way out from here," she said. "But you and Kyrkenall and I have to hurry."

The ko'aye called out once more, then looked down at her. "Hurry from what? Other enemies?"

"A great storm comes," she said, which was the simplest way to explain matters. "I've talked Cerai into letting you go, but we've not much time."

"I will kill her!"

Elenai had worried talk with the ko'aye would be difficult, and decided on blunt truth. "She'll turn you into a statue before you can even get close. And I can't stop her. But we can get you away from here if you meet me down by the stables."

Lelanc flapped her wings twice and set all four feet on the ground. Her eyes shone in the moonlight, eerie and unknowable.

"What you say of her powers may be true," Lelanc said. "But my heart cries for vengeance. For the city of my sister. For Rylin."

"Rylin lives," Elenai reminded her, and Lelanc's head rose.

"How can this be? This is not one of her lies?"

"I heard this from my commander, not Cerai. Rylin was wounded, but he escaped the city."

"That is a glad thing," the ko'aye said.

"Yes. But we have to hurry. A magical exit is going to be readied for us."

Lelanc's head bobbed back and forth on the end of her swanny neck. "I do not know your meaning."

"I'm not entirely sure I do, either," Elenai admitted. Rialla had died before the Ko'aye alliance, so there was no point in mentioning her name. "Kyrkenall's old friend, a sorceress, has come, and says it's our only chance to get out of here quickly. Lelanc, we're caught in the midst of . . . two storms, and the wind is heavy between them. I'm not sure where they'll take us, but I swear that if you come with me and Kyrkenall we will look out for you."

Lelanc's head lowered, then raised once more. "You have helped, and I am grateful. But I will find my own way." She turned to put front feet on an embrasure. Before Elenai could say anything more, the ko'aye pushed out and soared away, flapping to gain altitude.

Elenai cursed inventively as she watched the ko'aye climb toward the moons, a little surprised at her vocabulary. Too much time with Kyrkenall, she guessed.

There was nothing more to be done, so she hurried back to the stairwell and down, and out toward the stables, a two-story building built into an interior wall of the wide fortress courtyard. A group of Cerai's guards stood watching while Cerai spoke with the glowing figure of a woman in the midst of the compound. Kyrkenall was only a little distance from the stables, attention held raptly by the two women.

"What are they doing?" Elenai asked as she strode up, a little breathless after having run up and then down five flights of stairs. "Has Rialla said anything about what she's doing here, or what this is all about?"

"No! She keeps saying that she doesn't have time, and that we'll talk later! They've been going back and forth about magical theory now since just a little after you left." Kyrkenall seemed to take real note of her for the first time. "Where's Lelanc?"

"I don't know."

His voice rose. "You don't know?"

"She flew off! She said she'd find her own way."

"That's great," Kyrkenall growled.

"There wasn't much I could do about it," Elenai said, irritated by Kyrkenall's attitude. "Are you sure this is truly Rialla?"

That garnered another hard look. "She sure looks and acts like her. Apart from being glowing and transparent."

"But why didn't she know who I was when she's been talking to me in my dreams?"

"You're asking me?"

"Maybe you should ask her."

"I've tried asking her all kinds of things and all she'll answer with is a 'not now.'"

"And why is she here, now, rather than talking to us in our dreams?" The more she'd thought about it the less Elenai liked an already bad situation. "Before we walk into the middle of some huge spell," she said, "don't you think some clarity would be nice?"

Kyrkenall's brows drew together, then he brusquely nodded his assent and started forward.

Elenai came after and soon they stopped two spear lengths out.

Rialla turned and considered them. Somehow her ghostly image looked even more unnerving here under the moonlight. Cerai's nonchalant confidence was mostly absent. Now the alten was pensive.

"If you're ready," Rialla said, her voice once again reaching Elenai's mind while the ghostly alten's lips worked silently, "where's Lelanc?"

"We need some answers, Rialla," Kyrkenall said. "How do we know it's really you? And how are you even here? I put you in your tomb more than ten years ago! And why don't you know Elenai when you've been talking to her in her dreams?"

Rialla's head tilted a minute degree, birdlike. "So I will die," she said wistfully. "Or at least my physical form will."

"You already have." Kyrkenall sounded both confused and sad.

"I haven't done this in an order that would make sense to you." She looked at Elenai again. "If you said we've met before then I must have found something important to tell you I don't know yet. But please, you must hurry. It's vital you get to Darassus, or it will end badly. And I don't know how many times I can try this."

That left Elenai only a little less confused than before. She wasn't sure how to respond.

"Are you wanting me to leave Lyria?" Kyrkenall asked. "Out in the middle of nowhere?"

"Your horse is safer here." Rialla turned to Cerai, speaking to her with little warmth. "Watch carefully." She looked to the sky and stared. Elenai followed her glance and saw Lelanc circling.

Elenai watched from the inner world as Rialla worked her magics. The strange woman shone with diamond brilliance, glowing more brightly even than the hearthstones when they were active. With a complex cast of threads, Rialla shifted the winds ahead of them until they whipped furiously. Beneath their feet the ground lurched but she gave no sign of noticing.

Heliotrope energies spiraled before them and opened into a shimmering white tunnel through which sunlight poured, as well as the sound of screaming.

"Go," Rialla cried, her voice rising with the wind. "Go now!"

Kyrkenall flashed Elenai a resigned and faintly amused look and then walked through. His one step stretched impossibly long and then he stood at the far end of the tunnel, a tiny figure.

Behind her she heard the unmistakable call of a ko'aye and looked over her shoulder to see Lelanc gliding low, eyes bright red points, claws forward. She was trying for Cerai. As the would-be goddess threw herself flat, Rialla's mouth turned down in annoyance. She gestured and the portal stretched to catch the ko'aye's wing tip. It then swallowed the creature whole and Rialla turned her gaze upon Elenai. The phantom alten was silent but her meaning was clear—get moving!

And so Elenai started forward, and saw blurred land and skyscape rushing past on either hand even as that distant point rushed at her like an arrow.

She stepped through into the Arena Altenera, its center field set up as if for an awards ceremony, for the competition tools and ramps were vanished and a stage rose in their place. Lelanc was picking herself up from the floorboards near the edge. Her barbed tail rose menacingly behind her.

A quick glance showed her the hole in reality vanish in a wink, as though it had never been.

Elenai turned to take in the rest of the environment, discovering a heart-dropping scene of carnage. Much of the east end of the stadium had fallen in upon itself. The back arches had toppled onto the stands, pulverizing the benches beneath, as well as people that had been sitting there. The structure smelled of blood, dust, and fear. Trailing streams of people raced for the exits, leaving sprawled figures behind them, the dead and the dying and those who wouldn't leave them.

Stranger still, what she first took for the immense white carving of a winged lizard rested in the rubble of the western seating area, complete with lifelike statues seated upon its back. But its rear legs and tail moved feebly, and looking through the inner world she understood that the beast and its riders had been haphazardly struck with life-suspending magics

similar to those employed by Belahn and Cerai. This, then, was one of the
Naor dragons, in Darassus itself, and it must have been the source of this
terrible damage. Cerai had been right, and the Naor were already moving on the city. But who here had the power to petrify such an immense
creature?

She set aside unanswerable questions and walked toward Kyrkenall
and the bearded man in the khalat talking with him, whom she now recognized as Rylin.

On stage edge, a handful of exalts and men and women in flowery
white shirts were working themselves to magical exhaustion to keep
other fragile stadium walls from collapsing inward. Elenai activated her
hearthstone, sent tendrils of energy to revitalize them, then bolstered their
efforts with an ease that would once have surprised her, conjuring lines of
force from the artifact to lend support to the fractured stone.

One of the exalts, a lean, hawk-nosed man, used her magics to imitate and surpass her work. Perhaps because he was more practiced with
hearthstones, he stabilized the failing stone swiftly and sent his energies
around the stadium to address other strained areas.

Seeing that he and his followers had command of the situation, Elenai
left her hearthstone active for use and turned to join Kyrkenall. She was
almost struck in the face by Lelanc's wing as the ko'aye bounded up to
chatter excitedly at Rylin, who beamed at sight of her.

Kyrkenall summarized the situation without pause for pleasantries.
"The queen opened a rift and vanished through it with the hearthstones
right before we turned up in the same place."

Elenai ignored a host of questions that information inspired and offered a hypothesis. "Maybe Rialla keyed in on that opening."

"Maybe. It doesn't matter right now. The Naor are here in force. This
dragon must have been sent to scout ahead and spotted a target too
good to pass. It's not alone, because there are six more, and a small army
on monstrous ground-walking beasts. Our scouts reported that they're
something like eshlack, but about ten times larger, and there are men riding
on them. They're less than a half hour southeast and on a direct course for
the city."

"Of course they are." Elenai was a bit surprised at her equanimity and
supposed there were too many shocks to fully register.

"So. Rylin's going to try and get Lelanc into the air—"

"If you're willing." Rylin bowed to the ko-aye, who screeched fiercely
in return.

"And I think you ought to see if you can wake that dragon and ride it," Kyrkenall finished.

"You want me to ride a dragon?" Elenai asked. "I don't have the slightest—"

Kyrkenall spoke over her as if he wasn't aware of any particular difficulty. "The moment it attacked the hearthstones, the hearthstones trapped it, kind of like what happened with N'lahr. So maybe you can figure that out."

"You don't ask much."

"You told me not to treat you like a squire," he reminded her. "It only takes one dragon to take down a wall. And they've got six. I don't think Rylin and one ko'aye can handle six dragons, do you?"

"The dragons are kind of like puppets," Rylin offered. She eyed him for a moment, trying to accustom herself to his look with the scruffy beard. "At least that's what I gathered. The pilot magically controls them."

Lelanc cawed. "Come, Rylin! It is time to kill the nest rippers!"

Rylin nodded, then halted in mid-turn. "I'm going to fly to the captain of the south gate and consult, then take the fight to the Naor. I hope I'll see you up there. And that dragon can hold five—get some of the exalts to go with you. We'll need all the help we can get."

"You trust them?" Kyrkenall's voice dripped with scorn.

"Yes." The broad-shouldered exalt who'd been leading the repair efforts had already started toward them and Rylin waved him forward. "This is Thelar. He stood with me. And the others stayed to help Darassus."

"The archway will hold now," Thelar reported, then turned to Elenai before pointing up to the dragon. "If you mean to take this thing into battle, I mean to assist." His manner was a little challenging, as if he expected opposition.

Elenai wasn't at all certain she could get the creature moving, much less released from its hearthstone encasement, but she cut Kyrkenall off before he could object once more. "I'll be glad for whatever help you can give," she said.

Soon he and two more exalts were hurrying with her to the dragon. Kyrkenall came with them, grumbling under his breath.

Elenai reached the side of the beast and pressed her hand to its scaled maw. "Assuming I wake it, there are live Naor up there," Elenai called to Kyrkenall.

But she discovered he was already clambering along its back. "I'll be ready," he said.

She supposed he would.

Thelar eyed the dragon dubiously. "I'm not sure how we can get this casing off."

"Let me try." Elenai stretched out with her magical perceptions, threads of intent brushing the surface of the trapped beast. She'd learned a lot since she'd looked upon the hearthstone accident that had trapped N'lahr. This circumstance might be similar, but the execution was different. This time she had edges to work with, and this time, she had experience.

She sank her threads into the hearthstone, called upon its magics, and touched the surface of the restraint.

Elenai hadn't felt the pull of probability for long days, but it was there now, guiding her forward toward points of attachment upon the crystal. This had never before occurred when she or her companions weren't under direct threat. Whether pursuing other possibilities led to disaster or merely delay she couldn't know, but she worried this was not her own doing.

Rialla had shepherded them here, none so gently in Lelanc's case, almost as though they were game pieces that had to be arranged just so on the board if she were to win the match. She had steered Elenai through dreams. And once Elenai had begun working a hearthstone, Rialla's hearthstone, she had become aware, in moments of crisis, of paths that led to jeopardy. Elenai wished to be no one's instrument, even for a good cause, but now was not the time for hesitation. Later she would learn the truth. For now, she followed that line of probability toward success. And for once she did not smile in the wash of the hearthstone's power, nor exult as the crystal encasement fell away from the dragon.

She suddenly found herself in the presence of an immense, slitted green eye, and the head shifted to snap at her with teeth as long as her leg. She leapt back, falling into Thelar, who steadied her, then swatted it with a blast of pain. It moaned and moved its head away.

"Shall we?" she asked, and pointed to the rope ladder built into the saddle structure along its neck. She climbed up behind the trio of Exalted Ones as the dragon shook its head and struggled to rise off the loose and likely uncomfortable rubble.

Kyrkenall had already dealt with the Naor by the time she arrived. Five bodies lolled on the chairs stretching back past the pilot, an arrow through each. The driver himself had been stabbed through the neck. Kyrkenall was readying to take the same bloody blade to the straps holding the pilot in place.

"Just untie them," Elenai said quickly. "Don't you think we'll need to belt in?"

Kyrkenall grunted. "Right."

Thelar directed the others to the chairs at the rear. There were two banks of two chairs, and two individual seats along the neck, where the creature's spines were shorter.

Elenai quickly took in their surroundings, noticing then that the arena was close to empty, apart from a few still visible in the tunnel exits, and those attending the casualties. One of the exalts moved among the wounded now, joining a dozen others, some of whom appeared to be healers. Rylin had vanished upon Lelanc.

Thelar and the other exalts finished dumping the dead Naor overside and were inspecting the weapon caches built into their backless seat areas. One was a red-haired woman with a mole above her lip, the other a pale, balding man with expressive and intelligent eyes.

"If this works," she called out, "save your attacks until we're closer. They should see us as a friendly until then."

Kyrkenall turned and addressed them. "This dragon has spare warriors. So will the others. And that means that they'll be firing on us. Do you have defensive magics?"

The other two nodded. Thelar answered in the affirmative.

"Focus on that. Elenai's probably going to have her hands full driving this thing. And I'm going to be shooting the Naor mages controlling the other dragons."

"Understood, Alten," Thelar said, then looked back to his companions. "You heard him. Ready with wind gusts. M'vai, you guard our left, Folahn the right, and I'll fill in the gaps and look to above and front."

Rylin's friend seemed to have a decent tactical approach, Elenai decided. Now it was time to find out if all this clever planning would amount to anything. She reached into the dragon's mind with tendrils of energy. She'd never touched the thoughts of a creature like this—it seemed to lack a will or purpose of its own, though it exhibited some primitive urges and reactive reflexes. It was experiencing pain as a sharp stone stuck into a tender underpart, and that accounted for the restless shifting of its hind limbs. All she had to do was link threads of intent to the beast, and . . . There, she had it lift its weight from the offending projection and it stilled. This was a little simpler than she imagined. There were no branching futures to follow, no battle for control. She experimentally raised its left wing and brought up a cloud of dust. But how to get it to fly?

"Looks like you have it!" Kyrkenall said practically in her ear.

"Oh yes," she replied archly.

"Do you really have it?" Kyrkenall asked, sounding more concerned.

She glanced over her shoulder to find him gripping her seat, which was strapped into the leather band that encircled the beast's great neck.

"I can get it to move," she said. "Can I get it moving in a coordinated fashion? Can I get it airborne?"

"Looks like you'd better." He glanced behind him, then leaned forward so she could hear him better. "They're all strapping in."

"Shouldn't you?"

"I'm fine for now. But you ought to, right?"

She tied herself in with the cross braces and sought through the commands she guessed might set the monster in motion.

She sent impulses through the dragon's legs and got it to stand fully. Unfortunately, the rubble shifted under its weight and it took a moment or two to find a solid balance. It was more challenging still to get the legs to climb over the torn building, but after a little bit of wobbly experimentation she learned that rather than trying to control each individual leg she could simply command the thing to head in the direction she wanted, and it did the rest. She guided it through the destruction its crash had generated, arriving at the practice field just outside the arena. At the sight of the dragon, those still fleeing into the city cried out in alarm. She should have foreseen that. She certainly hadn't planned to panic anyone.

How to get it into the sky, though? She tried flapping the wings and that didn't do much except raise dust.

"Maybe you can have it climb back to the top of a stadium wall and drop off," Kyrkenall suggested.

"Not one of your better ideas," she told him over her shoulder. "And you really ought to belt in before I try to get it into the air."

"All right." He retreated, walking with ease along the animal's spiny back. She waited until she was sure he was buckled in, then set the creature's wings beating, and started it away from the people into an ungainly lope. Earlier she'd told it to move. Now she simply urged it to fly. Swinging its wings more and more strenuously, it ponderously rose into the air and over the field, just missing the roof of a house. It struck a chimney with a massive back leg and sent bricks flying. She felt that impact register as mild discomfort. They climbed until they were level with the top of the arena behind them. The wind streamed coolly into her face, bannering her hair behind her. Only then did she wish she had grabbed a helmet. She'd left it in her travel gear.

Kyrkenall startled her with a strange noise, and she glanced back to see him whooping with joy, one fist pumping the air. Behind, the other passengers were settled in. Thelar was serious and quiet. Beside him, the one Thelar had called M'vai seemed keyed up and avidly gazed to left and right, and Folahn, in the rear, looked as though he'd swallowed a bite of bad fish.

She set the creature climbing higher, exhilarated by the speed and the growing distance between them and the ground. Her magical endurance had more than doubled since she'd taken up hearthstone use, but she realized that every command she gave sapped her energies. She'd have to be careful, because she didn't want to have to draw on a hearthstone in the midst of battle. That Naor blood sorcerer, Chargan, might notice. She called to Kyrkenall. "You see the Naor yet?"

"There. On your left."

A great dust cloud climbed heavenward, about two leagues out. She banked the dragon over Darassus, stunned by a beautiful view of the great domes and the sparkling Idris in her channel. Soldiers raced down from the watchtowers on the high bluffs east of the capital, and squires guided the frightened masses through the gates into the inner city housing the palace and the Altenerai buildings. Those walls, at least, made a complete defensive circuit.

How long might the outer wall hold? How long did it *have* to hold? She didn't see many soldiers posted on its heights. Probably the defense forces had been deployed to Alantris or Vedessus. How had the Naor gotten so far, so fast, without word reaching Darassus? Fine questions, but right now she had only one task. She set the dragon climbing higher. The view was frightening and thrilling all at once, and she wished she had opportunity to truly enjoy it.

They spotted distant winged shapes in the sky beyond, not six, but seven of them, circling, and lumbering, fast-moving monstrosities on the ground at the van of the great dust cloud. Gods. There were so many.

She caught a movement to their right and turned her head to see Lelanc lifting up from the tower beside the south gate. She carried a single figure in a blue khalat. Rylin, who raised a hand in greeting.

Elenai responded in kind and took the dragon west, gaining altitude in a wind current above the bluffs.

"What are you doing?" Kyrkenall shouted up to her.

"Putting the sun at our backs!"

He let out a bark of approving laughter and then fell silent as she began the long swing back east, the bright sun behind her.

She wondered what the Naor would think of the return of this dragon. They'd have been too far away to see its landing in the stadium, so it was unlikely they'd expect their enemies to control it. They'd be surprised to see it flying from the west, of course, but maybe they'd hold their fire.

Or maybe they'd be incredibly suspicious. She shouted for everyone to be alert and ready.

She studied the seven opposing dragons as they glided high above the Erymyran farm fields. Though broadly similar in design, with leathery wings, long trailing tails, and fierce maws at the end of serpentine necks, the colors and characteristics varied. Each carried at least three riders, and four dragons were long enough that five Naor sat in metal studded saddles upon their backs. They came on in a wedge, with perhaps a hundred feet of air separating each. The largest, of a faded yellow hue, was in the lead.

Only a little ways behind, on the distant ground, great black beasts longer than most houses advanced across the farm fields southeast of the city. Apart from a few hundred Naor riding horses, the rest of the enemy soldiers had packed upon platforms fastened to the backs of the beasts. There had to be forty or more soldiers on every one of the horned monstrosities, and there looked to be nearly three dozen of the beasts in all. Calculating quickly, she estimated there were no more than two thousand Naor. Not so large a number, if the walls held, but capable of wrecking havoc if the walls went down. Was this just some huge destructive raid?

The drum of immense hooves upon the plains thundered like an unending storm.

She bore in on the leftmost dragon, a green-scaled monster larger even than their own. The Naor riding it wore furred jackets and hats. Only the pilot was armored, complete with a heavy helm with cheekguards. He and the five arranged on the dragon behind him turned to look as Kyrkenall let loose a flurry of arrows

The pilot tore at the shaft sticking out of his shoulder plate, only to catch one right through his helmet cheek piece. As he shuddered in his death throes, the dragon sank from formation, and Elenai heard the screams of the warriors seated along its length. Nothing, though, got the monster beating its wings once more, and it dropped like a stone.

The remaining dragon pilots were swift to react. Two broke formation immediately, turning to flank Elenai's dragon, and a smaller third one with pretty iridescent wings climbed.

Another flew straight on for the city, the domes of which gleamed in the light of the lowering sun.

Elenai glimpsed Rylin and Lelanc diving through the air above another monster, and then she was too busy turning her own animal to watch. Her stomach lurched during the speedy, winding drop. One of the pursuing beasts released its great roar as she swung out and away and their dragon shook beneath them. She'd hate to feel what a direct attack would do, and wondered how to command her own animal to roar.

Javelins fell from the beast above, and her team of weavers spread gusts of wind. The weapons dropped harmlessly to the right.

A blue beast swept in on their left, so close that its wing tip touched their dragon's. One of their warriors proved a fine marksman, for an arrow point struck Elenai's collar. It didn't pierce the highly woven fabric, but it felt like she'd taken a fist punch to the side of her throat. Elenai struggled to stay upright, alarmed when she felt her dragon wing-beat seize up. Pain or no, she retained control, raking her gaze left. One spear stood out along her dragon's wing, as Elenai detected a little of their dragon's irritation there, like a splinter.

The blue's pilot had whipped up a shield that now boasted several arrows, as did the warrior in back of him, slumped in his chair. One of the exalts must have attacked the Naor warriors to the rear, for they held motionless, hands clasping javelins they didn't throw.

"Hold steady," Kyrkenall shouted at her, even though she'd been doing exactly that. Then, with astonishing precision, he sent two arrows into the blue animal's largest wing joint.

Almost immediately it fell away and into a spiral, one wing hanging useless.

"Two down!" Kyrkenall shouted.

"Three!" Thelar corrected. "Rylin got one!"

It was then that the agile dragon with the shimmering wings bore down on them from above, right out of the sun.

Kyrkenall launched arrows at its underside as it swooped past. Elenai dived, and it felt as though her heart and stomach both caught in her throat. The barbed tail that swung down missed her head by a sword length. Behind her came a masculine shout of pain cut off in mid-voice. She twisted in her seat.

The bald exalt, Folahn, had been torn from his chair. He now hurtled limply through the air, blood streaming after.

Gods, she prayed, let him already be dead. She could too well imagine the terror of being conscious during that long way down.

A huge yellow dragon with great black spikes along its spine and jaw swept on for them from the right, pale wings slapping the air. The spearmen along its back lifted weapons expectantly. Elenai struggled to turn her dragon but its spear-injured wing made it sluggish despite that it registered little pain. Behind her Kyrkenall fired and cursed, for a sorcerous red energy wave, like vaporous blood, rose before the scaly beast, sweeping every shaft away. This, the dragon that had been in the lead, carried more than one sorcerer.

Its maw opened and Elenai gritted her teeth, activated the hearthstone, desperate enough for the extra spell energy to risk it. She felt M'vai and Thelar whipping threads of attack toward the enemy beast's pilot, only to be rebuffed.

She wasn't sure if the pain or the gleeful voice came first. This time Chargan sent her the feel of fire surging through her veins, and he laughed. *I had hoped we would meet again.*

He was somewhere nearby, either on a dragon or below, and had been waiting for the chance to key into her hearthstone.

She cycled the stone closed, saw the yellow beast nearing to fifty feet, and struggled to get her dragon to swerve. Any moment, she knew, the enemy monster would roar.

A savage screech rang through the air—the piercing call of a ko'aye. Elenai saw the Naor dragon pilot look suddenly over his shoulder just as a javelin drove through his side.

A flock of five ko'aye struck from on high, claws gleaming. Foremost among them was one of blue and white, with a scarred neck, and astride her was a lean, dark-haired man in a blue khalat.

N'lahr and Drusa had dropped out of the clear blue to join the battle. Elenai laughed in delight and relief at sight of them both, not just for their timely arrival, but because the commander was alive and well. She'd feared their last conversation had rendered him permanently immobile.

As the wounded pilot flailed, the dragon's wing-beats faltered and its deadly blast never came. The ko'aye ripped Naor warriors from their seats and sent them plunging, screaming as they dropped.

Elenai grinned in relief and heard Kyrkenall whoop with joy behind her. In moments the attack crippled the spiked yellow dragon and it followed its fellows to the earth.

Elenai scanned the sky and saw the other ko'aye racing to aid Lelanc and Rylin, locked in combat with a copper colored dragon. Below, the front rank of great black beasts had passed them by, and those that came after were half obscured by their dust.

Drusa and N'lahr glided in beside them. The ko'aye's head turned and she let out a caw of greeting. "The travel was long. But it is good to send our enemies into the red!"

Elenai saw the saddle holding the commander in place was a slap-dash affair with numerous buckles and ropes. A canister of javelins was strapped along his right leg.

"You're late!" Kyrkenall called over the whipping wind. "But the stylish entrance makes up for it!"

N'lahr smiled, then pointed into the distance with his javelin. "We've got to catch those headed for Darassus! The walls have to hold."

Two dragons were closer to the city every moment, one a huge silver, and the other, farther back, the lighter gray with iridescent wings that had slain Folahn. She felt her pulse rise and set her sights on the one closest to Darassus.

N'lahr saluted them with his weapon. Drusa screeched and bore him upward.

Elenai discovered she could still shout when she called to the mages behind her. "Conjure a wind at our back!"

The exalts did so in moments. She felt the push of it not only through her magical senses, but against the dragon's wings. They picked up speed almost immediately.

Kyrkenall shouted to her, his voice almost lost by the roar of the wind. "I'm out of arrows—dropped a bunch on your last dive! Two javelins left!"

She didn't bother shouting back that he'd better make them count. They passed over the front rank of the gigantic Naor beasts below, and she peered ahead at the shimmer of silver scales covering the dragon in the lead. What she'd first taken as blotches she now recognized as crimson hand-prints painted all along its serpentine body.

Thelar shouted something that sounded like a warning. She couldn't understand him over the wind. Then she saw a bloodred spike of energy from below rip a jagged slash through their dragon's left wing.

"What was that?" Kyrkenall shouted.

Elenai reached out with her senses and felt a second powerful sorcerous strike building below. She veered left, and her unnerving roll saved them from a strike against the dragon's belly, though the red slash tore a gap through the other wing. She felt her control slipping. The creature didn't seem to be capable of registering much pain, but it certainly was in distress. She forced their animal to fight on, beating its wings faster to compensate.

Ahead of them, the silver beast dropped altitude and speed as it closed on the outer wall, and Elenai knew with certainty they weren't going to reach it in time.

She heard its great roar. A thirty-foot span beside the closed Darassan gate blew into rubble. Only a three-to-four-foot height of wall remained. Beyond it lay a tract of blasted masonry. The attack didn't seem to have hurt many soldiers, who weren't present in large numbers. Probably most had been sent on to reinforce Vedessus and Alantris.

The dragon swept on, low over the city. Elenai swallowed in dread, knowing when it passed the titanic statue of Darassa the pilot meant to blast the inner wall as well. She funneled all the magical energies left her to build the wind behind them. They shot forward, closing quickly.

"Get me beside it," Kyrkenall shouted in her ear. "I've got this."

Weak from the exertion, she turned to find him out of his seat, grasping the straps of her chair with one hand and holding a javelin in the other. She could scarce believe it. "What are you doing?"

"Our exalts have their hands full keeping you airborne. Get me in close. I'm going to drop over."

"You're insane!"

"I'll be fine," he said with a grin.

They soared beyond Darassa's statue as the silver dragon passed over the spired dome of the temple of Kantahl, heading in a straight line for the wall about the palace grounds. Thousands still poured through the streets and into the inner city, and individual figures pointed up at them.

The dragon's rearmost Naor pitched javelins at them, but Thelar and M'vai used dwindling energies to direct them harmlessly away. In moments Elenai had their beast above the silver. Without so much as a farewell, Kyrkenall leapt over the side.

He landed near a prominent dorsal spike, rocked unevenly for a heartbeat, then advanced to slice the head from one of the rearmost riders as the man raised a bow. He jammed a javelin into his companion with his off hand. Kyrkenall leapt onto the saddle, whipped free the javelin, then drove it through the neck of another archer, turning too late to fire. Two warriors rose to fight him but he crouched under one blow and bowled into the man so he tumbled over the side, then sliced through the next and advanced on the pilot. He put his sword to the man's throat.

Elenai, flying above and aside, could only stare in amazement.

Kyrkenall's dragon veered up and over the center of the city. Elenai tried to stay just above.

"Elenai," Thelar shouted, his voice hoarse. "The little one's come back!"

Too late she saw the smaller dragon that had slain Folahn diving at them from above, claws outstretched. Three other ko'aye trailed it, along with Drusa and N'lahr.

She swerved, and the legs of Elenai's dragon struck Kyrkenall's. The archer's blade drove into his pilot's neck and his dragon began to drop. The ground lay yet a killing distance below.

Elenai turned hard, chasing Kyrkenall's dragon. The archer had latched onto the the pilot's saddle and she saw his eerie black eyes swing up at her.

"Grab the rope!" Thelar shouted breathlessly. The exalt had sliced free some restraining straps and used sorcery to stretch them toward Kyrkenall.

He could make that, she thought. That was a shorter leap than up to the ledge of their ko'aye cave.

Kyrkenall met her eyes, stepped back. And then, instead of jumping for the rope on his right, he whirled and threw himself into empty space to the left.

She gaped, knowing sheer horror, knowing her friend had just fallen to his death. A heartbeat later the talons of the little dragon struck just back of where Thelar sat. Elenai's dragon spun as she fought dizzily for control, the city a colorful blur below.

A smaller winged figure dove past, and as she righted their dragon she saw Lelanc snatch Kyrkenall's shoulder. The ko'aye might as well have grabbed a lead weight, for she and Rylin and the archer plummeted like a stone. Lelanc beat her wings frantically to slow the drop, but it looked terribly swift even still.

Elenai fought her dragon back into the air. Its strength was almost finished. She swooped to the left, to avoid smashing into Vedessa's temple bell. N'lahr and the flock of ko'aye climbed after the gray dragon. She didn't think she could follow. Her attention was still diverted by Kyrkenall's fate. Lelanc had angled left, and some twenty feet above a channel of the Idris she released her burden. Kyrkenall plunged and struck the water with a splash. The ko'aye's own precipitous fall almost ended the same way, but Lelanc pulled out of the steep descent and skimmed the surface before rising once more. People hurrying over a nearby bridge cheered as Kyrkenall surfaced, and a group ran to help him from the river.

Elenai struggled for control, tasting blood through gritted teet, as her dragon shuddered beneath her. She'd managed to bite her lip. She saw Kyrkenall's silver dragon smash into the cobblestone streets of the marketplace just back of the statue of Darassa. As Elenai flew past it looked as though the goddess had turned in sorrow to weep because the huge animal had fallen. A crash that would be her fate if she couldn't guide her failing beast. Blood sprayed with every lift of its wings.

"Its wings are bleeding badly," Thelar called up to her.

Behind her, N'lahr and the ko'aye still wove around the dragon with the iridescent wings. Elenai's own dragon was dying; she could be no aid to them. She wasn't sure she could be aid to herself. She managed a low path over the outer walls, thinking they'd done enough damage to the city already. Her gaze roved over the oncoming Naor, found them less than a half mile away.

"Help me steady the winds!" she cried. But there was nothing more to be done, and a moment later they met the ground at nearly fully speed.

32

The Army at the Wall

Rylin and Lelanc were only a few hundred yards behind Elenai's dragon when the beast cleared the outer wall. It dropped too swiftly, slamming across the surface of the grass blades, rippling them for a brief moment before it struck and slid for a hundred feet, flinging up clods of dirt and grass and rattling its three remaining passengers in their seats.

Lelanc landed only a few heartbeats after, just to the right. Rylin unstrapped to fling himself forward, dreading what he might find. At least the pale dragon hadn't rolled atop Elenai and the others.

Closing fast beyond the dragon were the horned, ebon Naor beasts, the front eight just visible in advance of their dust cloud. Somehow they were even larger from this angle. They'd picked up their pace, and Rylin guessed they had less than a few minutes before the first arrived. If any of his friends had survived he'd be hard-pressed to get them to the gate some fifty yards behind.

A glance over his shoulder showed him Exalt Meria rushing from the south gate with a handful of the city guard. From the walls, flaming bundles of pitch now arced out into the blue vault of the sky, trailing smoke.

As Rylin reached her, Elenai was struggling out of her seat. He'd been so distracted by first sight of her in the arena he'd completely failed to congratulate her on her promotion to the ring. Though she was leaner, locks and fly-aways escaped from her usually neat braid, and her stained clothing was well lived-in, the customarily tidy squire had changed in more startling ways. Gone was any trace of self-conscious awareness, replaced now with easy self-assurance, obvious not just in the way she carried herself, but in the keen-eyed certainty with which she approached challenges. There in the arena he'd noticed it in the way she held her shoulders while she moved; now he observed it in the way she checked on the welfare of the exalts as Rylin helped her down. A leader, ensuring the well-being of her followers.

Once, he'd found her attractive and full of youthful potential. Now, dirt and sweat-streaked and mussed, her confidence and capability had transformed her into an utterly beautiful woman and he'd have to have been dead not to notice.

Upon reaching the ground Elenai rocked unsteadily for a moment, blinking, then straightened, muttering thanks for his assistance. He helped Thelar and M'vai reach the ground soon after. Both looked pale and wobbly. Rylin felt Elenai draw power from her stone to send magic coursing into the nearest mages, including him. He grinned, feeling renewed. He turned to thank her, then saw her wince.

Even without watching from the inner world, he knew she'd shut off the hearthstone, just as he'd have known when someone closed the shutters on a window behind him on a breezy day.

"The Naor were trying to attack me through it," she said to his unspoken question. Her gray eyes held his. "It's their leader. Chargan."

"The sorcerer grandson of Mazakan," Rylin said. So he'd come here rather than Alantris. He wasn't sure how Elenai knew his name. "We'd best get to the walls."

Joined now by the guards, and Meria, they all hurried for the gate as the thunder of approaching hooves vibrated the air around them. Rylin waved for Lelanc to take the air, noting her wing-beats were labored. Small wonder, after the terrific fight she'd waged.

He glanced back once more as they reached the sally port, just in time to see one of those flaming balls slam straight into the long furry black head of the lead beast. There was an explosion of fire and flesh and gore and Naor bodies were flung far and wide as the creature staggered and blindly plowed into the earth.

Once through the doorway, a guard barred the sally gate and Rylin immediately spotted squire Elik in the wall gap the dragon had created, motioning dozens of Darassans forward with chairs, tables, and fireplace logs. They'd already gathered a fair pile of wood, and a guardsman was running along its edge, pouring out lamp oil. A clever idea, though such a blaze could only be a temporary obstacle.

As Rylin paused to quench his thirst from his waterskin, he heard footsteps beside him and turned to find Kyrkenall. The shorter man's dark hair was thoroughly wet, and water ran down from the edges of his robe.

"You jumped left!" Elenai said to him, sounding strangely pleased about it.

"Indeed I did." Kyrkenall smiled slyly. "If I'd tried for that rope Thelar held out I'd either have missed, or been flung into space once your dragon got attacked."

"I thought you'd gone mad," Thelar admitted, breathing heavily.

"I had prior knowledge," the archer said, mysteriously. Then his fathomless black eyes fixed Rylin, and he thrust out his hand.

Rylin shifted his waterskin to his off hand and clasped arms with his fellow alten, surprised by the strength of his calloused smaller fingers.

The archer spoke with quiet sincerity. "Thank you."

"We just barely got you," Rylin said, and passed over the waterskin.

Kyrkenall released his arm and took the offered drink. "Odd being thirsty after getting the outside so wet." He then raised the skin in salute. "'It seems your ring fits well.'" He drank long and deep.

Rylin felt a flush of pride. He couldn't recall the play Kyrkenall quoted, but knew it was from a famous scene when the veteran Herahn came upon his former squire, Tretiak, whose quick thinking had held back the Red One's cavalry force.

"And you exalts," Kyrkenall said, passing back the waterskin, "—well, we did all right together, didn't we?"

M'vai smiled at that, her sister's arm still supporting her somewhat. Thelar nodded soberly.

"We did," Elenai agreed. "But there's more yet to do."

Commander N'lahr glided into the boulevard upon his blue-white ko'aye, Lelanc shadowing. The rest of their winged allies kept to the sky, circling, and Rylin noted that two were missing from the flock. One he'd seen shot by an arrow, but he hadn't thought it a mortal wound. Perhaps it had landed behind the walls somewhere. He had no idea what had happened to the other, and hoped it hadn't been slain. Together, they had brought down the Naor dragons, and he felt a bond with the additional ko'aye even though they'd never been introduced.

Kyrkenall turned to greet both the commander and ko'aye, whom he called Drusa, with warmth.

"It's a sincere pleasure to see you both," Elenai said. The ko'aye cawed something at her Rylin didn't catch.

"A well-timed entry, Commander," Rylin told him. "What happened to the last dragon?"

"It went down in the northern suburbs after we got its wing. I think at least one of the Naor survived. I saw him running for cover but lost him in the narrow alleys." As the commander climbed from his patchwork saddle, Kyrkenall embraced him.

Looking both bemused and amused, N'lahr pulled back from his friend's arms. "You're soaking wet."

"I had to take a dive in the Idris," Kyrkenall answered. "I'd be road paste if Rylin hadn't turned up on Lelanc."

The commander nodded to Rylin. "Where's the queen?"

"Gone, with the hearthstones. She's planning to summon a goddess. And we think it will be bad if she does."

N'lahr nodded decisively, as if choosing not to ask for further detail. "How long do we have before she does?"

"Damned if I know. Our exalts might."

N'lahr took in the twin women and Thelar, all three of whom were staring at him in profound wonder. One of the commander's eyebrows quirked.

Judging by the rumbling ground and the shouts from nearby, there wasn't a great deal of excess time, so Rylin didn't bother with introductions. "Thelar—any idea where the queen went, and how long it will take her?"

"No idea as to location," Thelar answered as he might have Asrahn on the practice field. "But it may take her some time to put the broken pieces back together. And it will take her a lot longer without her full component of mages."

"Time estimate?" N'lahr prodded.

"At least a few days, Commander. Probably a week. And Rylin injured her—that may slow her a little."

"Or not at all," Rylin said. "I stabbed her in the heart and she didn't seem fazed."

N'lahr frowned.

"How'd you get here?" Kyrkenall asked his friend. "I mean, apart from the obvious way? What happened in Alantris?"

N'lahr answered quickly. "The city's ours. Tretton sighted dragons flying low in the south Fragments and monitored as they kept heading due west. We determined the Naor must be aiming for Erymyr. Then a big flock of ko'aye turned up and Drusa and her friends offered to help us hunt some Naor."

Her right wing held stiffly, Lelanc settled with awkward care to Drusa's left and the two fell into a twittering, squawking exchange. The blue ko'aye whipped her head around to face Kyrkenall. "Lelanc has hurt her wing saving you, black-eyed one."

"We will tend her with the finest healers," Kyrkenall said. "Have her take refuge in the stables."

"I wish to fight with my warrior brother," Lelanc said, her head turned to Rylin. "But I can barely fly myself."

"It was a splendid battle," Rylin said. "Rest for now, and we will take the air again soon."

Lelanc bowed her head to him.

"I like his spirit," Drusa said, and cawed. "Grab up your killing sticks, Kyrkenall, and take up the hunt with me!"

"Gladly," the archer answered, then asked N'lahr: "What's the plan?"

Rylin resented Kyrkenall's interruption a little, for he'd been wanting to ask about Varama.

The commander answered. "Organize the situation at the inner wall. And refill your quiver," he added with a glance at the archer's pack. "Drusa, if you attack the enemy now, they'll be able to fire with entire banks of archers and spearmen. Rest, and wait to strike when their attention's focused on us at the inner wall."

Drusa cocked her head at him and then bowed it. "You are wise. I remember. Though I wish to strike, I will do as you suggest and urge my brothers and sister to do the same."

"Let's go," Kyrkenall said. "I'll find you some water." He leapt lightly into her makeshift saddle. "Lelanc, come with us." Drusa took to the air and Rylin was troubled to see how hard Lelanc had to struggle before she made it aloft to follow.

The commander faced Elenai. "See if there are any other barricades you can set up between here and the best route to the inner wall. Anything to slow the Naor down once they get through this breach."

"Yes, Commander."

"You, Exalts, Rylin—assist Alten Elenai."

"Do you mind if I come with you, sir?" Rylin asked quickly.

The commander nodded, and in moments, he was hurrying to the stairs in the outer wall at the side of the commander, noting for the first time how tired the man's eyes looked. The thunder of the oncoming beasts set the stones vibrating in their mortar.

"How's Varama?" he asked as they started the jog up.

"No permanent injuries." For all that this was good news, N'lahr's answer was somber.

"The squires?"

Rylin saw the commander's downturned lip as they reached the mid-point on the stairs. "We lost a lot of good people, Rylin."

Before he could ask any further questions, they'd arrived at the landing, and N'lahr quickly assumed command from the small defense force, stunned to find him in their midst. Rylin appreciated how that would get tiresome for him.

The tower-mounted trebuchets scored several more direct hits before the beasts were too close to the walls. After that, six of the animals and the majority of horse troops headed for the breach the dragon had opened while the others spread out along the wall. Squires set fire to the wood in the gap to impede the enemies' progress, and indeed the beasts seemed reluctant to approach the flames despite frantic looking actions from their handlers. The black, horned monstrosities shambled off to look for weak points by ramming their heads at various places along the fortifications. The wall shook and dust was raised with each hit.

"That gate won't hold," Rylin said as ancient copper-lined wood rattled alarmingly in its hinges. The two-story portal hadn't been tested in centuries and if he survived this day, Rylin promised himself he'd see to a redesign. There were, at best, two hundred people along this wall. He doubted it could hold even with N'lahr in command.

N'lahr ordered the archers to fire at the eyes of the nearest mount, then spoke quickly. "We're just pruning their numbers and buying time. We'll have to retreat soon."

As a beast loaded with Naor javelin troops and slingers closed to exchange fire with a contingent of archers on a nearby battlement, N'lahr ordered the defenders to cut the ropes on the trebuchets so that they couldn't be used by the enemy.

As the south gate gave way with a sharp crack, N'lahr ordered the oil-soaked back side set ablaze, enabling the archers and surviving soldiers to retreat toward the inner city under his guidance.

Rylin and N'lahr followed after the last soldier, an older man cupping an arm struck by one of the Naor slingstones. As they neared the towering bronze statue of Darassa farther up the boulevard, they spotted Elenai, Thelar, M'vai, and Meria at the base of the goddess. N'lahr drew to a halt, motioning for the soldiers to continue their retreat past the dead dragon sprawled across the cobblestones beyond.

Rylin sensed the magic the four worked through his ring.

"Are you doing what I think?" N'lahr asked.

Elenai looked up at him. "I believe this statue can crush a few of those Naor monsters."

Elenai was planning to destroy the city's masterwork?

The idea apparently horrified N'lahr as well, for his eyebrows climbed. And then he relented with a single bob of his head. "Let Darassa herself go into battle."

"Can you aim it?" Rylin asked.

"I'm damned sure going to try."

Rylin looked to the commander. "I'll stay here and help."

"I'll see to the defenses beyond. Don't take the big risks here," he told them all. "We need you at the inner wall." As they acknowledged that, he wished them luck, and hurried away.

"I still can't believe that's really N'lahr," Meria whispered to her sister. Apparently those two hadn't known about his imprisonment, either.

Rylin stepped into the boulevard. He'd decided he'd be of better use monitoring the Naor than lending his magical assistance, for they already seemed to have things in hand.

At the sound of hoof clops to their rear, Rylin whirled and discovered Elik cantering toward them with a half-dozen saddled mounts. The animals snorted nervously as he brought them to a halt near the dead dragon.

"You don't have much time, sir," the squire reported. "Five of the monsters are coming in from the north. There's a regiment of archers whittling the Naor down, but there's not much else there, and nothing can really slow them."

"How close are you?" Rylin asked Elenai. To his eyes the wide bronze ankles of the monument looked just the same as ever.

Her voice was strained as she answered. "It's ready. Right now we're holding it in place."

For all that the statue looked undamaged, the mages were coated in sweat. Thelar looked up at him, his eyes showing equal parts fatigue and determination.

The Naor at the south gate must have made it past the fires. One of the immense monsters shook the wide boulevard as it advanced over the ancient cobblestones, its long black fur swaying with each tread. Enemy soldiers, their helms gleaming, their teeth white in snarls against their beards, swarmed to either side of it, ahead of a column of mounted troops.

"Almost," Elenai said tensely.

A second and third beast trailed the first.

Gods, Rylin thought, let this work and take them all.

"Now," Elenai said.

In a single moment, a slice from the front of the statue's ankles fell away so easily it seemed it had always been ready to slip free with a tap. The immense statue leaned only a little at first, as though Darassa had come to life and were lowering her head, and then it gathered speed.

Some of the Naor saw it coming, and shouted in alarm.

Darassa was too large to avoid. The lead beast and the men that rode beside it were squashed like bugs, and flesh and fur rained on the avenue with moist, sickening thuds. Men and horses screamed as they hurtled into the air, limbs flailing. The front portion of the second beast was struck as well, and the sudden impact flung up its back end so that Naor soldiers were catapulted even higher than their fellows.

Rylin couldn't tell if Darassa had struck the third beast or not, for there was not only a statue obstructing his sight, but a huge cloud of dust and debris raised by its fall. Though normally the grisly reek would have turned his stomach, Rylin smiled fiercely as he turned to assist his allies.

Elenai climbed into a saddle under her own power, but Thelar and the twins had to be helped onto the mounts. Rylin was the last onto a horse as a troop of Naor charged past Darassa.

The javelins they threw clattered against the stones only an armspan away.

"Hurry!" Elik urged.

But none of them needed urging. Rylin and Elik fled with the weary mages, their mounts' hooves clattering through the empty streets for the inner wall. Smoke rose as Naor set fire to buildings they passed.

Rylin had often jogged the perimeter of the inner walls when drilling as a squire. He'd never thought he'd see it actually used as a defensive barrier. Smaller than the outer wall, it climbed only fifteen feet, and was just wide enough for two soldiers to walk abreast. Guard towers that rose two spearlengths higher were set every sixty paces.

In total, the wall surrounded the Altenerai grounds, the palace, and a variety of related buildings. There was a little over two square miles of territory within, and now it was crowded with citizens. The wall itself was heavy with defenders, although there were no ballista or trebuchets.

It had been foolish arrogance to think no one would ever breach the outer walls.

As they closed on a postern gate, one of the monstrous animals let out a coughing roar and plodded after. Its handler guided it cautiously through the narrow streets. Even though moving slowly, its legs were so long it gained on their cantering horses.

Naor on the beast let fly with javelins and slings, and Rylin felt a stone slam into his middle back. The khalat protected him somewhat, but it stung, and he realized like an idiot he still wasn't wearing a helmet.

Defenders on the wall came to their rescue, launching arrows, spears, and hurling even clay pots. The monster slowed long enough they could duck their heads and ride through the postern gate. Elik hopped down to help slam it closed.

They'd made it inside. But the Naor were just beyond, and the shoulders of the black beasts were higher than the walls.

33

With Half of a Sword

It felt as though she had always been out of breath. Panting, Elenai and Elik pushed their way through the throngs, led by a squire urging haste. Only a few weeks ago, she had ridden past the palace at Elik's side and into the streets for the celebration of N'lahr's great victory over the Naor. She could never have guessed she'd return less than two months later wearing a khalat and a ring, or that there would be an army of Naor waiting beyond the inner walls.

Amidst all the changes, she was heartened to be in the company of her friend Elik again. They'd bonded early in their second year, recognizing in one another someone with the same work ethic and drive to succeed. Elik had been a master rider even before he'd joined the corps, and had always learned new information quickly, especially corps history, which he'd often helped her study.

He'd doffed his helmet and ran a hand through sweaty, curling brown locks as he walked beside her. One of the five brevets on his right sleeve was slashed. She didn't ask what had happened to it, and maybe the precise detail didn't matter, because the more general answer was the Naor attack. He'd survived that one. Soon they'd all be facing more.

With her and Elik came a scruffier, more valiant version of Rylin than she'd previously known, his shadow Thelar, and the twin redheaded exalts. Everyone had questions for them, mostly variations on the same two themes: what are the Naor doing and whether they thought Darassus would survive. A few asked if the queen had really fled, and others demanded to know if N'lahr had returned from the dead. Some insisted on impeding their progress to get answers.

She'd have to allay their fears. Elenai halted her companions, and when none of them seemed to catch on to what must be done, raised her hand for silence. A mass of citizenry cleared a circle about her while she sought and found the right words. "People of Darassus! Take heart! General N'lahr was never dead! The queen imprisoned him but Alten Kyrkenall and I set him free." There were gasps, murmurs, and cries of outrage at this, but mostly the faces were focused raptly upon her. "He saved Vedessus from Naor attack, and we destroyed their army there. He and Alten Varama defeated the Naor who had taken Alantris. And now he has come to aid us in Darassus!"

She paused, turning to take more of them in. "We six are going to consult with him right now. Stand firm and help one another. We will strike as one."

She turned then, and a squire came over to lead them through the crowd, which parted before him. A ragged cheer followed belatedly.

"Nicely done," Elik said from the side of his mouth.

Rylin flashed a grin at her.

The squire guided them to the practice field beyond the stables, where a row of hay bales had been tossed out to form a barrier separating them from the curious onlookers. They stepped through it, joining a band of grizzled men and women in the black-and-gold livery of the city guard, the dark-skinned exalt she'd seen tending the stadium wounded, a dozen men and women in white shirts she recognized as junior members of the Mage Auxiliary, and two lone third-rank squires struggling vainly to look resolute rather than overwhelmed.

N'lahr stood apart, watching as Kyrkenall trailed Lothrun through the sand where Elenai and Elik had trained under Asrahn. The archer used the point of the curved sword to draw an oval.

This, Elenai speculated, must represent the inner city. As she watched Kyrkenall finish, an older Alantran woman drew up beside Elik and squeezed his shoulder. Her friend brightened and made room for her. With the old woman were three Elenai recognized as city councilors.

"Elenai," Elik told her, "this is Governor Feolia, of Alantris."

Elenai bowed her head in respect and the woman returned the gesture. The youngest of the councilors, a stern man in a trim blue shirt and dark pants, with salt-and-pepper hair, pointed at N'lahr. "That's really him? Not some kind of magical trick to improve morale?"

"That's really him," the governor said. "Why won't you believe me?"

"You didn't tell me Kyrkenall the traitor was here," the councilor continued to Feolia.

Kyrkenall had just completed the oval only a few steps from him, and he glanced back.

"He's no traitor," Elenai said, voice sharp.

"You can arrest me later." Kyrkenall wiped the tip of Lothrun on his pant leg and sheathed the weapon as N'lahr stepped forward, carrying a short rake.

"I'll be brief," the commander said. "The enemy currently have a little over two dozen of those giant cattle, each carrying somewhere close to forty troops. There's also cavalry. All told we face somewhere close to fifteen hundred enemy soldiers. In case it isn't clear to you, this is not an invasion force. They mean to kill as many of us as they can lay hands on, and destroy anything they can't take away." He lifted his head and nodded into the distance. "You can see they're already setting buildings on fire."

He brought the haft end of the rake down to the oval Kyrkenall had drawn and slashed a line through its middle, then crossed it so the image was divided into four sections.

"Naor marksmen are already taking up posts in nearby buildings. Others are likely to remain on top of the black beasts, because once they come within sight of our walls they'll have a height advantage. Our ko'aye allies will aid us against the marksmen, and so will Kyrkenall, who will be able to shoot from the back of one of them."

N'lahr looked over to Elenai. "The Naor have at least one powerful mage among them, and they'll use him and others to sow chaos. But the Naor have ever and always relied more upon brute force than finesse. Their goal will be to gain the wall. And once they have part of the wall, their goal will be to advance across and start killing. So—we need the people off the grounds." N'lahr pointed to the councilors. "Get all noncombatants into the palace and Altenerai buildings. There should be enough room inside especially if you utilize the storage larders as well. Keep them out of the entryways, because those are our fallback points. Clear?"

"Clear," Feolia answered, beside Elenai.

N'lahr tapped the lines he'd drawn through the oval. "We'll divide the protection among four commanders. Rylin, you take from the main gate to the western sally gate. I'll take the western sally gate over to the north gate." He called to a bright-looking middle-aged woman in guard livery. "Captain Anaria, you take from the main gate to the gap by the Idris. And you," he pointed to the graybearded man in dark mail. "Captain Cercah, isn't it?"

The elder bowed his head in respect. "Yes, Commander."

"You take the last section. Each of you is going to need support teams below who can feed up extra arrows, spears, rocks, pitchforks, whatever you can possibly use against the Naor. Put teams together including volunteers from the citizenry. Each of you are going to have to keep at least two and preferably three banks of marksmen handy, capable of firing in volleys. Are you listening?"

The response was delivered with military precision, many voices speaking at once. "Yes, Alten."

N'lahr lifted the rake and pointed it toward the exalts. "Thelar." Elenai was impressed by her commander's retention of information—she was fairly certain Rylin had only mentioned the exalt's name once in front of him. "You're in charge of our magics. Apportion the spell workers on every wall. Spread mages among you. You exalts ought to know who's good at what and what strength everyone has. Make sure everyone has about the same force, right?"

"Yes, sir."

"Assign yourself to my wall, and keep Elenai out of your calculations."

Elenai wondered at that, but said nothing as N'lahr faced Elik. "Elik, you're going to command the mounted troop. Find us horsemen, and patrol the inner side of the wall. Come charging against any Naor who get over the wall, or through a gate. Get on that, now." She also wondered how N'lahr had learned that Elik was a natural for cavalry and inwardly applauded his choice.

"Yes, sir." Elik snapped a salute, gave Elenai a brief nod and a whisper of "luck" and hurried off, already calling the names of squires.

N'lahr pointed at blond-haired, brown-eyed Welahn. "You, third ranker. You're in charge of the armory. You first make sure that all of Elik's troop is armed and armored, and then make sure every weapon we have is in use. Clear out the place. Send an assistant to scour the palace and raid the Wall of Heroes. Alvor's axe is going to do us a lot more good in someone's hand than shining on the wall."

Welahn's eyes widened in surprise, then he snapped a salute. "Yes, sir."

"Get moving." N'lahr pointed to another city guard officer as Welahn dashed off. "You—" He snapped his fingers. "Your name?"

"Myllikar, sir."

"Myllikar, you find retired veterans and strong builders. Have them identify and ready near the weak points. Postern gates, the main gates, every kind of entrance. Erect barricades just inside them. Use whatever you need—barrels, stable siding, anything that's movable and defensible, even if you have to destroy buildings. Clear?"

"Yes, sir."

He faced them all once more. "I can't predict what other surprises the Naor might have, so we're going to have to think on our feet. Be flexible. Don't crowd the walls, but keep them occupied. Have people ready to fill in from below, because you *will* take casualties. Some Naor will reach the walls. Maybe a lot of them. When they do, take them back. Don't forget—we have more people than they do. Questions?"

Elenai's only question was why she hadn't been assigned a specific duty, but she waited, silent as the others.

N'lahr watched for a brief moment. "You have your orders. Dismissed." Without a pause he motioned Elenai forward. "Oddsbreaker, we need to talk."

He turned his back to the crowd, stepping close to the shadow of the stables. A sprinting first ranker arrived with multiple quivers of arrows, which he passed over to Kyrkenall, who immediately dropped to the sand of the practice field and began to inspect the shafts. The rest of the men and women raced off to their assigned duties. Some were already shouting orders, and one of the soldiers called for any hunters or marksmen to gather about him.

"Their mage is throwing some powerful spells," N'lahr said. "Any observations?" Understanding that N'lahr wanted a tactical assessment outside his own field of expertise, and quickly, she struggled to put her thoughts in order. "We've seen him work spells from a distance on multiple instances. He seems capable of keying in on a hearthstone and immediately countering it with something of his own that's just as strong. Possibly another hearthstone. I know of no other source that might sustain him."

"Blood," N'lahr said. "At least in part, he's using the black beasts as giant batteries to power his blood sorcery."

"Gods," Elenai said, wondering if that red spiking slash that had damaged her dragon had, in fact, been formed of blood.

"Once he has the beasts in place disgorging men he'll have less need of them, and they'll be even more useful as power sources."

"Of course," Elenai agreed more softly. Once again, she was astonished at N'lahr's finely honed perceptions. He might not understand sorcery, but he understood, profoundly, how resources were allocated in battle.

"Do you think he'll still be drawn to the hearthstone?" N'lahr asked.

"I'm pretty certain."

"Can you sense him if he's sensing you?"

"I haven't tried," she confessed, "but theoretically I should be able to do so."

"Chargan may not expose himself to direct conflict, so once we locate him we're going to have to go to him. And cut the head from the snake. We will have to wait for the right moment, which is why I want you on the wall beside me. Now let's get to it."

"Yes, sir."

Once again the populace was in motion, many retreating from the inner wall and into the palace and stone outbuildings. Women with babes in arms. Stooped grandmothers and grandfathers. Children, all kept in orderly lines by elders.

N'lahr was still arranging everyone, several dozen, upon his quadrant of the wall when the Naor moved in. A wide avenue lay just outside the inner wall, and all but one of the city's main streets fed into it. This meant that the horned Naor monsters had easy access to the palace walls themselves and came stomping toward them, parallel to the defenders.

A single drover sat in a roofed framework slatted with metal behind the head of each beast. The Naor troops rode upon platforms of wood and leather. Rounded shields hung along the lower sides, behind which the Naor crouched between attacks.

As one of the reeking animals swung sideways to the wall beside them, Elenai kept the first volley of slings and spears back with a great wind spell, and Thelar followed her example on the second, but as other animals moved in more stones flew, more javelins arced and it was impossible to shield everyone. Some weapons found a mark. The screams were one with the bellows of beasts and clatter of arms.

The warriors on the wall gave as good as they got, firing into the eyes of the Naor animals and sending some fleeing in pain. Many Naor fell finally behind their shields. Before long, though, a siege plank crashed down, landing with a solid thunk upon the battlement. A group of slingers rained stones down as Naor warriors ran howling down from the beast and stepped onto the wall.

And there they met N'lahr the Grim, bearing Irion.

Not so long ago, Elenai had fought at his side. Never, though, had she had such an unfettered view of the warrior in battle. Fluid, unlabored, he stepped between blows, somehow assessing the maximum length of his opponents' reach and remaining just beyond it. He advanced into battle almost like a ghost, impossible to touch, but slaying all that he passed with precise and deadly cuts. Here he thrust deep; here he parted armor with impossible ease, so that a Naor fell shrieking beside his weapon arm. Here he ducked so that an axeman brained another, and then brushed a throat with Irion's tip before tripping a rushing warrior and cutting an attacker's blade nearly in half as he parried.

Soon the swirl of combat encircled her, for a second black beast disgorged its hordes onto the wall, and then she was once more guided by that thread that enhanced her own blade skill, weaving past strikes to thrust home, ducking and rising with a slash, letting the incredible flexible armor of her khalat take the lighter blows. Thelar was in there beside her with a valiant second ranker and a band of archers whose arrows kept the nearest Naor marksmen too busy for concentrated volleys.

One moment she was facing a shouting bearded warrior; the next she was breathing heavily and her field was clear. Down the wall, N'lahr was still cutting a swathe through attackers, dropping them left and right. Closer at hand, Thelar finished off a downed Naor as the enemy soldier scrambled for a spear. The second ranker knelt beside a wounded archer. All up and down the wall beyond their quarter, as far as she could see, Naor fired from the black beasts or came rushing down planks to assault the defenders.

Elenai took note of the largest of the beasts she'd yet seen. It advanced to the corner of Altenera Way, a block to her west. If the others were twenty feet at the shoulder, this rose at least to twenty-five, and its massive horns were painted in scarlet. It paused briefly beside the great column with Queen Altenera at its capital that stood directly across from the famed Alteneran Gate. Then it advanced across the avenue, each step shaking the streets and puffing up gusts of fallen petals from the newly leafed trees.

Huge though the beast might be, it sat fewer Naor. Elenai saw only a handful upon its back. One was a trumpeter, even now calling signals that brought more Naor soldiers to the walls. Others were men-at-arms, broad of shoulder, their ringmail gilt with gold, their helms touched here and there with gold leaf.

She ascertained that the three Naor at the beast's head were sorcerers, even though they were as heavily armed as their fellows. Looking through the inner world she could not miss the glow of two active hearthstones, and something more—the life force of the huge beast they rode was threaded into the magic of the stones. Further, one of the three was better connected to those threads than his fellows. Chargan. It had to be. His helm boasted the most elaborate flourishes, and a gold crest. He carried a remarkable long-hafted sword, brandished now in the air—one side of it was saw-toothed, and the other smooth.

At sight of the enemy leader Elenai looked for N'lahr, and found him in the midst of a fierce fight with Naor toops.

Darassan soldiers fired steadily as Chargan's animal drew close. So, too, did Kyrkenall, for Drusa dived and he let loose a trio of well placed arrows as he swooped past.

But the moment missiles neared their target a bloodred dome of energy flickered into existence about the sorcerers; watching through the inner world Elenai saw the dark threads the Naor worked to manage the spell, and the mage that manipulated them. She reasoned then that each of the three must be apportioned a different task; one had threads into the animal's mind, and the other was clearly in charge of defense. Chargan, who as yet did nothing, was likely offense.

A peculiar furred hump stood up along the beast's back, directly behind its head, and Chargan drove that saw-edged blade down upon it. A gout of blood sprayed up, but the beast lowed only dully, as though it were removed from the pain.

Chargan raised his blade and swiped it through the air. Blood coating the weapon's edge slung out like a great whip and Elenai's eyes widened in horror. For when it struck the soldiers upon the wall, it didn't spray, but cut through flesh and into armor. Men and women dropped, crying out, or fell silent in death, and the whole of the battlement was clear. Chargan sliced once more and cast a deadly scythe of blood at soldiers advancing from the right.

This, she understood with grim clarity, was the kind of attack he had sent into the sky against her dragon. And she was not sure she knew how to counter it.

The beast plodded at the gate, lowered its head, and drove its horns into the thick wood. So strong was the blow that Elenai felt the stones sway beneath her even hundreds of feet away. Naor drawing closer upon their own animals took up a sinister two-syllable chant of their leader's name. Char-gan. Char-gan.

Below, she spotted a band of twenty Naor advancing across the park-like grounds of the palace until Elik's armored troop broke them with a charge. From what weak point the enemy had emerged she could not guess, but this break was further sign the defenders could not long hold them back.

Elenai called again to N'lahr and saw him fighting to disengage. For now, she would have to handle the enemy mage herself. She reached deep within her hearthstone and sent a wave of bright energies against Chargan and his beast. To her eyes it looked like a solid sheet of lightning, but it did not move swift enough to stop that bloodred barrier from flickering into existence. Her attack struck it and dispersed into the air in small sparks.

Elenai cursed, even as a familiar voice called out to her. It was amplified, ringing through the air like a thunderclap.

You are outmatched, Altenerai! You cannot last!

Sensing his reach for her stone, she turned it off, and she imagined him grinning in triumph. His beast backed away for another assault against the wall.

A winded N'lahr arrived beside her on the battlement at last, his bloody sword in hand. Over his shoulder was a stream of bodies. "It's time to take the offensive." And he pointed his dripping blade toward Chargan, before the gate.

Almost she asked him how he meant for them to get there. But she, too, was Altenerai. She spun to the bruised and battered second ranker, miraculously still alive beside her. She'd never learned his name. "Hold the wall!"

Thelar had apportioned a quartet of mages to their command. One had fallen to a Naor spear, and the remaining three clustered near her, two men in white, high-collared shirts that were the new official garb of the Mage Auxiliary squires, and an older woman in bright blouse and pants. She looked like a grandmother. Elenai called to them now. "Mages, with me!"

And with that, she and N'lahr were rushing over bodies and up the plank to the nearest of the ebon monsters. Its troops had already mounted the wall and been slaughtered by N'lahr, and its drover with a small force of guards still clustered near the thing's head. They were struggling to get the beast under way until N'lahr made short work of them, and she soon was brutally thrusting threads of intent through the monster's feeble consciousness. She discovered a little more there to work with than she'd found in the dragon, and recognition burst over her. The Naor monster was nothing more than an eshlack, twisted and reformed into this gargantuan shape. She should have guessed that sooner, from the familiar stench.

"You saw that shield the Naor formed from their beast's blood," Elenai said to Thelar. "Can you build something like it?"

"I've never made a shield," Thelar confessed. Yet as she reached into the stone and fed him energies, he gamely threaded them together, calling for the others to aid him.

They spun a glittering golden tapestry in a convex shape before the monster's head.

She braced herself for an attack against her hearthstone, but it did not come on the instant, perhaps because the enemy mages were so busy with their own work. She shut it down before Chargan sensed it.

As their own beast lumbered down the avenue parallel to the wall, gathering momentum, Chargan sent a blood strike against them. The attack drove partway into the protective screen, sheering into the threads without collapsing them, and the mages struggled to lend it greater strength as Elenai followed the curve of the wall and forced her animal into a run, driving straight for the side of the enemy beast. She urged it to lower its horns, fueling its confusion over the loud sounds and strange scents into a rage now aimed at the larger animal.

Kyrkenall swooped past, trying once more, but again his arrows struck the red dome that sparkled into place about the sorcerers and dropped away. He had already blinded the thing, judging by the shafts about the head, but that didn't seem to change its behavior.

Elenai's eshlack was but thirty feet out when Chargan's second attack cut partway through their shield. Most of the energies held, but a line of the blood broke through, passing within an arm's length of her and taking one of the Exalt squires through the chest. Blood spouted as though he'd been sliced deeply with a sword, and he collapsed.

Sickened, Elenai shouted to keep the shield up.

As they passed by, Naor soldiers hurled spears. Clever Thelar might be, but his shield proved no barrier to physical weapons. In a near effortless display of skill, N'lahr cut the two weapons that loomed closest from the air. He lifted his sword, the sapphire upon his ring gleaming, and Elenai heard the Naor shout his name in a mix of awe and fear.

Thelar seemed to have a better handle on what he was doing now, and she sensed a stronger resiliency in the barrier spread before them.

Chargan's next attack struck low into the animal's right front leg. The beast stumbled. Elenai forced the eshlack on through its pain. Unlike the dragon she'd piloted, this creature seemed to retain more of its senses.

She was alive to its agony, and shuddered with the animal as she fed that pain into its rage. She moaned as one with it.

She pulled her senses free from the beast in the split second before its horns rammed into the larger animal's side.

Many of the Naor bodyguards went down and two toppled right over the waist-high leather shielding and plummeted into the street. Chargan and one of the mages lost their footing and dropped to the platform floor.

N'lahr recovered before the rest of them and charged across the sloping skull of their beast. His helm gleamed in the sunlight, and his sapphire glowed. He leapt up to grasp the edges of the enemy eshlack's platform, already tilted toward him by the impact. In moments he was up and Irion shone in his hand. The elite guard suddenly had something much more troublesome to contend with than regaining their balance.

Chargan pushed himself from the deck to his knees and she felt his eyes upon her.

She had to act fast. "Thelar, I need the winds. Help me jump." She was already running onto the furry head of their beast as Thelar protested behind her.

As her feet pushed off, she sent a wind behind and beneath her and she felt Thelar helping shape the energies. She ignored a little spark of jealousy that he had learned so much from extensive training she'd never had.

Aided by sorcery, the impossibly high leap sent her up and up so that it was almost like flying. She dropped from above the trio of sorcerers, drawing her sword as she came, and slammed it onto the shoulder of the defensive mage. It drove deep and she had to release it as she went to her hands and knees. He fell with a shout of agony. The enemy beast shifted beneath them, still bawling pain from the impact of its smaller fellow. She swayed to her feet as the animal twisted itself. Chargan swiped the sawtoothed side of his blade at her, but he was still off balance and stumbled back toward the bloody hump, missing his blow.

The other mage, the graybeard in charge of guiding the black beast, retreated toward a quiver of javelins. The sorcerer with her sword in his shoulder clawed at her foot. She braced one boot against his face and yanked her blade free with a great gout of blood. He slipped back along the platform, slanting now as the beast shifted again, and he hit the waist-high guardrail and flipped over, calling out in dismay in the brief moment before he struck the street.

She abandoned caution and activated her hearthstone. As the graybearded mage sent a javelin tearing toward her with impossible speed, she sidestepped, navigating the way through her split-second glimpse of possibilities. At that moment she neither knew nor cared if it were some natural gift or insight from Rialla. She followed its guide path, then with an ease that astonished her, lifted a screen of energies even as Chargan scythed blood at her. The attack splintered to nothing on her magical shield, and then she struck out with her sword as the mage snapped another javelin at her. Her parry sent it twirling away.

The beast they rode forced itself upright, tearing free of the others' horns, its will subsumed to that of its master. The Naor sorcerers then alternated their attacks upon her: slices with the blood and a seemingly inexhaustible supply of javelins. Only her glimpse of the best path forward guided her between one calamity and the next. She leapt over one slow lash of the blood whip and then her sense of the future dropped away. The graybeard hefted another javelin and she understood she was off balance and wide open.

The man's mouth sprouted a feathered arrow and he staggered back, hands going to his throat. She heard a familiar mad cackle and glimpsed a winged form soaring past on the edge of her sight.

Elenai advanced on Chargan.

The mage's eyes narrowed. Behind her Elenai was dully aware of the shouts and screams and clang of weapons. It might have seemed ages, but so far this battle had lasted a minute at best. N'lahr was still engaged with Chargan's bodyguard. Over the sorcerer's shoulder she perceived a ko'aye diving at the Naor who'd now taken one of the walls. Naor had forced their way onto Rylin's wall as well, she saw, though the bearded alten was in the vanguard of the defenders fighting them back.

Others, though, had ceased their combat to watch her fight with Chargan. Perhaps they had seen N'lahr's jump or heard the bodyguard calling his name and thought it was he who battled their general.

Chargan laughed, and his sorcery lent him a godlike voice that echoed through the city. Elenai watched the threads of his spell coiling through the air with the words that followed. "You're not bad, fae girl," he called. "You just haven't had practice. And now you never will."

He brought the sword down at her head. She parried, saw the gleam of the sharpened blood on the slim side of the weapon. The strike notched her blade. He twisted it as he pulled back, trying to catch her chin with one of the projections on its saw-toothed side. At close range, she saw that the weapon's pommel was a fanged skull with glowing rubies for eyes.

Laughing still, he lashed out again and again with the blade. What he lacked in skill he made up for in the energy that burned within him, powered in part by the hearthstones carried at his back, and in part by the blood of the creature beneath him. She had used magic to sustain and even boost herself, but this was far beyond anything she had managed. As he said, she lacked practice with this kind of fight. Her next thrust was true, but the blade didn't pierce his well-made armor, and only a brief glimpse of possibilities swung her away from a savage slash that would have taken off her hand.

And her parry of his next blow sheered off half her sword.

She backstepped, wishing Kyrkenall were here, or N'lahr. She had done all she could, hadn't she? Where was Thelar?

But they were not here, at this moment.

Chargan laughed. "Nothing can stop this blade," he cried.

But that wasn't quite true. She leapt to the side, buying herself a moment, saw N'lahr battling a final pair of soldiers. The animal they'd ridden against Chargan was under assault by a second and Thelar and the older mage were retreating onto the wall. Kyrkenall was nowhere in sight.

She ripped the satchel from her shoulder and brandished it in her left hand as a weak shield even as she flung a powerful sleep spell at the advancing Naor sorcerer.

He laughed off the attack and strode toward her. She swore, wishing she had some better choice, and readied to face him, her broken blade in her right hand.

He came in with a slashing blow from the side.

And she interposed the satchel, with her hearthstone.

She felt the moment the blade struck, tearing straight through the bag and into the stone. Elenai released her hold on the artifact at the moment of impact and threw herself sideways.

Probably Chargan felt the immense blast of magical energy at the same time she did. She rolled away, coming to her feet, broken sword in hand.

The result was almost instantaneous. So it had been when N'lahr himself had struck a stone. So it had been when the dragon damaged one. The hearthstone itself surged against its attacker. Bloodred crystals erupted across Chargan's hands, spreading up across his armored limbs as spiky jets of blood erupted from his torso. Chargan wailed in terror and pain, his sounds cutting off sharply as Elenai passed her half sword through his neck and separated his head from his shoulders.

The crystalline transformation overtook his body, a warped rectangle of bloodred spikes. His helmeted head was left unscathed and she looked down to find its eyes fixed in a look of bewilderment.

The air was rich with the energies of the shattered stone. Her stone, she thought, and she scrabbled desperately to grasp at those powers, as one might pick up the largest pieces of a shattered pot. N'lahr had finished the bodyguards, for she found him panting steely-eyed beside her.

They had only moments to shape a victory.

Elenai tore the helm from Chargan's head and lifted the grisly trophy by the hair.

Three of the four walls yet held, but the Naor had gained one, and a hundred or more of their army were dashing for the palace steps even as Elik's cavalry troop led a handful of defenders to intercept them.

With her fading power she sent a mighty wind at the Naor on the nearest beast, blowing many from its back. She staggered the Naor running below. With a sweep of her hand she crackled a vast sheet of lightning over the heads of enemy soldiers on the far wall.

Nothing was left of her hearthstone's power but minute tendrils. She used its last remains as she called out to the farthest corners of the battlefield, her voice heavy with an anger just held in check, not just for the destruction wrought to the city and the lives lost, but for the sacrifice of her wondrous stone.

"Yield, Naor!" Her voice echoed through the city, as though Darassus itself had been given voice. "I have slain your general!" She raised Chargan's bloody head as proof. Though there was still the isolated clang of arms, most of the combatants had paused in their battles to contemplate her. "Surrender, and you may live! Defy, and you will be destroyed!"

N'lahr raised his own voice beside her. His gruff battlefield delivery sent his words almost as far as her own. "Hear me, Naor! I am N'lahr! Victor at Vedessus and slayer of Mazakan. This warrior Elenai brought me back from beyond the grave to oppose you! She has vanquished every power you possessed! This is your last and only chance! Surrender or die!"

It was a gamble. Perhaps their last. If the Naor pressed on, their numbers might carry the day. But did they know it?

The silence stretched on for what felt a thousand years, until a beardless Naor officer before the gate shouted up to them. Elenai knew that there were no women in the Naor ranks, yet she could have sworn the warrior shouted up in a woman's voice. "We will never surrender! But we will serve the stronger chief!"

"Then swear allegiance," N'lahr called back.

The beardless Naor looked to his fellows, then sank to one knee. "Hail, Elenai Half-Sword!" The soldier bowed his head. His companions stared at him. Then another beside him followed suit, crying out Elenai's name.

The ripples spread, and bit by bit the helmed heads sank, the numbers swiftly growing and spreading beyond the wall until almost fifteen hundred Naor knelt in fealty. They swore not to N'lahr, but to her, and she knew a terrible chill, a presentiment very different from those exhilarating glimpses of the best path forward.

Cheers erupted from the buildings and spread along the wall.

Still reeling from the energies she had wielded, Elenai looked to N'lahr. His eyes met her own. She saw pride there, for her, and maybe a little sympathy. What had he gotten her into? Was this how he'd expected things to play out?

No, she thought, this time he had improvised, just like her. She let out a breath she hadn't noticed she'd been holding. Some improvisation. A better mage might have defeated Chargan without sacrificing her only tool. How was she to wield meaningful sorceries without her hearthstone? It troubled her that amongst all the other tragedies, the loss of the stone plagued her most, and that she already wondered if N'lahr had brought Belahn's old stone, or if it would be possible to use Chargan's. She would resist the impulse to ask, or to look for them on his corpse. She had understood only at the end how close she had been to tapping the limitless powers that the hearthstone offered. But she had seen, too many times, that the hearthstone road led to madness. Though she might regret the sacrifice for the rest of her days, perhaps it was better that she had surrendered it before she became its slave.

Epilogue

A s Rylin took the switchback toward the cemetery, he deliberately kept his eyes forward. If he were to look left he'd see where the statue of Darassa should have risen above the city domes, at least two of which had gaping holes. He might have glimpsed the Naor camp, or the ruins of the stadium. So that evening, as the shadows grew long, he gazed only upon the city of the dead, for the present and future were far more painful to contemplate than the past.

He rode along the lane beside the cemetery ridge, stopping at last beside a little grassy square where two mounts grazed. Both horses, a brown and a light gray with a black mane and tail, looked at him curiously before returning to their own business.

Rylin left his horse with these and strode forward on weary legs. As he continued on, it occurred to him that this is where he'd had the first intimation that something strange was afoot. He hadn't really been paying close enough attention, of course, but he'd been sitting his lost horse Rurudan right over there, next to a now equally lost Lasren. And then, in the midst of a dull speech, Kyrkenall had galloped off with Elenai in tow, riding as though someone's life depended on it. Curious, he had thought then, and wondered what mad impulse had taken the archer from an important ritual he'd never before seen fit to attend. Rylin recalled losing track of the droning oratory to imagine a confrontation with the famed Alten if whatever he was dragging Elenai into went badly for her.

He trudged the final yards up to N'lahr's tomb and found the door standing open.

The last time he'd been here, Varama had opened the door and even smashed the corner of N'lahr's beautifully rendered sarcophagus lid to minutely examine his lifeless remains. This time the real N'lahr was there, but he was living and breathing and sitting on the bench, far less pristine than the perfect false corpse Varama had discovered within. Kyrkenall sat beside him, one leg up, his booted foot pressed against the stone coffer.

"Hail, Alten," Kyrkenall said, and lifted his bottle in salute.

"Hail, Altenerai," Rylin replied as he lingered under the lintel. He glanced to the right of Kyrkenall's dusty boot, where part of the relief of N'lahr's sleeping, carved face had been shattered by Varama.

"Come inside," N'lahr said.

"You're blocking the light," Kyrkenall added.

Rylin came through, glancing around the dim interior, and his eyes dropped to the sarcophagus. Even though he couldn't see the fake cadaver inside and he knew it wasn't real, the thought of it still disturbed him. He wondered if N'lahr had looked over the eerie duplicate of himself housed within.

He stepped around the stone coffin and its broken image of N'lahr reposed, and sat down on the other side of the living man.

"How did you find us?" Kyrkenall asked.

"Elenai thought you might be here."

N'lahr noticed the direction of Rylin's gaze. "I looked inside," he said.

"It's bad enough for me to look at it," Rylin told him.

"I think we should drag the thing out," Kyrkenall said. "We can pull some pretty great jokes with it, don't you think? Especially with the chunk missing on the face."

N'lahr silenced him with a look.

The archer leaned past N'lahr to better see Rylin. "Here to tell us to come back?"

"Mostly. But I wanted to hear more details about Alantris."

N'lahr sighed with regret. "It was bad. Two-thirds of the city is in ruins. Some are saying it should be abandoned. Others want to rebuild. But the Naor are finished there."

"And what about the squires?"

"They were a credit to the corps," N'lahr answered. "They steadily weakened and demoralized the enemy before we arrived, and opened the gates for us." He fell silent for a moment, then looked over to him. His voice grew somber and slow. "But they suffered terrible casualties. All of Varama's lead squires perished."

"All of them?" Rylin felt a sharp pang. "What about Sansyra?" Odd, that he should care suddenly for the fate of someone who had never liked him. At least, not until the end.

N'lahr looked as though that death had struck particularly hard. "She died after fighting a mage on a dragon. She killed the mage. Varama told me she planned to nominate her for the ring," he finished slowly. "I asked her if she wanted to award her a posthumous elevation."

A handful of those had occurred, over the course of the years, when a squire had perished heroicly in the line of duty. They were thereafter credited in the rolls as having reached the seventh rank despite never donning the ring.

N'lahr finished his thought. "But Varama wasn't sure Sansyra still wanted to be an alten, so she's finding a different way to honor her."

Rylin nodded, wondering that he should be so affected that he had no appropriate words. And then another thought came to him. "Aradel had a niece. Denalia. Did she . . ."

At N'lahr's slow head shake in the negative, Rylin swore. The only words that would come.

Kyrkenall handed him the wine. "I'm sorry about your friends," the archer said gently.

"It's the damnedest thing," he said after a long pull. It was overly sweet. He passed it back without comment, and wiped a tear from his cheek. "I barely knew Denalia. And Sansyra wasn't really my friend . . . Thelar and I *hated* each other. And yet . . . we had each other's back today. It's all different now."

"On the line you find out who your real friends are," Kyrkenall said.

Rylin's hand stretched up to his chin, clear of beard hair for the first time in days. Apart from a cursory wash, the shave was the only grooming he'd managed since the battle this afternoon, unless he counted the change of his undergarments. He hadn't yet had time for a bath, or a haircut, or a deep cleaning of his khalat. All of those would be nice, though what he really wished was to sleep for about a week.

He didn't want to sound as though he was challenging either man, who were not only senior officers but living legends, so he still hesitated a moment before finally asking the question he'd been wondering all the way out to the ridge. "What are you two doing out here, anyway?"

"You mean instead of rushing around the capital with a push broom?" Kyrkenall asked.

"No," he said, although there was a small element of truth to that line of inquiry.

"Me, I had to get away from all those people and all those questions before I killed someone." Kyrkenall thumbed at N'lahr. "And my friend here needed to rest after winning Alantris then racing overnight to get here."

"I didn't win Alantris," N'lahr said fiercely. Even Kyrkenall looked startled and N'lahr's tone quickly cooled. "You give me too much credit. Varama's the one who weakened the Naor. She set everything in place, through careful planning, and great risk. All she needed were the numbers I escorted. Nearly everything else was already laid out."

"Here's to Varama, then," Kyrkenall said, and drank.

Rylin suddenly missed her, terribly.

"As for why I'm here," N'lahr said, "I wanted to see my tomb."

"It's nice, isn't it?" Kyrkenall asked. "I thought Asrahn's husband did a great job with your image on the door."

N'lahr agreed lightly. "The view is extraordinary. The bench is uncomfortable."

Kyrkenall snorted. "I bet it's worse inside the box."

"If I was in the box, I wouldn't notice the view or the discomfort."

"Fair point. If you like," Kyrkenall said, "we can drag out some cushions next time."

"I don't intend to spend my free time here," N'lahr said dryly. "We probably ought to be going."

Kyrkenall's mouth twisted in annoyance and he took a pull from the bottle. "I know there's an awful lot to do, but is there any particular crisis we're needed for, just this minute?"

"Apart from the fact we may only have days before the queen summons a mysterious, long-vanished goddess, and we don't know what will happen if she does? And that no one knows exactly where the queen has gone?" Rylin was surprised by his own sarcasm.

So, apparently, was Kyrkenall, who stared at him, then laughed. "You're all right, Rylin. Did you have any luck getting the queen's location out of the exalts?"

Rylin shook his head. "They don't know. I've been searching the queen's office for clues. Thelar's looking into some stones on a shelf there. He said he thought they might be important."

"Stones on a shelf?" Kyrkenall repeated, instantly alert. "Gem stones?"

"Yes," Rylin said, and at the bowman's look of intense interest, added, "I found an Altenerai ring next to one of them, and I think it might be Kalandra's."

Kyrkenall swore and sprang from the bench, then sprinted out the door.

Rylin looked to the commander, who had climbed to his feet. In moments they heard hoofbeats receding.

"What has him in such a hurry?"

"He's been looking for Kalandra, and was told she might be in a gem, on a shelf."

Rylin wondered how that could be possible, then shook his head. After all that he'd seen in the last few days, very little defied belief now. "Here's hoping, then."

"Yes. I've stayed up here too long." N'lahr started for the door. "I imagine the councilors have their hands full trying to sort everything out."

"They're still trying to decide who's really in charge," he said as he followed the commander into the sunlight. "And the city sectors are picking councilors to replace the ones the queen killed." He fell quiet briefly at the thought of what he'd see in those council halls if he walked into that side of the building. "There's already talk of choosing a new queen."

"Have they nominated one of the councilors or governors?" N'lahr asked.

"No. But a big crowd of people was gathering outside the Hall of Ancestors when I left, shouting their choice."

"Who?" N'lahr asked.

"Elenai."

Acknowledgments

I am once again indebted to a team of people who were very giving of their considerable skills. Jennifer Donovan and Hannah O'Grady were always ready to assist behind the scenes. Kristopher Kam and Sarah Bonamino were invaluable for getting the word out. Edwin Chapman's eagle eye saved me from any number of little mistakes and from some big ones as well. Ian Tregillis was the guinea pig who read the rough draft and offered numerous brilliant observations so that the readers who followed him didn't have to suffer as much. Second readers, John Chris Hocking and Kelly McCullough, rode to my rescue with keen eyes and sharpened quills when I needed them most, and I'll be forever grateful for their timely and essential feedback. Pete Wolverton was an ever-steadying hand, keeping the story and characters honest and on the proper path. Bob Mecoy was always ready to assist, and helped with plot knots and sanity checks as the deadline ticked down. Lastly, an extra-special thank-you is owed my long-suffering wife, Shannon, whose work on this text was invaluable. A whole lot of idiotic things are absent thanks to her, and an untold number of passages are finer for her insight and input.